Riddled Worlds

Phil Coleman

For Maggie

But I have convinced myself that there is absolutely nothing in the world, no sky, no earth, no minds, no bodies. Does it now follow that I too do not exist? No: if I convinced myself of something then I certainly existed. But there is a deceiver of supreme power and cunning who is deliberately and constantly deceiving me. In that case I too undoubtedly exist, if he is deceiving me; and let him deceive me as much as he can, he will never bring it about that I am nothing so long as I think that I am something. So after considering everything very thoroughly, I must finally conclude that this proposition, I am, I exist, is necessarily true whenever it is put forward by me or conceived in my mind.

Descartes (Med. 2, AT 7:25)

Contents

1

THE HOLES

<Pock-fffftttt>

David snapped awake. The nylon walls of the tent vibrated against the gale outside. He didn't dare move. He listened and waited for a shift in the sand around him. The sound of the Hole still echoed in his ears. It had been close. Very close. But not directly below him. If it had opened beneath him, he would have already been taken. Perhaps he had only imagined the sound. Perhaps it would simply go away. But the Holes never went away. And that was the problem. That was why he and his brothers had come this far, to the very end of the world.

Not fair, David thought for the thousandth time. *This isn't fair.* He was only fourteen, after all. He should be at home, thinking about homework and school and movies and baseball, or whatever it was that used to be important. Someone else should be huddled out in the middle of nowhere. Anyone else.

David kicked his sleeping bag aside and rolled to his knees. As he eased down the tent's zipper, a blast of hot air hit him. Sand stung his cheeks, embedding itself in his thick mop of dark hair. He turned to shield his eyes from the mid-morning sun. Several seconds passed before the world rolled into focus.

Outside, the plains looked like the cracked expanse of the salt flats, dusty, red, and parched. Jagged canyons splintered through the arid land, spawning dust devils as the wind howled. In the distance, rolling hills gave way to foggy abstracts obscured by blowing sand. Even the sun appeared as only a smudge of light through the haze. But that was only how the plains looked.

What the plains *were* was something else entirely—something only David could see. Because what they actually *were* was covered, riddled, burrowed, chopped, and Swiss-cheesed with Holes. Some were small, no larger than a dropped penny. Others were massive, as wide as the cradle of a stadium. But the majority of the Holes were the Hula-Hoop to school bus-sized openings that David saw now. And whether large or small, they were all perfectly circular, so dark they swallowed the surrounding light, and as bottomless as they were unrelenting.

<Pock-fffftttt>

David flinched as another Hole sucked through the landscape, this one a mere five feet from the tent. He thought the sound was the worst of all. When a Hole formed, Goliathan or mouse-sized, it was preceded by a single, hollow "pock," like when someone placed a finger into their mouth and plucked their cheek. The second sound wasn't from the Hole at all, but the rush of surrounding air. The "fffftttt," started low, before growing so shrill a person couldn't tell if the noise had stopped, or just risen past the register of human ears.

No one except David could see the Holes, but that didn't mean they weren't there. After all, the first Hole back home had claimed fifteen people before he'd found it. He had only been nine at the time, and no one believed what he saw. At least, not right away. Only after one of the doubters jumped onto ground that only *looked* like it existed—and was never seen again—did the townsfolk listen. Now, five years later, David was still looking for Holes. Though now he was alone.

He stared out at the Holes, his eyes drawing back to the one that had taken Newman. Over time, the men he called his brothers had all made the mistake of veering one step from the path of their guide. And in that misstep, they had been yanked into the void. Once you set foot in a Hole, even if only an inch, it had you. There was no pulling back again, only fighting and fighting until it dragged you down. And though they had sworn to walk exactly in David's footprints, the mistakes still happened. One-by-one-by-one.

David corrected himself. Newman hadn't done anything wrong. He'd hadn't strayed from the path; he'd just been unlucky. A Hole had opened below him. There was nothing he could have done.

With a heavy sigh, David stepped out of the tent and broke camp. He folded the segmented tent poles against one another and then rolled the rest of the tent around the bundle. It was a sloppy job, and he had to rewrap it three times to make it fit inside the bag. That wasn't his fault. He'd be better at this if they had ever let him practice. But they'd always dismissed him with the same excuse: *You're our guide, that's the most important job there is. Just leave the tent to us… leave the water to us… leave the cooking to us… leave the…*

He dropped to his knees in the ocher sand; a lump formed in his throat. He choked it back. No one would have seen him cry, but no good would come from crying either. After all, someone had to finish this.

Rising once more, he pulled his backpack across his shoulders. The knapsack was too large for him, each strap pulled as short as possible to make it fit. At first, David hadn't carried his own pack. But when his brothers started falling into the Holes, they had given him a bag with all the essentials. In the long run, items like the compass were more important than the life of any one of them.

David removed the compass from his pocket and held it flat on his palm. He might not know all the ins and outs of the instrument, but he didn't need to. The important thing was that he follow the red arrow. East. And that was where he was going. East, east, east, east, until he got to the end and found the reason for it all. He didn't know what he'd do when he got there. No one had made it that far.

Then he saw it, swirling only a dozen yards away. His brother Michael had called them "dust demons," while Kevin had called them "tornadoritas." They had never agreed on the name, but they meant the same thing. They were like the granddaddy of a dust devil, though shy of a full-scale tornado. And while the phenomena weren't deadly in their own right, they could hurl a man fifteen feet across the desert. Out here, with Holes all around, any misstep could be deadly.

As David watched, the dust demon shimmied, then split in two, a second identical demon next to it. Then each dust demon trembled and split once more. And then again—until eight meandered in lazy circles. They paused, then started toward him.

Impossible. They can't see me. That's impossible. That's… he paused. They *can* see me.

Sweat trickled along his back. He kept his eyes locked on the approaching windstorms, trying not to panic. After all, the winds could shift in his favor. And he didn't want to veer from his path unless necessary. But as David watched, the dust beneath his feet sank. He leaped aside just in time.

<Pock-ffffttt>

A newly formed Hole, just as black and just as bottomless, appeared where he had stood. *At least it wasn't one of the big ones*. He looked to his left and saw another indentation, then another, then another.

<Pock-ffffttt, pock-ffffttt, pock-ffffttt, pock-ffffttt!>

David sprang forward, and then forward once more. The Holes weren't simply forming, they were driving him. Caught between Holes and the dust demons, he was left with nowhere to go. He only had moments to act, to decide.

This is the end, he thought. The ruined world had finally had enough of him, his brothers, and their fool errand. And they had been so close. But he had one trick left. He had one wild card he'd been warned to keep secret—even from his brothers. He reached into his coat and removed the vial.

The capsule, as long as David's pinky, was made from tinted green glass and filled with liquid. The vial curved inward at the middle like an hourglass, needle-thin at the waist. He held the capsule to his eye and remembered what the sage had said:

Now David, those men, your brothers, are as good and honest and true as any thirteen men ever were that walked the good green earth. But you got to remember that if we lose you, a boy who can honest-to-god see the Holes, then we've lost a major weapon in this here battle. So I'm going to give you something special. Very special. But it's only for you. When the game is run and the gig is up and you're staring death in the face, you break this vial. And then you come find me. One last Hole, boy. One last Hole.

"One last Hole," David whispered. As he bent the capsule between his fingers, the glass gave way in a hollow crunch. Liquid spilled onto the sand.

<Pock-fffftttt>

A depression formed, then sank downward. He stared in disbelief. It was a Hole, to be sure, but not the hollow voids surrounding him. This Hole glowed with ethereal yellow light… and it didn't look empty. David knew exactly what the sage would want him to do.

"One last Hole," he said. He jumped in.

●

The sage huddled shirtless over his cook fire, cursing the grease that popped from the skillet and landed on his exposed skin. That had been the trade-off, and one he'd weighed for a long time. For while the sage was an incredibly learned man, he had a vain streak as well. From his meticulously shaved head and manicured goatee to his chiseled physique, the sage cared deeply for his appearance. And while skin may heal from grease burns, all the wishing in the world wouldn't get him another vintage green 1976 Rolling Stones T-shirt. Better to suffer than to risk such a treasure.

The sage glanced over his shoulder for the fifth time in as many minutes. The light peeking through the cavern wall flickered once more. He thought there must be some sunlight out there, some way out of the cave he hadn't seen before. More importantly, the passing of shadows told him the chimera were moving.

A pop of grease drew him back to the task at hand. The bacon (the *last* of the bacon) sizzled on the skillet he had carried down a hundred and fifty-seven worlds. Each had brought him closer to the bottom, each had brought him closer to the center. The bacon smelled slightly sour from being packed away too long. But to the sage, it was the most wonderful smell in the world.

He flipped the frying pan with a snap of his wrist, deftly switching the bacon from one side to the other. The act spat a single drop of grease which flew toward the book in his hand. The sage jerked back. After all, truth (ultimate truth) is a particularly rare and valuable thing. And he was convinced this book contained such truth.

"*Cogito ergo sum.* I think, therefore I am." The sage snorted in disgust. "It couldn't possibly be that simple." After all, if that was all it took, then the Holes, the boring, the crumbling, and the fading wouldn't matter in the least. Such a theory had been disproven on countless occasions in countless worlds. The sage flipped the book to glance at the cover. Everyone, even *Rene Descartes: Collected Works*, should know that. But if that wasn't the truth, then what was? And it had to be in there—it had to be. You look at things through enough angles and through enough layers of reality, then it would come out. The truth *always* came out. The sage felt he was closer than ever. He may even be at the bottom. Why else would he be held captive?

He snapped the book shut and returned to his dinner. One thing at a time and all would be clear. He needed only his own patience, and—of course—the patience of those *things* outside.

He shivered at the thought of the chimeras on the other side of the wall. Waiting, watching, waiting, watching to make sure he didn't try anything. The sage had no delusion about their intentions. He had no hope of compassion or pity. If they were benign, they wouldn't be working so hard to keep him trapped. And if they wanted his destruction, they wouldn't have kept him fed. The creatures wanted him kept, nothing more.

Maybe, the sage mused, one of those hunters he'd met would show up. In the stories he'd collected, the hunters and the chimera were never far apart. Maybe the deepest cave in the world wouldn't keep the hunters from finding them and finding him. Would that count as destiny? The sage shook his head. He didn't buy into that old theory. Perhaps he should stick to his Descartes.

He scribbled a few thoughts in the book's margin, then returned to his reading. Perhaps the passage was important. After all, it couldn't hurt to be hopeful. And hope and bacon were a lovely pair on which to feast. On the other hand, the sage would have given all the bacon in the world for the chance to see David, just one more time.

2

Lofton's Net

When it came to hard work, determination, putting your nose to the grindstone, and god-help-ya just gettin' the job done, Walter's father was the best there was and the best there ever had been. But when it came to imagination, old Mr. Lofton fell a little bit short. So when Walter heard his father talk about seeing ghosts in the oyster beds, he started asking around. He asked his sisters, he asked his friends, he asked his wife, he asked his three sons, and finally, he asked the old man himself. Just as he expected, his father denied seeing anything at all.

But Walter also knew that whatever his father lacked in imagination, he made up for in curiosity. And so when the oysterman started scheming with his fishing buddy, Douglas, when the two of them spent long nights in the tool shed, Walter made sure to keep them in his sights. But he didn't have to push very hard. After all, Lofton's plan included him. *Someone* had to man the oars.

And so, with the shadows growing longer, he found himself in the marshes with two old fools and a mess of fishing nets. He had been rowing for an hour, and still hadn't the slightest idea of his father's plan.

"Walter, boy, why don't you just pull the boat aside that shelf over there and let your betters out. Come on. Put your back in it."

Walter gritted his teeth. That tone of command hadn't changed since he was eight. Even though he was now *thirty*-eight and a half foot taller than the old man, you couldn't tell it from the way his father spoke. Douglas, of course, only made things worse.

"Now Mr. Lofton," Douglas said, his voice a graveled rasp, "do they always fall out the same place, or is it just all around here?"

Walter paused from rowing. "Does *what* fall?"

"Hush now, Walter boy," Lofton snapped. "You said you'd be quiet if we let you come. So now you just go on doing that. But if you must know, Douglas and I are out to catch something. That's what you do with nets. Even a farmer should know that." Lofton turned to Douglas and removed his wide straw hat, the only protection between his wrinkled head and the afternoon sun. "Well, Mr. D., they fall all around, but always right around these parts. Now let's just get on shore and stretch these nets, and hope the Lord God grants us fortune."

Walter landed the rowboat and set anchor. Then, under his father's direction, he suspended each of the fishing nets above the marsh grass. Each net was held up at eye level, suspended by long poles sunk into the black mud. He stretched thick bailing twine from the top of the poles and then staked them into the surrounding oyster beds to hold the lines taut. The end result was a collection of nets scattered around the marsh, and looking much like an army encampment.

"The plan is simple," Lofton said as he marched the perimeter. "You see, each of these nets is specifically designed for the purpose of catching. But not on the falling side, Mr. D., the rising one. So when the next thing comes a-shooting out the marsh, we'll have it! Just as simple as you please."

Walter gritted his teeth. He should be in his fields. He should be getting the crops ready. This whole exercise was ridiculous. But when his father got an idea in his head it took less time and less effort to help him see it through than to argue.

Douglas called out, "Toss me that water there, Mr. Lofton." He, like everyone in town, never called Walter's father by his first name.

Lofton unslung the canteen from his neck and handed it over.

Douglas took a sip and then passed the container back. "People'd a think us two right foolish old fools if they'd of seen us out here today. Your boy ain't gonna say nothin', is he?"

"He promised as much." Lofton's face grew suddenly stern. "But don't you say nothin' either, Mr. D. I know you're one to talk, and my daughters already think I'm crazy. Heck, why do you think they have Walter babysitting me?"

"I'm not here to babysit—"

"Shush, boy. I know why you're here. Just you remember that one day it'll be you out in the marsh with one of *your* young'uns trying to decide if you should be chained to your rocking chair."

Douglas grinned. "I hear that, Mr. Lofton. My boys wouldn't let me off the porch if they had their way. Time enough for that when we hit our later years."

Walter declined to comment.

<Pock>

Lofton tilted his head. "You hear that, Douglas?"

"I heard it," Walter said. "What was that?"

"Shush, boy." Lofton raised his arm and pointed out into the marsh. The green stalks swayed from the sea breeze as it rippled across the landscape. "Listen."

The sound came again, the tiniest hollow pop. It reminded Walter of the squish of oysters as the shell split open. The pop was followed by an outrushing of air, like the hissing of a cat.

<Pock-ffffttt>

Walter dove aside just in time to avoid the creature that rocketed up from the ground—completely missing the nets—and past their heads, squirming and barking as it went. The projectile diminished to a speck as it vanished overhead. In disbelief, he collided with his father and they both fell into the thick marshland mud.

"There! See? See, Walter? See, Douglas?" Lofton clapped his hands. "I told you I wasn't crazy! Now get off me." He pushed Walter aside and struggled to his feet.

"Oh lord, oh lord almighty…" Douglas shook with nervousness. "That was a damned animal! That was a damned dog, it was. A damned dog just shot out the damned marsh." He pointed at the ground below then traced with his finger to the sky above. "And into the damn sky! Why didn't you done tell me?"

Walter stared in disbelief. "Did that really just happen? Is *this* what you've been seeing?" He lumbered to his feet.

Lofton grinned and knocked the mud from his pants. "I've been trying to tell you two all the livelong day. What you think we been doing out here?"

Douglas shook his head in disbelief. "Well, to tell the truth, Mr. Lofton, I thought you'd gone 'round the bend. I wanted to make sure you didn't go and hurt yourself."

Walter nodded in agreement.

"On the other hand," Douglas continued, "I don't want to catch no mad dog either. They all dogs? What you want to catch a dog for?"

Lofton shook his head. "They're not all dogs. But I've seen just about everything fly up from the grass there is to see. Now, are you two ready to catch something?"

"What for?" Walter asked. "I believe you now. I don't believe it myself, but I believe you."

Lofton smiled. "We are not here to prove things, Walter. I'm too old for that." He folded his arms across his chest. "We are here to catch things. Now, boy, move one of those nets to where that thing came out."

Douglas asked, "And what then, Mr. Lofton?"

"Then we wait."

●

Yellow light engulfed David. He could feel himself falling, but the brightness was so all-encompassing that he had nothing to use for reference, nothing by which he could judge. He was sure he was falling, as the wind rushed past his body and whistled across his ears, but speed and direction were gone. The only constant was the light.

The wash of color faded from yellow, to green, to blue, to indigo, to violet, to red, to orange, to yellow, to green… He felt he was falling through the layers of the rainbow, and couldn't help reciting the old mnemonic he had learned in school. ROY-G-BIV, ROY-G-BIV, ROY-G-BIV. The chant rattled through his mind and for a moment he wondered if this was the way he was destined to spend eternity, falling through an abyss, driven mad by cycling colors and his own lack of bearings.

Suddenly darkness, an impenetrable black.

The transformation was so sudden that David had recited five ROY-G-BIVs before he registered the difference. Then, as quickly as the light was gone, it had returned. This time the colors cycled faster, nearly three times more quickly than before. Blackness again, then light. The colors hastened (roygbivroygbivroygbiv…). Blackness, light, blackness, light, until the colors flashed so quickly they melded into a single indistinguishable blur. Brighter, brighter, brighter… Black.

This time, the darkness lingered. He could see his own body, somehow lit, yet nothing else around him. He wiggled his fingers in front of his eyes but was soon distracted. For the first time, he saw a *something* in the distance. This was a small light as well, but distinct. It had color and the tiniest wisping of something that looked like... clouds.

My god, he thought. *I'm about to fall through the sky. And then... and then it's Splatsville for Davie. So long, bye-bye.* He looked at the steadily approaching blue. The image was two-dimensional, as though he was not hurtling toward the sky, but rather a *picture* of a sky. Closer, closer, closer...

●

David collided against the woven twine of a foul-smelling net. The rope creaked against him, the strands imprinting a waffle pattern on his face and skin. And then he had stopped. Bewildered, he stared through the mesh of the net at the clouds below, trying to determine both why there was a net to keep him from falling, and why the object of his salvation was so extraordinarily rank.

"Lord Almighty, we got something!" A voice called from above him. He rolled onto his back and looked up. For a brief second, he could see the passage from which he came, shining with yellow light. But as soon as he glimpsed it, the opening vanished. In its place was a ceiling covered in long, thick-bladed grass.

Where am I? Have I...? I've fallen clear through the planet! No. That's ridiculous. It doesn't work that way, and I know it. But if I didn't fall through the planet, then why is there grass above me? And why am I still being pulled down, if down should now be up?

This last thought triggered a twist in his bearings. Panic seized him as the world flipped. He plummeted up (or down, according to his new perspective) into the marshes, landing face-first in the cool, black mud. As soon as he hit, he scrambled to a crouch. His veins felt as though they were on fire; his heart raced. He snapped his head from side to side, looking for Holes, seeing if any were close by. But whether they were obscured by the grasses, or simply absent, he didn't see a single one.

The air was thick here. Every breath drew a lungful of water both pleasant and exceedingly strange. As far as he could see, marsh grass swayed in the humid breeze. Channels of water meandered around him, broken in places by oyster beds, piles of detritus, and the occasional sea bird. This was, he thought, quite different from the *other* side of the world. That was the only way he could reason it. But there was little time to reflect further. For not ten feet away, three men—two old, one younger—were eyeing him closely.

One of the old men stepped to David's side and helped him to his feet. He was dressed in canvas pants tucked into knee-high rubber boots. He wore a faded flannel shirt with sleeves pulled past the elbows and secured with braided rope. His face was dark, a deep ebony creased with wrinkles by his broad smile. The man rubbed a finger along his dappled gray mustache, his eyes shining with delight.

"Are you sure it's safe to touch him, Mr. Lofton?" the other old man said. This one was a few inches shorter than the smiling man, and dressed identically, except in clothes much more ragged and generally unkempt. He had a worried frown that contrasted his companion's smile. David was reminded of the twin masks of comedy and tragedy on the walls of the school theater.

"Now, that's ridiculous. He's just a boy, see?" The smiling man offered his hand again, this time not for lifting but for shaking. "My name's George Samuel Lofton, but folks in these parts call me Mr. Lofton. Or just Lofton, if you prefer. How do you do?"

David tentatively shook the man's hand. "Fine, thanks. Nice to meet you. Um… where am I?"

"Just a minute there, my boy," Lofton said. "We're not done introducing yet. That's my good friend Douglas, and this here's my son Walter." Lofton jerked his thumb at the younger man. Walter appeared in his late thirties and may have been the single largest person David had ever seen. He stood well over six feet tall, his arms thick with muscles, and his head shaved clean. The man's arms were folded across his chest and a scowl rested on his face.

"Uh… my name's David." He cast his eyes down.

Lofton smiled, "Don't you mind those two, they never seen nobody drop out the ground before."

David didn't respond. His head swam with incredulity. The buzz of flies and the thick scent of marshland air was so… so very *real* he could barely take it in. He looked from Lofton, to Walter, to Douglas, and back to Lofton again. "It's my first time too," he mumbled. "Where am I?"

Lofton smiled knowingly. "This here is the low country, boy. We are in the marshes outside of Greenwater's End, which I do humbly call my stomping grounds. I'm an oysterman, though slowed down a bit from the rheumatism. And where are you from, boy? When you're not falling up through the ground an' all."

"I'm from Bailey, Colorado, sir." David looked at Lofton's puzzled face. "It's about an hour from Denver. But it's been a long time since I was home. My brothers—not really my brothers, we just called ourselves that—anyway, we left to find the source of the Holes. And we—"

"Now wait a minute," Walter interrupted. "This is going too far." He directed his words to the old men as though David wasn't there.

"I've never heard of a place called Denver, or Bailey, or Colorado. And we don't know if he's dangerous." Walter looked at his father. "Do you trust that boy? We don't have any reason to trust him."

"Shush, now," Lofton said. "What's this 'dangerous' talk? He's just a boy. Wherever he's from."

"Oh, yeah? What if he's a chimera?"

The old man leaned back and roared with laughter, huge, belly-shaking heaves. "Good Lord, Walter boy. And they say I'm the crazy one. Just look at him."

David blinked once. Even before the Holes, and even before phones, TVs, and the radio broke down, he was pretty sure most people knew where Denver was. And certainly Colorado. On the other hand, if he did fall straight through the world, then maybe he was...

He paused. There was no way of telling where he was or even how long he'd been falling. He knew that things got weird after you had spent too much time near the Holes. And well, what if a long time had passed? Maybe there wasn't a Denver anymore. For that matter, what was a chimera?

"Well," he said tentatively, "I don't think I've ever heard of Greenwater's End either." David paused. "Is this... is this Australia? Did I fall the whole way through? You don't sound Australian."

Lofton rubbed his eyebrows once again. "Australia? Now that at least sounds a little familiar. But this ain't there neither. You ever hear of an Australia, Mr. D? Walter?"

The two men shook their heads.

Lofton continued, "You're on the Carolina coastline, boy. That help?"

David nodded. He knew where that was. In the southeast. One of his friends from school had grown up in Virginia and talked about going to South Carolina to visit his grandparents. But to have not heard of Colorado? Either these three men were from deep in the woods, or something was very wrong. And why not? He had just fallen through a Hole. He should be ready for anything.

Lofton said, "Well boy, sounds to me like you got a tale to tell. But I know it's the kind of story a boy like you is only going to want to tell once. I, for one, am a man who knows storytelling's hungry work. So, how about we head on home? I think if we get some food in you, then you going to be ok. Now go clean up while I get these nets." A pause. "Walter, get the nets."

David made his way to the water's edge. He dunked his head under, hoping the fuzziness would clear, then scrubbed off the mud in the warm salt water. Within a few minutes, the men had gathered their things and secured them in a rowboat covered with peeling paint and a veneer of algae. Lofton waved at David to climb in, and they were off. Walter manned the oars, his gaze fixed on the newcomer.

"How old are you?" Walter asked.

"Fourteen."

"And you said you haven't been home in a while? I imagine a boy your age doesn't travel alone. Who are you with? What are you doing out here? Where's everyone else? And *why* are you here?"

David opened his mouth to respond, but Lofton put a steady hand on his shoulder. "Shush, Walter. This is my catch, and I'll decide what to do with him. Now, how many times do you want to hear his story?"

"At least once," Walter muttered.

"Well, so do the rest of us. And I'm sure he has a few questions of his own." Lofton grinned. "But let him go first. I don't want to gang up on the boy."

The creeping unease which had settled on David's shoulders finally reached a breaking point. He had to know. "Are the Holes here?" he blurted.

"Holes?" Lofton raised an eyebrow. "What kind of holes? I suppose everywhere has a few holes. I've got one in my roof. Douglas has more than his fair share in his shirt. And Walter here? Well, his farm ain't nothin' but holes."

David shook his head. "Not that kind of hole. The kind you can't see. That's why I'm out..."

"Hold on there, boy." Lofton frowned, his wrinkles forming deep grooves in his face. "We'll be home in a spell. You can tell us then."

David gritted his teeth in frustration. "I don't want to wait! This is important. Just 'cause you don't call them Holes, and just 'cause you can't see them, doesn't mean they're not there. Have people been disappearing? And no one knows where?"

The three men stared at him, blank expressions on their faces.

David continued, "Nothing strange has happened? Phones not working? Cars not starting? The weather acting weird?"

Walter asked, "What's a phone?"

Lofton looked at his son with reproach. "A telephone, of course. You're showing your ignorance again, boy. And sorry, David, but we ain't had telephones out here since the second war. Maybe up north, but not down here. You want to tell somebody something, you use the radio. Or write a letter. Course, nobody writes letters quite like they used to. A lost art, if you ask me."

"You're not answering me," David said. "Has anything weird been happening? Anything you can't explain? Anything at all? You seriously don't know about the Holes?"

"Look." Walter quit rowing. "The only thing I can't explain is how you wound up in that net. You want to tell us about that?"

David dropped his voice low, "I don't know everything."

"But you do know something," Walter said.

David took a deep breath. He proceeded to tell Lofton, Douglas, and Walter everything he knew about the Holes. He told them about how people had started disappearing, then how the telephones, radios, and cars quit working, cutting off his town from the rest of the world.

He told about how he could see the Holes where others couldn't. And that for everyone else, they just saw an illusion of something that wasn't real anymore. Then he told them about the sage, and how the old man convinced him and his brothers to go to the edge of the world to find where the Holes started. Lastly, David told about how his brothers had been lost to the Holes, each and every one, until he jumped into the one that brought him here.

Through it all, the men asked only a few questions, usually when they didn't recognize the things he described. They knew about radios, but not televisions, and certainly not computers. They knew about cars but were surprised his family had owned two. They'd heard of airplanes but never seen one themselves. But most disturbing of all, they didn't recognize the places he described. New York? Yes. Baltimore? Yes. Atlanta? Yes. But nothing to the west. Not Colorado, nor California, Texas, or Oregon. After a while, the men quit asking questions. They looked at him with suspicion.

By the time David had finished his story, they were at Lofton's dock and had been sitting in the boat for twenty minutes. At first, no one said anything. Then Lofton spoke. "I think… it's probably best if you don't go telling too many people what you just told us."

Walter snorted in disgust. "Why? Because it's ridiculous? Invisible Holes and sages and everyone having three cars and flying in planes and talking on the telephone? It's obscene."

Frustration welled inside David. This was like back home all over again. No one believed him at first. He was determined that this time he would make people listen. "Well, how do *you* think I got here?"

Walter's face darkened. "I… I don't know. It's just impossible. All of it."

"Son," Lofton said, his voice calm, "you saw him arrive. We all did. And why would he lie? I believe every word this boy says is truth. And my gut tells me we all should. Or don't. Believe what you want.

But that's not what we need to decide." Moving stiffly, Lofton exited the rowboat and climbed onto the dock. "We have to decide who else needs to know about this. Because if we start telling the whole town, who knows what they'll do?" The oysterman paced the dock, hands clasped behind his back. "You remember Sammy Jenkins, don't you? Remember what happened last summer when he told everyone he saw a chimera? Remember how he was almost run off when no one ever found it? It's the same thing. So the important question is: Are there Holes here or not?"

While Walter simply frowned, Douglas raised his hand. "Well Mr. Lofton, ol' Fensterbacher just up the road keeps losing his sheep. And no sign of wild animals around his place. Ain't no bones or nothing. Think that might be a Hole?"

David shrugged. "Could be. Animals can't see Holes either. They can fall in like anything else. I could go look."

Walter cast his eyes at his father. "What do *you* propose we do?"

"Just what David said," Lofton replied, "though you might not like it. We ain't going to put that boy out there to be questioned. So we don't say nothing for now. We got boys his age coming into port all the time, so he'll blend right in. We don't say nothing, and ain't nobody going to ask."

"And then?"

"Then he does what he needs to do. Looks around, sees what he can see. If we've got Holes, well then, we've got a problem. And we don't keep it a secret. But we make sure first. Because if I walk into church with a wild story in one hand, I want to be holding proof in the other one."

Walter gritted his teeth. He dropped his eyes to the floor of the boat. "I'll take care of him. He can stay with me, Bethany, and the boys. I'll do it."

Lofton shook his head. "No, I think he should stay right here with me. Safer that way. Your mother and I—rest her soul—raised all you kids together. She may be gone, but I think I can handle one boy."

"And what do I tell Beth?" Walter asked.

"Why, everything!" Lofton grinned. "She's your wife. You tell her and those three sons of yours what we just heard. No secrets from family. I'll let your sisters know too. But I don't want this story going further than that." Lofton's face turned stern once more. "And Douglas?"

"Yes, Mr. Lofton?"

"I better not hear 'bout *you* talkin' to *anyone*."

●

David lay awake. The heavy ocean air weighed against his skin, turning his clothes damp and salty. A thin layer of sweat covered him, and only partly from the heat. The greater issue remained. This place wasn't home. It was twisted, shifted to one side, out of sync. Those men seemed nice enough, but they didn't understand. They hadn't seen what he'd seen. They weren't the same as his brothers.

The pang of loss crept into his stomach once more. Time had been a blur since he used the sage's potion. Now, the feeling of loss flooded back. With his brothers, he'd felt a sense of belonging. They had been in a war, of course. But they'd all been in it together. And over time they went from being just companions to brothers. Lofton? Walter? Douglas? They would never understand.

The sounds of Mr. Lofton in the next room had diminished to low, rhythmic snoring. The only other noise was the rush of wind through the palmettos and the constant chirp of cicadas. David held his breath, counted to thirty, then snapped his eyes open.

Pulling the sheet to the side, he slid to the ground, careful not to squeak the floorboards. He wriggled into his pants and shirt, then shuttled the rolls he had pocketed during dinner into the middle of his blanket. He wrapped the bundle together and tied it tight.

The old man's shack had broad open windows on all sides, with thick shutters pinned back against the walls. David dropped the bundle through first, then his shoes, and finally wriggled out himself. He flinched as the salt-blasted wood groaned under his weight. He crept to the end of the porch and onto the damp marsh ground.

The seaside air tickled his nose, gentle and comforting. The breeze invited calm, acceptance, complacence. David gritted his teeth. Carelessness had killed his brothers. It's not what he needed here. He wriggled into his shoes and set his sights west. Walter and Douglas had gone that way, walking down a footpath now faint in the moonlight. That way was town. It had to be. And from there? A highway? A car? Anything?

David set off down the trail, at first in a tiptoe and then faster once Lofton's house was behind him. A plan formed. Wherever he was—whenever he was—it was at least *somewhat* like home. Lofton said this was the Carolina coastline, which meant he was in the east. That was similarity enough, and maybe there were more. Maybe the Holes weren't here. Or maybe they just weren't here yet. So if David could get to Kansas, if he could get to the source before the Holes spread, then perhaps he could find out what caused them.

He stopped. His breaths were hot and heavy in the night air. The lap of water against the shore drifted just beyond the trees. He wondered if determining the source of the Holes would be enough. There was, of course, the matter of getting home again. But if he'd made it here, he could make it back. After all, unless he did *something*, then there wouldn't be a reason to go home at all.

Readjusting the bundle on his back, he set off again. He kept his eyes forward and soon could see the first traces of light through the trees. As he came closer, voices joined the light and he saw the first glimpses of people.

He had reached a wharf. Lanterns were strung from the masts of ships lined along a dock. A group of people lingered around the piers and sat along the open-air bars. There was laughter in the air, muffled and indistinct, but hearty. He drew close to the sound, alien in his ears after his time in the wastelands. With no Holes in sight, and people enjoying themselves, he felt more a stranger than ever.

David heard a rumble and retreated into a shadow. A rickety truck pulled out from the end of the wharf and turned to head up the hill. There were more lights up there. That must be the real town and the way out.

Turning from the conversation and laughter, he started up the road. He had gone only a dozen yards before a gruff voice sounded behind him.

"Up and running away? My cooking's not that bad."

David turned to see the weathered face of Mr. Lofton. The old man wore his same torn trousers and checkered shirt from earlier. His bare feet were muddy up above his ankles. He smiled softly.

"I can't stay." David swallowed hard. "I don't have much time."

"Course you don't. Don't any of us have enough time. But running away don't solve anything. You got to face your troubles."

David's ears burned with indignation. "I'm not running away. That's why I'm going. I can't just sit here."

Lofton pulled one hand out of his pocket and rubbed his wrinkled head. "I kind of think you are. You drop in, talking doom and whatnot, and skirt off again. You're running for sure. You just not admitting it. You think you can do all this on your own? Think it'll be faster that way? It might seem simpler now, but sometimes a body needs help. You're taking the easy road and you know it."

"No, I'm not."

"Fine. Then you're taking the hard one. You got to recognize that if you want to do this—whatever it is you're out to do—you got to trust some folks. Turning out by yourself ain't gonna help nobody fast."

"I did trust people. And…" David shook his head, pushing away the memory of his brothers. "It's too dangerous for anyone else. And I can't just stay here and wait."

"And I can't have you running off if those things—those Holes— are right under my nose. I got a son and daughters and grandsons, nephews and cousins. I can't forget them."

"But I *have* to do something."

"Of course you do. And I'm not saying you don't. You give me three days. You look for Holes around here first, and I'll find that you have a way to get to where you need to go. I'm too old to take you myself. I barely hobbled this far. But I can help."

David gritted his teeth. "You promise?"

"On my life. And you?"

He nodded.

"Then you rest up. We got a long day tomorrow."

3

TOOTH

The hunter dropped low and listened. The tip of her readied arrow brushed against the top of the verdant ferns, causing them to waver before coming to a rest. She held perfectly still, not risking the tiniest motion which would betray her position. The chimera had fled, and with luck, had lost track of her. But it would be back. It wouldn't dare leave a witness.

Behind her, a tree creaked as though bending in the wind. But the lack of breeze in the humid air made the hunter think twice. She pivoted on the balls of her feet, keeping the arrow taut against the string. Another creak, this one closer, and she saw it.

The chimera was forty feet up, pressed against the trunk of a long leaf pine. Its skin had assumed the color of mottled bark speckled with green. The chimera shifted, then leaped, passing in front of unbroken sky for an instant before landing on the trunk of the next tree.

The brief silhouette betrayed its form. Two arms, two legs, widespread hands with fingers as long as its forearms. It also had a pair of wings, translucent and sleek, like a dragonfly, sprouting just above its hips. With each jump, the wings would flit once for stability before folding again against its body.

The hunter exhaled. The chimera wasn't fleeing; it was stalking her. Each diagonal leap reduced the distance between them. The progress was too deliberate, too measured to be random. The chimera had found her. But, perhaps, it didn't know that it had been seen as well.

The hunter allowed a smirk to touch the corners of her mouth. She twisted once more, deliberately stepping on the dry sticks at her feet. She turned away from the chimera and began to walk.

Behind her, the hunter heard a "fwip" as the chimera's wings cut against the air. And then once more, closer. And then closer.

The hunter snapped around and released the first of her arrows, which coursed through the air to hit the chimera just below its neck. She dove hard to her right, rolling into a readied crouch. She caught sight of the creature as it collided with the ground where she'd stood a moment earlier. It shrieked as it tumbled, first in pain from the arrow, and then in fury. By the time the chimera had returned to its feet, the hunter had shot another arrow, this one embedding in its hip. The chimera bellowed, and as it did, the color of its skin melted from foliage green to deep black. Its shape changed as well. The wings became scythes, the webbed fingers, claws.

The chimera sprang forward, but the hunter was ready. She twisted her bow around, deflecting the strike. One of its scythes cut into the hunter's side. She was aware of the pain, but only from a distance. Drawing her knife, the hunter closed the gap between herself and the creature. In a single arc, she brought the blade down, separating the chimera's head from its body. And then she crouched, poised, left arm up in defense, right arm low and ready.

Ezra breathed deep. The woods were silent once more.

Ezra contemplated the remains of the chimera. She rubbed the bandage on her side, to remind herself it hadn't been a dream. Shortly after the kill, the creature's body had dissolved into a puddle of organic sludge. They all went out like that, as if the muscles comprising the beast relaxed at once, not only their strength but their cohesion. The only thing that remained were its two precious fangs, now tucked into the pouch around Ezra's neck.

Nothing remained but to burn the body, to make certain the creature wouldn't heal itself, coalesce to form a shape—any shape—and continue its search for prey. Ezra lit the fire and watched the flames grow.

The corpse stank as it burned, dank and acidic. The smell overpowered the verdant humid air. That much hadn't changed in all these years. Ezra covered her nose with the loose bandanna hanging around her neck. The cloth was woven of fibers from the silkwood plant. And though decades old, the bandanna gave off a clean scent that masked the smell of burning flesh. But Ezra could hardly leave the kill now. Not until the job was done and the last bubbling pile had been thoroughly charred and mixed with earth. Twenty-four years had passed since her last kill, but she still knew enough to follow custom. Even if the rest of the hunters were gone. Even if the time for tradition had passed.

Ezra examined the arrows she'd removed from the chimera's body, one intact, one now splintered. The arrowheads would have to be discarded as the creature's blood corroded most metals quickly. But arrowheads were replaceable. Or were they? Did anyone use a bow these days? Dismissing the thought, she removed a new arrowhead from the pouch on her belt. She carefully unscrewed the old point and fastened the new one in its place. She sat her lean frame down on a mossy stump and propped her chin against her fist.

The chimera. Ezra hadn't seen one in over two decades. Not since the creatures had vanished, ending the war as they went. Like many hunters, she'd never quit searching. She'd traveled to the southern continent, into the northern tundra, though didn't cross the ocean to Europe or Asia. No civilization remained there anyway.

She had returned home in defeat. Only a hunter had no home. For that matter, a hunter had no family, no possessions, no gender, no age, no friends, and no name. The name she did bear, Ezra, was merely one more decoration, just like the faded canvas pants, the dusty leather boots, the thick woolen shirt, or the wide-brimmed hat. Only the last did she truly consider hers. That had been earned, the rest only tools.

Ezra examined the short ash and bone bow. There had been a crack when the chimera had struck it. The act may have saved her life, but now the bow was ruined. Replacing it would be her first concern. And she must act quickly. Just in case the chimera were coming back.

That, of course, was a passing fancy. There were no more chimera than there were hunters these days. Most of Ezra's compatriots—the few she'd asked after—had taken real names, had real possessions, real families. Without their enemy to face them, they forgot the old promises. Or simply faded, without purpose.

A crash snapped Ezra to wariness. She slid a knife from her belt and prepared to throw it. At the same time, she flicked her left wrist so that her battle chain uncoiled from her arm to drop to the ground. She gripped the chain just below where it was attached to the manacle on her left wrist. But as she saw who approached, she returned the dagger to its sheath. She coiled the chain back into place.

"Did you... did you get him? Huh? Did ya?" The boy crashed into view. He was dressed in rough canvas shorts passing just beyond his knees, and a shirt which had been mended so many times it looked to be nothing more than stitches and patches.

Ezra frowned. For the boy to have been so close, he must have been following—which she had forbidden. She knew all too well that news of a kill fell on sour ears if there had been a casualty. The hunter pulled her shoulder-length white hair behind her ear.

"I told you not to follow me."

"But you got him, didn't you?"

"I did," she said, the utterance ending with lips parched and teeth bared.

The smile dropped from the child's face. "Sorry, I only meant to…"

"Off with you. Tell your people the chimera is gone. Run, before I bury you along with it."

The boy turned and fled, crashing through the underbrush. Ezra smiled. There were few reputations better than "ornery and mean" when it came time to collect a bounty. Hunting may be a destiny, a calling, a sacred oath, and an obligation, but even hunters needed to eat. Maybe one time she'd have been carried by charity, but not anymore.

After all, the age of hunters had passed. Some of the old ways must pass as well.

●

The town of Regalwood sat on the lower swampy reaches thirty miles from the coast. It didn't have the worn and salted ways of its more oceanic brothers, and yet the speech and mannerisms indicated this town was not far removed from a fishing village. The houses were the combination of old and new Ezra had come to expect. The newer dwellings were of cut timber with shingled roofs, while the old buildings were of brick, likely shipped in before the war. Both were squat, built to withstand the fierce winter winds and the monsoons of spring.

The entire village had the feel—all too common these days—that its moment of glory had passed. Fences rotted in disrepair, paint peeled from the shopkeepers' signs, and rusted trucks limped noisily through the streets. Ezra had always fantasized that after the end of the second Chimeran War people would embark upon a golden age, free to live as they wanted. Instead, the world had become complacent.

As Ezra entered Regalwood, people poked their heads out to watch, to look to see how the day had gone. As she had expected, the first person to greet her—bounding from his old but well-maintained automobile—was Mr. Crouse. He was a thickset man, in clothes that must have come from the mills up north. He had a smirk on his face and confidence in his step. He'd been the one to call Ezra here, and so he likely considered her victory to be his own.

"Welcome back, Madam Hunter," the man oozed. "I trust you were successful?" He looked from side to side, relishing the attention of the townspeople. "The boy said you were, but who can trust a kid? So did you find it?"

Ezra reached into the pouch around her neck and removed the chimera's fangs. She allowed the man to glimpse the bloodied stumps for only a moment, then put them away. She waited until the eyes of the townsfolk drifted back to her, and away from the rich man.

"There was no wail," she stated. The hunter's voice was no louder than a whisper, and yet her words carried easily throughout the street.

"Beg pardon?"

"The wail. The chimera did not cry for help. Either the creature was too surprised, which I find unlikely, or it was simply too far from its burrow. I suspect it was alone."

Mr. Crouse parted his lips, but Ezra continued.

"The body has been burned, buried, warded, and sealed. I would worry yourself no more on this. The kill was clean."

The man's face glowed with happiness. "Good. Good! That's great news. Tonight we'll throw a party. We'll celebrate, and dance, and—"

"My bow was broken." Ezra kept her voice low. "It will be months before I can find a worthwhile replacement. We're hundreds of miles from a hardwood forest. I must increase my ransom."

Mr. Crouse scratched the back of his neck. "Hmm, yes, er… about your reward. I was told that in the old days hunters took no fee for their work, a charity to one and all?"

"Perhaps, when the chimera were numerous, and hospitality more generous. But honor is no longer the rule of the day. I can't replace my bow on gratitude. Were I to rely on charity, I would have given up hunting long ago."

"Well, certainly, but this is a mighty poor town after all. I myself try to keep up appearances… someone needs to speak for them. But we've all had a hard time, what with the drought and the cold winter before that. You understand, of course."

"Poor?" Ezra raised an eyebrow. "Tired perhaps, but not poor. Given the number of trucks I've seen, you must be sitting on some oil. But that isn't my concern. In normal times, I would take only what was promised, as that is what a promise means. But if you cannot compensate me for my things, I'll take both teeth instead."

At this declaration, Mr. Crouse frowned deeply. The courtesy left his voice. "Now wait. You get one tooth, of course. But—and I'm talking about custom, now—the other tooth is mine."

Ezra jerked her head to meet the man's gaze. "According to custom, a casualty like my bow is remedied. But surely, sir, this was never about the tooth? You called for a hunter to deal with your chimera. I have done that."

Mr. Crouse shook his head. "I will see what I can do. Wouldn't want to break tradition, now would we?"

●

Since before the war, hunters used the local blacksmith for the site of purification. Regalwood, however, didn't have a smithy. Few towns did anymore. Instead, Ezra settled in the machine shop. The building had been annexed to a double-sized garage where a man named Hank Coe worked. Hank was the town's catch-all as a mechanic, welder, repairman, and at times even picking up where the missing blacksmith left off.

Ezra could feel the mechanic looking over her shoulder as she worked. The local doctor, contrarily, waited patiently in the corner, his eyes averted. The two men had helped her move aside the old tires, coils of wire, and rusted auto parts so she could access the forge. After the space was clear, she used an air compressor as a billow to stoke the flames. Then she addressed her two major concerns, neither one more important than the other. A hunter's body and a hunter's tools were equally valued.

She tended to her weapons and clothing first. After removing her clothes she dropped them into the boiling water in the cast iron pot. The heat would remove both the smell of the chimera and ensure that if any poison remained it would be rendered harmless. As her clothes stewed, she laid each of her knives in the embers, purifying them one by one. Next, she addressed her wounds, starting first with the scratches on her arms and belly, then the deeper cut on her side. They were all scratches, really, but unless treated, rubbed, and seared, the risk of infection was too great.

"Bloodwart, wolfsbane, peroxide. Hand me those vials." Ezra issued orders to the doctor without turning around. He had been nominated, quite against his will, to help with treating her wounds— and moved slowly as though to remind her of that fact. She had already determined the man to be useless as anything but an assistant. His hands shook as he handed her each bottle. She mixed the items into a paste and spread it on her scratches. The pain was searing, yet it would only be a tickle compared to what came next. As Ezra waited for the mixture to set in, she cast her eye at the trembling man.

"Is something bothering you, doctor?"

"No, I, it's just that... I'm not sure this is decent."

Ezra glanced at her bare, scarred torso. She forgot that these days, people didn't think of her only as a hunter. These were the new times, the soft times.

"I thought you were a physician."

"Oh no, I'm just a pharmacist. The doctor doesn't come through town but once a week and... I, I don't..."

Ezra snorted. She turned to the mechanic. "And what about you, Mr. Coe? Do I make you uncomfortable?"

"No, ma'am... I mean no, sir. I was in the war too. This is all part of it." The mechanic paused. "And don't think I don't appreciate what you did out there. That thing would have taken down twenty of us without you. Helping you is an honor."

Ezra allowed a hint of a smile to touch her lips. The mechanic was three times as broad as she, and yet she didn't think him exaggerating. She could see the scars on his cheeks. He probably had seen a fight or two himself. He knew where the battlefield began and where it ended. For her, it had never truly ended.

The hunter reached a long iron into the fire and removed her clothes from the boiling pot. She let the water slow to a drip and then set them on a rack to dry. There was only one task left.

"Have you done this before, Mr. Coe?" Ezra asked the mechanic. The man nodded, his face grim. He slid the poker from the fire. Ezra pulled a leather strap from the table and clenched it in her jaws. She nodded to him.

Pain coursed through Ezra's body as the mechanic seared the cut on her side. The process took only seconds, but staying conscious was a battle. When the flare of pain diminished, she dipped her finger in the cool water and chilled the wound.

Now, with tools, body, and mind cleansed, she could finally relax.

●

"A hard one, she is. Damn near the hardest woman I've ever seen."

Ezra's ears perked as she heard the men behind her begin their talk anew. Despite the festivities in her honor, she had kept to herself. Whenever the townsfolk approached, she had answered their questions, quietly, politely. The old men had sought her first, those who had met other hunters during the war. The second to come were those too young to have remembered the fighting at all. Ezra did not dissuade them, but neither did she encourage their attention. Nevertheless, she kept her ears open.

The lantern light waned as the celebration wound down. In twos and threes, the townspeople returned to their homes. All that remained were a few pockets of revelers, and Ezra herself. Despite the bone weariness from the day's battle, her mind was charged and alert, buzzing with the excitement of seeing a chimera once more.

She felt a presence behind her and turned to see four men gathered, smiling nervously as they gripped their drinks. "Please, gentlemen," she murmured, "have a seat."

The men plopped down in the vacant chairs of the table, the checkered nylon tablecloth shifting as they settled. They rustled nervously until one worked up the courage to speak.

"They say Mr. Crouse tried to pull your reward. That's what they say, at least."

Ezra showed no expression. "He made mention of it, but we worked out our differences. He received his tooth, and I what had been promised." She could feel the pouch at her side, now thick with cash.

"Of course you did," the man replied. "A tooth is a prize, ain't it? He didn't want to let it slip out of his hands. Am I right there, Madam Hunter? A tooth ain't something you let go easy."

She set her mug down on the table and met the eyes of each man in turn. "If you have something you'd like to ask me, then by all means, ask."

The men shuffled in their seats. "Do you… do you think they're back?"

"Not in the way you mean," Ezra replied. "But I also doubt the chimera were ever as gone as most think. That one today was a juvenile, so somewhere, the chimera are breeding. Our enemy has always been one to hide, so I expect they are still among us. But are they returning? I have my doubts."

The man frowned and shook his head. "Well, I think it's just a sign of more to come. Too many odd things have been goin' on lately. Why you probably saw it yourself. People weren't even shocked to hear about a chimera showing up."

Ezra raised an eyebrow. "What sort of things?"

"Things have been… disappearing, I guess is what I'd say. Sometimes people, sometimes dogs, sometimes cattle. The first time the chimera was seen, we thought that was what was causing it. But it hasn't always been messy like when one of them attack. Just eerie, really. Why just the other day…"

"Now that's enough," one of the other men butted in. "Don't nobody need to be telling a hunter when something strange is goin' on. They know before we do. Ain't that right?" The men looked intently at her, the question shining in their eyes, and the subject brought up once more.

"I suppose, gentlemen, you wish to know about the tooth?"

No response.

"To be honest," Ezra continued, "I haven't used a tooth in a very long time. After all, if there is no rumor of chimera, why should I waste my stores?"

"But what about today? How did you find that one today?"

Ezra smiled, a genuine smile. "You forget a hunter has other ways to track and trap than simply a tooth. Though it's a powerful tool, to be sure. The tooth is an edge, a way to get close. But our strength is here," Ezra pointed to her eyes, "and here," she touched her ears, "and here," she tapped her nose. "After all, you shouldn't believe everything you hear." She looked into the dregs of her tea. "And yet gentlemen, I must retire. For it has been a long day, and if the chimera are on the rise—as you suggest—then rest will be a fleeting luxury."

●

Moonlight streamed through gaps in the shingled roof. The night was warm and hot, pleasant even. Things would be different if a rainstorm began. If that happened, Ezra was prepared to raise her tent among the bales of hay and broken tools. But the thought of rain wasn't what kept her awake. Her blood still ran hot from the encounter with the chimera and the thought of the prize around her neck.

The tooth. Ezra hadn't been entirely honest when she spoke of the tooth earlier. True, she hadn't used one in years, but her reasons were false. She didn't abstain from the tooth out of fastidiousness or propriety. Her supply had simply long been exhausted. She had used her last tooth seven years ago following a rumor of a burrow. Yet that time had been as fruitless as all the rest.

But now, with actual evidence the chimera still lived, Ezra's thoughts turned again and again to the ivory prize. She longed to taste the searing burn of a tooth's powder, and yet she knew she must not do so without reason.

There had been no wail. The chimera, when it felt the tip of her arrow, should have wailed. If any other chimera had been close, the creature would have called for help, or vengeance. The only rational reason was that there was no help to come. And yet... and yet...

Ezra sighed. The tooth could erase those suspicions, but only with a full dose. To use anything less would be a waste of potential. If she were to use the tooth, it should be all or nothing. But if there had been no wail...

"Strange things," she whispered. That's what the farmer had said. He said people had been vanishing, no evidence left behind. He said no one was surprised a chimera had appeared. Perhaps there weren't chimera about, but what about other things? Other beasts? Other oddities? A hunter, after all, was not devoted to the chimera, though that was their original purpose. If something else was out there... something new...

She had to know. She had a tooth in one hand and rumors in the other. If she didn't use the tooth, then she may lose her chance. But if she was wrong, how many years before she saw another chimera? Would she *ever*? She had to know.

With her decision made, Ezra knew sleep would be impossible. She rose and gathered the rest of her belongings. Though late, she made two stops on her way out of town. The first was to give a nod of thanks to the mechanic, the only man who had shown her respect. The second had been to the pharmacist to replenish her supplies. That was all she needed for now. This town had nothing left for her.

North she traveled.

She walked for two hours before hitching a ride from a passing truck. Ezra wanted to be at least sixty miles inland before she used the tooth, and Regalwood had been too close to the coast. She had no desire to waste the reach of her eye by looking at lifeless ocean. After all, the chimera avoided salt water.

When dawn had come, Ezra thanked the driver for the ride. She could see in the distance the location for her vigil. It was a hill, certainly not a mountain. The rises and falls of these lands could in no way be considered mountains. But it was still high ground. Slight, rocky, covered with amicable green shrubs and a smattering of pine and laurel.

Perfect.

●

Mortar, pestle, file, scalpel, needle, fire, and cup. Ezra laid the tools before her on a silk square of black cloth. She first cleaned the instruments, then put each to diligent use. She scraped the tooth along the file, making long splinters of bone. Once the strands were ready, she commenced grinding until the fragments were reduced to powder. With the needle, she pricked her finger and introduced a drop of blood to the mix. This was the hidden part, the secret part. No doubt Mr. Crouse would stop at the grinding. The rich man would drink the powder and receive a leap in stamina, awareness, reflexes, and strength. But that was only one way to take the drug. To truly gain the benefits of a tooth, for full potency, blood and fire were also needed. And Ezra desired the full effect.

She placed the stone bowl over the smoldering coals. Slowly, the white powder reduced to a pallid, bubbling liquid. Ezra waited until the time was right, when the color shifted to pale olive, then she acted. Wielding the scalpel once more, she cut a long slit in her thigh. That portion of her body had never been marked by the chimera, and yet was overrun with scars. When the first drop of blood appeared, she rubbed the formula over the wound. As she had seen countless times before, the liquid sought the injury. It seeped in and disappeared. Moments later, the cut had healed. The only trace was a thin line.

The hunter sat back. She could feel the fire running within her veins as the tooth worked its way through her body. The weariness was coming as well, the overpowering desire to sleep. But Ezra knew she must fight this, for the trance would begin in moments. Ten, nine, eight... she struggled to count down, to make herself focus.

Then it began.

Her mind rocketed upward. Below, her unconscious body could be glimpsed for only a moment before shrinking to obscurity. Her eye soared, then paused, seven miles above the land, the green carpet stretching below her. This was the last of the simplicity, the last of the natural, the last until—

The world changed.

Ezra's mind blinked as the eight layers of existence peeled off one by one. Every time a layer was removed, the color of the world dissolved, revealing a baser, stranger, more abstract hue. At each stage, the existence of nature was removed as well. The first strip removed rocks, dirt, rivers, and the mundane. The second strip removed grass and trees. The third, fourth, and fifth strips removed fish, fowl, and beast. The sixth strip removed man. This was where the vision truly began, when the world of humanity and the world of nature were peeled back so only the supernatural remained.

Her mind scanned the surface, looking for the flares of brightness indicating the chimera. And yet there were none. She searched furiously. Only seconds remained until this layer of reality disappeared, and with it, the ability to locate her enemy. The next layer, the one beyond this, had never shown her anything. That layer was the fabric of reality, the governing laws of nature. Light, darkness, gravity, and mathematics: immutable properties of no use to a hunter. For a brief instant, she thought she saw a flare, far, far to the north. Was it a chimera? Before she could be sure, the penultimate layer was swept away.

Ezra had expected the pale phosphorus of the final layer of the world. She had anticipated the maddeningly uniform appearance, where existence shone as a featureless glowing globe. She did not get what she expected. The final layer of reality was anything but constant, anything but calm. The world looked like a sunburst of ethereal light, so bright and so powerful that she tried to shield her mind's eye. Yellows, greens, bright blues, savage reds, iridescent pinks. There was no uniformity here. And yet it did have reason.

The starburst had a center, in what was beyond her mind's eye, far, far to the west, past the great river and beyond the borders of civilization. That must certainly be the center of it all. But the starburst was not alone. On the coast, not far from her—at least what she remembered as the coast from before such things dissolved—there was an intense point of light. She fixed her gaze on the point and focused.

Her vision shifted. The layers of reality began to return again, each piling back on top of the last. Ezra watched as the layer of chimera, man, beast, bird, fish, plant, and rock returned, careful not to shift her eyes from where she had seen the light. And with the landscape returned, she knew its location, a small fishing village, resting at the mouth of the river winding east across the low country.

The hunter fell. Her mind plummeted from the sky as she returned down, down, down to her motionless body.

When Ezra hit, the layers of ultimate reality lifted suddenly and terribly. And yet in her mind, the image of the white-hot light in the seaside town remained. And on her lips, a name formed.

"David."

4

GREENWATER'S END

David darted into the alley behind the general store. He could hear his pursuers closing in as they scrambled over the junk scattered in the street. He knew he couldn't outrun them, but maybe he could outmaneuver them. Vaulting over a pile of boxes, he charged for the chain-link fence blocking the alley's exit. If he could get up and over fast enough, then he could escape. He jumped and began to climb, but—

"Got you!" A hand locked around his left ankle. Another hand grabbed his right leg and pulled hard. Rather than fighting, he released the fence to fall backward on top of Anthony, Lofton's oldest grandson. They tumbled to the ground in laughter. David looked up to see the other cousins round the corner to meet them.

"Dang, you're slippery," Anthony exclaimed as he pulled himself to his feet. "Where'd you learn to run like that?"

"My brothers and I used to play football together," David replied. "I was the littlest, so I had to be quick."

"Well, you're quick, all right."

Anthony pulled David to his feet. He murmured thanks and brushed off his pants. The rest of Lofton's grandsons gathered haphazardly around.

"So, do y'all want to play again?" one asked.

Anthony shook his head. "I promised grandpa we'd be back by noon. You guys can go again, but we're done."

Like David, Lofton's oldest grandson was fourteen years old. He was tall, but not yet beginning to fill out. His curled black hair stood out about an inch all over his head, and he always seemed to wear an easy smile. Before today, David had only talked with Anthony once, as the boy was usually out fishing with his father. But there had been no fishing today. Anthony's dad was concerned about the weather—and to David's benefit. Now he had a guide who could show him the ins and outs of the town.

Before now, Lofton had been the one who led David around. Together they had inspected every inch of Walter's farm, the land surrounding Lofton's daughter's homes, and the old man's property itself. For two days they searched, and in that time, David hadn't found a single Hole. But he had been anxious to look at the rest of the town, the roads, the docks, and the boatyard. He wanted to be where the people were. He wanted to be where the danger might be as well. Finally, after pleading with the oysterman, Lofton had let David go, but only with Anthony as an escort.

David turned to Lofton's grandson. "We can't go back. We haven't even started looking."

"Don't worry. I just needed a good excuse to get away." Anthony winked at him. "If we didn't tell 'em something, they'd just have followed us. So, this is Greenwater's End."

The town's main street looked like something from a postcard. The road was lined on either side with shops and craftsmen's tables. A few alleys splintered from the main road, but little was beyond them.

There was a general store, a tavern, a blacksmith, a post office, a butcher, and a few shops that sold tools, fishing equipment, and grain. Anthony was most excited to show David the electronics store where lamps, flashlights, alarm clocks, and power cords were strung up as though in an art gallery. Each building had stone foundations on which wooden framing sat. The only exception was the church, which rested atop a small hill at the very end of the main street. The church was constructed of stone and brick, with a high spire containing a circular stained glass window.

David pointed up the street. "What kind of church is that?"

"What do you mean?" Anthony asked.

"I mean, like, is it Catholic, or something?"

Anthony shrugged. "Church is church. Go on Sunday, pray to Jesus, all those things. We also have town meetings there. Don't you have church back home?"

"Of course we did. Just asking."

"All right, then let's keep going."

In the two days since David had traveled through the gateway to Greenwater's End, he'd pushed to learn as much as he could—but without causing too much of a stir. This wasn't home, that was certain. This was a different *world*. A lot was the same—a whole lot. But significant chunks were missing. To hear Lofton tell it, there was no Europe, no Asia, no Africa, and no Australia. The continents still existed, but no one lived there, and hadn't for almost two hundred years. There had been a war, or a plague, or *something* that decimated the population. The very few survivors abandoned their old homes for the Americas. Only they didn't even call it that. As far as David could tell, there weren't countries at all anymore, just towns here and there. And with fewer people in the world, everything was a little behind the times. They may say it was the same year he did back home, but things looked more like the way his grandfather described life from when he was young.

"So over there," Anthony said, "is where they set up the farmers market. That only happens on Saturdays, though. And really mostly folks just trade with each other."

David listened with half-interest. He was distracted by the sky. Heavy clouds had rolled in from the east. They were thick, weighty, infusing the air with anticipation. He had asked Anthony about the storm earlier and whether they should get home. The boy had just shrugged it off. He said if there was a problem, the church bells would ring in warning. David hadn't thought about any danger, he just hadn't wanted to get rained on.

"And back here—you'll want to see this, David—this is the gallows. They haven't hanged anyone in a long time, though. I think the last was Mr. Gregor. He used to be the mechanic until he went crazy and burned down the library. A few folks got trapped in the fire."

David nodded. "Uh-huh. Right." He looked around and finally asked what he'd been wondering all morning. "So where is everyone? It looks empty."

"On the water, of course. Or out in the fields. Come on, I'll show you the docks."

Anthony led David to the end of the street, where the road split in two directions. Heading to the right, the road set off toward the farms. Going left, down the hill, led to the wharf. As they walked, the buzz of voices and the smell of seafood grew stronger.

The wharf was set on a long channel that wound through the marshes before heading out to the sea. A cement barrier stretched the length of the waterfront, with wooden docks bristling from the seawall into the channel. Most of the slips were empty, their occupants still on the water. The remaining ships were primarily trawlers, their diesel engines rumbling as they entered and left the docks. There were a few boats under sail-power alone, but those were much less numerous.

Men swarmed both decks and docks. David didn't know exactly what they were doing, but they all seemed busy sanding, scraping barnacles, sorting ropes, and conducting any number of repairs. Like Lofton and his family, most of the men were dark-skinned. As for the rest, some were pale and blond, some olive-skinned with straight black hair, and some short and swarthy with hair hanging in thick curls. All of them had a sun-worn look. These were men of the sea.

"When will the other boats come back?" David asked.

"Anywhere from about now till dark, depending on how far out they sailed. The fishing's been pretty bad these last few days, so some came home early. And who knows if this storm is going to do anything."

"Sounds good. Where to next?"

Anthony laughed. "There's not a whole lot else to see unless you want to check the farms one by one. But you're the expert. Where did you look for Holes back home?"

"Let's go back to town first," David said. "I want to recheck the streets, make sure I didn't miss anything. Then we can loop around a few times, maybe come down here when we're done. We'll stay where it's busy for now. I can check farms tomorrow."

They turned and started back up the road to the town center when a voice called from behind them. "Hey, Anthony! Anthony, hold on a second."

David turned to see a collection of eight boys stroll up from behind. They were all dressed in knee-length canvas pants and plain shirts marked with the refuse of a day's fishing. Most were at least his age, though some were slightly older.

"Back already?" Anthony asked.

One of the older boys shrugged. "It's the storm. East is a bad direction this time of year. Everybody's heading in. Too early to tie it all down, but we'll listen for the bells."

Anthony turned to David. "Sorry, forgot you for a second. Everyone, this is David. He's staying with my grandpa." While a few of the boys nodded, no one paid him much attention.

The largest of the boys spoke up. "We were going to play some ball to kill time. You want in? The new kid can come too."

"Yeah, we'll play," Anthony said. "Behind the church, or what? Who's got the ball?"

David flinched. A strange electricity was building in the air, an anticipation he didn't feel from the darkening clouds above. The anxiousness hit a peak, and then—

<Pock-fffftttt>

David's eyes went wide at the sound of an opening Hole. Adrenaline surged through his body. He darted his eyes left and right searching for the anomaly. And then he saw it. Perfectly round and totally black, a Hole had opened in the middle of the road. The Hole was relatively small, only two feet across, but that's all it took. He watched with horror as a heavyset boy with curly red hair, walked toward it unaware.

David lunged forward. He tackled the redhead, shoving him out of the way. The surprised—and far larger—boy went sprawling to the ground. David, however, neither hesitated nor apologized. He snatched a triangular rock from the ground and traced a circle around the Hole. He looked up with fire in his eyes.

"Back! Everyone get back! Don't cross the line. Get back… Now!" He brandished the stone like a knife. The other boys were too confused to react.

The redheaded boy jumped up, fists clenched. "What's wrong with you?" He took a step toward David, and inadvertently toward the Hole.

"No!" David yelped. "It's a Hole! If you touch it, you'll be sucked in!"

The boy steamed in frustration. The other kids started to chuckle.

"You have to listen to me!" David looked around at them. "Just stay back. I've seen these before, I've—"

David wasn't ready for the punch. His vision went white for a second as his legs gave way. The stone tumbled from his hand as he landed hard on the dusty road.

Anthony stepped over to help him back to his feet. "Listen, Henry," Anthony said. "Everyone, listen to me. He's telling the truth. My granddad told me all about it."

The laughter only grew. The look in the redheaded boy's eyes turned cruel. "Mr. Lofton's a drunk and everybody knows it."

David slowly rose once more. He wasn't angry at the boy for hitting him, only that the others wouldn't listen. "You don't believe me? Just watch." He picked up the stone again and held it over the Hole. He dropped it, and as the rock fell, it disappeared into the Hole. He knew the other kids would have seen it pass right into the ground itself.

"What kind of trick is that?" Another boy reached forward with his hand.

"Don't touch it." David's voice was stern. "If you so much as brush against it, you'll get sucked under. And it will never let go. Ever."

"That's a load of bull," Henry sneered. "This kid is trying to make us look stupid. I'll show you." The boy stepped forward once more. David tried to stop him but was held back on all sides.

"See," the boy said. "It's just dirt." The redhead stepped across David's line and directly into the Hole. But where he stepped, there was no ground. Henry was yanked forward as his leg was seized. It whipped him to the ground. The violent jerk hyperextended his hip, snapping the tendons in a horrifying wet rip as his leg bent behind him.

The boy howled with pain. Shrieks of panic filled the air. He called out, but the words were indistinguishable amid his frantic sobbing. Anthony and the other kids darted forward. They grabbed his arms and tried to pull.

"All of you! Help!" Anthony shouted. "No one cross that line!"

The group of boys wrapped around one another, each pulling as the trapped boy wailed. Snot ran down his nose, tears gushed from his eyes, and blood trickled from his mouth from the injuries within. But not one inch was yielded by the Hole.

"My arms!" he screamed. "You're pulling off my arms!"

The boys yelled at one another to pull harder, to not let go. Each and every one of them tugged to help their friend.

Except David.

He backed away, his eye throbbing from where he'd been hit. His heart raced, and his arms felt electric with anticipation. But he made no move to help. There was no helping. A Hole never let go. David barely heard the wails of the boy or the yells of the others. He could only wonder if the Holes had followed him here. Was this somehow his fault?

Another wrenching of sinew and the trapped boy slipped further in. As his head disappeared into the Hole, his screams were silenced. Shocked, the other boys let go and tumbled backward.

David walked forward. He pulled a stick from the ground and drew another ring around the Hole. "No one crosses this line." His words were flat. And this time, no one laughed at him. He looked around to see a crowd had gathered. A roll of thunder echoed from over the water.

"What you do to him there, boy?" an old fisherman asked. "Where'd he go?"

"A Hole got him." David pointed at the ring. "Does anyone else see it?"

The fisherman ignored his question, asking again, "But what did you *do* to him? He ain't 'round here. So where is he?"

Dread poured over David. These people thought he was responsible. They thought this was his fault. Should he run, try to make it back? No. He was too tired; he had nowhere to go.

A heavy voice boomed through the crowd. "Everyone stop. Everyone be easy." David looked up to see Walter, Lofton's son, push through the onlookers.

"What happened, David?" Walter asked.

"There's a Hole." He pointed. "Right there. One of the kids got sucked in."

Anthony whispered, "It was Henry."

Walter nodded. His eyes were fierce but his face calm. "Ok then. Anthony?"

"Yes, Uncle Walter?"

"Find the mayor. Call an emergency meeting. We've got a problem. We need David to tell everyone what he told us. People have to know."

"Have to know what?" someone called.

Walter shrugged off the question. He looked at the crude line around the Hole, then over at David. "Is there a way to fill it in?"

"No, but we can block it off. Build a wall. It's the only thing to do."

An old fisherman cackled. The sound was without humor, dry and grating. "They ain't gonna be no town hall today, Walter. We got a bigger problem."

One of the kids looked up. His eyes were red and angry with fear. "Henry's gone. He's gone! What could be bigger than that?"

As if in response, thunder rolled once more. Then the bell at the church tower rang. And rang. And rang.

5

WINDS

Ezra tilted her nose to the wind. Until now, she'd been too far away to smell the ocean. But with a breeze rising, the brackish air raked her nostrils. Something else rode on the wind besides salt. The air had weight. Not just humid, but drawing a presence with it. A storm was coming. And that meant trouble in late summer.

The hunter knelt to tighten the laces on her calf-high boots. Both were already well-bound, but the habit was unshakable. At the first hint of danger, check your boots, prepare your weapons, know your ground. Ezra ran through the list. The terrain was simple, a mixture of straight pine and the occasional copse of gathered oak. A survey of her weapons was less than satisfactory. Her hunting knife, its blade long enough to be considered a sword, was strapped tight across her right thigh. Her arrows, replenished to a full thirty, remained ready in their quiver. She still needed a bow, though. And until she could replace hers, her only ranged attacks would be from her throwing knives.

Ezra rose to her feet. She had two other weapons, of course. Her body was the first. Despite her injuries, she was healing well. And her last weapon? She smiled. The chain attached to the manacle around her wrist was always there as a last resort. Both crude and elegant, it served as a reminder of the day she had earned it.

Pausing for but a moment more, Ezra checked the cord holding her shoulder-slung pack. The long, fat roll, bound in sinew, was positioned to hang just beneath her quiver. The knot resting against her sternum was secure for now, though the slightest tug would release the satchel. Satisfied she was ready—or as ready as possible—she resumed her pace. She wove through the pine forest and to the town whose name she knew not, but to the man whose name she did.

David.

●

When Ezra reached the edge of the forest, she saw thunderclouds building in the distance. Out of habit, she extended her left hand to point at the storm, thumb outstretched, then glanced to her right. The old sailors had taught her that. The thumb pointed to what part of the storm was the real concern. What would "getcha." She chuckled. She was now older than the "old salts" who had taught her the trick. Nevertheless, this storm couldn't be avoided. The thunderheads spanned the horizon to the southeast, boiling and roiling. Ezra turned her eyes to the north instead. A tendril of smoke emerged from beyond the marshes. Finally, civilization. And perhaps the home of this David.

Ezra quickened to a loping run, only to realize the marsh resisted such direct travel. Dropping her speed, she wove through the low, wet land. She kept her eyes down, searching for patches of firmer ground while avoiding oysters. As she snaked through the marsh, the first of the clouds stretched their fingers overhead, and rain began to fall. Not heavy, but constant. Her broad hat kept the rain from reaching her core. Yet as the ground became saturated, she was soaked from the bottom up. Her boots found less purchase on the softened ground, and her pace suffered.

By the time Ezra reached the trees on the far side, the breeze had tripled in strength and clocked around to her back. But with a trailing wind and stable ground, her lope became a run. She also accepted the storm for what it was. The island peoples had called them *tai'fun*, the God Winds. Closer to this side of the world, they called it a hurricane.

The hunter ran until she reached a split-rail fence at the edge of town. She vaulted the ties and slowed to an even pace. Ahead, she saw the townsfolk were deep into their preparations. Bags were being hauled, ropes tightened and knotted, and every item in the village was being staked and secured. She sniffed the wind once more. There was fear in the air, dank and palpable, but it wasn't coming from the storm. Something else troubled them.

A voice called from behind her. "Excuse me, sir. It's not safe out here."

Ezra turned to face her hailer, a man with skin as dark as the tribesmen of the southern continent. He was large—very large—but with muscles toned from physical labor instead of battle. She raised her whitened brows in question.

"Oh, sorry… ma'am. If you'll be looking for shelter later, we'd appreciate a hand now. Storm's coming." He nodded, though did not smile. Ezra waited for a moment, and the man began to fidget. "Sorry… I wasn't trying to be rude. My name's Walter."

"Ezra."

"Ezra, then. Storm's coming, big one. Bales to the left, sacks to the right. Pile what you see together, but pile it low. We'll handle the nets if you can help with the haul. I don't mean to be curt, but…"

"But a storm's coming." She spoke no more. Without pausing to remove her pack, she fell in beside the others. She received a sidelong glance, then a nod as she took their lead. As she helped, Ezra examined the townsfolk. Most appeared to be farmers or fishermen. None had weapons at their sides, save for the odd fishing knife or awl. Their hands were—without exception—calloused and cracked. And whether blackened in soil or reeking of fish, the people embodied shipboard discipline. Even now, despite the threat of the storm, the stacks of goods were orderly, the tie-downs precise, their motions efficient. During the war, Ezra would have sacrificed much to have worked with people such as this.

Down the hill from the town center, something caught Ezra's eye. In the middle of the road stood an odd, circular barricade. What made the structure peculiar was not that it blocked the path, but that it was built of scraps of wood, broken furniture, and jumbled refuse. The haphazard construction was in sharp contrast to the fastidiousness elsewhere. What's more, a wrongness emanated from within that wall, one as present and evident as a slick of blood on a schoolhouse floor.

Ezra turned to those around her, but all avoided her gaze. The feeling of uneasiness had heightened. She set back to her task, patient for now. She would lift one bag, place and secure it, then return for the next. As she worked, the rain shifted from a light drizzle to falling in sheets. Then easing up once more, then heavy, then nothing. The winds, however, only grew.

"Listen up everyone." Walter leaped atop a pile of sacks. Rainwater glistened across his mahogany brow. "Surge is on the way. Listen. I say the surge is coming! Last ties and out of there, everyone."

Not understanding, Ezra turned to grab another sack but was stopped by a firm hand on her shoulder. The knife at her side was half drawn when Walter's voice stopped her. "You get inside too. It's the storm surge."

Another nod, and Ezra angled to where the townspeople swarmed, a broad stonework building in an otherwise wooden town. The church, of course. And where else in a time of crisis? A priest in sodden robes gestured the sixty or so people through the doors. She paused at the base of the steps. This, too, was a habit, a last survey of the land. She took stock of both the supply piles and the placement of cottages and stores surrounding the square. She wondered how much would remain when the true winds came. But these were strong folk, and this wasn't their first storm.

As the villagers flocked inside, Walter stood back to help the others. Ezra lingered on the steps until he sent her in as well. Once through the entrance, the men began to swing the heavy doors closed. Another pair of men stood to the side, ready to bar the door.

"Wait," a woman's voice called from behind. "There're more people comin'. I see 'em there."

Ezra turned to follow the woman's fingers, her eyes joining those around her. A group of four people shuffled toward the church's entrance, hats pulled down over their eyes, sacks slung across their backs.

They almost didn't make it, she thought. Ezra wondered whether the great doors would have been reopened once shut. Maybe, maybe not. Maybe not even if the preacher was out there. Her stomach tightened, the same pit she'd felt so many times before. She faced the pointing woman.

"Do you know those people? Do you know their names? Their parents? Their homes?" She kept her voice tight. "Answer me."

The village woman's eyes filled with fear and suspicion. "No, ma'am. They look to be travelers, same as you. The Lord says all shelter in a time of…"

Ezra called to the men, "Shut the door, now. For your lives, shut the door!"

Walter turned to her, his brow wrinkled. He laid a strong hand on her shoulder. "Now listen, we can't turn anyone away. The storm surge is…"

Ezra jerked from Walter's grip. Her hand darted to the knot on her chest. With a tug, the pack fell free. Her other hand dropped to her weapons, removing one of the many throwing knives. With a few quick steps, she darted through the church doors, rolling forward and into a crouch to let the dagger fly. The blade buried itself in the forehead of one of the travelers. The wide straw hat dropped as the traveler crumpled.

A scream sheared the air behind her, then diminished to stunned silence. The traveler disintegrated into a shambles the moment he hit the ground. His companions did not react with fear. They simply peered with odd curiosity. Their faces showed no pain, no sadness. And then… recognition.

Ezra snaked her hunting knife from its sheath and rose into a crouch. As the blade came bare, she flicked her left wrist and the chain wrapping her arm dropped from the sleeve of her coat. The metal clanged on the granite steps of the church. There was no longer doubt. The villagers knew what she was. A hunter. The things out there knew it as well.

The first of the travelers lifted his arms. The tattered cloth, at one moment flapping in the storm, turned dark, becoming an oily black, only to explode, splinter, and then coalesce as the traveler hunched. Spikes, scales, and wings erupted from the man's back. Soon the man had no back at all, only an armored carapace. Ezra heard the screams grow behind her.

"Chimera! The chimera have come, the…"

The creature shot forward, darting to where Walter blocked the doors. The leap became flight as its slick wings buzzed in fury. The four segmented arms hooked their oily claws. But as the demon came close, Ezra leaped. She flipped her chain into the air with viper speed. The links snapped around the chimera, catching it on the rise. She twisted her body, swinging the weight of her prey in the air, and smashing it hard onto the church steps. Her knife came down as the creature hit, bisecting its head.

Ezra charged back into the church, bowling Walter over as she entered. "Close the doors!"

Walter moved first, the others a moment behind as they shut the doors and set the bar. As the wood cracked down, something heavy hit the frame. The door bulged inward, eliciting screams from the townspeople.

Ezra looked at Walter. "Does this church have a rectory? Somewhere belowground you can hide?"

He shook his head. "This is low country ma'am. No basements, 'cause they flood. Besides, these walls are strong and—"

The chimera shrieked outside, the call coming from above. Ezra shot her eyes upward. A large rose window, a beauty of stained glass and stonework, was fixed high on the wall. A shadow passed across the window, and then vanished. Moments later, the window exploded inward as a chimera barreled through. Shards of colored glass rained on the townspeople. Screams filled the air as the chimera crashed into the wooden altar, reducing it to splinters.

Ezra darted forward once more, her blade ready. But she didn't reach the creature before it was upright and striking at the nearest person. An oily foreleg snapped down, eviscerating a refugee. The creature jumped, a single beat of its wings propelling it into the air. The serrated legs spread wide as the chimera fell into the thick of the congregation.

The hunter leaped as well, her boot finding purchase first on the back of a pew, then a bystander's shoulder. She cracked the chain, and the links coiled around one of the chimera's legs. She jerked hard, and the limb ripped from its body, disappearing into the crowd. The creature flailed. Townspeople fell wounded and bleeding as it struck out. Seeing the gap widen, Ezra hurled her knife into the crowd. Once again, her aim was true. The blade found its home in the head of the chimera.

And then all was still. Even the severed leg ceased its twitching. In the shocked silence, whimpers and murmurs grew.

"One more, damn you," Ezra said over the sobs. "There is one more out there! Arm yourselves and open the doors. We must take the fight to—"

Something heavy smashed into the front doors of the church. And this time, it broke through. Though not because of the chimera. The storm surge had arrived, the hurricane—a threat half-forgotten in the madness—was here as well.

The doors buckled inward under the force of the wave. Knee-high, frothy water filled the church, lifting both pews and the bodies of the fallen.

Walter called out, his voice steady. "Grab for the walls, make for higher ground."

Shrieks filled the air, but they faded into the background. Ezra turned toward the doors and pushed her way to the exit.

"What are you doing?" Walter asked. "You can't go out there."

Ezra spit through gritted teeth. "There's still one left."

"Forget those things. It's the storm we need to worry about now."

"Not yet," she snapped.

She looked out through the hollow frame of the splintered door, the storm surge lapping knee-high, no longer pushing, but ever-moving in a constant slosh. A survey of the courtyard gave no sign of anything living. Bits of houses, fallen trees, smashed wood, and debris bobbed over the flooded ground.

But there was no sign of the chimera.

Panic seized Ezra, a pain as sharp as the sting of any whip. The water had already swept away the bodies. Two chimera, four teeth. All lost.

Ezra spun away, her eyes roving the church for the corpse of the other chimera. There, the shiny black carapace, already beginning to dissolve, bobbed among the townspeople. Ezra waded to the body. She grasped the hilt of the knife still embedded in the skull and twisted the head toward her.

The face of every chimera was unique, and all unsettling. This creature had taken its last instant of life to mimic its attacker. Ezra looked at her own countenance on the creature's body, her features rotting in fast decay. This was not the first time she had seen her dying face. Though the last time, it had been a face twenty-four years younger.

Reaching to the back of her belt, she removed a pair of pliers. She peeled back the creature's lips to reveal its gleaming white teeth. Her heart sank. Only one of the two fangs remained. The other must have been lost long ago. But even a single tooth would be sweet. Ezra gripped, then pulled swiftly down. The fang came free with a hollow slurp. Smiling, she dropped her prize into the pouch around her neck.

Next, she dragged the floating body across the church floor and to the great husk of double doors. She put one boot against the chimera's head and kicked it into the deluge. The knife came free, and though it dripped with ichor, she sheathed it.

Ezra turned back to face the church. Everywhere people clutched to the rails mounted along the walls, or to one another. The water had not risen past her knee, but the danger remained. Human blood, mud, and the foul sap of the chimera mingled together. They could all have been poisoned. No way to be certain.

She surveyed the room. Walter was huddled to one side with a woman and three young boys, no doubt his family. They looked uninjured, though shaken. The large man caught her eye. He spoke a few words to his wife and then walked toward her. His face grew ever more grim as he approached. "That what you came for? Were you looking for them? Or were they looking for you?"

Ezra shook her head. "I wasn't followed. And save your scolding for later. As you said, we've a storm to mind. But first, where is David?"

6

THE EYE

David gritted his teeth. He tried to ignore the howling outside, and the relentless battering against doors and windows. The hurricane was just a distraction. Even once it passed, there was still the matter of the Holes.

Lofton, however, refused to be concerned. "Can't do a thing but hunker until the winds stop," he said. There was a quiet fatalism to his words, which reminded David of the way most people had reacted to the Holes back home. Wait it out. Sit it out. See what may come.

The old man walked to him and placed a gnarled hand on his shoulder. "Now listen here, boy. That face is sour enough to curdle milk. I'd offer you whiskey, but I'd catch hell if Walter or the girls found out."

David forced a smile. Lofton had clutched a bottle in his hand since the storm began but had yet to open it. Occasionally, he'd set his eye to a hollow where the boards didn't quite meet, mutter at the storm, then look at the bottle before shaking his head.

"Where's your family?" David asked. "You think they're ok?"

"Lord have mercy. Walter's been tying bales for something on twenty years. My daughters too. They'll be fine. And it's ebb tide right now, which will help with the storm surge. Us low country folks can handle a storm now and then." Lofton smiled. "I suppose you didn't have hurricanes out west, huh?"

David shook his head. "No. We'd get some blizzards in the winter, though. Sometimes the roads would close and no one could get through. But nothing like this. We kind of liked it, you know. Sometimes they'd close school too."

"Snow, huh? Haven't seen snow fall 'round here in three years. And even then it didn't stick. But don't you worry, David. For your first storm, this is as safe a place as there is."

A crack of thunder outside—too close—and David flinched again. He and the old man were alone, and without other voices, ignoring the hurricane was difficult. Most of the other villagers were either riding out the storm in their homes, or in the church. Even Lofton's grandsons, sons, and cousins—who always seemed present—were with their families.

And then the wind *died*. The rush calmed to nothing. The howl became a whisper, still present, but not battering at the door.

"What… what happened?" David asked.

Lofton winked. "That's our sign. Eye's come! Come on. We don't have long, but best to check our ties while we can."

●

Ezra's ears perked as the wind ceased. "What's happened? Is the storm finished?" She looked to where Walter stood. While the rest of the townsfolk had been huddled and crying, he had taken action. He directed his sons and his wife to bandage the injured and to try to restore some semblance of order. Walter's skin glistened from both sweat and the stormwater. Ezra could tell the man was scared, though tried not to show it. He had seen storms, that was for sure. The way he moved and the way he talked was evidence enough. But before today, he had never seen a chimera.

"Storm's not done, ma'am," Walter muttered. "This is the 'eye,' the calm at its center. We'll have ten minutes, maybe fifteen, before the winds start again. We should do a run of it while we can."

"You'd run?" She raised an eyebrow. "But how can you outrun the wind?"

Walter took his turn to smile. "Not a run *for* it, a run *of* it. Check the shutters, lashings, and such. Tie down anything that may have burst loose and—"

"Count your dead?"

Walter frowned. "Check our friends. There's a difference." He motioned to the men around him. They slowly rose at his command. He pushed toward the door when Ezra stopped him.

"There may still be chimera."

"Then come with us."

"David." She spoke the word, not as a question or request.

Walter shook his head. "The flood waters may have dropped, but he's too far away to make it in the eye. I'll not have you risking yourself."

Ezra did not reply.

Walter folded his arms. "And I need to know a few things first."

"I've told you what I know."

"You didn't say how you knew his name."

Ezra didn't reply, and she wouldn't. Not until she saw for herself who this David was. All Walter would tell her was that he was a boy, a castaway of sorts. Nothing more. Walter, too, had secrets. Ezra could read that as easily as the worry on his brow. "I'll come with you," she said. "There may be more of them. I'll keep watch."

"And work?"

"Yes. And work. But first, there's something I need to do." She pulled the chimera's tooth from the pouch around her neck, stuck it between her jaws, and bit down hard. Walter covered his ears at the sound of crunching bone.

●

Outside of Lofton's shelter, fallen branches and debris scattered the ground. The ubiquitous layer of brown pine straw was now mixed with vibrant green needles shaken from the trees. And while the shelter stood strong, many of the surrounding dogwoods, oaks, willows, and poplars were twisted and split. The breaks, all halfway up the trunks, looked to have been severed by an angry colossus swinging its hand across the forest.

David followed Lofton as the old man stumped around the squat building of interlocking timbers. He paused every few feet to inspect where blowing limbs had left marks. But there was no real damage, and nothing needing immediate repair. Lofton's house on the water may be a different story. David guessed that in earlier years the old man might have scurried down from the knoll to check that as well.

<Pock-ffffttt>

David dove to the side, the action a reflex. He skinned his knee, but the pain was nothing more than a dull throb—nothing compared to his rising fear. *Another? And why now?* As he stared at the Hole, Lofton called from behind him.

"Hello out there! What're you doing?" the old man yelled.

David turned to answer, but saw the old oysterman wasn't speaking to him, but rather a figure sliding through the trees.

Lofton continued, "What you doing out there? Best come in now. Winds'll pick up again soon."

A shape emerged from the tightly bunched pines. The person—possibly a man but difficult to tell—had a dusky brown trench coat with hands thrust deep into his pockets. The stranger wore a rounded hat that reminded David of those drawn in pictures of Pilgrims, and leather boots as faded as the coat. Something about those boots bothered him. When the traveler walked, the strides didn't quite match the footfalls. Instead, it was like watching someone move across ice, feet rolling backward, as though with each full step taken only a half one was gained.

Lofton called again, "I say, what are you doing out here? You come from town?"

The figure stopped twenty feet from them, though his boots continued to take one step more. He pulled one black-gloved hand from his trench coat. The appendage looked uncannily shiny, and to David, may have had one finger too many. The traveler pointed.

"Davvid?" The question garbled past the his lips. "Davvid?"

"What's your name, sir?" Lofton asked. "Now you can wait the storm out with us, but you've got to tell us your name."

The speaker turned his head, and David flinched as he saw that the eyes were the same pale color as both boots and cloak.

"Arre you Davvid?"

Sweat trickled along his back. And with it, an epiphany. This quaint town, with its farmers and fisherman, its warm-hearted townsfolk, its bustling dock, and idyllic church—all of this was just a corner of a much larger painting. This wasn't a more rustic version of his own world. It was a different world altogether.

David opened his mouth to respond, but Lofton beat him to it. He stomped up to the traveler and pointed at the man's lifeless eyes. "Now listen here, stranger. This here's my home, and I'll…"

The traveler *twitched.* And as it did so, the left hand blurred into a folded pincher. The segmented arm snapped up, then back once more. David flinched as a thin red line appeared down the bridge of Lofton's nose.

"Run, David," Lofton rasped. The oysterman dropped to his knees, then pitched forward.

●

Walter watched as the hunter convulsed where she stood. After Ezra had bitten down on the tooth—the grinding of bone still echoing in his ears—her eyes had rolled back into her head. She shuddered once, twice, then her eyes opened. The whites were bloodshot, her pupils dilated. He shied away from the madwoman's glare.

"The chimera are looking for David." Ezra's voice was maddeningly calm. "And another… Lofton. We need to find them."

"How'd you know who—?"

"Now, Walter!"

He recoiled. "They're on the south side. But the storm could be back any minute. We can't go out that far…"

Ezra sprang to her feet, shifted her gaze south, then took off at a run. Walter raced behind.

●

David ran without direction, only away. He didn't hear the demon behind him, and yet he didn't slow down. His breaths came in huge, gasping heaves, partly from exertion but mostly from fear. But beneath that terror surged an indefatigable desire to live. Crashing through a mess of vines, he stumbled, falling hard on the broad, damp leaves. He scrambled back to his feet, not pausing to see if he was bleeding.

Thunder rolled overhead, followed by rain. The misting grew steadily stronger to transform the woods into an unfamiliar realm. David scanned the downed timber for a place to hide, but there was no familiarity here. Nowhere to turn.

Then he saw it, a toppled tree, with roots pulled from the ground to leave a crevice beneath them. Reacting with awakened animal instinct, he dropped to his belly and slithered inside. He flipped around to peer back through the opening. Outside, the drizzle had become a hard rain. The heavy drops struck the ground, splattering his face with mud. David fought to control his gasping breaths, to stay quiet. He scanned the woods, looking for some sign of the thing chasing him. And then he found something. Not the creature, but a Hole. This one was only twenty feet from his hiding place. Compared to the panic brought on by the demon, he regarded it dully. His senses were already stretched to their limit, beyond rational capacity. With the low whirr of a locust, the creature came into view, hovering above the bushes on oily black wings.

Despite his fear, he took a moment to examine the monster. It no longer looked human at all. Eight segmented legs sprouted from a shiny black carapace; wasp-like wings beat hard against the air. The face of the creature, however, was in flux. While first resembling a housefly, it shifted in color and shape to look like that of Lofton, and then David himself. Only the teeth remained constant. Whether staring out from a human-like head, or behind an insect's mandibles, two ivory fangs were always present.

A gust of wind batted the creature to the debris-covered ground. The wings transformed, becoming a fifth pair of legs as it crawled forward. David watched as it crossed back and forth over his tracks, steadily moving to his hiding place.

"Davvid?" the creature rasped in an over-slow voice. Then the tone changed—even as the creature did—to become the voice of Lofton. "David, you out there? I say, where are you? Give us a word, now."

David remained perfectly still, afraid to make a sound. The creature held its head low to the ground and inhaled with a great snuffle. When it looked up, wearing David's face, savage teeth poked beyond the lips of what would otherwise have been his reflection. Rain dripped down its face and plopped from its chin.

"Come out, David." The monster's voice was a mirror of his own, the voice that sounded within his head. And even worse, he wanted to listen. The surreal nature of being called by name diminished his fear to a throbbing unreality. Then a thought crept through the haze. If it knew his name, then it must know something about why he was here. It must know something about the Holes.

David crawled from beneath the roots and then stood to face the creature. He clenched his fists and tried to sound brave.

"Who are you?" he asked. The howl of the wind carried the words away, and yet he knew the creature heard him. "*What* are you?"

Its lips spread, a grin revealing the fangs. "It *iss* you. You finally made it, as we knew you would. As he ssaid you would. I have a message. The answer to your Holess is out there. You must keep looking… but you must not find your answser. Ever. That'ss the ssecret of the linchpin. No one can win. No one musst ever win." As the creature spoke, it changed: first to Lofton, then to the insect, and then to an amorphous black mass.

A glint of steel caught the corner of David's eye as a knife flew from the trees to strike the creature. Screeching in pain, it transformed into an insect once more. David shied back as a woman, weathered and gaunt, stood suddenly beside him. She held a long knife in her right hand and a length of chain in her left. Her eyes were set forward.

The beast took flight. Even as it shot upward, the woman reacted, moving so quickly that he saw nothing but the blur of metal as an object flew from her hand. The creature howled as the knife struck. It changed its course, darting for the Hole.

"No!" David screamed. He tried to dash forward but slipped in the mud.

The monster, however, was not slowed by the attack. It disappeared into the Hole, and as it did, the awareness that had pulsed within his mind winked out as well.

The gnarled woman released her own cry, this one tinged with longing, but only for a moment before becoming collected once more. She turned her eyes to him and dropped to a crouch at his side. "You're David?"

He nodded.

"I am Ezra. You must come. Quickly." A leathered hand reached out. "That's the last of the chimera. Only the storm is left."

No, David thought. Only the Holes.

7

VIGIL

David flinched as Ezra wrapped her arm around him. Where he had expected frailty, he found none. The woman was sinewy, with knots of muscle over toughened skin. He didn't know what she'd seen or where she'd been—but he knew she'd seen *worse*. And yet, there was a weariness in each step, though he couldn't tell if from a lifetime of trials, or simply the day's.

With Ezra supporting him, David made his way back to Lofton's home. They hunched low as they pushed through the crosswind and the sheets of rain. When they finally reached the shelter, the old man's body was gone. Then he saw why. Walter stood in the doorway. His hands were stained red.

David's knees buckled, though he was steadied by Ezra's firm grip. He could feel her fingers tight around his arm, but the sensation was distant, numb. He opened his mouth to speak, but the words wouldn't come.

Ezra stopped him. "We need to get inside. Can you do that?"

David nodded. He steadied himself and made his way through the door. Ezra followed, closing and barring the entrance behind her. She strode past him and settled on the floor against the far wall. She pulled off her wide-brimmed hat and then curled up in the folds of her cloak. Without another word, the woman's eyes were shut fast. But he couldn't tell if she was sleeping, or simply blocking the storm from her mind.

He looked across the room. His vision filled with white before settling once more. On the far side, Walter knelt over his father's body. Blood was everywhere, soaking the bandages wrapped around the old man's head. Walter's movements, however, were not frantic. He methodically removed the bandages and wiped his father's brow clean.

David crossed over to where Walter knelt. "Is he… going to be ok?"

"He's gone." Walter breathed deeply. His gaze lingered for only a moment before he shifted it to the inert form of the hunter. When he looked at David once more, his eyes were filled with anger and pain.

David gritted his teeth. "What… what was that? What was that thing out there? It chased me, it came for me. And Mr. Lofton, it got Lofton and, and…"

"That," Walter replied, his jaw set, "was a chimera. Surely my father told you about them."

"No! I mean… yes, I guess. He mentioned them once or twice, but I kind of thought it was a fairy tale. I thought they weren't real."

Walter's voice was choked. "They're very real."

David asked, "Is that why things here are the way they are? You know—different. Is that why there are so few people and cities and things?"

Walter nodded. "In the first war, those things killed half the world. Millions died. Whole countries, whole continents. We lost everything to them. We barely escaped the old country." He looked over at Lofton. "Is that real enough for you?"

"It's…" David shook his head in disbelief. "Those things took out everything? *All* of Europe? *All* of Asia? Africa too? Everything? There is no one left there at all?"

Walter snapped, "What did I just say?"

David swallowed hard. In truth, he couldn't imagine it. How could he?

Several seconds passed before he worked up the courage to speak. "Ever since I got here, I wondered how so much of this place could be the same, but so much could be different at the same time. It's the chimera. Back in my world, we didn't have them. Here you do."

Walter answered with a harrumph. David looked down, picking his words carefully.

After a few minutes, he spoke again. "You said 'the first war,' was there another one?"

A double crack of thunder echoed outside, and David flinched. The wind howled, the baleful whine starting shrill then fading in the distance. Walter gritted his teeth, seeming oblivious to the sounds of the tempest. He turned his eyes back to David, looking at him for a long moment before replying. "Yes, there was a second war. That one started right here. My father and his generation—that was their fight. I was just a kid, too young to fight. You can ask the hunter when she wakes up. You can ask her question after question after question, and I'm sure she'd love it. But I'm done with my history lesson."

David turned to look at Ezra. The woman lay curled against the wall. Her eyes were shut fast. She looked to be sleeping, but would occasionally twitch and jerk. He walked over to her, then turned to back to the farmer. "Do you think she's ok?"

"She'll be fine."

For a moment, Walter didn't move. He sat with shoulders hunched and eyes downcast. Without meeting David's gaze, he rose and walked to the cupboard. He removed two wool blankets, tossed one to David, and draped the other over Ezra's unconscious form. Walter paced around the shack, occasionally peering out the window or cocking his head to listen to the winds outside. After several minutes, he turned back to where David sat, his arms folded across his chest.

"My turn to ask some questions. Now tell me the truth, did you call that woman here?"

"Ezra? No. How would I have called her?"

"And the chimera? Did you know they were coming? Like you knew about the Holes?"

"No. If I'd known, I'd have told you."

Walter's eyes were flat. "That hunter, she knew your name. How'd she know that?"

David winced. "I don't know. I really don't know."

"You... you have to know *something!*" Walter's cheeks were flushed. "You can't have told us all there is. You can't. And maybe you didn't know about the chimera, and maybe you hadn't met that hunter before, but you have to know a lot more than you're letting on. If not about those things, then at least about your Holes." He dropped his voice low. "You remember that boy this morning? Henry? The one your Hole took? His father is a friend of mine. Now his son is gone, and he's going to ask me why. So I'm going to ask you again. In all that time you were out there, looking for Holes and trying to figure them out. You didn't learn anything?"

"Only," David whispered, "that they never go away."

"Nothing else?"

"No."

"And no one knows more than you?"

David looked up. Maybe someone did.

●

The wind from the hurricane beat against the side of Lofton's shelter. The gusts would surge, then die, then surge once more. The damp had crept through the cracks in the walls, turning the air hot and clammy. Only the hunter seemed not to notice. She hadn't moved since she'd collapsed in the corner, save for the slow rise and fall of her chest.

David looked up at Walter. "Do you remember when I told you and your father about the sage?"

"Remind me."

"Back home, after the Holes got bad, this old man came into town. From the way he talked, he'd known about the Holes for a long time."

Walter folded his arms across his chest. "So what did he say about them?"

"He said they meant the world was ending. He said unless we found out why, we couldn't stop it from happening. He thought since I could see the Holes, we had a real chance too. That's why we set out in the first place, because of him. We were going to save everyone." David paused. "But that's not what was weird."

Thunder pealed outside. The rolls were growing steadily more distant. In the corner of the cabin, Ezra shifted in her sleep. Her hat toppled to show her eyes were still shut tight.

"So what was weird?" Walter asked.

"Well, for all the sage knew about the Holes, he didn't talk about them much. What he was interested in were stories. He would listen to story after story after story, every one anyone could remember. He told his own stories too. And he was good at it, doing the voices and being dramatic. Since we didn't have TV or internet by then, a lot of people got together to listen whenever he talked. But I bet for every story he told, he probably listened to ten."

"So he's a storyteller. Great." Walter gritted his teeth. "What's that have to do with the Holes, or the chimera?"

"Nothing, I guess. But the sage *is* the reason I'm here."

"I thought you jumped in one of your Holes. Isn't that why you're here?"

"Yes. But the sage is the one who told me how to do it. He told me not all Holes were empty. Sometimes when you went through one, you'd wind up in a different place, a different time—maybe even a different world. He told me if I ever got trapped, I should jump in one of those Holes and try to find him. He even gave me something that would open that kind of Hole."

Walter looked at David with wary eyes. "What did he give you?"

"This little glass tube with yellow stuff inside. When I poured it out on the ground, it made this—I guess a kind of portal or gateway or something. And when I jumped through, well, now I'm here. He was the one who got me here."

Walter raised his eyes to stare at David once more. "What did he look like?"

"Who?"

"Your sage."

"Oh, um. Kind of crazy, actually. He was old, but he was strong. He was like a bodybuilder or something. He looked kind of Asian, had this long mustache, always wore a T-shirt no matter how cold it was. Oh, and he was always carrying around books."

A whisper from the corner of the room. "I've seen him."

The hairs stood up on David's neck. Ezra had stirred from her sleep. The hunter opened her fierce eyes and sat upright.

"I've seen your sage. Met him. Told him my own stories, just as he asked. I even heard him talk about your Holes. He didn't say a thing about being from another world."

David's eyes grew wide. "Where did you find him?"

"I saw him in the south, near Portsmouth. People said he'd been there for a few days before I came."

"Do you think he's still there?"

Ezra shook her head. "He left before I did. Said he was headed north. But if we can get back on the highway, maybe someone will know something."

Walter leaned forward. "Nobody's going anywhere. Not yet." He pointed at the far wall where Lofton was wrapped in tarpaulin. "That's my father over there, and I want answers."

"Answers?" There was scorn in Ezra's voice. "You think I owe you answers? What do you think would have happened had I not been in that church? I saw no other weapons drawn. No one else joined that fight, not even you. You should answer *me* with payment."

"Then what about him?" Walter asked, jerking his thumb at the boy.

David said, "What *about* me? I'd never seen those things before. Just the Holes."

Walter slammed his hand down. "The Holes, the Holes, you and your bloody Holes! Maybe those Holes are what brought them here? Maybe those Holes follow where you go? Ever think of that? Even during the war, we never had a chimera come this way. Never. Not once. And now *four* show up, and just days after you."

David raised his hands in protest. "I don't have anything to do with—"

"Yes, you do." Ezra's voice chilled the room. "I didn't come here looking for chimera, David. I came looking for you. But *they* can see a lot of what I see. They came looking for you too." She cocked her head. "It talked to you, didn't it?"

"Yes." David shuddered. "It told me… Well, it didn't make any sense at all. It told me that the answer to the Holes was out there, but that I shouldn't find it. It told me we can't win. It sounded like that was really important, that we couldn't win."

Walter snorted. "Of course it said we can't win. It was a chimera. They hunt us and they kill us. Of course they don't want us to win."

David shook his head. "No, that wasn't quite it. It didn't say we weren't going to win. It was more like we *shouldn't* win. Not us or it. But what does that mean?"

"Perhaps," Ezra murmured, "your sage will know."

8

BROKEN

The three spent the rest of the night in Lofton's shelter. David, stretched to exhaustion, tried his best to stay out of the way. He soon found himself in a half-awake, half-asleep limbo, unsure of how much time had passed. During his waking moments, he listened to the murmur of conversation—sometimes heated, sometimes calm— between Ezra and Walter. The exchange of almost-familiar names and places washed over him until they, too, faded into the steady thrum of rain. He drifted to sleep.

When he awoke, pale light streamed through cracks in the boarded windows. The beating of wind and rain was absent, as were Ezra and Walter. And Lofton.

David crossed to where the old man's body had been laid the night before. He felt a pit of loss in his stomach for Lofton, who—for however brief a time—had been his anchor in this insane new world. Last night, David had fantasized that the three of them—himself, Walter, and Ezra—gave Lofton a proper burial. The thought was silly, he realized. Lofton had more friends and family than David could keep track of. And yet, for the body to be gone before he had even woken up, made the emptiness that much worse.

Shouldn't this be getting easier? he asked himself. He had watched each of his brothers fall, one by one. Shouldn't he be getting numb? Instead, the load was getting heavier. But he had to keep going. That was the first lesson he'd learned.

David lumbered to the door and pushed it open. The sun was peeking low through a sky strewn with bursts of clouds. Fallen limbs, stripped leaves, mud, dirt, and debris lay everywhere. And all of it damp. Moisture hung in the air, as though the expanse of the hurricane had not passed, but merely been absorbed.

Perched on the trunk of a tree so bent it nearly touched the ground was Ezra. The hunter looked very different in the morning light. Her broad hat was balanced on her knees; her silver hair wreathed her shoulders.

"You're up," she said. She hopped to the ground. "Show it to me."

David nodded in response. He knew what she wanted to see. He ambled to the far side of the shelter, carefully stepping around the fallen debris. When he got to the Hole, he pointed.

"Can you see it?" he asked. There was no trace of hope in his voice.

"I cannot."

Mechanically, David picked up one of the branches at his feet and threw it into the Hole. He watched as it vanished.

Ezra murmured, "I came within a few feet of that thing earlier. How big around is it?"

David picked up a windblown limb and drew a circle around the Hole. Then, feeling the marking was insufficient, built a barricade with other fallen branches.

Ezra regarded him thoughtfully. "You've done that before, haven't you? Many times."

"In the beginning, I did. But when there started to be a lot more Holes, I'd just mark them off. Others would build the walls. We used chicken wire, mostly, since that kept the animals out too." He paused. "Chicken wire, it's like this metal—"

"I know what it is." Ezra raised an eyebrow. "You're very calm about this, David."

He shrugged. "I guess I've grown numb to it." He glanced around, wishing the old woman's eyes would lift from their stare. He also realized something peculiar about her. She didn't talk to him like most adults did. His brothers had always regarded him as someone to take care of. Lofton had believed his stories, but that wasn't the same thing. She was different. "Where'd Walter go?"

"He went to town. I helped him move his father's body this morning. Then I came back for you. I thought it best he—"

"Be alone?"

She nodded.

"How long should we wait?" David asked.

Ezra's face turned grave. "Are you sure you want to go back at all?"

"What do you mean?"

"Holes, chimera, and a hurricane. These people will be looking for someone to blame. I know from experience. And they know I was looking for you. That won't help your case."

"How did you know I was here, anyway?"

"Sometimes I see things. It's part of what I am. For now, answer me this: Do you want to go back? We can travel together if you'd like. We can find your sage. That's what you want, isn't it? The people here can't help you. You should stay away from them." Ezra shrugged.

David's head swam. He'd never been feared before. Back home, his ability was seen as a blessing, something to be praised.

"What'll they do to us?"

"Maybe nothing. Probably yell. Certainly curse. There will be tears and crying, and angry voices, but I wouldn't expect anything rash until nightfall. Such passions fear the sun."

"You'll come with me? To find the sage?"

"Yes. And if you are set on going, and I can see by your eyes you are, we shouldn't linger. It's mid-morning already."

David nodded. "Ok, but first I need to say goodbye."

"If you must."

●

The path from Lofton's shelter to Greenwater's End was difficult to follow. Downed branches made detours necessary, and the layer of needles and leaves often obscured the trail. David led the way, his eyes open for Holes. Being a guide again felt natural. Falling into old patterns kept his mind off the stranger and more frightening things—like the chimera, or the loss of Lofton.

The thought of the old man caused the pain of loss to resurge. David had only known him a few days, and had expected to leave again soon. But the loss of another friend still stung. Perhaps, he thought, this journey would be one he'd be better off taking alone. There would be less chance of anyone being hurt. He tried to bury the thoughts inside him. There was far too much he needed to be aware of.

David tried to focus, but there was something undefined in the air. As he grew closer to the town, the feeling grew stronger, a sense of *wrongness*. The feeling was not unfamiliar. He'd felt it hundreds of times whenever Holes were nearby.

"What is it?" Ezra asked.

He pointed through the grove of trees to where the first buildings could be seen. "Something's wrong down there."

"Tell me."

"It feels wrong. It just…"

Rounding the last bend, his fears were realized. The town of Greenwater's End was a wasteland. Buildings lay crumpled from the floodwaters. Trees had been thrown across the village square, annihilating the structures they hit. David, who had no experience with such disasters, thought it looked like a bomb had exploded in the square.

But the force of the storm wasn't what made him gasp. Littered throughout the town, Swiss-cheesing the wreckage of buildings and debris, were Holes. There were hundreds scattered about, ranging in size from two feet across to more than ten. There were none of the "monsters" that could swallow entire buildings, but the danger—if unaddressed—would quickly claim victims.

"Quite the mess," Ezra murmured.

David wheeled around. "Holes! There are Holes everywhere! We have to get down there. I can guide them out. I can get them out! We just need to get down there, we have to—"

The hunter stooped to look David in the eye. "Remain calm. Stay focused. You say there's danger?"

He nodded.

"And is there a way to tell? Are Holes always on empty ground? Are there signs I can look for?"

"No! There's no way. Everything looks the same. Houses, fences, roads, bricks. The illusion is still there, but it's not real. It's only after the Hole opens that you see things fall in." He clenched his jaw. "The rest just isn't real anymore."

"Then lead. You keep me safe from the Holes. I'll protect you from anything else. Have we got a deal?" The hunter reached out one leathered hand. David paused for a long moment, then shook firmly.

"Step exactly where I step," he said. "I'll stay center where I can. My brothers and I had some hand signals and stuff which I could—"

"Later."

"Right, later," he agreed. "Let's go."

David burst into a run as he scrambled down to the village. Inexplicably, there wasn't one Hole beyond the split-rail fence that encircled the town. But within the fence, where the buildings began, they were everywhere. He wove through the Holes, staying as far from each as possible. Ezra followed behind.

Glancing over his shoulder, he could tell the hunter was taking his suggestion to "step where he stepped" quite literally. In fact, there was only one set of footprints visible behind them. When they reached the main street, the screams of the villagers became more apparent. On the steps of the church, a throng of people watched with fear. They were crammed together, peering out desperately over the town, but not one person left the steps.

Ezra pointed. "Can you get us over to them?"

"Yes. But they're *thick* over there. The Holes, I mean. Step exactly where I do." David dropped from his run to a careful walk. The Holes were dense, spaced no more than ten feet apart in places. His heart jumped as the other villagers saw him and Ezra coming their way. Their yells became more fervent, approaching a near din. But David didn't answer. He just worked his way closer until he was within earshot.

"Nobody move," Ezra ordered. Her command dropped the townspeople's voices to whispers. "This town is hurt. I know you know that. This boy can lead you out. But we need you calm."

A yell issued from the crowd and a red-faced man stomped forward. His face was strewn with scratches, his clothes torn and his eyes wide. "Don't listen to them! It's them what did this! Kill the witch and kill her boy!" The man launched at them in fury. Ezra readied her weapons, but there was no need. The man toppled forward into one of the Holes between them. His cry of surprise snapped to nothing as he was jerked into the darkness. The people gasped, a few squeaking, a few beginning to cry once more. And behind those first sounds of despair, the murmurs rose, building with the frenzy.

"I am no witch," the hunter boomed. "I am Ezra Jenova of the Scarlet Arm. I am a hunter. And those of you who saw the chimera know I speak the truth. The demons have left, and my business should be done. I help only for the sake of this boy. Now, will you listen?"

Another man spoke, this one with the salted look of a sailor. His voice held a low contempt. "Not a witch, she says. Then what's happened here? Where did those chimera come from, and the storm, and…" As the man grew more agitated, he stepped from the church stoop. David's eyes widened.

"Stop!" he shrieked. "Back up! You're right in front of one. Don't come any closer."

The color drained from the sailor's face as he pressed back into the crowd. But before another protester could step up, a familiar face emerged. Walter stood tall, solid, his face bearing its usual look of concern.

"They're telling the truth," he boomed. "They both are. David can get us out, and he is here to help. Listen to them." Walter leveled his eyes at David. "Will you help?"

David nodded. He made his way to the church, stepping carefully through the infestation of Holes. When he reached the steps, he took a deep breath.

"First off. No one move until I say. Do. Not. Move. These things that are taking people, they're called Holes. And they are very, very dangerous. They don't look like anything. And whatever used to be there will still look real—but it's not. And if you step in one…" he let the words hang, his eyes drifting to where the man had fallen. "I can see them. I can get you out."

The huddled group murmured to one another. Perhaps fear had replaced their anger.

David continued, "I'm going to lead you out of town. Once you're past the fence, you'll be safe. If you step exactly where I step…" he looked back around. "Um, I need something to draw with."

He felt a tap on his shoulder and turned to see Ezra offering him her oversized machete. He took it with a nod and then started a slow circumnavigation of the crowd. He dragged the knife behind him as he went, creating a clear line in the dust.

"Ok, as long as you don't cross the line, you'll be ok. But don't move anyway." David glanced around. "Does anybody else have something like this? I need another one." More shuffling within the crowd and soon an object was passed carefully from person to person, until David had another machete in his hands. Correction. This was truly a machete. What Ezra had given him was polished, engraved, and ornate. Hers was a cross between a ceremonial dagger and a short sword. The machete was just that, a thin blade and a single sharpened edge.

David nodded in thanks as he took the machete in his left hand and Ezra's sword/knife in his right. "Ok, here's what I'm going to do. I'm going to make a path, like so." He walked forward, dragging each blade beside him in the dust. "Stay in the middle of the lines and you'll be ok. Remember that if you step on the lines, the people behind you won't know where to go. So *don't* do it. Oh, uh, and stay single file. That means one at a time. And walk, don't run and…" He struggled to think of the other things he'd heard from his days in school and the fire drills. "And try and be calm. Does everyone understand?"

Murmurings and a few nods drifted from the crowd. David hoped they'd listen. Not that this was complicated, but if anyone panicked… He shook his head. Dropping the tips of the blades into the dirt, he drew his path, careful to move where the Holes stood the farthest apart. Behind him, and allowing for several feet of breathing room, came Ezra, and after her, the procession of seventy-odd townspeople.

The silence was unnerving, broken by the occasional snivel or cry of a baby. More unnerving was that David realized how many of the villagers were missing. The Holes must have swallowed a dozen people before they realized the danger. No wonder they were so subdued. But Ezra was right about another thing, tensions were too high to stay here for long.

David navigated until he reached the fence encircling the town, and then a good distance past it just to be sure. When finally they were all safely away from the Holes, he stopped. "Ok, we're out now. As long as you don't go past the town fence, you'll be safe. So stay here, ok?"

He turned to walk back the way he'd come.

"Where are you going?" a woman asked. Her voice cracked with anxiety.

David was surprised by the question. "To see if there's anyone else."

The woman's eyes widened. "Don't leave us! What if there are more out here? We can't see those things!"

The crowd murmured in agreement. And though David didn't know how to respond, Ezra spoke for him.

"Stay here for a while and be safe. We'll be back." Ezra looked over at David. "How long will the Holes remain?"

"Forever."

She turned to the villagers. "Think upon what you will do from here, but know you cannot ever cross that way again."

Another man spoke up. His clothes were clean relative to those surrounding him, but he, too, looked worn down. "Then what are we supposed to do? Those are our homes."

Ezra set her jaw. "Decide for yourselves." She paused. "Walter? Will you speak with them?"

"He ain't our leader. He ain't the mayor."

"Pick your own masters, then." Ezra scanned the crowd. "Or none. Discuss, decide. We'll return when we can. David, your lead."

David started back toward the village, afraid to look behind him. Ezra was on his heels, and though he was unsure what to make of the world-weary hunter, he felt safe having her there. He stepped quickly and had reached the edge of the farm when he heard a crashing of footsteps behind him. He wheeled in surprise to find Ezra had already drawn her hunting knife with her right hand, and a throwing knife with her other.

"Wait," a small voice called. "I'm coming with you. You might need help." The speaker was a girl, perhaps two years younger than David. She had a ruddy, freckled complexion, and although her clothes were now soiled from the storm, he could tell they were once of finer stuff. There was something strange about her eyes, but he couldn't put his finger on it. "I know my way around, and I'll follow you exactly. Cross my heart."

Ezra replied, "And you're not afraid?"

"I'll stick close."

"What do you think, David?"

"I could use a guide."

Greenwater's End was desolate when they returned. Before, the murmurings of the townsfolk had filled the quiet. Now there was nothing. Ezra turned to the girl.

"You know who was missing, don't you? Do you know where they could be hiding?"

"Yes. And I…"

Ezra raised an eyebrow. "Yes?"

"Never mind. Um, first let's check the storehouse. I know some people were going there before the storm."

"Which building?" David asked.

"That big gray one."

David nodded and turned to select a path through the Holes. As he led, Ezra and the girl called out to the survivors. "Hello! Is anyone there? If you are, call back. Don't move. It's dangerous. Hello! Is anyone there? If you…"

For two hours they combed the village. They found two dozen people hiding, and led each back to the safe place next to the ruined church. When finally they had searched all the buildings, they started back, following the same double border David had drawn on his first exit from town. When they neared the fence on the edge of town, the hunter turned to face the girl.

"It was brave of you to come with us," Ezra said.

The girl toed the dust in front of her. "It was nothing. You needed help, and I knew the town. Wasn't nothing.'"

David looked at the girl, and though her head was lowered, he could see the strange flicking of her eyes. Something that didn't quite make sense unless…

Ezra smiled. "Oh, but I think it was. It takes a strong spirit to face the unknown. And your people are going to need someone to help them. They can't go back to their village. I think you know that. They will need leaders. And guides. Yes, David? What were you going to say?"

The thought crawled across the surface of his brain, moving from conception to realization. Her eyes were flicking, because… he released a yelp. "You can see them! You can, can't you? Why didn't you say anything before? Why didn't you tell me?"

The girl's freckled face turned crimson. "No… I can't. Not like you, I mean. I can't see them. I can, well, smell them or think them, or… I don't know. I just kind of know where not to go. Does that make sense? But I needed to go with you just to make sure I wasn't crazy. And…"

David's voice grew animated. "This is amazing! You're the first person I've *ever* met who could see them besides me. Don't you understand how incredible this is?"

Ezra kept her voice low, "David…"

"No! Seriously, me and my brothers traveled all over the place, and even through Denver, which has like a million people there, and no one could see the Holes but me and—"

"David."

"What?" He shot a look of indignation at Ezra.

"This is not your home. And this is not your world." The hunter kept her voice calm, though impatience bubbled in her tone. "I believe you will find many things to be different here, and likely the chimera and this girl's ability are the least of them. With luck, we may find such gifts in every town we visit. But our time grows short. So it is very important we understand each other. Please. This is important."

He dropped his head, the excitement diminishing. "I understand. It's just… No. I understand."

Ezra turned to the girl. "This is a gift. Your people will need someone to help them rebuild, to find a safe place. And David and I cannot stay. Do you understand?"

She nodded, her eyes fearful, and then grinned shyly. "I'll do what I can."

●

David did not expect a warm reception when he, Ezra, and the girl returned to the group. He saw the accusing look on their faces. Too many of the villagers had fallen, and the beginnings of blame were in their eyes. They stood to the side, just beyond the crowd. Soon they were joined by Walter.

The large man looked at them with worry in his deep brown eyes. "You two have done more than your share. And now—"

Ezra interrupted, "Don't bother. We're leaving."

"I was going to suggest it." Walter pulled off his worn hat and massaged his shaved head. "These people… you've seen 'em. They're jumpy. They've been through a lot."

"They'll be fine. That girl there, she can sense the Holes, if not in the same way as David. You will all find somewhere safe to begin anew. But don't go back."

Walter asked, "And what about you? You're off to find this sage?"

David sparked. "Yeah. You've got some ideas, right Ezra?"

She frowned. "Best I not say. Not until we're on the road."

Walter swallowed hard. David could feel the tension mounting, but he didn't know the source. This was more than fear, more than the unknown.

"Then I'm coming with you," Walter stated.

Ezra squinted. "You don't trust me with him."

"No, ma'am. I do not. That's why I have to go."

David broke in. "This is about me?"

"Yes," Walter and Ezra said together.

"He thinks I'll use you," the hunter replied. Her voice was chill.

"And I'll make sure you don't. You've shown yourself a hunter, Ezra. You've shown you can fight. But that wouldn't be enough for my father. I'm going to see to it that I've done him right. I've already spoken with my family about this. I just need a minute to get my pack."

Ezra asked, "And your wife, and your children? You would leave them alone and homeless? After—as you said—we have asked so much of them?"

Walter set his jaw. "This is bigger than just me or just them. They understand that. They're not helpless, you know. Right now, my wife and my sisters are making plans. They had better things to do than mill around waiting for the high and mighty hunter to come back. And my boys…" His voice grew softer, "I think one day they'll understand as well."

"Of course they will. I imagine they'll be just fine." Ezra smiled. The baring of teeth was more lupine than friendly. "Very well. If it makes you comfortable, you can accompany us. I'll give you five minutes. Then David and I walk. If you aren't behind us, you'll never find our trail."

David felt his stomach drop. His world was changing again. And what's more, he knew the town of Greenwater's End, with its marshes, singing, bustling docks, and smiling faces, had been a fleeting dream. And what remained for him? His new companions weren't like his brothers. They weren't the strongest, brightest, most agile, and most capable people his hometown had to offer. This was an old has-been soldier and an ordinary farmer. How could they succeed where his brothers had failed?

And as they walked, the words of the chimera played over and over in his mind. *No one can win. No one must ever win.*

9

Air Waves

Everything happens for a reason. An oft-said maxim, and one of solace for those in suffering. A comfort, yes, in times of strife, but no one asks what the reason is. The greater good, or God's will? The fulfillment of the universe? Perhaps. But worlds are not made simply to be fulfilled in obscene and abstract ways. Consider, for a moment, that the truth is far closer, far simpler. A single time, place, struggle, event. What is the world if not constant struggle? I have seen in my time that each of a world's struggles leads to another, and then another, until at last a final struggle. A conflict between forces of the utmost immensity. And yet, that struggle, too, must one day end.

What then of the other pieces? The pages, the colors, the props, sets, and supporting actors? Where do they go once their purpose has been fulfilled? To a greater life? A better destiny? Up? Away? Beyond?

Or are they simply forgotten?

The sage read over the words he'd scrawled in the book's margins. After musing the point for more than a few minutes, he decided to lowercase the "G" on the word for divinity. After all, he didn't want to offend anyone, and a capital "G" god had implications. He wasn't writing about implications. Then again, maybe he was. Maybe the whole capital "G" / lowercase "g" conundrum would go a long way to solving this mystery. Or perhaps he'd just been in the cave too long.

Months. It felt like months, though the hash marks on the wall—in a deliberate nod to the prison tales he loved—showed only six weeks. Of course, when first he arrived, he had *meant* to settle in for a while. He'd gathered a lot of data and needed to make sense of it. The chimeras' offer of a place to study had been attractive. And with the creatures nearby, he had hoped to fill in some missing facts. The chimera were, he surmised, a large piece of this equation.

The sage spat in disgust—a thing he would never do in polite company. He should have paid more attention. But those chimera were convincing. At least some were, like that fellow that always showed up dressed in a black suit, looking somewhere between an undertaker and a mariachi player. The sage had been calling him Johnny Cash for just that reason. In private, at first, and lately to his face. Yes, Cash was very convincing. But still, the sage knew he should have recognized the trap.

The buzzing beyond the edge of the cave had ceased. But the sage had no reason to believe the creatures had forgotten him. After all, they didn't want him dead. Perish the thought. He was too important to be dead. Too *fundamentally intriguing* as the wild buggers put it. They just wanted him contained. He'd tried to slip into another world, of course. He'd tried the moment he realized he was trapped. But there was nowhere to slip. His technique for crossing worlds didn't work here. Did that mean he had reached the bottom? Or were the rules here just different?

The sage had asked the chimera the same questions. But whatever their theories on the Holes, they had seen far less than he had. They were native to this world, or so he believed. Because if they hadn't started here, then all of their theories about "not winning" were just a whole lot of smoke.

Frustration swept over him, and the sage leaped to his feet. He charged to the pile of rocks sealing him in and pressed his face against a gap in the rubble. "Hey! Hey, is anyone out there? I thought you were keeping me alive."

First silence, then a scuttle, then the ruffling as he heard several chimera changing their shapes and approach his prison. For whatever reason, they preferred not to speak his language when they were in one of their bug forms. He wasn't convinced that was even their real shape, perhaps just the most popular.

"Yess? You called uss?" The chimera's voice, slow and raspy, butchered the "L's" so that they were more gargling than sound. What's more, the accent was telling. Not one of the smart ones. That was good.

The sage stomped his feet. "I said, you're *supposed* to be keeping me alive. But I'll be dead in a week unless I get some real food."

There was a ruffling, and then a great quantity of chirping as the chimera discussed the point with each another. Another ruffling, and then the response. "You have the fruitss. You have tomatoess. You have soupss. What else do you require?"

"Bacon! God damn you fluttering beetle brained-octopod. I need bacon, salt-peter, sulfur, and ammonia." The sage grinned, though the effect was lost with the rubble between them. "I've got to have my vitamins. And keep 'em separate. If you mix 'em, you could poison me, terrible cooks that you are. I'll do it myself. You hear me?"

Another series of chirps, and one last fluttering. "We will see. We will try to find your… bacon."

The sage repeated his list again, and then once more until he was certain the chimera had it down. And if they fell for it? Well, he was on his way to freedom. And if they didn't, maybe he'd at least get his bacon.

●

The transmission tower had stood for a hundred years, and for forty-nine of them, Joby stood at its side. The tower's care, maintenance, upkeep, and attendance had been his life's passion, his work, his purpose, and his love. Never mind that only the bottom of the tower had been painted. (Joby had run out of paint and didn't know how to make more.) Never mind that the control shack had a roof of tarpaulin. (Joby was a radioman, not a roofer.) And never mind that some of the wiring was exposed. (Joby knew to avoid a shock.) In fact, the only thing that truly concerned him was that the oil reserve was down to the skinny—at least as skinny as Joby himself, and apt to disappear even sooner.

That, Joby mused, was a problem. He'd been begging for a refill for two years, but supplies were scarce. If the tank ever ran completely dry—truly bone-dry, nothing left in the barrel—he didn't have a chance of being heard. So Joby hadn't turned on the generator in three weeks. Because when he did, he wanted to be confident the right folks were listening. That time was close at hand. Tomorrow was the autumnal equinox. And on that day, just as in the spring, and on the winter and summer solstices, every radio tower east of the Mississippi would crank up at once. They'd check-in, exchange greetings, a snip of news, and then become silent once more. Joby would get out his request, and in doing so save himself the hassle of making the trip in person.

Joby could still *listen*, of course. He didn't need to turn on the generator to listen to the airways. The receiver's batteries lasted for months even without the generator turning. He could hear the news as it flowed across the sky: riverboats and politics, storms and crops. And most recently—and most interestingly—he'd heard of the chimera. Apparently, a hunter had bagged one in Regalwood far to the south, and a group of miners had run across one west of Atlanta. Of course, two chimeras were no reason to panic. Some were seen each year. But two in a single month was worth paying attention to—and it gave Joby an excuse to do the one thing he loved almost as much as maintaining his tower.

The pistols had been given to him by a fellow radioman, relics from the Chimeran War. They were heavy, boxy, and cool to the touch. Each pistol held fifteen rounds of large-caliber ammunition. Each shot was enough to send Joby reeling. After the announcement of the second chimera, he had taken the pistols out on a daily basis, to practice his aim on tin cans from the provision shed. The gun belt, however, had gotten in the way of his work chaps, and so he fashioned a sling that crossed over his back, the holsters resting just below his arms. Joby liked the way the guns complimented the dull iron of the hammer, wrenches, screwdrivers, and circuit testers on his tool belt. After a few days of target practice, he started wearing the guns every time he put on his tools—which was nearly all the time except when he slept.

Joby looked at himself in the long workshop mirror. He practiced his poses: left hand on a wrench, the other holding a gun, then his right hand on a circuit tester, and his left on a gun. Then both hands on guns, then both on tools. He smiled, the cut of his squared-off beard exaggerating the expression. He was a good-looking man, he admitted. Guns and tools brought that out in people. And in him more than most.

The midday sun beat down overhead. Joby walked outside to assess the tower. He'd cleared away most of the fallen trees and brush left in the wake of the hurricane. Now all that remained were to check and recheck the guy wires stabilizing the antenna. The tower hadn't given way in the wind, and yet the groan of stretching steel had made his stomach turn. He thought the groans were louder this year, louder every year. Could these be the tower's final days?

"No way. Not going to happen. Not on my watch," Joby declared. But in his heart, he wondered if the signal wouldn't go through. And if no one answered that call, then he would have to make the long journey up to Brighton himself. Old man Carrig lived up that way—or maybe young Carrig had taken his place. No matter. If they didn't have fuel to spare, they could at least put out the call for help. Maybe he'd have better luck the second time around.

Joby smiled. It was a fine day, and he had work to do. One way or another, this old girl would sing her song. And if the chimera showed up, or some other beastie? Well, he would be ready for them. Because Joby stood for the tower, for as long as the tower was to stand.

●

"Will you tell me about the hunters?"

David had been waiting to ask the question all day. Actually, he'd been waiting since he'd first heard the term. But every time he opened his mouth, Ezra would shush him without ceremony. Until they stopped for the night, and she declared them safe from the chimera, they were all to remain as quiet as possible.

David, Walter, and Ezra had traveled west from Greenwater's End until the sun dropped low and red on the horizon. For that entire time, David led the way to scout for Holes, followed by Walter, and lastly Ezra watching the rear. As they walked, questions brimmed in his mind. And for the first time in a long time, he thought not just about the Holes. Now he had the chimera to consider as well.

According to Walter, there had been two Chimeran Wars. The first war, humankind had lost. They'd barely survived, having to abandon Europe, Asia, and Africa in the process. But in the second war, twenty-four years ago, the people had won. But Walter hadn't told him any details. He said the story of the hunters was for Ezra to tell. And the hunters, David believed, were at least as interesting as the chimera themselves. And now, with the sun setting, he wouldn't take excuses.

"Come on, Ezra," he pleaded. "It's going to be dark soon, and I don't think I can walk much farther. And it's about time I get to know what's going on, especially since I'm the only one who doesn't. Where did the hunters come from? How did you become a hunter? How did the hunters beat the chimera? What's it mean that the chimera are back? Catch me up."

Ezra smiled her thin smile. "Yes. I suppose that would be fair. But it's a very long story."

"Well, then you should start so I can hear it all."

"Soon. We're almost there."

The hunter pointed a gaunt finger through the trees. David could see the object in the distance. The crisscross of steel held fast by retaining wires was a familiar sight. A radio tower. He had noticed the tower, but he hadn't thought anything of it. Towers were common enough back home. He hadn't been surprised before, and yet now he was. The thought of radio in a place where hunters had knife fights with gigantic bugs felt both inappropriate and fitting at once.

"The tower?" Walter asked. "That's where we're going? Why didn't you say so?"

"I didn't know until now," Ezra replied. "We needed miles between us and the mob. Things could have turned bad back there. I think you know that."

Walter asked, "But are the networks still active?"

"They should be. After the war ended, keepers were assigned to them in case of emergency. The radiomen were a proud lot, and I don't expect any to have abandoned their posts. At least not willingly. But if I was a chimera, and I'd known what these towers were for, then I'd make them early targets."

"You're cheery today," Walter said.

"That I am." Ezra pursed her lips. "But it has been such a lovely day."

The sun's rays streamed through the trees ahead of them, a ruby glow reaching tendrils of light into a sky misted by the hurricane's aftermath. The sight was beautiful, though the devastation caused by the winds made David sad. But not too sad. There was something natural about this destruction that felt appropriate versus that left by the Holes. All in all, the damp in the air, the colorful sunset, and the prospect of reaching their goal kept him in high spirits.

"What's at the tower?" David asked as they continued their march. Thoughts of hunters and chimera had subsided for the moment.

"Shelter at a minimum. The radio, if we're lucky," Ezra replied. "But you're our guide. You tell us how we should use it."

David nodded. "The real problem's the Holes. So we need to find out if it was just back in Greenwater's End, or if anyone else has had an issue."

"Anything else?" Ezra asked.

"I'm not finished." David scratched his head. "The problem is the Holes, but I don't know if that's the solution. We need to find the sage. He'll know what's going on."

Walter spoke up. "You mean the story collector?"

"He's not just a story collector," Ezra said. "He came from the another world, just as David did. And he knows how to travel between them. He's been studying these Holes, so he should know something. And if he's causing as much of a stir as he did when I met him, then he shouldn't be hard to find."

Walter frowned. "Why do you care?"

David snorted in exasperation. "Why do I *care*? I lost my friends and who knows if my family is ok. And he's probably the only one who could ever get me home. And—"

"Not you, David. Why does *she* care?" Walter turned to face Ezra. "You're a hunter. Always going to be. Even with the war gone twenty-four years, you're still looking for chimera."

"And I've found them."

"Right. Then why look for these Holes? Why do you care about that? Go back to your old life."

Ezra adjusted the wrap of her battle chain. "I believe the two are connected. If I can help David find the Holes, then perhaps I can learn more about the chimera. Where they've been, and where they are now. He says our world is dying. I don't know about that. But I know what my purpose is."

"So you're using us," Walter said.

"We're all helping each other."

●

David, Walter, and Ezra broke free of the woods and into a wide field covered with squat, broad-leafed plants emitting a dank aroma like coffee. David didn't like coffee, though he'd tried it once at his brothers' urgings. They'd asked him to try a lot of things. At first, it had been kind of a joke to watch him spit out coffee, or go into a coughing fit when they offered him a cigarette. Some of it was fun, of course. But when his brothers started to fall victim to the Holes, things changed. One day he was the brunt of their jokes, and the next he was their talisman. Some of the kidding stopped. More respect crept in. As for how things would shift between himself, Walter, and Ezra, it was far too early to tell.

The radio tower was three hundred feet tall. It stretched straight up, with four heavy beams that tapered together to a point. Triangular girders crossed between the beams, the reinforcing wedges drawing closer together until fading out of sight. The tower was two-toned, rusted orange at the top and a dark gray on the bottom. A dilapidated building stood beside the structure, the roof covered in places with bits of tarpaulin. Both building and tower were surrounded on three sides by rusted coils of razor wire, though the gate lay face down.

"Doesn't look like it's running," David remarked.

Ezra replied, "I disagree. This one's in pretty good shape, all things considered. The bottom of that tower must have been painted recently."

"What about the rest of it? This whole thing is a piece of—"

A gunshot boomed across the late afternoon sky, dust from the bullet springing up in front of them. David dropped to his belly, as did Ezra—with Walter following suit a second later."

A creaky voice called from ahead. The accent reminded David of Yosemite Sam from his morning cartoons back home. "Don't you be takin' one step closer. Raise your hands an' state your names. I want to hear you *an-nun-ci-ate*, now. Leaping lemurs and such."

Ezra was the first to respond. "I'm Hunter Ezra. These are David and Walter from Greenwater's End." She winked at David. "And leaping lemurs lay lines of lemon lozenges in Liberian languages."

David's jaw dropped in incomprehension, but whatever nonsense she'd just said, the reply was immediate.

"Well, why didn't you say so? Come on in, come on in!"

Ezra hopped to her feet, with David and Walter more reluctant to rise. Once upright, they saw a short, bony man covered in grease and tools. He had threadbare blue jeans and wore a toolbelt containing wrenches, screwdrivers, hammers, awls, wire cutters, and many other instruments. The man's sleeveless shirt and face were smeared in grease down to his squared-off beard. The man smiled and then returned his two enormous pistols to holsters beneath each arm.

The three walked forward, as the man did the same, meeting them halfway across the field. He wiped his hand on his jeans and then offered it to the three travelers. "Name's Joby. I'm the radioman, as you might have guessed. Pleased to meet you."

Ezra shook hands and reintroduced the three of them.

David squinted one eye. "I don't get it… leaping lemurs?"

Joby smiled. "Leaping lemurs lay lines of lemon lozenges in Liberian languages! You're too young to know that one, but surely you know the reason?"

Ezra responded, "The chimera, David, can take most any appearance, but very few mastered our speech." She leveled her gaze at Joby. "But if you're asking, and if you're armed, you must have seen a chimera yourself. Are they in these parts?"

"Seen 'em, no. But I've been listening to the airwaves. There was one killed in Atlanta, and another down south in Regalwood."

Ezra nodded. "The Regalwood one was mine. And another three in Greenwater's End yesterday. I hadn't heard about Atlanta."

"Hah! So I was right to be careful. Five in one month is somethin' worth talking about. But come along now, you must be hungry. I'll get you something to eat."

David, Walter, and Ezra followed Joby to the tower. Once they'd stepped over the fallen gate, they entered the aluminum building. The inside was open, with no walls serving as dividers, and yet contained three distinct areas. The first was the generator, occupying most of the space. The cogs, pistons, and messes of wires stuck out at chaotic angles, though the machine seemed otherwise well maintained. Where metal was exposed, it gleamed. Where the pistons connected, the joints were greased with no hint of either corrosion or disrepair. In relation to everything else, the contraption sparkled.

The rest of the building was an amalgam of workshop and living space. Among the mess of tools, there hung a faded red hammock and an overturned wire spool covered in pots and half-filled tea cups. A collection of six folding lawn chairs in various states of decay circled the spool as though the radioman had been entertaining. The cobwebs, piles of old books, buckets filled with once-used nails, and dirty rags atop them told a different story. Joby bustled to the makeshift table. He unceremoniously cleared the chairs and bade them sit.

Walter clicked his tongue. "Did the storm hit hard? Or was all this from before?"

"The fence got knocked down, you saw that. And I lost a fair amount of the roof. I've got a tarp for a quick patch, but need to fix it for real before the rains come. As for the tower herself, she's been silent for a while, but she'll get tested tomorrow."

"Your machinery looks in order," Ezra observed. "Why haven't you been broadcasting?"

"It's not the equipment that's the problem, it's the fuel. I'm down to fumes, I am. Next time I fire her up could drain 'em dry."

"Seems odd to run so low. Haven't you any reserves?"

"Sure I did, once. But times are lean, you know. Gas ain't cheap, and it ain't exactly wartime when a tower's a priority. I take what I get, and I do as I'm told. I'll put the call out for a resupply tomorrow. And then I wait."

"We need to use the tower," David blurted. "We have to find the sage."

The grease-covered mechanic squinted one eye at him. "Listen, kid. I've got just enough fuel for one transmission, and I need that to make my quarterly report. But what, my friends, do you have in trade for an old radioman?"

"We've got something for you," Ezra replied. "A story. And this is one you'll want to hear. David?"

●

David told the radioman all about the Holes. Despite cautions from Ezra, he left nothing out. In his mind, the more people who knew about the Holes, the better. But while Joby had heard tales of an odd disappearance here or there—and he'd even thought it peculiar—there hadn't been enough to worry him. He was more interested in Walter's tales of the hurricane, and Ezra's news of the chimera.

But now, safe for the moment and with his story told, David's impatience returned.

"Well," he said, "that's all there is to tell from my side. So it's my turn to hear your side."

Joby raised an eyebrow. "What do you want to know?"

Ezra interrupted. "He's not talking about you, he's talking about me. Our friend David is still quite new to this world. Literally. Many of the things we take for granted, he is only beginning to learn."

"Like what?" the radioman asked.

David sighed in exasperation. "Like the chimera. Or these wars everyone keeps talking about, but I don't know a thing about. And I've been walking next to a hunter, and I still don't even know what that is."

Walter smiled smugly. "Well, Ezra, you heard the boy. Tell us what it's all about. Go on."

"Very well." She set her jaw. "But I must first ask our host for a bite, and a drink."

●

Joby stoked the wood-burning stove and threw a kettle on top. While David couldn't see what the radioman had put in the pot, his stomach growled at the thought of food. Joby adjusted the burner, then walked to a shelf on the far side of his workshop. After no small amount of clanging and pushing aside wrenches and cogs, he returned with a dusty bottle. He passed the jug to Walter and Ezra and even offered it to David, who refused after one whiff set his nostrils to burning.

Ezra looked at Joby, then Walter, then David in turn.

"To tell my story," she said, "and to tell the story of the hunters, I need to go back a very long time and a very long way away. Across the ocean and to the time of the first Chimeran War. Because there wouldn't be hunters if there weren't any chimera. More specifically, you wouldn't have any hunters if it wasn't for the tooth."

"The tooth?" David asked.

"Yes. The tooth. You see, David, when a chimera dies—killed or otherwise—most of the body dissolves away. All but its teeth. Much like eagle feathers, boar tusks, and rhinoceros horns, the teeth were prized and collected since the first chimera was slain. It didn't take long to discover the teeth were more useful than simply as trophies."

Ezra's eyes closed. "Crushed, powdered, or burned, the tooth induces a strong narcotic effect."

"So it's a drug."

Ezra nodded. "In a sense. Medicine is more accurate. If prepared in a particular way… and used by those susceptible, it is quite powerful. To some, it can bestow the ability to locate the chimera. In others, second sight. Before the discovery of the tooth, people were helpless to know when or where the chimera would strike. But afterward, the people were not so blind. Those who could use the tooth became guides. They helped the survivors flee the chimera. They escaped across the ocean to this new continent.

"When the refugees arrived here, they were relieved to find no chimera. And so their highest priority was to keep things that way. The users of the tooth, their guides, became sentinels. And when the chimera arrived on these shores—as eventually they did—the people were alerted. The creatures were hunted down and destroyed before they could gain a foothold. Over time, the guards became the hunters they are today. Hunters were trained to seek out the chimera and destroy them. No matter what form the chimera took, or how far they tried to run, the hunters would find and stop them."

Walter frowned. "So the hunters started out as guides? That's not how I heard things."

Ezra gave a dismissive wave. "Many people like to think hunters have always been warriors. But it isn't the whole truth. From the beginning, hunters fought out of necessity. Over time, we grew better at it."

Joby cackled. "And it didn't hurt you had guns by then. Bigger, badder, and better guns!"

"I agree. Advances in weapons certainly contributed to our success. Even if the hunters themselves stuck to the old ways."

David spoke up. "So what happened? If the hunters were so good, why was there a second war at all?"

Walter's voice dropped low. "Good. But not perfect. The chimera eventually slipped through in the north."

Ezra chuckled to herself.

"What's so funny?" Walter snapped.

"I laugh," Ezra replied, "because you said this was my story to tell. And yet you give the southern version. Every place I've ever visited says the chimera slipped through somewhere else. Truth is, no one knows *where* they came through. But we do know *why*."

"What do you mean?" David asked.

"You see, David, the hunters' effectiveness at keeping the chimera away was due to the tooth—no other reason. Over time, the hunters used more tooth than we obtained. When we ran out, the chimera could move undetected. They remained hidden until they were strong—and we were blind. Then they attacked. The second war began."

Joby tapped his chin. "I remember hearing about the first attacks over the radio. My daddy was an operator back then, and I was just learning. Must have been sixty years ago."

Ezra nodded, "Correct. And that is where my role in the story begins. You see, my village was one of the first to be attacked by the chimera. And a lone chimera at that. Without the hunters to warn us, we were taken by surprise. Many, many people were killed before the creature was stopped. When the hunters finally arrived, they tested the newly orphaned children, to see if any of us could become hunters. I was recruited."

She paused. She looked across the room where David and the others sat in rapt attention. "You know, Walter, you have that spark as well. If you'd been born in a different time, perhaps we would have fought together."

Walter flushed. "I, yes… I…. You're right. I was tested when I was young. But I wasn't old enough to fight. But how did you know that, Ezra?"

She smiled wickedly. "I saw it yesterday when I used the tooth. How do they say, 'it takes one to know one'?"

David asked, "So what happened next? After you went with the hunters?"

"Well," Ezra continued, "they trained me. I learned not only how to use the tooth, but also the weapons of the hunters. Chain, knife, bow—"

Joby interrupted. "Now that's something I never understood. All you hunters out there with bows and arrows and knives, like you'd never seen a good solid six-shooter in your life. Didn't make any sense to me."

"We asked the same questions," Ezra replied. "Suffice it to say our training was one of tradition. Whether tooth or bow, we followed our protocol. Hunters have little appetite for change."

Joby shook his head. "Ok, ok, just always wondered, and getting' a straight answer from your kind—begging your pardon, ma'am—ain't the easiest thing in the world. Please, go on."

Ezra leaned back in her chair. "By the time I joined the front lines, I was seventeen. Skirmishes had turned to full-out war by then. The battlefront started to the west, then moved east as the chimera gained ground. I took my orders and joined the fight, going wherever I was asked. I fought for twenty-five years and in many, many battles. By then, everything beyond the Mississippi River had been completely lost. We were losing ground one battle at a time. We were fatigued, and running low on bullets, food, and willpower. Then, two weeks before my forty-third birthday, came the event I will never forget."

Joby said, "September 22nd. The day of the calm."

Ezra squinted. "The date may not be quite so precise, but it was late September, to be sure. One day, the chimera disappeared. There were no more skirmishes; their burrows had been emptied. And no matter how much of the tooth the hunters used, there was no trace of them anywhere. The war had ended."

David looked up. "Just like that, they were gone? You mean completely gone?"

Ezra nodded, her face grim. "We assumed it was a trick, that they had simply learned a better way to hide themselves. But as days turned to weeks, and weeks to months, when we had repaired our walls, re-provisioned our outposts, and restocked our ammo, there were still no chimera to fight. Slowly, we accepted they were gone.

"At forty-three years old, I was left without a purpose. And in that, I was not alone. And while the years passed, I searched. All the hunters searched. Every once in a while you'd hear of an attack, just often enough for us to look all the harder. But I never found one myself. Not until a week ago."

Joby cleared his throat. "Here's the thing though, David. And it's important you know this. The chimera never completely disappeared. I don't know about on the ground, Madam Hunter, but I heard of one attacking every few months on the radio. They'd still show up in twosies and threesies, onesies and twosies. They weren't all gone-gone, just not many left. I bet that's what you saw. Four may be a lot in a month, but it's happened before. I wouldn't get too worked up quite yet. I wouldn't say the chimera are back."

"But now things are different," David protested. "Now you have the Holes. The chimera don't even matter anymore. Nothing else does."

Joby looked up, a skeptical look in his eyes. But before he could speak, Ezra replied.

"Perhaps he's right, Mr. Joby. The Holes could be a greater danger than the chimera were. But I also don't believe this is coincidence. I think the two are connected. And while I may be familiar with the chimera, these Holes are new to me. That's why I follow David now. And that's why it's important we find this sage. You can help us do that. You can call anyone on this tower. Surely you can hear the news of the world. Someone like the sage is bound to be noticed."

Joby screwed the lid back onto his jug in quick practiced turns. "I told you once before, I ain't got but enough fuel left in this old girl to start her but one more time. And I need that to put in the request for gas."

Walter said, "But if you get *your* request in, then you can make *our* request. You can still hear what everyone says, right? All you have to do is ask the question. You can listen for the answer later. Am I right?"

Joby frowned for only an instant before his face lit up. "He's right, dagnabbit. The big fella is completely right. I ask for fuel first—that's my condition. But then I'll ask about your storyteller. Why not?"

"Story listener," David murmured.

"Beg pardon?"

"He doesn't tell stories, he listens to them. He collects them."

"And books," Ezra said. "When I met him, he collected books too."

David asked, "Well, aren't books stories?"

Ezra shrugged. "Some are, but not all. The man I met didn't just want tall tales, but works of thought and thinking, speculation."

"Then he's a philosopher." Walter chuckled. "He should have spoken to my father. He could have heard stories drift into philosophy and back to stories without ever knowing where the first ended and the second picked up."

A rare smile lit Ezra's face. "I understand. He's not a storyteller, he's not a historian, and he's not a philosopher. He's a collector of ideas as well as tales. He *is* a sage. A sage gathers all knowledge, not just one kind."

10

SIGNALS, SIGILS

Night settled around the radio tower, and with it the cool damp of the forest air. For Walter, his slumber had been so deep and so dreamless that when he did wake, he felt time had jumped from evening to morning without a second between. He'd woken before the sun, a habit so ingrained in him that no matter how tired he was, he could not alter his routine. He wanted to take a walk, clear his mind, try to relax. But relaxing would not be easy. Walter had too many things to ponder, too much to consider, too much information pouring in. He also had a secret.

Actually, Walter had many secrets. In a way, he was more a man of secrets than he was of anything else. He collected them, hoarded them, protected them, and when the time was right, he might even use them. And while he knew secrets about almost everyone he'd ever known, his personal closet was not without its skeletons. And that was something he'd just as soon the hunter not know.

Ezra had found one of his secrets already. She knew if times had been different, maybe he would have become a hunter. That bothered him. It had always bothered him. And though he had been flustered by one secret revealed, there were others he knew the hunter would be more eager to find. Two secrets in particular. Two small, *ivory* secrets sewn into the lining of his jacket. Because if he had ever been able to read someone, he had read this: If Ezra knew he had two chimera teeth, then all else would become forfeit.

Walter hadn't thought about the teeth until Ezra told her story. There had been something in her voice when she described the chimera he hadn't been able to pinpoint. At first, he thought speaking of the beasts dredged up old fears. Then he thought the gleam in her eyes was in remembrance of the thrill of the hunt. Finally, he recognized it. Longing. Pained, anguished longing. She didn't just want the chimera to return, she needed them to. She needed the tooth.

At least Ezra didn't have the sweats or trembles. Or maybe she did at one time, and now they were long past—even if the mental addiction remained. Walter knew what drove the hunter. Not the chimera, but what the chimera could bring. And so if Ezra thought helping David would lead to the creatures? Well then, Walter imagined she would follow him to the ends of the earth.

Above him, the tower struts groaned. The reverberations shot down the stays and through Walter's spine. He tilted his head back, his eyes tracing the steel from the ground up to the heavens. The night, still clouded from the trailing storm, darkened the sky above. He examined the faint smudge of light behind which the moon was hidden, and then looked out to the forest. The sun would come soon. The gloaming was tingeing the sky to the east. And from that small hint of light, he saw movement.

Alert, he lifted his head from the tower strut. There was motion in the trees, lithe shapes drifting from one to the other, then settling, then moving once more. He squinted to determine whether what he saw was animal, human, or chimera. But he couldn't tell from here.

"I see you've found our audience."

Walter lurched in surprise, then settled himself. Ezra stood beside him. Her tone was low, wary, but not nervous.

"Chimera?"

Ezra shook her head. "No. They move entirely too much. The chimera blend and hide. When they stalk, they will appear as trees, a bush, a stone. These are men. Though I trust our host is unaware he has visitors."

Walter shook his head. "Don't underestimate him. He caught us."

"Yes, but it was light still, and we weren't trying to hide. For now, he's sleeping soundly. I would guess a man of Joby's age makes no hurry to greet the day."

"Joby's age? You're not far behind him. Maybe ahead."

Ezra's smiled. "That's how I know. Nevertheless, he is an easy target. And I don't believe these men mean well."

"So what then?"

"The very question I've been pondering." Ezra waited a long moment. "Joby has told us he has very little fuel remaining. Thus our opportunity to get David's questions out is also quite limited. And for all his hospitality, he doesn't seem to think much of David's Holes, certainly not as a pressing issue. I think he tolerates us as visitors, no more. So I don't wish to have him distracted when he broadcasts."

"What if our 'friends' decide to try something?"

"We must take that risk. When the broadcast starts, you stay with David and Joby. I'll continue to stand guard."

"Continue?"

"What do you think I'm doing now?"

Walter recalled the fight between Ezra and the chimera. If whoever was out there wanted trouble, they would certainly find it in her. "Ok. Fair enough. So we just wait?"

"For now. Until the radioman makes his broadcast, we say nothing to him or David. We need them both focused." Ezra raised an eyebrow. "Can you keep that secret, Walter? Do the people of your village believe in secrets?"

"Of course I can. We all have secrets."

●

David rolled over in his cot as the sun shone through the eastern window. He'd been awake for an hour but had relished the moment of peace.

"Getcha up, and getcha movin'," Joby called. He swung a crescent wrench around, clanging it against pipes and dragging it across the fence surrounding the generator. "Lots to do and a short time to do it. We've got…" the radioman glanced at his oversized wristwatch, "two hours until the signal flares. Getcha breakfast and then come and help me."

Walter leaned against one of the long, copper pipes. His muscular arms were folded across his chest. The sheer brawn impressed David. "What do you need doing, Mr. Joby? Many hands make light work. On the farm, or I reckon, around here."

"Most of it's done, prepped, and ready for days. Storm didn't change that. Just tests and tests until the hour comes. We'll start the gennie—generator, that is—a few minutes before broadcast. By the time she's warm and humming, it'll be our turn to talk."

"I've already eaten," Walter said. "So put me to work."

David ambled over to where Ezra tended the cast iron stove. The hunter shifted back and forth between scraping at a frying pan and stirring some sort of thick porridge. Her eyes kept drifting to look out of the window.

"Sleep well, David?" Ezra asked without turning.

"Not really. Too much to worry about."

She gave a slight nod. "About your Holes? Or my chimera?"

"Your story." He wrinkled his face. "I didn't like the ending—where the chimera just disappeared. Stories aren't supposed to just end with nothing happening and the problem going away. That's not an ending at all."

"Why should life need an ending like a story?"

"It doesn't have to… but there's no closure. I mean, what *happened* to them? Where have they been? Did they really just scatter? Doesn't it kill you not to know where they are, or what really happened? Or why they're back? Doesn't anyone know? No one has any guesses? No clues?"

Ezra's smile disappeared. "Of course it bothers me. I've spent my life trying to answer those questions. And all I've learned is some stories don't have endings. Or maybe the ending hasn't come yet. Your sage would know. Stories are his trade, not mine."

David's frown deepened. "I think he'd hate this story. Why would he care about a story with no ending?"

"I don't know." Ezra sighed. "Maybe it's not important, or maybe it is. But if I thought the story didn't have an end, then I wouldn't be with you."

"And you think the Holes will give you an answer?"

"Perhaps. I told the truth yesterday. I believe your Holes and my chimera are connected. Neither is completely natural, and their appearance at the same time can't be a coincidence." Ezra removed a pewter plate from the table next to the stove. She scooped in a few strips of bacon along with an ample dollop of porridge and offered him the plate. "Now eat, and let's help Joby so we can find your sage."

As if in response, a crash sounded from across the room, followed by a barrage of curses from Joby and protests from Walter. David popped to his feet, plate still in hand. Crossing toward the generator, he could see one of Joby's many, many toolboxes had been overturned.

Wrenches, nuts, bolts, and ball-bearings lay in a swath of shining/rusted metal across the floor.

"You gad-nabbit, enormous stinking oaf of a dirt farmer!" Joby leaped up and down, his already sunburned face turned crimson. "Didn't you see my tools? They're right there, right in front of your oversized colossal head and below your ogre's feet! Are you blind, or just too thick to move your feet without looking at them?"

"What were your tools doing on the hand railing?"

"Nothing! Sitting there! Ready to be used because that's where they belong!"

"But it's the railing to the stairs…"

"Which is where the tools go!"

Ezra cleared her throat, turning the gaze of both men. "We've got a job to do, right? And little time, right Joby? You're the professional."

"I am? Ah, yes…" Joby puffed out his chest, his face relaxed. "Yes, I am. Ok, David, collect what the oaf knocked over. Madam Ezra?"

"Yes?"

"Remove those wooden chocks around the gennie so it can turn free. Walter?"

The farmer raised an eyebrow.

"You… are enormous. Go get some more kindling from the shed, and then start pulling the tarps free of the lower struts. I'll test the connections."

David shoved the bacon in his mouth while leaving his porridge untouched. He scrambled beneath the railing to do as the radioman asked. But he soon discovered that once one task ended, another began, then another, and another. And none of them had much to do with the radio tower so much as tidying up Joby's workshop. And so, when he finished scrubbing the stove, he braced himself for the next chore.

"It's time." Joby's eyes glinted. "It's time, it's ready, it's come. Five minutes until transmission." He pointed in triumph at his wristwatch. "And here… we… go!"

The radioman turned to the generator. He took step after deliberate step, his footfalls changing from hurried stomping to a reverent tiptoe until he faced a metal box with padlocks lining one side. He produced a small, bronze key from his shirt. He held the object to his lips, kissed it, then pulled the chain from his neck. With precise movements, he unlocked the top, middle, and lower padlocks, returned the key to his neck, and swung the box open.

Inside were rows of switches: red, black, and gray. Next to each switch was a piece of masking tape and an illegible descriptor. "Hold on to yer butts," Joby muttered. He pinched the topmost breaker with his grease-covered fingers. *Flick.*

With the flip of the first switch, the lights of the workshop blinked and then returned. The orange glow was replaced by pale neon. *Flick, flick, flick.* Breakers snapped, engines hummed, and pistons turned. The tower thrummed to life, power radiating throughout. *Flick, flick, flick.* More lights and more clanking, steam puffed from pipes and corners. *Flick, flick… FLICK.*

The generator groaned, and then began to turn. The revolutions were slow at first before building to a speed where the individual nuts, bolts, wires, and fastenings were only a blur. David watched in fascination until Joby called to him.

"Phase one complete," he barked. "Only moments to spare, friends. Follow me." He leaped from the top of the steps, clearing the short flight in a single bound. As he landed, he released the clasp on his tool belt. The collection of pouches and instruments clanged to the ground. Joby skipped to the far side of his workshop where a rusted ladder led straight up and through the ceiling. He scurried through the hole, his face reappearing moments later. "What are you waiting for? Come on up!"

Ezra shook her head. "Looks a little tight. I'll wait down here."

The radioman grinned. "It's tight all right. But I need you in case they ask about the chimera. Leave the biggun' down instead. Probably just knock things over anyhows."

Walter and Ezra exchanged a look, ending with the farmer nodding in agreement. Then, Ezra darted up the ladder, slinging her satchel aside to fit through the narrow opening.

"Go ahead, now," Walter murmured. "I'll be fine down here. Wouldn't make it through that hole anyway." David nodded and ascended. He squirmed through the hole and onto the floor.

The walls of the chamber were covered in lights, knobs, and buttons. Wires crossed from circuit to circuit and hung from the low ceiling. David sat cross-legged on the floor beside Ezra, hoping he was suitably out of the way. Even with only the three of them, the space was cramped.

Joby flicked a toggle, and white noise filled the room. The hiss narrowed before focusing into the soft whine of a violin playing classical music. David forced himself to exhale. They had made contact.

As quickly as it began, the music ceased. A baritone voice crackled across the speakers:

"This is Alert Control Central with the quarterly test call. All stations respond when addressed and establish status. Lack of response indicates non-connectivity or peril. The test begins now. Station One Baltimore, respond."

"Station One Baltimore, confirm all green," a woman's voice responded.

"Station Two Boston, respond."

"Station Two Boston, confirm all green."

"Station Three Charleston, respond."

"Station Three Charleston, alert yellow, damage to main tower, require assistance for repairs to mid stays."

"Roger that, Station Three. Request confirmed. Station Four Dover, respond."

"Station Four Dover, confirm all green."

"Station Five…"

Joby turned to face the others. "We're Station Forty-six. We'll broadcast fuel reserves and your message. After that, we'll switch to receive-only. Once the checks are complete, we'll listen for their response. If we're lucky, our fuel will hold out that long."

"Station Nine Fayetteville, confirm all green."

"Station Ten Greensboro, respond."

No reply.

"Station Ten Greensboro, second request, respond if able."

No reply.

"Station Ten Greensboro, registered no response. News from Greensboro? General inquiry open."

"This is Station Twenty-three Fort Bragg. Greensboro reported zero percent fuel stores by courier last month."

"Roger that, Twenty-three. Dispatching crew to respond. Station Eleven Holleman, respond."

"Station Eleven Holleman, confirm all green."

"Station Twelve Jacksonville, respond…"

David held his breath, craning his ears as station after station gave their report. When finally station forty-five confirmed they, too, were 'all green,' the speaker crackled once more.

"Station Forty-six Mayfair, respond."

Joby leaned forward over a polished silver microphone. The buffed chrome contrasted the rust covering the other instruments. "Station Forty-six Mayfair, alert red, fuel reserves below one percent. General dispatch, reports of four chimera attacking town of Greenwater's End. Priority red, request word of sighting of person calling himself 'the sage.' Cutting transmission, pending emergency. Over."

"Roger fuel warning, Forty-six. Roger chimera sighting. Request for information confirmed. Hold for response after check. Roger unable to respond." The voice over the speaker paused. *"Sounds like an eventful month out there, Forty-six. Continue report. Station Forty-seven, Morristown, respond."*

"Station Forty-seven Morristown, all green."

"Station Forty-eight…"

Joby reached to the wall and flipped a switch, the sounds of generators and machines tapered significantly. "Ok, we're checked in and have our mayday out there. We'll be at receive-only for now."

David shook his head. "I don't know what that means."

"It means we can listen but can't talk back. Fuel's too low to broadcast. But if we're lucky, you'll hear something on your sage, and I'll have gas coming my way in no time. Now sit tight, and keep your ears open."

The speaker from the radio box continued, with seventy-three towers reporting in. Eight didn't respond at all, twice that number reported critical fuel levels, but only one other had a sighting of chimera. When the signoffs were finished, the rigid cadence of call and response shifted, becoming more conversational. Beginning with Station One and continuing up, each radioman reported the weather, current events, a touch of politics, and a smattering of rumors. The names of places were vaguely familiar to David, but the people and events were not.

David thought his request had fallen on deaf ears until Station Sixteen responded. The radiomen told of a fire at the local tavern, that a reverend was running for mayor, and that the season for goose had been better than usual. And then the operator said something that made his ears perk up.

"This is Waterville here. One more rumor and a response to Forty-six. We've heard of your sage. Old guy, bald, kind of strange. Tells a lot of stories and writes a lot down. He left town heading west across the foothills. Said he was going to

Cinderwood, though can't imagine why. Also, we've had lots of reports of strange disappearances. People just vanishing, no explanation, no warning. May just be a rumor, but anyone else seen something like that?"

For several seconds there was no response, then the board behind Joby lit up in an erratic flare. The flood of lights turned the dim room frighteningly bright.

"This is Station Fifty Richmond, report seven disappearances last month. No trace."

"This is Station Nine Fayetteville, report three disappearances, no trace, and no evidence."

"This is Station Twenty…"

Station after station, report after report, each radio operator announced that people had gone missing. No one said Holes, but the signs were there. David waited quietly until the broadcast was complete and the news shared. The operator gave a final farewell with a promise to respond to the requests. Then the switchboard went dark.

Joby returned the silver microphone to its stand and hit the master switch on the board. The last of the lights faded away. The radioman had a satisfied look on his face. "Well, I think you got your message out, and you know where your sage is. You know how to get to Cinderwood?"

"Unfortunately," Ezra murmured.

Inspiration surged through David. "Do you have a map?" he asked. "I want to check something."

David, Ezra, and Joby descended into the workshop. The generator had crawled to a halt, though Joby never hit the switch to cut it off.

"Must be out of gas for good," he muttered. "Where's the big guy?"

David looked around, but Walter was nowhere in sight. He shrugged the thought away as Joby handed him the requested map, a yellowed and cracked thing dotted with names and scribbles, both printed and handwritten. Once he spread the map out on the table, Joby tapped the center with a grease-stained finger.

"That's the spot right there. Cinderwood. Too far to walk. Straight shot on the main road, though. You wait long enough, you'll get a ride, at least part of the way. Might be a few days before a truck passes, unless you're lucky. No one much goes that way on purpose, but you could get close. You see, we're right here, and…"

David interrupted him, his excitement building. "Joby? That station in Waterville, they said seven people missing, right? Where else had people disappeared?"

Ezra pulled the map from Joby and smoothed it in front of her. "Do you mind?"

"Not at all," Joby responded.

Ezra reached into a dish on the side of the table containing a variety of colored pins. She started by putting a white pin where they were, then another in Lexington. She grabbed red pins and stuck them around the map, then the blue ones, then the yellow.

"The red pins," Ezra said, "had more than two disappearances. The blues more than eight, and the yellows over ten. Notice anything, David?"

The pattern was clear. Reports of people missing grew steadily the farther west on the map. And if the reports were accurate, if they traveled in the direction of the sage, then they would go into the thick of it. David knew in his heart the Holes would increase as well. What's more, he knew where the center would lie. Just then, the door flew open, crashing hard against the wall. Walter stood in the entryway, his eyes wide.

"Ezra! David! We've got trouble. We need to get out of here."

Leaving the map behind, David leaped to his feet. He rushed to the door and crossed through into the sunlight, momentarily blinded by the glare.

In a great billowing of smoke and dust, accompanied by the deep rumble of engines, a procession of vehicles was barreling toward the radio tower. Any hope that they might be friendly was dashed by staccato bursts of gunfire from men perched atop the vehicles and hanging from the windows. The men laughed and yelled, white teeth and white eyes shining from faces smeared with mud and oil. There were at least two dozen vehicles in the procession, from battered vans, to jeeps, to pickups, to dune buggies.

"Friends of yours?" Ezra glanced at Joby, her tone low.

"This is bad," Walter said. "I've heard of these guys. They've been running all up and down the southeast. They take what they want, then head out again once nothing's left. Greenwater's was too far off the path, but I've got a cousin up near Charlotte that had a run-in with them. Best thing we can do is clear out before they know we're—"

A gunshot rang out beside them. David dropped low and saw Walter do the same. The shot had come from Joby, now standing astride a piece of toppled scaffolding. He had a pistol gripped in each hand and a sneer on his face.

"Patrice, you damned she-devil! Call off your dogs if you don't want a few extra holes in 'em!" Joby fired a shot into the procession. But instead of the bandits backing away, their reaction was one of laughter, followed by returned fire.

"Inside. Now," Ezra barked. David wasted no time following her directions. Walter came in just behind, trailed by Joby.

The sound of bullets striking the shack, from roof to door to tower struts, continued sporadically. Though his heart raced from being shot at—actually *shot* at—David could tell this wasn't an all-out assault. The bandits, or whatever they were, meant to intimidate.

"What do they want?" he asked.

"Hell if I know." Joby spat on the floor. "Unless they're in the radio business, ain't much here except my tools. That, or they just need a place to hang out. I suppose this would be as good a base as any."

Ezra was stooped over, tightening the laces of her boots. When she looked up, her eyes had returned to the hard, serious expression she'd worn during the hurricane.

"Master Joby, will you fight these men? What do you seek to gain?"

"What do I...? Seek...? How can you...?" Joby's flushed. "This is my tower! Mine! It's my responsibility and has been all my life!"

Ezra turned and raised an eyebrow. "David?"

He shook his head. "Sorry, but the Holes are more important. Let's get out of here."

No sooner had he spoken, the front door exploded inward, crashing to the ground as the hinges gave way. Crowded in the doorway, guns at the ready, were four armed men. The bandits' earlier grins had been replaced by stony, determined faces.

"Drop 'em, old man," one of the men barked, his rifle trained on Joby.

David didn't dare move, and his friends seemed equally paralyzed. Walter was in a half-crouch, his fists balled. Ezra had her weight back on one foot, her hunting knife drawn and by her side. Joby was the first to move. Slowly, he lowered his pistols and set them on the ground.

Four more bandits filed in, spreading out to either side. Two had their guns focused on Walter, one on Ezra, and one on Joby. David, it seemed, was not the most immediate threat.

He heard a chuckle, and a heavyset woman pushed through the door. She had a sadistic grin on her scarred face, and a long-barreled revolver in her left hand.

"Well, well, Mr. Joby. That wasn't too hard now, was it? And if my timing is right—which it always is—I suppose you made your distress call." She winked, her small, intense eyes scanning the room. "So when can I expect my fuel delivered?"

11

REUNION

David flicked his eyes to Ezra, expecting her to do, well, *something*. Instead, the hunter slid her knife back into its sheath and folded her arms across her chest. Walter stood up from his crouch.

Joby reacted differently.

"*Your* fuel! Dagnabbit damn thieving rustling bunch of..." Joby's voice dropped to silence as the bandit pulled the hammers back on her revolvers.

The bandit didn't blink; her hand was steady. The smile stretching her lips neither grew nor dissipated. "Yes. *My* fuel. On order, awaiting arrival, and enough to keep my crew rolling for the next few months. Then on to the next one, I suppose."

Joby wailed in frustration. "But the tower, the signal, our line of defense against the damned chimera! I've kept this old girl for forty-nine years, and I'll be damned if..."

The bandit's smile widened. "Exactly. You are damned, Joby. Your tower as well, and you know it. Your years are done and this hunk of metal is way past useful. Now be polite and introduce your friends."

David was surprised by the familiarity Joby and the woman had with one another. They were not strangers. That much was clear.

"Very well," Joby gestured around the room. "Everyone, this is Patrice. She used to be friendly, well-liked, and respectable. Now, she's a dirty thief. Patrice, these are my guests. The biggun's Walter, farmer from the coast. That's Ezra. She's a hunter, which you can see unless you're as blind as you are dumb. And the kid's name is David. He fell through a Hole in some other dimension and is on a mission to save the universe. Or something. Happy now?"

Patrice nodded, though her eyes did not even drift in David's direction. "Been a while since I saw a hunter dressed for the big fight. What are you doing here?"

Ezra stretched her neck and leveled her gaze. "Hunting." She paused. "And you? Where was your chapter—before you abandoned your duty?"

Patrice's eyes flared with rage. "Abandoned? You forget yourself, Hunter Ezra. Times are changed and passed. The chimera are all but gone. The world has no use for hunters."

Walter cleared his throat. "Is she a hunter too? Are you *all* hunters?"

Ezra replied, "She used to be. Not anymore. But I think she still remembers. She wears the chain, after all, even if she does keep it hidden." Ezra tapped the metal links on her forearm. "She hasn't truly forgotten. I imagine she longs for the old days. She wishes she was still useful."

Patrice grinned. "Oh, I'm useful all right. Useful to myself, useful to my men. And if the chimera return? I'll fight again. I keep my skills sharp."

"By robbing radiomen? Those who keep watch? Those who would tell us of a return?"

"Sometimes. And sometimes…" the bandit's smile widened, "I even rob the odd hunter." Patrice ran her eyes up and down Ezra. "If you give me trouble, I'll shoot. First you, then your friends. Don't think me foolish. I imagine you still have your edge. And from what I overheard, you may have run into some chimera yourself. Intriguing. If that's true, then there's something I need from you." The bandit bared her teeth, then tapped twice on her right canine. She turned to the armed men. "Search those three for weapons, but *her* I want scoured. Every pocket, every seam, every stitch, and every scrap. If she's carrying a chimera tooth, I want it."

Ezra snorted in disgust. "Then you'll be disappointed."

Patrice stared back with deep, unblinking eyes. "We'll see about that. Your hands look too steady to me, your eyes too sharp. You aren't hurting, not as much as you should be. But…" the bandit leaned close, her face inches away, "…perhaps *I* am."

The bandits marched their captives outside. Walter and David were put in handcuffs, which were in turn secured to a long chain, looped around the fence. Ezra, on the other hand, was not handcuffed at all. As her battle chain was permanently attached to the manacle welded around her wrist, they simply padlocked it to the fence directly. Only Joby was unrestrained, though not out of mercy. The bandits ushered him inside as soon as the others were secured.

Ezra, Walter, and David leaned back against the chain-link fence and watched their captors as they stripped the station of anything worth taking. And as the workers worked, the rest of the convoy convened. More battered and decrepit trucks arrived, each covered in rust and bearing cracked windshields and bullet-ridden panels. There were some twenty-odd vehicles in all. One school bus held the bulk of the troops, while the other vehicles were outfitted with crews of three or four men each. The marauders laughed and joked as they dismantled what Joby had fought to preserve. And yet, David thought they acted with a hope and purpose he'd seen before. Their camaraderie reminded him of his brothers.

"Kind of sad, I think," he mused. He glanced left and right at his companions. "I mean, the tower might be out of gas or whatever, but it's still kind of sad. You could tell Joby cared about the place. What do you think they have him doing?"

For a moment, neither Walter nor Ezra spoke. Eventually, Walter looked over, shrugged, and returned to watching the caravan. David fidgeted with anticipation.

"They have trucks," Ezra said. "They have trucks, and we have a destination."

Walter squinted at the hunter. "Wait. Is that true? Did you find out where the sage is? I mean, I forgot to ask, what with the shooting, and yelling, and guns pointed at me, and all. But do we know?"

Ezra turned, but not to look at Walter. She settled her uneasy gaze on David. "Not for sure. But I wasn't talking about the sage. I don't think we need him anymore. Am I right? You know where we're going, don't you? You saw it on the map."

David's mouth had gone dry, not because Ezra knew what he thought, and certainly not because of his strange predicament. What made him sweat was she saw the truth.

"What's she talking about?" Walter asked.

"She's right." David's voice was tiny. "Joby had a map and… it's the same as my home, the same oceans, the same land."

"We already knew that," Walter replied.

"Right. But the *pattern* was the same too." He crouched in the dirt and began to draw. "On the radio, we heard about people disappearing, and in some places lots of people."

"Holes."

"Exactly. And the farther west you went, the more people had gone missing. That was just like back in my world. I think that the center where my brothers and I were going is the same place we need to go here. It's too close for coincidence."

Ezra smiled her thin smile. "What have I said about coincidence, David?"

He shrugged her off. "We're going here." He tapped on the center of his drawing. "It's called Kansas. There was a town there back in my world—Salina—but I'd be surprised if there was one here." He looked up. "Why isn't anyone out west again?"

Ezra replied, "It was beyond the hunters' guard."

Walter rubbed his chin. "That's the middle of nowhere, David. Nobody lives that far inland. No one lives past the Mississippi for that matter. If we head out there, it's not just the Holes we'll find. Probably chimera too." He squinted up at them. "So, we've really given up on the sage, then?"

David shook his head. "No. We still need him. He probably knows more about what's going on than anyone. Without him, it might not be enough just to make it to the center. And when it's over, he's the only one who can send me home. At least, he did get me here."

Ezra nodded. "Very well. We escape. We take a vehicle. Extra fuel if we can. Head west. First, we find the sage. Then, we go to Kansas to find the source of these Holes. Try to see if there is a way to fix all this." She paused. "Is that enough of a plan for you, Walter?"

David raised an eyebrow. "I don't think it's gonna be that easy."

"Yeah, like the escaping part," Walter grumbled.

Ezra looked back at the commotion around the radio tower. "Watch. Wait. Opportunity will come."

●

As the day dragged on, the sun intensified. David wasn't used to the heat, and certainly not the choking humidity. After a time, the sweating stopped. He wanted water, needed water. But despite his pleas, the bandits paid him no mind.

Ezra and Walter had their own ways of dealing with the heat. The big farmer huddled as best he could, as unmoving as a statue. His plain white shirt was spread to cover the top of his stubbled head and broad shoulders. The man's eyes were glazed-over slits, his chest barely moving as he breathed. Ezra also remained still, all but her eyes. Her gaze darted back and forth from the bandits, to the trucks, to the buses, and always back to the bandits' leader. David still knew little about what it meant to be a hunter, but he'd seen the way Ezra had moved. He wondered if Patrice was just as dangerous. Ezra, for one, always had a trick up her sleeve. Except for now. He had expected the old hunter to pick the lock or somehow worm from the shackles—but all she did was watch. She didn't even acknowledge his weak pleas for help beyond giving him her wide-brimmed hat. She looked strange with her head bared, vulnerable in a way being restrained didn't touch.

The thought drew David's eyes to Ezra's battle chain—now being used to shackle her. The oiled links were a sharp contrast to the rusty chain running from his handcuffs, around the fencepost, and to Walter's hands. Walter had told David that hunters used the battle chain like a whip, and were as skilled with the weapon as though it were an extension of themselves.

And there they sat, until all of Joby's belongings had been hauled from his workshop into the trucks. When the last box had been moved, Patrice swaggered up to where Walter, David, and Ezra sat.

"And how are my guests today?"

"Water?" David croaked. "Can we have some water?"

"Soon. Soon enough, once the sun is down and you won't sweat it off. I've my men to consider first. This here is a hierarchy of sorts. I'm at the top, then my lieutenants, the cooks, the handlers, the grunts, and then way down at the bottom, well, I suppose we've got you." Patrice shifted her gaze from side to side. "We'll be here a few days. At least until the tanker arrives." The bandit moved to stand directly in front of Walter. "But you know, you could be a whole lot more useful—and a whole lot less thirsty—not chained to that fence. If you wanted to be, that is. Of course, I don't know if I trust you enough to let you go. Shows remarkable bad judgment traveling with a has-been like your hunter friend. Why are you trotting together anyways?"

Walter stirred from his statue-like torpidity. "You done with your speech, ma'am? I don't really think you care too much about who we are and what we're up to. Not even a little bit."

"You're right. My crew is here for the gas. That's all. You three are a distraction, a curiosity. But since there is time to kill, why are you here?"

Walter cast a sidelong glance. "David? You want to answer that one?"

He looked up. "It's because of the Holes."

"What?" Patrice became alert. "What are you talking about?"

Though his voice rasped, David dropped into the familiar tone of explanation. "Not everyone can see them," he whispered. "But they're there. As black as night, and if you fall in, you're gone for good. They can take a car as fast as a person, and I've even seen big ones that could swallow your bus."

The smirk on her face, affixed since their first encounter, had vanished. She brought her eyes to bear on David as she dropped to one knee in the dust. "Ah, the Pits. So you can see them too?"

David opened his mouth in surprise, but it had already happened. Ezra jerked forward, turning a full somersault before striking out with an extended leg. Her worn boot cracked against the bandit leader's cheek, eliciting an oomph of pain. The hunter twisted her body, wrenching her shoulders as she yanked against her restraint. It was enough. The chain stretching from her wrist to the rusty fence strained; the lock broke. Ezra pivoted to face her opponent. She crouched with her right hand in front of her like a claw, and the fighting chain on her wrist slung low. Her index finger twitched in readiness.

"Bitch!" the scream tore from the bandit. Patrice rolled to a three-point stance, two feet down, her left knuckles keeping her balance. She dropped her right hand to her holster and drew. But even as the gun rose, Ezra lashed out with the chain. The tip cracked into the bandit's fingers and knocked the pistol away.

Ezra drew her chain back, and then swung once more. But this time her opponent was ready. The bandit rocked onto her back foot and blocked the strike with her left forearm. David expected to hear the thump of the chain and a breaking of bones. Instead, there was a mighty clang as the links struck something metallic.

The bandit's sneer returned. With a single motion, she grabbed her left sleeve and pushed it up above her elbow. There, wrapped around a broad manacle encircling her forearm, was her own fighting chain. The color, the construct, even the links were identical to Ezra's. The bandit shook her arm and the chain dropped to the ground. She adjusted her crouch and raised her right hand into a half-claw. Her true colors as a former hunter were revealed.

"I'm ready, old woman," Patrice sneered. "Are you?"

The two hunters paced one another, their stances matched, their forms mirrored. They could have been the same woman facing herself in a mirror to see her body dressed in different clothes.

Ezra moved first. Her chain swung with deadly purpose, but was again blocked. Patrice struck back; Ezra feinted to avoid the blow. The strike, the parry, the dodge. The fight mesmerized David with both its fluidity as well as its brutality. Whenever a blow landed, the thud of impact and wince of the fighters was terrible. The two women lashed and parried, and though their determination never flagged, he saw that each strike was slower than the last.

Walter must have seen it too. David's hands jerked backward as the large man strained against his shackles. He heaved against the chain, muscles bulging with the effort, but there was no use. And the next time he flexed, he was met with a leveled gun from one of the other bandits. The fight had been noticed, and the onlookers were crowding around the two hunters. At least thirty men, in their ragged clothes and scuffed leather boots, now watched. They laughed with delight as they cheered their leader, shaking their knives in the air and occasionally firing a pistol. But they did not join in. And now David saw why.

The battle's dynamic had changed. Ezra still lashed, stroke after stroke, but her art was shifting to frenzy, her strikes becoming sloppy. And though she swung three times for every answer from Patrice, she was losing ground. At the next blow from her opponent, Ezra flailed with her right arm—her unprotected arm—to block the chain. The crack of bone sounded as the links connected. But she didn't hold back. She made a final, furious strike. But whether dulled by pain, or simply fatigue, she faltered. Patrice sidestepped the blow, and brought her chain around, the links coming to bear against Ezra's unprotected skull. This time, the strike landed. She crumpled.

The bandit leader dropped to her knees beside Ezra. The battle chain fell limp at her side. Patrice took a few labored breaths, then struggled to her feet. She walked to recover her pistol and replaced it in its holster. She looked back at her fallen opponent.

"She's alive." The bandit's voice cracked from strain. "Keep her that way." She pointed to her men. "Her arm is broken, maybe more. Splint it, just in case."

Patrice turned her eyes to David, and his heart sank. "And get these two some water."

The last time David had been in a van, he was given the honored position in the front seat. Newman, the oldest of the brothers and the unofficial leader of the expedition, always took the first shift as driver. While Newman navigated the shiny green vehicle down the highways and byways, he'd tell stories of the times from before the Holes. He'd talk about football games, corn mazes, pretty girls, and ski trips. He'd talk about the summers full of barbecues, fishing, hiking in the mountains, and the jobs he'd held at the local summer camp.

David's brother Alex, on the other hand, dealt exclusively in dirty jokes and tales of getting into trouble—which no one believed. And whether Carlos, Ernie, Federico, or George, David's brothers made him feel as though he belonged. Brotherhood and teamwork enveloped everything they did—despite the reasons they did it. Those were high times.

And then a shadow fell over his soul. He'd been so caught up these past few days, he'd barely thought of home. He wondered if his parents thought about him. He wondered if they were still among the lucky ones. He wondered about his brothers' families. Had they fallen to the Holes? Or did they simply wait for their sons who would never return?

And now David was in a van once more. But this time he did not swap stories as the world streamed by. No. He was huddled on the hard aluminum floor in the back. There were no windows, no seats, no mats or coverings. The only fixture, apart from a cage separating the front seats from the passengers, was a metal U-ring welded to the floor. Chains spread from the ring like an industrial spider's web. At the end of one chain was David, and at the other, Walter. As far as they knew, Ezra and Joby were in their own impromptu prisons.

"Walter?" his voice was weak, "do you miss your family?"

The large man looked at him with deep, dark eyes. "Yes. Of course I do. But it's only been a day, you know. I miss them less than I'm just worried about them. Tully, James, and Marcus. They're too young for all this. But I'll tell you, David, my wife is really smart and as strong-willed as anyone I've ever met. Between her and my sisters, they'll be ok. And who knows, we could be back in no time. Once we get out of here, of course."

David remained silent. The thought of going home was so distant it could barely be conceived. And yet, if the sage was out there, maybe there was hope after all.

"But what about the Holes?" he asked. "Aren't you worried about those?"

"I came with you, didn't I? Doesn't that prove it?"

"And the bandits? Do you think they'll let us go?"

Walter's face darkened. "Well, I suppose we'll know soon enough. I don't think we're worth a ransom. And we're not exactly dangerous. If they can't come up with a use for us, then maybe they'll let us go. They could leave us somewhere. Or..."

"Or kill us?" David's voice cracked under the strain. "But why? It doesn't make any sense. What could we do to them?" He dropped his head into his hands. "There must be something else."

David lurched in surprise as he heard a knock on the van's side, followed by a rumble as the metal door slid open. The bandit leader Patrice stood there. The smile, once permanently affixed to her face, had not returned. She'd changed into a fresh set of clothes, but he could see from the way she moved that she suffered from the fight. To her right stood a hard-looking man with a sawed-off shotgun curled in his hand, his finger on the trigger.

Walter frowned at the newcomers. "You were listening?"

Patrice propped one foot on the step of the van and folded her hands on top of her thigh. "Of course. So let's cut to it, shall we? It's a valid question. What *can* you offer that is worth your lives, or the life of your hunter friend? Don't look so surprised. She's still breathing. Hunters are a hard lot to kill."

David looked uneasily at Walter, but neither responded.

"Oh come now, don't sell yourselves short. You, boy, you can see the Pits, the Holes as you call them. It would be extremely useful to have another lookout. And you," she turned her gaze to Walter, "you're a big fella in your own right. Joby said you're a farmer, but I think you could learn other trades."

"Thank you for the offer, but I have a family. A wife, kids."

Patrice grinned. "All of whom would rather have an absent daddy than a dead one. At least, that's my bet."

David shook his head in disbelief. "So you want us to join you? Help you rob and drive around and stuff?"

"And watch for Pits."

Walter started to speak, but David cut him off. "No! This isn't about surviving the Holes—it's about beating them. Where I came from, there is hardly a world left. Our only chance is to get to the source of it all—before there's no turning back. You should be helping us, not locking us up. We're not going to turn you in or anything, because you're not important. Only stopping the Holes is. So let us go."

Patrice snickered once, then clapped her hands. "Sorry kid, but like it or not, you're an asset. You join my crew, you earn my trust, and then maybe I'll hear what you have to say. There's time. Have patience."

Walter gritted his teeth. "I've seen how you operate. You take what you want, and to hell with the rest. We could be with you for a month or years. Your kind doesn't care about the rest of us. So why should we believe you?"

"You don't take a hunter's word?"

"Of course not," Walter snorted. "I've met hunters before. On the other hand..." His eyes widened.

"What?"

Walter frowned. "Ok, maybe we *can* work something out. The kid's right, we're in this for other reasons. I'm in it for my family, and they don't care about this radio tower, or what you take, or any of it. We just want to be on our way. So maybe we can make a deal."

"And what could I possibly want from you—that I haven't already taken? Or couldn't take?"

Walter set his jaw. "A chimera tooth."

"You lie." Patrice's voice had dropped to a whisper.

"It's the truth. I didn't tell Ezra I had it. I needed something to bargain with." He grimaced. "And it seems that's the only thing you hunters care about."

"Is that so?"

"Have I got your attention?"

"Undivided." Patrice paused. "What do you propose?"

"You give us a ride to the next town. Today. Not in three days, or whenever you get your fuel. Once we're there, I tell your man where I hid the tooth."

"No deal. I need it now."

Walter shook his head. "If you had it, you'd never let us go. Just like you said."

Patrice asked, "And how can I trust you when you show so little trust for me?"

"Like I said, I've got a family. I've got more to lose."

"Fair enough. But I still need collateral. The hunter stays until I get my tooth."

"No," David cried. "We need her. It's too dangerous for us alone. We're not fighters. And we've got too far to go."

From outside, in the dark of the humid night, a thud sounded as though something heavy smacked on the top of the van. The sound was dull, hollow, and then went silent. And yet, it wasn't unnoticed. Patrice's eyes narrowed. She rested her hand on the pistol at her side and glanced at her shotgun-wielding companion. "Check it out. Be careful."

Patrice watched as the armed man disappeared outside, his shotgun raised as he went to investigate the noise. After he had moved out of sight, she crawled into the van and sat opposite them. She pulled the door shut, the privacy somehow disturbing. Her focus changed, her pupils constricted. She tilted her head and then studied Walter closely, saying nothing for several long seconds. For a moment, David thought she might start sniffing him.

The bandit said, "You have it with you, don't you? The tooth. I can feel it in the air; I can sense it." The bandit's eyes widened. "Freedom can be yours. Life can be yours. Just show it to me. Just, just show it to me and you can have anything. I... I know. I've got an idea. I'll give you a truck of your own. There's no need for messages and secrets or traveling back and forth. I'll put you and your friends in a gassed-up vehicle. Hell, I'll start the car for you myself. Just give me the tooth. At least show me it's real."

David looked over at Walter. The big man frowned, then narrowed his eyes. "Do you swear it? Do you swear it on all the honor you ever had? And the lives of your men? And all else in the world?"

"Yes," she hissed. "I swear it and more."

"I want a gun. For protection."

The bandit's fever pitch ebbed, but she didn't refuse. Patrice removed the long-barreled pistol from her belt. She flipped it around so the stock was toward Walter. "How's that for a show of trust? Now where is it?"

Walter took the gun and tucked it into his belt. He unbuttoned his heavy canvas shirt. His fingers probed around for several seconds, and when his hand emerged, a long, ivory tooth rested in his palm. Patrice snatched the tooth. She brought it to her lips and kissed. But as she did so, a voice sounded from the still-open door of the van.

"Seems you've lost your edge. I'll take that."

Standing in the doorway, her form outlined by the pale glow of the half-moon, was Ezra. Even in the dim light, David could see the bruises covering her face, and the sawed-off shotgun balanced across the splint on her forearm. Even more shocking than her injuries was her expression. Any hint of kindness, empathy, or control was gone. Her eyes were as red as dripping carmine, her teeth bared.

Patrice's fist snapped shut around the tooth. "No. It's *mine*." She clutched it to her chest.

Ezra said, "Don't move. Just give me the tooth."

"Enough!" Walter shook his head. "It *is* hers, Ezra. I traded it fair and square, and you being here doesn't make a difference." The farmer advanced on the bandit leader. He gently removed the keys from the ring on her belt. He undid his shackles and then locked them to Patrice's wrists.

Ezra, her aim unwavering, spoke though gritted teeth. "We'll need that tooth where we're headed. We'll need it. I'll need it. I'll…"

David shook his head. "No, Ezra, Walter's right. It's her tooth now. Guns or not, the deal is the same. She was going to let us go in exchange, and that's what we'll do. We both swore to it. And she'll keep her word. Isn't that right?"

The bandit leader nodded, her face a twist of emotions. "Of course. Otherwise, I'd have already called my men. You can't fight through us all."

Ezra tore her eyes away. "Good point. Walter, can you tie a gag? We don't want her making noise once we're gone."

"Sure." The large man ripped his shirt sleeve then tied it fast around Patrice's mouth. "Sorry 'bout this, but it's the only way I know."

Ezra nodded in approval. "Ok, now all we have to do is…" The hunter moved in a blur as the stock of the shotgun came down against Patrice's head. The bandit folded, her body falling motionless against the floor of the van. Ezra looked down at the tooth where it lay on the ground. She huffed and turned away. "Follow me and be quiet."

●

Walter followed Ezra as she wove through the caravan of vehicles. He was aware of the boy as he struggled to keep up. He was aware of the thatched metal of the pistol grip in his hands. He was aware Ezra's shotgun had come from the hand of a guard both unseen and unmentioned. And he was aware of the remaining chimera's tooth still sewn into the lining of his shirt. Walter had seen the look in Ezra's eyes. She needed these teeth in an all-consuming way. The time may come when he'd need a bargaining chip again.

"Hold," Ezra said. "That's it. That's the one."

The hunter had stopped in front of a large misshapen form covered in canvas. The hunter pulled on the cover and the fabric rustled away. There, beneath the worn cloth, was an impossibility. It was a car: not a truck, not a pickup, not a rusted collection of scrap metal and bullet holes. This was a machine. Black and chrome glistened as though waxed the day before. The vehicle bristled with tailpipes, spoked rims, and was painted with yellow flames tinged with iridescent blue.

"Whoa," David whispered.

Walter held up Patrice's key ring. One key stood apart, as black and polished as the vehicle before them.

Ezra asked, "Can you drive, Walter?"

"Sure. Trucks and combines. You?"

Ezra shook her head.

"Then I guess it's up to me." He climbed into the driver's side, sliding into the scooped leather seat. He palmed the chrome gearshift and slid the key into the ignition. The vehicle was a far cry from the pickups in Greenwater's End. But the controls were the same: clutch, gears, brake, accelerator. He glanced at Ezra beside him, and then at David in the back. "This is going to be loud."

Ezra turned to David. "Are you ready?"

"All buckled up."

"Walter, do you know where you're going?"

"The road runs through, east to west. We head west a little farther and the service road should hit the county road, then the highway. We'll need a little luck."

Walter pressed in the clutch, and turned the key. The machine roared to life, the twin exhausts churning so loudly they put the radio tower's generator to shame. He looked over at Ezra. "What about Joby?"

"No time for him now," Ezra said. Her voice was no longer a whisper. "His part in this story has come to an end. And our time is short."

Walter eased the car into reverse, and then shifted into first. He rolled toward the access road running alongside the radio tower. A few of the bandits were crawling from the cabs of their trucks, or up from cots scattered around the vehicles. The pale light from the half-moon gave them cover for but a second, and then they heard a scream of disbelief.

"Hey! It's the damn hunter! She's gotten out! And she's got the Hoss!" A pause… and then the inevitable: "Get her!"

Walter slammed down on the accelerator, his head thrown back as the muscle car leaped forward. Slamming up to the next gear, the car charged toward the access road, slid, and they were off.

"Yee-hah!" David shouted in delight.

The car sped from the radio tower, plowing down the access road like a hellshot demon. From the rearview mirror, Walter could see the headlights of other trucks flaring to life.

"Careful, now," Ezra said, her voice steady against the roar. "We have to survive until the highway."

Walter eased back on the pedal, and just in time. A deer darted in front of them, though he was able to avoid it. The road steadily deteriorated, craters and ruts becoming more widespread, rocks more abundant. He wove through the debris and fallen trees. But even as he angled, the bandits were gaining. And yet, despite the raw power of the car, he was too shaken by the near-miss to risk going any faster.

And then they were gone.

The light behind him vanished. The sound of other engines was absent, as though the chase had never happened. And in a way, Walter found himself unfulfilled.

"Did they just… did they just quit?"

He was answered by a frantic plea from David.

"Stop! Stop, stop, stop, stop, stop!"

Walter slammed on the brakes. The car tires squealed as they shuddered to a stop. The engine stalled, dropping to silence.

Ezra asked, "Yes, David? What is it?"

As always, Walter found the calm infuriating.

"A Hole… a Hole in the road." David sucked in his breath. "I'll need to drive."

Walter opened his mouth to protest, then sighed. He exited the vehicle and crossed to the passenger door. "Ezra, would you take the back? He may need a hand." Walter watched as David crawled over the divider to sit in the driver's seat. "You know how to drive?"

"Not a stick. Just an automatic."

"What's an automatic?"

David's face wrinkled in confusion.

"Ok, I'll teach you."

With steady words, Walter explained the operation to David. He could see Ezra paying just as close—if not closer—attention. But even so, the hunter kept one eye behind them to look for their disappeared pursuers. After a few stutters, the car roared to life once more, and David eased it into gear. He angled the muscle car far off the road, rolling through a fallow field, before finally swinging back around, and returning to the highway.

For a minute, no one spoke. The rumble of the engine was the only sound.

"That must have been a big Hole, David."

"Yes." Tears streamed down the boy's face. Walter thought all of David's grown-up ambition and strange perseverance had melted away. "It was a big one."

"And our friends? Do you think they gave up?"

Ezra leaned up from the back seat. "In a way. If Patrice spoke the truth, she could see the Holes like David. They knew what we were headed for. They couldn't risk it without their guide. No matter what we took from them. And if they do follow…"

"They go right into the Hole." Walter wrinkled his brow. "So, we're free?"

"Maybe." Ezra leaned back once more. "Maybe not."

12

Roads and off Them

I must concede I've been mistaken. Through my travels, I saw again and again, that once the great fate was realized, the world would fade and die. One after the other, stacked like records on a shelf. One by one, dropped and broken. But there was always another world beneath, always another opportunity. So perhaps we must assume that even this layered reality is incomplete. Perhaps there is a final reality, a reality binding them together. But if I have truly reached the end, the deepest there can be, then how could that core reality fade?

Either I have not reached the end, or I am yet to understand it.

The sage watched as the man in black read through his notebook. As usual, there was no hint of a reaction. And why should there be? The man in black, who the sage had been calling Johnny Cash, was not human at all. He was a chimera, and a clever one at that. But like all chimera, there was a gap of culture between them that could only be acknowledged, never crossed.

Mr. Cash closed the notebook and handed it back to the sage. His movements were smooth and unhurried, nearly human. Even his appearance: black shirt, black dinner jacket, black leather boots, looked *almost* human, if not for the incongruity of being worn in an underground hornet's nest.

"This ink is rather faded," Mr. Cash mused. "How long ago was it written?"

The sage took the notebook and tucked it in his bag. "It's been quite a while, some twenty layers back. I got stuck in a world for a while, and let's say I became pensive. But the question of an ultimate reality is still relevant, don't you think?"

Mr. Cash clasped his hands behind his back. He paused for several seconds. When he spoke again, he didn't answer the intended question. He did that quite a bit. "So this isn't the first time you've been stuck. Interesting."

The sage shot a look of indignation. "Who says I'm stuck?"

"Oh, no one. No one at all. Clearly, you remain in this place due to your great love of my company. And the opportunity to write and think, provided as promised. Along those lines, have you made any breakthroughs?"

The sage hopped to his feet and shook a finger at his captor. "Not locked up here, I won't. But I'm close to a few. And if I was free to move about, maybe I could figure this out once and for all. We want the same thing, Cash, so let me out already."

"I believe," Mr. Cash paused for several seconds, his generally flat eyes twinkling, "that we prefer you right where you are. After all, we can't have you in harm's way. No, we can't have that at all."

Mr. Cash stepped forward to meet the sage's stare directly. His body then rippled as it elongated and changed. His basic appearance was the same, but he loomed nearly a foot taller. Mr. Cash turned away. He strolled around the cave, occasionally lifting a book and returning it to its place.

"I'm told," the chimera said, "that you've made some rather odd requests lately. Care to explain?"

The sage thought of the supplies the chimera had brought him. In addition to his repeated pleas for bacon, fruit, and tortillas, he'd been given the last few ingredients necessary to start building his bombs. The sage had tried hard not to show any surprise at the delivery. He hadn't considered the chimera would fall for the trick. Nevertheless, he should have expected Mr. Cash was watching the requests.

"There's nothing to explain. We have different tastes in food, that's all."

"True, but some of those things weren't even food. Sulfur, for example?"

"Look, Cash, sometimes you forget I'm not from around here. And even if I was, we have different palates. But since you asked, I put sulfur in my soup back home. It's vitamin-rich, it is. But that was a hundred worlds back so I'm not surprised you'd never heard of it before."

"Thirty pounds of it?"

The sage grew red in the face. Sometimes anger was the best way to deal with the chimera. "You think that's too much, huh? And why is that? A second ago you said I'd be here forever. What's a finite quantity divided over infinite time, anyway? Riddle that one out. You want to talk reason? Fine. Let's talk reason. Just as soon as you let me go."

Mr. Cash smiled and walked to the jumble of rocks blocking the exit. "Perhaps some other time. My family and I have a… previous engagement. It's important at times we remind the world we are not truly gone." He chuckled to himself. "But for now, keep up the good work."

Don't worry, the sage thought, watching the chimera ooze through the gaps in the boulders, *I plan to keep busy.*

●

In this world, David observed, the Holes were getting larger. Back in Colorado, there were big ones too. But they tended to be more numerous than expansive. Not here. The farther they moved west, and the closer they got to the center, the bigger the Holes became.

He had driven through the night, several times taking detours to evade them. No wonder the bandits chose Patrice as their leader. No one else could have kept them safe. But that raised other questions. In a week, David had met two others with his particular gift for—if not seeing—at least detecting the Holes. In his own world, he'd been the only one. Did that mean he was less special here, or did it mean something else?

And if the Holes were this big, how come no one from Greenwater's End had heard about them? Either Holes—like the chimera—actually did stay away from the coast, or else they were a new thing. And were spreading fast. As if in echo of his thoughts, David heard the pop of air preceding the forming of a Hole. But this time, the sound wasn't the subtle "thwock" of a ping pong ball. This was a gunshot. He darted his eyes to the left. A field of abandoned wheat sank. The land distorted as it curved down, and then dropped farther, farther, until the ground had descended to nothingness. Wind sucked the air in a violent rush. And then was still. Where a field had been, nothing remained.

"Whoa! Did you hear that?" Walter opened his eyes and looked around. "What was that?"

David didn't answer. No need to provide an answer, and no good could come of one. He pointed ahead at the shadow breaking through the fog to the west. "We're almost to the mountains."

The hunter, though asleep moments before, had no hint of weariness in her voice. "The Appalachians," she said. She picked absently at the splint on her arm. "Did you call them the same?"

"Yeah." David sighed. "I never saw them, myself. Where I lived was in the Rocky Mountains. That's way past where we're headed. Maybe if we make it through this, then we can go see them."

"We'll see," Ezra murmured. "We've a long way to go until then."

●

Walter kept a steady eye on their fuel. By the time the sleek, black car had reached the mountains, they had used the first of the gas cans carried in the vehicle's trunk. He reasoned they had a day's worth of driving left. After that, if they couldn't find any fuel in the passing towns, they'd be on foot. And they'd had no luck so far. Whether they inquired about fuel, or the Holes, or the sage, they were met with blank looks and shaken heads.

The muscle car wound over the first of the Appalachians, across the Tellico Pass, through the Ocoee Basin, and beyond the Firegizzard Gulch. This was new territory to Walter, but Ezra seemed familiar with the names. And every time she pointed one out, David would either nod in agreement or simply shake his head.

"Where are we now?" David asked.

Walter leaned forward over the back seat. He and Ezra had taken turns in the front though David stayed at the wheel. "West Tennessee, still. One more crest of hills and then we'll be in the Mississippi Valley."

"The Mississippi!" Excitement filled David's voice. "I know that one. Back home you'd hear stuff like 'Come to Eddie's Smokehouse for the best burgers west of the Mississippi!' You heard things like that a lot. It was always 'east of the Mississippi' this or 'west of the Mississippi' that. Is it the same way here?"

Ezra shrugged. "In a sense. The Mississippi is the last great river, and the border of the civilized world. Most of the towns this far out have been abandoned. The Mississippi River marked the edge of the chimera's domain—back when they were still around. There were a few towns on the river, of course… but always right on the water, safer that way."

David glanced at the hunter. "So chimera don't like water? What about them showing up in a hurricane? I'd never seen so much rain in my life."

"The chimera," Ezra said, "are not normal creatures. They aren't just flesh and bone, but also spirit. And so their dislike of water is not merely that of the cat. Tell me David, in your world did anyone ever speak of the eight layers of reality?"

"I don't think so. I think I'd remember that."

"The eight layers are central to our understanding of existence. As hunters, we can see those layers when we use the tooth. The first layer is the mundane. Dirt and stones and the lifeless physical things like wind and water, rocks and mud. It's our tangible surroundings and the foundation.

"The second layer consists of grass, plants, trees, and flowers. It's the tiniest living thing floating in the seas, the mold in the earth, and other hints of life. Next comes fish, then fowl, then beast. Three layers, each more complex than the last, though few know what makes one animal cross from the third plane to the fourth, or fourth to fifth.

"The sixth layer is the layer of man. Conscious people and thinking beings. This is our layer, David, but it's not the final one. Because on top of that is the supernatural. And it's on that level that the chimera exist. The chimera are halfway beings, somewhat flesh and somewhat spirit. They shy from water, as water is the basest and most pure of the levels, the most different from their essence. Water makes them weak."

Walter held his tongue. This may not have been the exact version he'd been told as a boy, but the essence of the story was the same. Water was pure. And that purity kept the chimera—the impure—away. He'd never thought to question it further. But David did.

The boy chewed his lip then looked back over at Ezra. "So why didn't they care about the rain? That's water. Did it make them weaker?"

"Oh yes, it very much did. Those chimera were dangerous, but they moved a hair too slow. It's one reason for our survival. If we were to find a chimera out here on the plains or in the mountains—and me without a tooth—we'd have a different story on our hands."

"So you were lucky?"

"We all were."

David nodded then looked over again. "That's just seven layers, what's the last?"

Ezra continued, "The eighth and final layer consists of the rules tying the world together. Light, darkness, gravity, motion. It's the ultimate piece and the binder of everything."

David snorted. "Well, that doesn't make sense. It seems like that would be the first layer, not the last. Do you have them mixed up, maybe? Or does what layer something is really matter?"

Ezra smiled softly. "You're counting in the wrong direction. When I say the eighth layer, I mean the most essential layer, the greatest of the foundations, the purest in spirit. Each lesser level edges further from the spiritual and more into the physical, until you're left with nothing but rock and water."

Walter snorted. He leaned forward between the seats. "So wait a minute. You mean to say the chimera are *higher up* than people?"

Ezra shook her head. "No. Not higher or lower. It's not a matter of one being greater or less than any other, it's a matter of balance. Yes, they are more spiritual, just as humankind is more natural. It's a continuum."

Walter wrinkled his brow. "Ok, that may be. But the way you tell it. Gravity and light are less natural than people."

"More celestial. Less natural. There's a difference."

David asked, "And you understand the difference?"

"I understand the order. And that's the order."

For several long minutes, no one spoke. The landscape limped along outside the muscle car. Finally, David broke the uneasy silence.

"Ok, Ezra. I have a different question for you. Where *is* everyone? We've been driving a long time and there are no towns, no gas stations, just a few farms and cows here and there. It doesn't make any sense. If there aren't any people, then why is there even a road?"

Ezra smiled. "Had enough talk of the mystic, David?"

"This seems more relevant."

"Very well. There are few towns and few people, because of the chimera. After the war, people were slow to come back west. The road was built before then, and so gets little use."

"Will it take us the whole way?"

"Just to the Mississippi River. There's nothing beyond."

"Nothing at all?"

Ezra wrinkled her brow, the tanned skin turning to a series of furrows. "Well, there is a great deal of land beyond—forests, plains, and deserts, as I'm sure you know. But very few people. Have you heard differently, Walter?"

"Oh? So now you need my advice on travel?" He paused. "I've heard a little. Every once in a while someone would claim they went past the river. Never any word of chimera, though, just a few empty burrows."

David swerved a little as he turned to face him. "Burrows?"

Ezra nodded. "The chimera make tunnels, caves. Caverns in places, pits in others. They dig down to make their nests. The way this is done—"

"Maybe save that for another time." Walter pointed ahead. "We've got ourselves some civilization."

As their vehicle crested the hill, the valley floor spread out beneath them. Farmland and houses, winding roads and stone walls filled the area. And at the center, a walled city. The buildings looked old and cobbled. History was evident in the stonework of the churches and the smokestacks of the factories.

Walter swallowed hard. This had to be Cinderwood. He'd heard as many horror stories about the people of Cinderwood as he had about the chimera. He shuddered.

"All right!" David honked the horn in delight, the muscle car eliciting a deep bullhorn rumble. "Food, gas, and maybe the sage!" He scanned the horizon. "And not a Hole in sight."

Ezra looked at Walter. "You want to head down there? I'd be up for it, as we don't have a lot of choice. But we could possibly make it to Memphis on the gas we have. That is Cinderwood, you know."

"I know." Walter gritted his teeth. "But if David's sage is in there, we need to risk it. I'm not thrilled about the idea, though."

Ezra nodded. "I agree."

"Wait." David swung his glance between Walter and Ezra. "What's the matter?"

"That's Cinderwood," Ezra said. "It's one of the few cities this far west that never fell to the chimera. It was no accident. They're isolationists."

Walter snorted. "I think you mean xenophobic bastards." He turned to David. "Back before the war, they had these purges. 'Cleansings' they called them. They threw out anyone different. It didn't matter if it was the color of your skin, the way you spoke, or what religion you followed. If you didn't look like them and you didn't think like them, out you went. Got violent too. Kicking people out quickly turned into fighting. Now jump forward a few decades to when the chimera showed up. Even in disguise, they were different. And so the Cinderwoodans didn't let them in. They never let down their guard."

Ezra interjected. "You see, David, for the people of Cinderwood, the chimera proved they were right. Proved that anyone different couldn't be trusted. They'll know we don't belong."

Walter had to agree with her. He knew his dark skin was enough to set him apart from the much paler people of Cinderwood. And Ezra probably had an ancestry that stretched back to the islands. Even if David happened to look like them, whenever the boy opened his mouth, he would be immediately pegged as an outsider.

"But," David ventured, "you're a hunter."

"Yes, but not their kind of hunter. It doesn't matter. We can't hide who we are, so we'll just have to hope for the best."

"And what if something goes wrong?"

She didn't reply.

●

David guided their car into the valley, keeping his usual slow crawl. He kept his eyes open for Holes but didn't see any nearby. As they got closer, the wilderness turned to farmland. Walter would point out the different plants: corn, wheat, tobacco, and indigo, but David paid little attention. The farmers they passed stopped to gawk at them, and especially their car.

"It's too much attention," Walter mumbled.

Ezra shrugged. "At least we won't surprise them."

The road wound down and toward the city gates, massive, steel-plated doors on monstrous hinges. Though both gates were open, there was a checkpoint in front, manned by armed guards.

While the guards were in crisp uniforms, the people passing through the gates appeared to be working folks not unlike those in Greenwater's End. Some wore threadbare blue jeans and earth-toned shirts, while others were bare-chested except for the straps of their overalls.

By the time David, Walter, and Ezra reached the point of entry, there was only one vehicle in front of them, a horse-drawn wagon laden with sacks of corn. Once the wagon had gone ahead, the guard huffed toward them. He was dressed—oddly enough—in the same kind of police uniform David recognized from home.

"Hoo-wee, boy. If that ain't the finest automobile I've ever seen. Where'd a boy like you come up with a vehicle"—he pronounced it vee-hickle—"like that?"

David shrugged. "I'm just the driver."

"It's mine." Ezra's tone was flat. She folded her arms to display the links of her battle chain. They'd discussed their strategy during the approach. At times, Ezra's status as a hunter should remain below the surface. But on occasion—like this—perhaps it would garner respect.

"Well hello, Madam Hunter." The policeman's smile wavered between politeness and thinly-disguised contempt. "And I thought y'all didn't believe in possessions and things."

"It's on loan. But still my responsibility."

The policeman's eyes had settled on Walter. "And where would you be going, Miss Hunter, with such a fine automobile, and such"—he sniffed with contempt—"eclectic companions?"

David's skin crawled. Despite the surface civility the policeman radiated contempt. The feeling was evident from the tilt of his head, to his narrowed eyes, to the mocking tone in his voice. Oddly, the loathing emanating from the man triggered David's need to run in a way that even the chimera did not. He looked behind him to see that Walter had his jaw set and teeth gritted.

"We're headed west, to Memphis. But a friend of ours is in the city, or so we've heard. Joby here," Ezra nodded to Walter, "is a radioman. His colleagues told him this is where we should look. If our friend is in town, we need to speak with him. If not," Ezra shrugged, "we hope to resupply."

"Memphis? Ain't nobody come outta Memphis in weeks. And who's this fella you're looking for?"

"He calls himself 'the sage'. He collects stories, tales, histories. Shaved head, wild eyes, mustache. Looks like a monk. You know him?"

The policeman did not reply. He turned and walked to another uniformed man—this one wearing the wide-brimmed hat of an old-west sheriff. The two exchanged a few words before the sheriff mounted his horse and trotted toward the open gate. The policeman returned, his swagger more pronounced.

David spoke up. "So can we go inside?"

"You have a license to drive that thing, boy?"

"No." He doubted driver's licenses existed in this world.

"Then maybe you stay put, and I ask the questions."

Ezra kept her tone low. "Pardon. We've been on the road for quite some time. Travel can hinder etiquette."

"Etty-cat? Tell me, do all dirty outsiders talk like that, or just dirty, has-been hunters? 'Cause it's starting to get just a little bit on my nerves."

Walter leaned forward. He dropped his voice low. "Ezra, I think this is getting bad."

"Hey, you. You need to talk, big-boy, you do your talking to me. But there ain't a got-damn thing I need to hear you say."

The tingle along David's spine turned to a full-fledged surge of panic. He eased his hand back down to the gearshift, the movement casual, and glanced over at the hunter. She gave him the smallest of nods. His panic shifted to adrenaline.

David thrust the car into reverse and stomped on the accelerator. The muscle car rocketed back, smashing through a wagon filled with fruit and sending people diving for cover. He sped back the way they had come.

"Stop! Halt! I'll shoot!"

He barely registered the policeman's demands. He ratcheted the car back into first and slammed down on the gas once more. The car leaped, sped, and launched. After three hundred miles of slow cruising, the muscle car flexed.

Crack, crack-crack, crack. Gunshots snapped behind them, then stopped abruptly. David didn't dare look back, his knuckles white from gripping the wheel, his jaw clenched hard. He could see a frenzy of motion from the guards in the mirror, but with the car's speed, the town quickly shrank from sight. The onlookers, however, flocked to the roadside. While before the muscle car had drawn looks, now it incited yells. But David didn't care. He knew that just up the next hill, he would be fully out of sight. Safe.

He swerved left and right, dodging the farmers as they approached the road. He could tell he was getting farther away as the number of onlookers diminished, and then he was free. Though the city walls were still visible in his mirrors, the farmland had once again become countryside. And with a final twist around the bend, the city disappeared behind them.

"Ok, David. That's enough." Even over the roar of the engine and the whip of the wind, Ezra's words remained steady. He slowed the car to a halt. The vehicle stalled, then shuddered to quiet.

"Holy Lord!" Walter cried from the back seat. "Are you trying to kill us? I mean, what was that all about?"

"I... I... I just..."

Ezra rested a steady hand on his shoulder "It was a bad situation. David got us out. It may not have been our best move, but it was a good one. Would you care to be back there and in chains? Would you care to be tried by a Cinderwood judge?"

Walter slumped in his seat. He shook his head. "All I'm saying is they were shooting at us. That's all I'm saying. And, I might mention, now they'll be looking for us."

Ezra nodded. "Perhaps. David, can you find somewhere to pull off? Be careful we don't leave tracks."

●

Another mile along the road, David found a rocky stretch of ground and pulled off the highway. He navigated through the brush and rocks until the muscle car was out of sight. They left the vehicle and followed Ezra to a small cliff where they could look down on the road below. But though they waited and waited, no trucks came.

David looked over at Walter and Ezra. He kept his voice to a whisper. "Why didn't they follow us? They seemed pretty upset."

Ezra replied, "They're isolationists. We left, and so they were satisfied. They aren't trying to conquer the world, just live apart from it."

"Then why are we hiding?"

"In case I'm wrong."

Several minutes passed before Walter broke the silence, this time not at a whisper. "We went the wrong way. If we'd gone west, we could be on our way to Memphis."

"What about the sage?" David asked.

Walter shook his head. "Your sage sounds like a smart guy. He wouldn't hang out in a place like that for too long. He'd have kept right on going. We've got a better chance of running into him out here than in there."

Ezra nodded. "Perhaps. But we don't know that. This is where we have to decide."

David looked up. "Decide what?"

"We know where we're going—at least we think we do. Kansas, as you call it. I don't think we need the sage to get there. But he may have the knowledge we're lacking."

David glanced back and forth between Ezra and Walter in disbelief. "I think you're missing the point. There is another reason to find the sage."

"The chimera?"

"No, not the chimera. I'm talking about going home. What good is finding out what causes the Holes if I can't make it back home to tell my family? What if we *do* find what causes the Holes? Or even how to fix 'em? I need to be able to tell everyone. That's the whole reason I'm here." His words came faster and faster. "And the sage, I *saw* him back in my world. If anyone knows how to get me home, it's him. He got me here, remember?"

Walter protested, "We can't go back to Cinderwood now, David. Even if we snuck in, Ezra and I would stick out like sore thumbs. And they'll be looking for us for sure."

"I might blend in," David said.

Ezra nodded. "That could work. But we can't drop you off at the gates. That would be foolish. It's probably best if we… hmmm."

Walter looked at Ezra in horror. "You're not thinking of sending him by himself, are you? Are you insane? They'll roast him alive. They'll take him for an outsider in less than a second. Then they'll—"

"It's all right, Walter." David smiled. "No one will even notice me. I'm just a kid. No one pays attention to a kid. I should know."

"You really want to do this?" Walter looked long into David's eyes.

"I have to."

Ezra smiled with satisfaction. "Ok, then let's get you ready."

13

CINDERWOOD

The muscle car thundered over the mountain pass, careening down the valley and to the gates of Cinderwood. Walter gripped the wheel in both fear and exhilaration. He was tripling—no, quadrupling—the top speed of the pickup he'd once driven back home. And though David had driven this fast before, now he was in control. He was the one guiding the beast. And Holes be damned, he was lord of the machine.

Beside him, Ezra maintained her calm passivity. Feelingless wench. Walter wished she'd occasionally show something other than an ache for a chimera's tooth. That hadn't been a human emotion, anyway. Just animal need. Even her arm—the arm whose bone he'd heard crack— even *that* didn't bother her. She picked at the splint from time to time, but never once complained.

"Here we go." Walter stamped on the accelerator, the pedal smacking hard against the floorboard. The muscle car lurched forward. And now, they could be seen.

Past the farms, past the outlying areas, past the vegetable stands dotting the sides of the road. Pedestrians and livestock leaped to avoid the raging automobile. Walter saw people scrambling, heard the clang of a warning gong. He knew the guards were aiming their weapons, waiting only to see what he'd do next.

As they neared the gates of Cinderwood, Walter knew they were with range of gunshot. Now was the gambit. As Walter jerked the wheel to the left, the muscle car careened off the road. The wheels rumbled against the rough ground. The car's suspension lurched and banged as they plowed through a newly planted tobacco field. But they weren't slowing down. The muscle car charged through irrigation ditches with impunity. Faster, faster, the far end of the field was in sight. And on the other side? The road led past the city and into the west. Walter eased the wheel right, preparing to angle back onto the highway. But the steering did not respond as he'd hoped. They hit the embankment too fast, and they were airborne.

One, two, three, the seconds stretched by. And then they landed. The shocks bottomed out with a clang of metal on metal. But the race wasn't over yet. Walter wrenched the wheel left, and they went into a skid. The wheels caught, and the car lunged forward once more. Up, over the embankment, and there! They were back on the highway and headed in the right direction. Cinderwood shrank behind them.

●

Two miles back, crouched behind a juniper bush, David watched the spectacle. The guards of Cinderwood had not been prepared for their return. They gave a brief chase, turning around once it was clear the car would not double back. David had no doubt these people thought what they were meant to think. The sleek black car with its impossibly polished chrome and roaring engine was gone for good.

One hour later, blending into a gaggle of children, David was inside the city walls.

●

The city of Cinderwood was the closest thing to development David had seen since Greenwater's End. But the differences from home were still there. The people wore that same collection of jeans or canvas pants topped with checkered and earth-tone shirts. That much had been consistent since arriving in this world. David, with his borrowed clothes, had little difficulty blending in. Other differences were more pronounced. For instance, there were only a handful of cars on the streets. A few trucks rolled by hauling goods, but everyone else was on foot.

One thing, however, stuck out clearly. And that was the guns. Everyone, from the younger kids playing in the streets, to mothers pushing their strollers, was armed. The weapons weren't inconspicuous either. A grandmother carried two six-shooters on either side of her walker. A street performer had a shotgun across his back. A vendor selling hotdogs was wrapped in a bandolier. In fact, David was certain he was the only one on the streets *not* armed.

He brushed the observation aside. There wasn't anything he could do about it. Not without money. What was important was to find the sage or some word of him. David hoped he could find him at his usual game. Stories, tales, histories—those were the things the sage found important. So should he check the library? A school? Ezra said she met the sage in a bar, but David thought he'd be unwelcome there. And if he showed up at a school, he'd be recognized as an outsider. The library it was.

David walked up to a man selling hotdogs. The man's round form and cheerful smile made him look—despite the guns—to be one of the friendlier characters on the street.

"What can I get you, boy?" The man shot him a grin.

"Just directions. I'm trying to find the library."

The smile became a scowl. "I'm working here."

"But I don't know how to get there."

The hotdog vendor put his hands on his hips. "And do I look like an information booth? You want information, go to the information girl."

"And where's that?"

The vendor narrowed his eyes to slits, a look reserved for the most ignorant of the ignorant. He jabbed a chubby finger above his shoulder. David turned and saw a kiosk on the opposite side of the street. A twenty-something girl sat there, sipping idly from a clear cup. "Help?" was painted on the sign above her head.

David thanked him and skirted across the street. When he reached the information girl, she beamed down at him with what must have been the most perfect set of teeth he had ever seen.

"Why hello! And what can I do for you?" The girl's words were drawn out, "dewwww for yewwww."

"Uh, I'm looking for someone. He's from out of town, but I'm not sure if he's still in the city. I don't even know his name, but he calls himself 'the sage.' He was collecting stories, books, history, and things. And," he paused, "where should I look? Is there a library around somewhere?"

The girl's smile transformed to a puzzled look. "Listen, sugar. I may be here for information, but I don't know everything. But if your friend isn't from around here, he'd have to register with immigration. And if he's left town, well, immigration would know about that as well. Do you know where that is, pumpkin?"

He shook his head.

"Well then, I'll just have to give you a map."

●

The immigration building was located next door to the Cinderwood city hall. The hall was a majestic structure of white marble and fluted columns surrounded by topiaries. Immigration, by contrast, appeared designed for utility. The front was plain and the windows no more than hewn squares. Even the sign out front was now so rusted it looked as red as the bricks around it.

David took a deep breath, hoping that those inside would be at least a little more hospitable than the guards had been. But as he took his first step forward, he felt a stern hand on his shoulder.

"You don't want to go in there, son."

David turned to look into the face of a man in his late fifties. The man had a full head of hair that sprang from the top of his head like a puff of cotton. His eyes were bright green, nestled in the folds of his skin like emeralds in a beggar's palm. Though his face was weathered and his hair unkempt, he held himself with poise. Like the other inhabitants of Cinderwood, he carried weapons. Two sawed-off shotguns bristled from his back in twin holsters.

"Who are you?"

"I'm Levi. I'm a friend." The man's voice rumbled in much the same manner as the muscle car. "And you must be David. Remus told me to be on the lookout for you—though I thought you'd never show. Don't look so surprised. I've had my eyes peeled since I first heard of that stunt at the gates. I suspected someone might sneak in—just wasn't expecting you. You were easy enough to find, though."

David shook his head in disbelief. "You followed me? How did you follow me?" A pause. "Wait. Who's Remus?"

Levi glanced around. "It's not safe to talk out here, especially not with the *event* coming. But that's not important right now. As for Remus, I believe you know him as the sage."

●

Levi led David through the back alleys of Cinderwood to an unmarked basement door. The man refused to speak to him as they walked, ushering a warning of secrecy. And indeed, he didn't even turn around to ensure David was following until they entered his apartment.

Despite the squalid exterior, Levi's home was maintained with the utmost fastidiousness. There was a low table surrounded by four woven straw mats and a row of stainless steel pots and pans hanging from a rack on the wall. There were no pictures, no decorations, and no knickknacks scattered on the shelves. Then David saw something that made him gasp. On the wall opposite the door, hanging in a manner both haphazard and refined, was a battle chain, an oversized knife, a bow, a quiver of arrows, and a broad straw hat.

"You're a hunter!"

Levi smiled. "Yes, but not the way you mean it. I am a philosopher. I'm a hunter of truth, not of the chimera. I keep these relics to remind me there is much in the world we do not know or understand. Most importantly, they remind me there are limits to what can be known using one's intellect. The man I knew as Remus, your sage, believed ultimate truth was obtainable, that all you needed were enough clues, enough pieces of information. I heartily disagree. I embrace my limitations. And in doing so, I found peace. Sometimes, one must give in to see truth."

Levi gestured to the straw mats on either side of the low table and David settled into place. The man turned on the stove and put a teakettle on the burner. He removed two green ceramic cups then took his seat.

David scanned the sparse apartment for some sign the man was not what he appeared. Finding none, he looked up. "So how did you find the sage?"

"I didn't find him; he found me. Twice actually." Levi removed a pipe from his coat and packed it with leaf from a box on the table. "The first time he was simply looking for stories. I had a reputation as one who'd chased a few stories myself. I suppose it was only a matter of time before he landed on my doorstep. I told him my tales—not just the ones I'd heard, but about the city, the war, the chimera, and such. He gathered them all. Clinically, I should say."

David nodded fervently. "That's him all right. He sought me out too. I didn't have much to tell, but I told him what I'd seen."

Levi smiled knowingly. "Ah, yes. Of course you did. We all did." He gazed at David thoughtfully. "Different question. Do you consider yourself a religious person? Do you believe in a higher power?"

David scratched his head. He hadn't thought much about it. Ever since he first saw the Holes, the supernatural seemed all around him. But he'd never been religious in the traditional sense. "I guess sometimes. I really haven't thought much about it. Why do you ask?"

"Later. Let's move back to Remus, shall we? Do you know, David, *why* he was collecting stories? Surely you know there was a reason for his search. He isn't just another in a long line of inquisitive minds. There had to be more to it. Why else would he travel across worlds?"

David's pulse quickened. "How did you know…?"

"He told me, of course." Levi settled back into his chair, lifting his pipe to gesture as he spoke. "But not until his second visit. He told me of his origin, told me he was from a different world and had visited countless worlds in search of stories. At that point, I naturally asked him why. Why was a man, with talents such as his, so single-minded in his pursuit? He told me he was looking for something."

David leaned forward. "What was it?"

"Truth, like me—though our approaches differed. Remus said every story, every tale, and every slice of wisdom was a piece in the puzzle. He felt himself a detective asking the same question of a million and one witnesses. Where the stories matched from world to world, there could be truth. When a story wavered, the detail must not be important. By visiting different worlds, he could see what stayed the same, and what was unchangeable. Those universal truths, the truths unchanged from world to world to world, to him that was *truth*. But surely, David, you know why he sought truth with such diligence. He wanted to know not about truth itself, but to learn about its opposite."

David wrinkled his nose in thought. The sage was looking for ultimate truth because it was the opposite of… not lies. That was too simple. The sage was looking for something else. He gasped in realization. "The Holes. Of course, it's the Holes. I never made the connection. He thinks if we understand one, we understand the other."

"Precisely." Levi grinned warmly. But something in that smile bothered him. "Now tell me, are the Holes here yet? You can see them, right? Just as Remus said you could?"

"Yes… I can. And yes, they're here too. Not in the city, but I saw a lot of them on the way here."

Levi's smile finally wavered. "So my world is dying like the others." The man's eyes glassed over.

David looked up at him. "I don't understand. The sage told me who he was because I can see the Holes. But he made me promise not to give him away. He said if I told anyone, people would think he was crazy. And no one listened to a crazy man. So why did he tell you?"

"But David, I thought you knew. He told me all that because he had nowhere left to turn. Your sage, you see, is trapped."

●

Walter covered the muscle car with a thick layer of pine boughs and shrubbery. While they were pulled far off the road, he didn't want a stray glint of light to give away their location. Or perhaps, he admitted, he was just staying busy to avoid the hunter.

Ezra had disappeared not long after they stopped, returning in less than an hour with a newly slain doe. She had skinned, dressed, and cut the meat into filets with a speed that left him astonished. Oddly, Walter had never thought being a "hunter" would translate to other prey than chimera. Nevertheless, with food secured and the camp hidden, they had nothing to do but wait.

Walter looked over to where Ezra was wrapping the last of the meat. "How's your arm?"

She didn't reply. Either she hadn't heard him or chose not to acknowledge the question. He tried again.

"Ezra, do you think we should head back to the road and make sure they're not following?"

This time, the hunter looked up. "No need. There's more risk of being seen than could be gained by forewarning. And if they were intent on chasing us, we'd have heard them by now. I'm not concerned about the Cinderwoodans. Not for us at least."

"David, then."

"Correct."

Walter glanced at Ezra. But when his gaze met her eyes, he looked down. "I thought you wanted him to go."

"It was his decision to make, and I supported that. In his mind, the trip was necessary."

"But not to you?"

Ezra narrowed her eyes. "I believe our destination is important—not this sage. He may have come from where David did—perhaps he can even cross worlds—but I don't think chasing him is the answer. I suspect we are heading to the same place. These side journeys are distracting. Dangerous."

"But David thinks he could help him get home."

"Perhaps. But, David won't leave until he has his answers. Otherwise, his journey is for nothing."

Walter looked at Ezra. He didn't look at her, so much as took her in, all of her. He saw the scars, the taut muscle stretched across a weary frame. He saw the years riding on her shoulders and the need that poured from her eyes.

"Ezra… what do *you* hope to find out there? I'm here because of my family. I made my father a promise, and I want his death to mean something. As for my wife and kids, those Holes ate right through our town. I want to stop that. But what are you here for? Forgive me if I've misread you, but the Holes don't seem your top priority. So why bother?"

"The tooth."

Walter's face twisted in scorn. "That's what this is about? Finding another chimera? Finding another damn tooth? You'll use David to get your fix and toss him aside?"

"Calm down. Sit. I'm not finished." Ezra took a deep breath. "I'm not here to find a tooth. I'm here because of what one showed me. Tell me, Walter, what do you know of the world?"

"I may not have spent much time outside of home, but I know people. I've seen what matters to people, what's important. I know right and wrong. Or at least do my best to tell them apart."

She shook her head. "I mean of the nature of the world. The eight layers of reality."

"Back to that again, huh?"

Ezra clenched her fist, the joints cracking loudly. "I don't believe you are as simple as you pretend, but I'll explain as I must. If prepared correctly, the active agent in the tooth allows you to see each of the eight layers of reality, one after the other. That's what a tooth does. That's how I found David."

"Ok. So what?"

"'So what,' is that when I used the tooth, I could see differences I hadn't seen before in the final layer. Since my first tooth, I have never seen it altered. It's always complete, uniform, and unwavering. But not anymore." The hunter closed her eyes. Walter watched her slow her breathing. "About a week before I came to Greenwater's End—before the storm, before the Holes, everything—I tracked and took a chimera. I used a tooth, my first in years. And when I saw that layer, the world was falling apart. I know now I was seeing Holes. But I also saw David. The world screamed his name."

"You were looking for him?"

"No. I was looking for the chimera, just as you suggested. And I was looking for them for the very reason you suggested. But what I found instead was David. He shone brighter than any of it." Ezra exhaled. "What I don't understand is why."

●

David held his tea untouched in his right hand. He could feel the liquid's warmth through the ceramic mug but didn't drink it. His appetite, voracious only a short time ago, had dropped to nothing. He shifted his gaze from the mug to look at the philosopher. "Trapped? How can he be trapped? I don't understand."

Levi puffed on his pipe, then set it on the table between them. "Remus—your sage—said there was a knack to crossing dimensions. Science in some worlds, magic in others, but the result was always the same. A Hole would open, and he would pass through. You've seen this firsthand?"

David nodded. His fall into Greenwater's End seemed a distant dream.

Levi continued, "Well, whatever the trick—magic, science, or otherwise—it doesn't work here. Remus believes—and I have no reason to accept or deny this—that this world, my world, is the bottom."

"The bottom?"

"Correct. There is no world lower, no world to slip further down to. Perhaps this is the main world, the foundation world. Or perhaps it's just the lowest on the totem pole. Either way, this is it. He has nowhere left to turn. No more information to pick and gather. And that, my dear boy, is why he was hoping you'd arrive."

"Because I can see the Holes."

"In this case, yes." Levi pursed his lips. "He needs all the weapons he can gather. For the time has come to solve his riddle. What, my dear boy, are the Holes? What causes them? And most importantly, how can they be stopped?"

David set down his tea and folded his hands in his lap. If the sage couldn't leave this world, were they all stuck here? Was it possible nothing he did could save his family?

"Why are you telling me this?"

Levi released a guffaw. "Because Remus asked me to! I imagine as long as you're on his trail, he'll have left lookouts and guides."

"Will he come back?"

The man shook his head. "No. It is only onward and forward for him. He's done with Cinderwood. He's headed west to Memphis, to the edge of the known world. After that, he'll keep going. Though if you ask me, there's nothing beyond."

"Was he going to Kansas?"

"I don't know that name." Levi sipped his tea. "But he said you knew where to go. And there you would find him."

For a long moment they sat, neither speaking. David tried to absorb the words of the philosopher. He felt he should trust this man, if for no other reason than the sage had done the same. And as such, he should take what Levi said as being the truth. But something about the philosopher raised David's hackles. Something in the air told him to leave.

David looked up at Levi. The white-haired man's eyes shone with sardonic light. "Ok, well, then I guess there isn't much reason to stay around here. Will it be hard to leave?"

"Oh no, getting out of the city is easy enough. But I won't send you away empty-handed. You'll need supplies. Food, water, ammunition, things like that. That, and I want to show you something."

David let loose an uneasy chuckle. "Ok, but first I have a question. What *is* it with all the guns around here?"

"What would you suppose?"

"Um, something to do with the chimera?"

"And you'd be right. Cinderwood was one of the few places in the war that stood strong. If a chimera ever shows its face here, we plan to be ready."

David nodded. The last thing he wanted was to be seen as an enemy. "All right, lead on."

●

David followed Levi through the streets of Cinderwood. And though the philosopher made it clear he would not accompany him past the walls, he intended to see him well provisioned. They stopped at a local market. And while David stood awkwardly to one side, Levi bustled around to gather dried beef, dried fruit, dried soup, and dried noodles. He felt out of place among the normalcy of the town. Part of it was that he couldn't shake the memory of the gates, but there was more to it. A chill permeated the air. And it did not emanate from his guide.

After Levi checked out and packed the food into David's pack, he looked at his watch for what must have been the hundredth time that day. The old man shifted uneasily, then shot back a too-friendly grin at his companion.

David adjusted the strap of his knapsack. "You've been very kind, sir. But don't you think this is enough stuff? I'd like to get back to my friends."

"Just one last thing. Not to get, to show you. Consider it the price for my assistance. It's my hope that you will catch up with Remus. When you do, I want your help convincing him. To settle an argument, if you will. It's a running dispute between us, a disagreement of principals. And if you meet him again, you will of course let him know."

"I don't understand."

Levi continued, "It's an old argument, and about the very thing he seeks: Truth. I'm afraid he has the whole thing wrong. And what I will show you will prove my point."

"And what's that?"

"I dare not spoil the surprise. But I assure you, it will be quite unforgettable. After all, I've been waiting half a year for this myself. I'd say the timing of your arrival is not a coincidence. Now come on, we don't wish to be tardy."

As they walked toward the center of town, David and Levi joined with a crowd heading in the same direction. Indeed, the masses all flowed toward the great coliseum. The structure rose high above the hordes of brick and sandstone buildings. From majestic marble arches to flags streaming from the parapets, this was a work of beauty.

"Come, David. We're almost there." A mischievous twinkle shone from Levi's eyes. The man smiled, glanced down at his watch, then looked up again. "Let's hurry."

David followed the philosopher as they moved en masse with the crowd. They passed through the first of the great marble arches and into a tunnel so low the ceiling reached only a few feet overhead. As the passage stretched, the light within became dimmer and dimmer. For a moment, he lost sight of Levi until the man's grip found his wrist and pulled him forward once more. And then, the strange birth canal reached an end. They were out.

A cheer roared from the crowd, setting the air to buzzing and pressing in on him from all directions. On the other side of the tunnel an arena opened to the sky. A mosaic of red, white, and grey tiles formed the stage, which curved up and outward to become seating. Crowds had already occupied the lower half, with the upper-level filling just as rapidly. David wondered if the whole of the city was present, or if not, on its way. They passed through the tunnel to step away from the flood of spectators pouring into the arena.

Levi glanced at his watch. "No time to look for a seat. It will be starting any moment."

"What's starting? What kind of game is this?"

"Why, my boy, this isn't a game."

David swallowed hard. He recognized the glint in Levi's eye. Conviction. Complete and utter certainty, without room for argument.

Seconds ticked by, the sounds of the crowd muddled together like the roar of a waterfall. David turned to look at Levi, but the man's eyes were fixed dead ahead.

"Do you know why your sage will never find his truth? It's because it cannot *be* found."

"What do you mean? It doesn't exist?" David glanced over his shoulder, eyeing the exit.

"Oh no. It exists, all right. But it cannot be found through research or reasoning. Are you familiar, David, with the name Rene Descartes?"

David shrugged. "He's the 'I think therefore I am' guy, right?"

Levi nodded. "Not a literal translation, of course. It is much more appropriate to express as 'I think, I am.' It was his crowning achievement. Descartes said even if you can't trust your eyes, your ears, or your senses, there is one thing you can trust, and that is your existence. If you can think, then you must necessarily exist."

The philosopher continued, "But that's the limit of reasoning. It's the only thing that can be proven, and thus proves something that is apparent already. Once you have established that, you cannot go beyond. You are stuck. And that, David, is the 'Cartesian Crux.'"

David looked over his shoulder once more. "Levi, I kind of want to get back to my friends. Can't you just give me a message? Do I have to see whatever this is?"

Levi ignored him. "Descartes didn't give up, of course, but he never solved his dilemma. Your sage couldn't either. He thought by gathering stories and looking for similar truths he could bypass the problem instead. He thought maybe the 'practical' approach could serve him where logic broke down. But the issue remains."

David shifted from foot to foot. "Ok. But why did you bring me here?"

Levi smiled. It was not a knowing smile, but one tinged with condescension. "Earlier, I asked if you were a religious person. I myself am, as was Descartes, incidentally. I am here because I had a vision. A premonition of things to come. Very soon there will be an event that will shake the whole town. The reason I know this is not because of logic. I didn't put together the pieces one by one and arrive at a conclusion. No, I was shown. I was given a revelation by a power greater than myself. The message you need to take to Remus is that questions of ultimate truth cannot be solved by reason. Only through submission to a higher power can we ever know anything worth knowing. Only with the intervention of the divine, can we know truth."

"But why are we here?"

"We are here, because once you see the event, and once you realize that logic did not forewarn me of it, you will know the power of revelation. You will know the power of faith."

"What's going to happen?"

"That, David, you will see for yourself."

●

Walter and Ezra left the muscle car and picked their way back toward Cinderwood on foot. For most of the hike, they had not spoken. Each was concerned with keeping hidden, and for Walter, at least, it allowed him to think about what she had said.

There was a rumble from the road beside them, and both Walter and Ezra dropped to their bellies. For the first time, he saw that when prone, the hunter's loose poncho and straw hat made her melt into the landscape. By comparison, his own clothes stood out like a beacon. They waited until the vehicle passed before continuing on.

Walter whispered. "We could move the car closer if we wanted to."

Ezra lifted her head, her leathered face appearing once more beneath the conical brim. "No. Once we have David, we can send a runner. We stay hidden until then. We are close, anyway. Two more miles and we'll be at the edge of the farmlands. I've no interest in moving beyond the trees where we can be seen."

"But what if we need to get out fast?"

"Better to stay hidden than to ruin our cover. Two times they let us get away. I think a third would be pushing our luck."

"And what if something goes wrong for David?"

"If we don't see him by nightfall, we'll know there's a problem."

"And then what?"

Ezra lifted a finger to her lips. She pointed into the forest away from the road. Walter took the cue and followed her as she crawled, then crouched, then walked through the leafy vegetation. When they came to a halt in a small clearing, she sat down on a fallen log.

"I need you to understand, Walter, that we are hiding. Our presence is undesired by those who are heavily armed. If you wish to speak, we move away from the road. There may be others on foot we cannot hear, just as we ourselves wish to remain unheard." She paused, cocked her head to one side, and then frowned again. "Now, you may speak."

"David. I'm concerned about David. I know we said we'd wait until it's dark, but I have a bad feeling."

Ezra nodded. "It is good to trust one's instincts, but we have few options left. We can wait, and we can watch. But we have little cover remaining and several miles of farmland between us and the city gates. I would prefer darkness, as we are hardly welcome. There is also the matter of Holes. Every step we take risks encountering one." She opened her mouth as if to continue, then closed her lips and looked down.

"What?" Walter demanded. "What is it?"

The hunter exhaled deeply. Her eyes bored into his skull. "There is…" Another pause. "There is a way we can be sure. You have a bad feeling, an intuition. In my experience, these things are not to be taken lightly."

"What are you talking about?"

"I know of the tooth, Walter. I know you have it sewn into the lining behind the breast pocket of your shirt. We can use it to find

David, to see if he is all right. And if what Patrice said was true, we can use it to avoid any Holes."

Walter snorted in disgust. "I knew it! I knew it would all come back to this. This is why you wanted David to go on alone, isn't it? You needed a reason to get us apart, a reason for me to give in. That's what all this talk of visions and layers and everything is all about. You wanted me to offer it up. And if I don't give it to you, what then? You'll take it. Oh, it'll be for our own good, of course. All to save David and protect him and see what lies ahead. And when he comes back, no matter what happened to him, you'll have an explanation. Well, I don't buy it, Ezra. It's a little too convenient." Walter stared into her snake-eyed gaze. No emotion reflected back.

"Are you done?"

"No. I don't think I am done. I think I'm in the middle of the woods, with no one around and trapped with a damn, deadly addict. That's what I am."

Ezra did not lower her eyes. "You don't trust me. Very well. You don't need to. The tooth is too precious for me to use anyway. Especially as it is the last one."

"So it's *not* the answer? Which is it, Ezra?"

"The tooth is still the answer. But not for me."

Walter felt the blood drain from his face.

"I assume, farmer, that sometime in your rich and varied life, you've had alcohol."

He nodded.

"And I would imagine the first time you took a drink was a little different than the second, or the third, or the last. The effect was different each time, diminished."

"Go on."

"We have one tooth, Walter. One. Every speck of that tooth is precious. For me to have a vision, far too much would be wasted. Like any narcotic, the effect diminishes over time and with greater use. But not for you. Just a pinch, a small taste and you can see for yourself. We can look for David and the Holes. We can give form to your intuition." Ezra smiled; the expression did not rest easily on her face. "Or we can simply wait, as was our plan."

Walter hadn't a chance to respond. Ezra was on her way once more, weaving soundlessly through the brush. He hesitated before following. One thing was certain, waiting wasn't enough. Whether using the tooth, or hatching some other plan, they had to do something.

Smug old coot, Walter thought. Surely she could feel the doom hanging in the air. And if Ezra felt it, then one of them would have to use the tooth. The concept terrified him. He'd had his battles with alcohol in the past. The thought of losing control scared him. That was why he was on this maddening expedition in the first place. Nothing was more unknown and out of control than these Holes.

"This is a good spot," Ezra murmured. They had come to a ledge blanketed with thick brush. Just beyond the ledge, the bushes dropped away to grassland. But from here they were still covered. What's more, they had an unobstructed view along the highway until it rounded the corner and to the city gates.

"I don't see him." Walter dropped to a crouch beside Ezra. "Didn't expect to, but it's still a few hours till night, I suppose."

Ezra sat cross-legged among the bushes. Seated, Walter could only see the tiniest glimpse of highway through the trees. He edged forward to get a better view of the valley. "Something looks a little strange here."

"What is it?"

He furrowed his brow. "I don't see enough farmers. The fields aren't fallow—you can tell from the plow lines. But for this time of the day, and at this time of the year, I'd expect to see everyone out."

"Perhaps it's a holiday."

"No. We saw them this morning."

"Shhh, listen. Do you hear that?"

Walter strained his ears. There was a muffled swell of noise in the distance. "Sounds like cheering. Maybe they're having a festival. That would explain it." He sat down across from Ezra. "You think that'll make it harder or easier for David to get out?"

"Easier, if he's with the crowd. Very difficult if he's not." She paused. "So what do you think?"

"I think you're right. He can always blend in."

"Not about that."

A chill ran up Walter's spine. He had known exactly what Ezra meant: the tooth. He could use it himself, give it to the hunter, or wait. Each choice could be a disaster. But what if they took no action? What if David needed their help?

"Ok," Walter said. "I'll do it."

14

SEEING IS

As Walter watched, Ezra prepared her instruments. The hunter removed a rolled leather bundle tied by two cords on either end. She loosened the knots and unrolled the case. Inside were a variety of instruments, each carefully secured in a fitted pouch. She removed a square of black silk and laid it next to the toolkit. In measured movements, she wiped each implement with a second silk cloth. Mortar, pestle, file, scalpel, needle, and cup. She looked at Walter, her eyes alight.

"The tooth."

It wasn't a question or a demand. Walter's hands trembled as he unbuttoned his shirt and opened the compartment sewn behind his breast pocket. With a twist of his knife, the threads parted. He fumbled for a moment, then removed the tooth.

He studied it carefully. The tooth was ivory, curled, sharp as a razor on one side, serrated on the other. The base, where the flesh of the chimera's mouth held the canine in place, had dried and blackened. The remnants soiled the otherwise pearly color. Walter closed his hand over the tooth, squeezed once, and then handed it to Ezra.

"I thought you just chewed on it," he said.

Ezra cocked her head. She pulled back on her cheek to show him her molars. Each of the teeth was capped in metal. She went back to her preparations. "That's one way, provided you have no other choice. To prepare like this, the effect will be many, many times stronger."

The hunter rotated the tooth, examining it. She then pulled out her file, holding it above the bowl of the mortar and pestle. One, two, three, four, each scrape shaved a thin strand from the tooth. After a dozen strokes, the bottom of the bowl was covered with splinters. Ezra placed the remaining tooth on the silk, then went to work with the pestle, grinding the strands into a fine dust. She set down the bowl then picked up the needle.

"Give me your finger."

Walter did as he was told, wincing as Ezra pricked him. She squeezed a few drops of his blood into the mixture.

Ezra kept her eyes on the bowl as she stirred. "I prefer to heat this over coals, but a candle will do just as well. Hold this." She handed the bowl to Walter and removed a short, fat candle from her pack. The candle had five wicks versus just one, so that once lit the flame was as wide as the palm of her hand. Retrieving the bowl, she held it over the flames, stirring as blood and bone bubbled and coalesced.

"Now place your hands on your knees, breathe deep, stay calm."

Ezra removed the scalpel and made an incision in the exposed skin of Walter's forearm. She poured the insipid mixture over the cut. He gasped as the liquid bubbled and moved. It beaded along the cut, then filled his veins with fire as his body absorbed it. Just as quickly, the cut disappeared, replaced by a thin scar.

"Stay calm," she murmured. "Whatever happens, stay calm."

The effect of the tooth was not immediate—neither a flash, nor a rush. Instead, a tingle spread from his legs, to his belly, to his chest—like sensation returning to a numbed limb. By the time the feeling had reached his head, Walter no longer sat on the forest floor. He had returned home, seated on the three-legged pine stool in his father's shanty. A half-empty bag of potatoes sat beside him, the skins littering the ground all around.

He looked at his hands. The blisters and scrapes from crawling through the woods were still there. But on top of those remnants were details more perplexing. Potato skins were jammed beneath his fingernails, and the dank odor of the tubers filled his nostrils.

There was a thud of footsteps behind him, and Walter turned to face his father. Mr. Lofton looked quite healthy. His limbs and face appeared twenty years younger than when he had last seen him. This was how his father looked when Walter was young. This was the person who taught him his manners, how to rake oysters, plant a seed, and showed him the heavy strike of his hand. Then his father's face shifted. It darkened, tightened. The skin loosened as furrows formed, becoming wrinkles. As the seconds passed, Lofton aged. His back became bent, his fingers lined and crooked. At the exact moment when his father reached his current age, he jerked violently. A bloody score slashed his face, and he fell.

The body toppled on the cabin floor, but the changes did not stop. Lofton's body decayed. And as it did, the hut, the furniture, and the pile of potatoes disintegrated as well, turning to dust. As trees faltered and the surrounding grass withered, Walter heard a pop and sucking sound. He could see indentations in the landscape, impossibly dark, each a circular gap of nothingness. Holes.

As the Holes ate through the ground, Walter left his body behind. He rose to the heavens, though he kept his eyes down to watch the Holes consume first the ground, then the stars, then the sky. He hung suspended in the abyss. Not black, not darkness. Nothing. A true absence of form and matter. Time passed. Then the world shifted again. First one star appeared, then another. The heavens returned and the Holes began to fade, revealing scraps of land beneath. Time had reversed. The land was regurgitated from the blackness. But Walter did not return to the shack in Greenwater's End. His mind soared without form, to the west, following the road they'd traveled since leaving his home. When he finally stopped, time stopped as well. He hung suspended above the stadium of Cinderwood, the crowd frozen in mid-step. Each person's face was twisted in horror as they looked at something behind him. But bodiless as he was, he couldn't turn his head to look.

And then Walter saw a face he did recognize. David was there, his eyes wide in terror, his lips parted in a frozen cry.

And then Walter was free. He could again move his head. Time had resumed. He looked into the hard eyes of Ezra.

The hunter spoke, her face expressionless. "Yes?" The words snapped Walter to reality.

"I saw the world end." He closed his eyes to avoid the hunter's gaze. "I also saw David. And he's in trouble."

●

The sun passed behind the rim of the Cinderwood coliseum. There was a general nervousness riding on the murmurs of those thousands, though David's thoughts were elsewhere.

"Mr. Levi," he asked, "are all of these people here because of you?"

"Not at all. Today is the festival of the equinox. These people are here to listen to the mayor. As you might imagine, he has a lot to explain these days."

"So we're not just here to see him?"

"Of course not. We're here to see something more unexpected, the first of two amazing things shown to me in my dream. The first is here, the next by the sundial not far away."

David gritted his teeth. He was growing weary of Levi, the man who called himself a philosopher. That wasn't the right term for him at all. Someone who predicted the future wasn't a philosopher, but a prophet.

The thought was snatched away as a crackle of electricity surrounded him. It began with a tingle along his skin, charging the atmosphere. Then the charge was gone, not just vanished but sucked from the air, leaving the world lonely in the absence of the once-great energy. And in that void, came a great sound. Immensity itself, a colossus, one billion peals of thunder echoing in a single hollow blow. David was first pushed back against the people behind him, and then yanked forward, along with the rest of the crowd, as a great wind ripped through the crowd.

Throughout the stadium, violent gusts of wind hurled onlookers into the center of the arena. Some people were thrown a single row, some several. Screams of surprise and panic filled the air, followed by groans and wails of the injured. The wind shrieked all around him. David pulled himself to his feet. And as he regained his bearings, his heart dropped. Covering three-quarters of the field and stretching onto the far side of the stadium was one of the largest Holes David had ever seen. Easily two hundred yards wide, the void sucked the light from the air. As he stared, the screaming horde diminished to a mumble in his ears. The people were being pulled into the Hole in the hundreds, and there was nothing he could do to stop them.

And then the wind stopped.

The Cinderwoodans gasped again, this time in surprise. But the electricity had returned to the air, a sudden wave of heat as if from a flashbulb. David felt two firm hands on his shoulders. He twisted his head to see Levi had come up from behind. The prophet had a gash on his forehead. A stream of blood trickled across his nose to drip from his upper lip.

"There, David. That wind! Was it an earthquake, a tornado? Have you ever seen anything like it? There's no way I could have guessed that would happen. Revelation, my boy. You tell Remus not all truth can be deduced. You tell your sage about this."

David couldn't believe his ears. He shifted back to look at the gargantuan Hole. The people were still falling into it, disappearing forever. Was it possible Levi couldn't see—if not the Hole itself—then at least its effects? Surely he could see the—

A shadow rocketed from the Hole and into the sky above. David's heart skipped a beat. He had seen that fury of buzzing once before. A chimera.

Shouts of confusion transformed to screams of terror as more and more shapes erupted from the Hole. Chimeras spewed into the sky. The Hole below found deathly symmetry in the swarm filling the sky.

●

Ezra led Walter from the safety of the forest, taking careful note of their path as she went. She tried to walk with purpose, as though she belonged. But she knew if someone came too close, they would be easily found out. Luck, however, was on their side. The fields and mills were vacant. The only greetings were the warning barks of dogs. With this realization, she and Walter hastened into a slow jog. The pace helped mask her worry. After all, Ezra took Walter's vision quite seriously. And though what he saw may have been mostly a dream, it was a vision all the same.

KA-THUD

A thunderclap smashed through the air, answered seconds later as the echo reverberated from the mountains in the distance. Walter dove for cover, his eyes wild. Ezra dropped to one knee. This wasn't thunder, or a gunshot. She stooped to lace her boots. That was a lesson she'd never forget.

"What the hell was that?" Walter sputtered. "Was it dynamite, or was it…" the farmer's words died in his mouth. Straight ahead, in the heart of the city, a cloud of black billowed upward. Ezra's jaw tightened.

"Chimera." The word poured from the hunter's teeth like falling sand. She realized she was smiling and hurried to smooth her face. That bothered her most of all. She was staring into a fountain of chimera, a swarm larger than any she'd seen in the war. Yet she didn't feel danger. Her mouth salivated with the thought that with each chimera, she could obtain the sweet burn of the tooth.

"Holy Christ!" Walter's words snapped her back to alertness. "Chimera? All of them? Jesus, what do we do? What about David? What about the town, what about everyone? That many here, at once?"

"Calm down. Prepare yourself. We have to get there as soon as we can." Ezra paused. "For David. Now follow me."

She took off at a dead sprint, but not toward the town. She angled to the nearest farmhouse. She rounded the porch on the far side. Success. A horse was tethered there. And though most certainly a plow animal, it would have to do. Ezra swung her knife to cut the tether. Just as quickly, she had mounted.

"Come up. Hold on," she ordered. Walter scrambled up behind the hunter, quite nearly pulling her down with him. The hunter dug in with her heels, and the horse took off. They galloped toward the city as screams, gunshots, and death rose to meet them.

●

Walter gripped Ezra's waist in desperate fascination. He was no stranger to horseback, but he'd never ridden like this. He clutched tight as they charged across the fields to the gates of Cinderwood. As they neared the entrance, he could see people pouring from the gates. Children, mostly, but all terrified. Ezra pulled the horse up short and signaled for Walter to dismount. He nodded. If they continued mounted, they might trample someone. But if they didn't, they could be caught in the wave as well.

"Come." Ezra jogged to the gates with Walter in tow. Giant turnstiles ensured that traffic only flowed in one direction per side. And while the masses poured from the town exit, only he and Ezra sought to enter. They pushed through the turnstile and into the city. The chaos of the mob was replaced by a far darker, and far more violent scene.

Chimera were everywhere. But for each of the swooping and striking creatures, there were three armed Cinderwoodans releasing a hail of bullets. They *all* were armed. The streets were alive with gunfire, yells, cheers, and terror.

"Jesus, Ezra, how are we going to find him in this mess? How can we even try and…" But the hunter did not answer. She lunged forward, the arc of her knife swinging to bifurcate a chimera as it passed. The creature was severed up the middle. The left half dropped motionless, while the right half continued forward to seize and impale a running man. Ezra took a few quick steps, struck at the still-animate half, and the head dropped neatly off. She kicked a fallen pistol toward Walter, then turned back to the creature.

In a motion both fluid and violent, Ezra seized the fallen head. She pulled a pair of pliers from her belt and then ripped the chimera's teeth free. Without pause, she dropped to her knees. She set the teeth on the cobblestones, then slammed down hard with the butt of her knife. After three blows apiece, each tooth had been reduced to splinters. She snatched the fragments and swept them into her mouth.

The hunter chewed with deadly purpose, determined but measured. Her body went into a shock of spasms. Her eyes lost focus, her limbs twitched. And then it was over. She ripped the splint from her arm and flexed her hand.

"Follow me."

Ezra took off along the cobbled streets of Cinderwood. She would dart forward, swing to the side to strike at one of the chimera, and then leap ahead once more. She moved with the fluidity of the bluefish back home. Dart, strike, dart, strike. Walter tried to keep up, his hands wrapped tight around the stock of the pistol. But he never fired. Every time a chimera came close, Ezra would intercept it.

"We're close," she snapped. She spun, her knife cutting through the air to decapitate another chimera. And, as she had done with the others, she moved in distinct bursts to yank the teeth from its head. She tucked them into the fattening pouch around her neck.

Ahead, Walter saw an open town square. The carnage had increased since entering the city, and this looked to be its epicenter. Bodies of bullet-riddled chimera lay intermingled with the fallen townsfolk. And the battle continued. Men, women, and children with shotguns, pistols, rifles, and automatic guns fired at the swarm. Walter also saw—to his great dismay—that many people only *appeared* to be human. The chimera were shifting their shapes—but not to completion. He saw an aged grandmother with a scythe for an arm.

Another looked like a small boy, no older than his nephews, but with a grasshopper's legs, and the mandibles of an ant.

"No…" Walter shook his head fervently. "We can't go through there. Most of them aren't even human—and I can't tell which is which!"

Ezra glared back at him as she ground more teeth fragments in her jaws. Her body convulsed one more, her eyes becoming one shade more red. "I. Can. Tell." The hunter spun and leaped forward. In long lopes, she ran through the courtyard, her blade constantly moving, cutting, striking. Walter sprinted to keep up.

And then they were across. The hunter didn't even look back to see if he followed. She darted into an alley and disappeared.

●

Levi, the prophet, gripped a shotgun in his right hand and the cuff of David's shirt in the other. The other Cinderwoodans had either raised their weapons to fight, or had simply run. David wasn't sure what Levi was doing. For though the man occasionally fired his gun, he wasn't in a panic. Not like David was. Not like the whole town was.

"Move your feet. Faster," Levi ordered.

David tried to comply, but his legs were numb. His mind was overwhelmed by the size of the Hole, and the impossibility of the chimera swarm.

Gunshots sounded. Not for the first time, bullets hit the wall behind them, fragments of brick showering the side of his face. He winced, but kept his feet moving. He had to. Levi's grip was unwavering, as was his sympathy.

"We've got to get out of here," David pleaded. "I have to get back to my friends."

"Just keep moving. We're almost there."

"Outside?"

"No. To the second half of my vision."

Amidst the fear, amidst the panic, a chill ran up David's spine. Levi was a changed man, and David was more than a little uncertain where he fit into all of this. "What did you see this time?" he managed.

"You'll see for yourself. There it is."

Levi pointed down the length of the alleyway. Sandwiched between the shops and just beyond the vendor's carts was an immense stone structure, a sundial. The dial sat atop a raised dais, which stretched twenty feet across. It had been carved of polished granite and inlaid with bronze. David suspected the sundial served more as a piece of art than an actual timepiece.

"Up, up there. This is where it happens. It's just as I was shown!" Levi released his grip on David's collar. He scrambled onto the dais. The prophet cradled the shotgun in his hands and dropped to his knees. He called to the sky. "Show me! I'm ready! I'm ready to meet my destiny!"

David had seen enough. He had to escape this madman. He backed away, then froze. A great whirring filled the air. As shadows surrounded him, he cowered in fear. Five chimera, four bug-like, and one which looked human except for onyx wings, rushed at the sundial. The first to arrive, with a head like an alligator, aimed directly at Levi. The creature collided with the prophet, pinchers impaling him as he swept him from the dais.

Panic ran across David's skin in electric currents. The four remaining chimera landed, their talons clicking on the cobbled street. When the fifth chimera returned, Levi was no longer in sight. The alligator-faced chimera stepped forward. It looked at David with its glassy black eyes, then shuddered. As the beast twitched, it rippled and discolored, until he found himself looking at a perfect facsimile of Levi.

The creature was identical in all ways except for its eyes, which remained dark as ink.

"David. We must speak." The voice was clear, with no trace of hissing S's like the chimera in Greenwater's End. But it was not Levi's voice.

David inched backward, only to find himself pressed against the sundial. He dropped to a seat, hands clutched on the stone rim. "How do you know me?"

"Others have seen you. At the seaside town. And before. We've heard of your gift, your quest." The creature emitted a series of clicks. David wondered if this was the speech of the chimera, or if it was just clearing its throat. "It's too dangerous for you to be here. We would never have attacked this place if we'd known it would put you in danger."

"Why do you care about me? You don't care about anything else. Does this have to do with the Holes, or the sage?"

"Everything is connected. You must continue your search—but you must not find your sage. He holds no answers. If you find him, your story could end. We mustn't let it end. For the sake of the world. All worlds."

"I don't understand! Why look for him but not find him? It doesn't make any sense. Tell me why! That's all I want."

The creature nodded, the gesture quick and jerky. "It's the linchpin, David. We are the linchpin for this world, but we believe you are part of one even greater. Do you understand?"

"No! What's a linchpin?"

"Your search is the linchpin. And it will be so only as long as it continues. And that is all you can know."

"You are so damn—"

David didn't get a chance to finish. The five chimera shot into the air. He watched the ascent, and soon they were joined by others, the entire swarm rising at once, massing, and then funneling as they traveled back in the direction they had come. They were going back to the Hole, back into the black.

A yell rang from the far end of the courtyard. "There he is! David, hold on! We're coming!"

He twisted to see Walter and Ezra running his way. Walter clutched a pistol in one hand, his body drenched with sweat and splattered with blood both red and vermilion. Ezra kept stride behind him. The hunter's face was caked with gore, her eyes so red she appeared to be bleeding from both sockets.

"Walter, Ezra! You're here!" He paused. "What the heck is a linchpin?"

The hunter's eyes widened in surprise. "Not now, David. Not until we're safe."

●

Walter pulled the rusted truck to a stop next to where the muscle car was hidden. In the aftermath of the chimera's attack, there had been so much chaos and so much madness, that slipping away had been easy. David didn't even consider taking the truck to be stealing. The Cinderwoodans would find it soon enough, even if the gas had been drained for their own purposes.

After transferring their supplies to the muscle car, they set off along the road again. They drove for several hours before pulling to a stop just off the road to build a small fire. There was a relief at being away from the madness of Cinderwood. And they had a lot to discuss.

Ezra sipped from her waterskin before passing it to Walter. "We should talk about what happened, before the memory fades. David, what did you find out?"

"That could take a while. You go first. What did you do? You know, before the…" He trailed off.

"Mostly, we waited," Ezra murmured. "Then we came for you. Now speak."

David hung his head. "I learned a lot. It's almost too much."

Walter nodded. "Then start at the beginning."

●

David told them what he'd learned. He told of how the sage was collecting stories to see what truths existed across all worlds. He explained how the sage was stuck here, unable to leave this world. He also told how Levi, the prophet, believed truth could not be deduced, and instead found only in revelation. Apparently, Levi and the sage had only agreed on one thing: By understanding truth they could unravel the secret of the Holes.

Walter rolled his eyes. "So we're not searching for the sage anymore? We're searching for truth? Well, that should be *much* easier. You still think that's in Kansas?"

David shrugged. "I don't know. And, I think we *are* still searching for the sage. I think he's still a part of this. Maybe he's learned something Levi didn't know. But there's more to consider."

Ezra looked up. "The chimera. They spoke to you again." The hunter's eyes were still red from the effects of the tooth. Her face glistened with sour sweat.

"Yes. They told me I should keep looking for the sage and for answers, but I shouldn't find them. They said it several times."

Walter raised an eyebrow. "A chimera told you that? They talked to you? Specifically to you? They knew who you were?"

"It wasn't the first time. I talked to one during the hurricane. It said the same thing. It said I had to keep looking, but that I should never find anything. It doesn't make any sense to me."

Walter grew agitated. "Now just wait a minute. You're saying the things that killed my father, murdered countless people in Cinderwood, and are somehow connected to your Holes, gave you advice? And you're listening to it? They come from the Holes, David. They're probably what causes them! It all makes sense. This has been about the chimera all along."

David shook his head. He closed his eyes tightly. "That might be simpler, but I don't think it's right. But listen for a second. They mentioned 'the linchpin'. They said they were the linchpin here, but maybe the search for answers to the Holes was too. Does that mean anything to you?"

Ezra, strangely silent through the talk of chimera, stirred once more. "Perhaps. The hunters used that word as well. It was a metaphor for something that held other things together. A linchpin was a focal point, a critical join. During the Chimeran War, the hunters called our leader the linchpin. Even when the rest of the world was falling apart, he held it all together. When one leader died and another succeeded him, they called it the changing of the linchpin. Seamless, unbroken."

Walter asked, "So what happened?"

"Years after the war ended, no one stepped up after the old linchpin retired. And with no one to replace him. Things fell apart."

"So if the chimera said they were the linchpin, what does that mean?"

"Well," Ezra replied, "if they use the term like we did, they think they're holding something together. Maybe themselves, maybe something else." She chuckled mirthlessly. "They were right about one thing. At least for the hunters, the chimera were more of a linchpin than our leader ever was. Without the chimera, there wouldn't be hunters. That's the real reason my colleagues died out. There was no enemy to fight. Maybe now, after Cinderwood, we'll start to come back."

David felt his face turning red. "But what does that have to do with the Holes? Or the sage? Why is getting answers bad? It doesn't make any sense."

"Does it need to make sense?" Walter asked. "Maybe there isn't always a reason. Maybe this truth you're looking for—this truth with a capital 'T'—maybe it doesn't exist. Maybe both the sage and this Levi guy were wrong. Maybe the world is just dying. Maybe things just die. Ever think of that? It might not be a great mystery, some kind of puzzle to put together. Maybe it's not a matter of finding the truth like your sage thought, or sitting on your butt and waiting for someone to tell you the truth like that prophet thought. Maybe there isn't any reason at all. You have to consider that too."

For two long minutes, the three remained silent. Walter's brow was wrinkled in contemplation, while David struggled to come up with a response.

Ezra broke the silence. "Perhaps there is no purpose, Walter. Perhaps there is no truth beyond what we make. But that doesn't mean we can't have purpose."

Walter sneered. "Really? And what's your purpose, Madam Hunter? To find your next tooth?"

"At times. What's yours?"

Walter clenched his jaw, the muscles rippling up the side of his head. "To do what my father asked. To help David."

"And David, what is your purpose?"

A strange feeling washed over him, a feeling that at once everything might be all right. He looked from Walter's wrinkled brow to Ezra's bloodshot eyes. "For now, it's to find the sage. After that, to stop these Holes once and for all."

15

MEMPHIS

David leaned back against the windshield of the muscle car, legs outstretched on the hood. The sun was cresting over the eastern hills. This was a dawn he was used to, a slow warming of light, ever-growing until the sun finally peeked over the highlands. The mountain sunrise was not as dramatic as those over the ocean, but it was familiar. He'd accept a hint of home whenever possible. At the other end of the camp, Ezra and Walter began to stir.

Walter yawned once as he lumbered over to David. "So, Memphis it is, huh? You think the sage'll be there?"

"Not anymore," he replied. "But someone may have seen him."

"We'll need fuel and supplies either way," Ezra said as she tossed their belongings into the trunk. "It's only a guess we have enough gas to make it. You ready to drive?"

"Yeah, I guess. But watch that I don't fall asleep."

The three climbed into the muscle car, David at the wheel, Ezra beside him, and Walter in the back. They eased onto the highway and soon were up to speed. As they drove, the landscape changed. On the drive to Cinderwood, David had seen a few Holes—some very large—

but they were scattered. As each hour passed, and they moved farther and farther west, the more common the Holes became. Now, with the sun directly above their heads, they would scarcely leave sight of one Hole before the next came into view. David also noticed something else. Ezra's eyes followed the Holes as they passed by. At first, he thought it was a coincidence, but now he wasn't so certain.

"Ezra?"

"Yes, David?"

"Are you watching the Holes? Can you see them?"

The hunter shook her head. "I can't see them exactly, but I think I can feel them. It's from the tooth. There is something of an aftereffect. I'm not surprised, though."

"Me neither. That hunter with the bandits said the same thing. What does it look like to you?"

"Hard to describe. It's like the color is off, a little washed out, grayer, less together. But not like it's in a shadow, just indistinct. If I didn't know of the Holes, I probably wouldn't even notice it."

David's breath caught in his throat. In the distance, he saw a Hole. But not just a Hole, it was the single largest Hole he had even encountered. It didn't even look like a Hole, but a sea of darkness. A plain of nothing. "Ezra," he whispered, "can you see that?"

A yawn issued from the back seat. Walter leaned forward between them. "What are you two talking about? Oh look, we're almost to Memphis. Good thing too, I'm starving."

David glanced back at Walter, then at the abyss that lay ahead. He didn't see a city at all, because he saw the truth.

Memphis was no more.

David dropped the muscle car to a crawl as he neared the Hole. And though Walter and Ezra both claimed they could see the city as clear as they could see him, David saw only black. When he told them about the Hole, they didn't question him. They never did anymore.

Walter lurched forward in his seat. "There. Right there, David. Can you see that?"

"What am I looking for?"

"The combine. The tractor, can you see the tractor? I'll bet that thing still has fuel in it."

At the edge of the Hole, no more than ten yards from where the nothingness began, was an enormous piece of farming equipment. The tractor was three times the size of a dump truck, and except for some rust and cobwebs, appeared in good repair. David slowed the car to a stop.

"I see it. It's not in the Hole. You two stay put. I'll check it out." He exited the driver's seat and walked toward the machine. Something else was strange here. Little pieces of debris, scraps of tires, splinters of wood, old cans, and torn clothing formed a line in the sand. He followed the litter of trash and saw it roughly traced the perimeter of the Hole. The border sometimes swung wide, and sometimes came very close to the edge. David carefully stepped between a smattering of broken bottles and a pile of toys. A yell echoed behind him. He turned to see a girl with frighteningly wild hair running in his direction.

"Stop! Don't cross it! It isn't real. You'll get sucked in!"

The blonde girl sprinted to the edge of the trash line. She wore a ragged dress held together by the will of its threads. Her hair jutted out in all directions. David placed her at about seventeen years old, but between the torn clothes, the feral hair, and the dirt on her cheeks, he couldn't be sure.

"Don't go any farther," she said. "Come back toward me. It's not safe. You've got to believe me."

He smiled back at her. "Can you see the Hole? Do you know what happened here?"

The girl stopped short. She frowned, her bright green eyes watching him. "If you've got a name for it, then you've seen this before. You should know better than to get close. I saw your car back there. Where do you come from, anyhow?"

David opted for the shorter response. "From the coast. We've been on the road a few days. We just left Cinderwood yesterday… they are having some problems of their own." He watched her eyes for a reaction. "They weren't too friendly either."

The girl's scowl turned to a grin. "Hah… hah! Wow, that's quite the understatement. I used to have to go there every once in a while to pick things up. Never my favorite errand. Oh, don't look so shocked. You think you're the only ones they've ever picked on? Now if you promise to tell me what's going on out there, I'll fill you in on things on this side of the world. Sound good?"

"Yeah, that's sounds great." He walked away from the edge of the Hole to where she stood. "My name's David."

"Melanie. Nice to meet 'cha. Who are your friends?"

The girl did not budge from her wide stance until David was fully across the line of trash. But once over, she opened her arms as if to embrace him, then punched him in his right shoulder.

"Ow! What did you do that for?"

"Just makin' sure you're really, really real." She grinned. "Can't be too careful these days. I've seen weirder stuff out here than a kid in a fancy car." She shrugged. "But what can you do, right?"

David heard the chunk of car doors opening and saw his friends approach. Walter's arms were folded across his chest. Ezra rested one hand on her belt, the other hung by her side. David recognized the stance as one of readiness.

Melanie punched him in the shoulder once more, eliciting another squeak of protest. "Aren't 'cha gonna introduce me?"

"Melanie, this is my friend Walter. Walter, Melanie."

"Afternoon."

"And this is Ezra."

The girl shook each of their hands then glanced over at the muscle car. "That's quite the ride you've got there. Looks a little banged up, but nothing you couldn't pound out with the right tools." She jerked a thumb at her chest. "I couldn't do it myself, mind you, but a couple of the kids here are pretty handy. We've got a mechanic, a farmer or two, and a plumber. But most of us are just scouts when it comes right down to it." She winked. "Except me, I'm the pilot. Come on, I'll show you."

David, Ezra, and Walter followed the girl away from the enormous Hole. As promised, the walk was short, a little less than a quarter-mile to what she explained was once a fire tower. She said that from her perch she and her friends (all absent) could watch for new arrivals. Visitors, however, were somewhat rare. Even before the Hole, most people didn't come this far west. All the land past the river was chimera territory, or had been during the war. And even though the creatures hadn't been seen here in years, no one went farther.

The top of the fire tower resembled a tree house built by a master welder. The roof was of corrugated metal, the tables were metal, as were the chairs, and even the odd dresser or two. The floor was covered with straw mats and littered with books, tools, clothing, and bean bags. Melanie plopped into the largest of the bean bags and gestured around the room.

"This here's home. Take a seat anywhere that looks good. And don't mind all the stuff. Cleaning's not my strong suit. But I've got some cheese and crackers on the table if you want."

David plopped down and let the questions flow. "So how long have you been here? I mean, when did it happen? The Hole, that is."

Melanie's smile dropped. Her green eyes watered behind her tangle of hair. "It's been a while since Memphis quit being real. Me and my friends were on a field trip for school. We were supposed to go tour one of the old mines that used to be around here. No one mined much anymore because of the chimera, so it was, you know, just educational.

"We'd been gone for maybe an hour when the boom came. Loudest thing ever. Like big hollow thunder… Boom! My ears rang for about ten minutes. But that's not the point. After the boom, came this wind. We ended up huddled back in the mine as trees and bushes, sticks and trash were blown around."

The wild-haired girl paused. She chewed on her fingernails. "So after the wind finally died down, we headed back to town. But by then, it wasn't real anymore. It all *looked* normal, but there weren't any people left. And if somebody got too close, they'd get sucked under as well. A lot of folks disappeared trying to cross that line until we figured out where the edge was. That's what all that trash is. It's how we know not to go any closer." Melanie looked at each of them in turn. "You don't seem surprised."

"I've seen Holes before," David said. "Like I said, we just came from Cinderwood. There was a big one there too. Nothing this big, but…" His eyes went wide. "Oh no!"

Ezra asked, "What's the matter, David?"

"The Hole at Cinderwood… I didn't warn them! I didn't block it off!"

Melanie squinted at David. "What do you mean, block it off? Do you know how to close these things up? Can you fix them?"

"No, I can't. I meant mark it off, kind of like what you did here."

Ezra said, "There's little we can do now. Melanie, can you tell me how many people are left here?"

"There were maybe a few hundred outside of town when it happened. Of those, most everybody went back east."

"But you stayed."

"I had to. This is my home. It *was* my home, at least. And I have my reasons."

"Oh, and what's that?"

"I'm going to make things better. It won't be easy. Memphis may be done for. But what if it isn't? I met someone who was trying to figure out a way to help us."

The hairs on the back of David's neck prickled. "You mean the sage! You talked to the sage. Can you tell us where he went?"

Melanie's eyes blazed with delight. "Aha! So you're *that* David. Of course I can tell you where he went. And I can do you one better. I'll take you there."

●

Ezra stood on the tarmac, arms folded across her chest. She could feel the heat radiating from the asphalt. Acrid smells filled her nostrils, mixing with the humidity to form an oppressive mixture. This was a human smell, a smell of industry and technology—what many folks coined as "progress." Ezra considered it unnatural in its own way, just as unnatural as the chimera. This was unnatural in the same way shoes were unnatural. Or guns. Or the terrifying contraption behind her.

"We can just ferry over the river," Ezra offered. "That way, we'll still have our car. It's safer."

Melanie grinned at the old hunter. "That's too slow, and you know it. Not to mention roads aren't exactly common past the river. It's been a good fifty years since anyone tried to build one over that way, much less keep it up. Trust me, this is the fastest way to get there."

Recently, Ezra had seen a lot of things she didn't agree with, things that made her nervous—though she took pains to hide it. This new development unnerved her more than the others. She'd heard of airplanes, of course, even seen a few take flight during the war. But it had been years since she saw one aloft. And she'd never been in a plane herself. And this particular aircraft, though the polished aluminum gleamed, didn't look safe to her. Not safe at all.

David scrambled up to the airplane. He ran his hands over the wings and inspected the propellers. He circled and thumped along the fuselage, before finally rejoining the others. "It's beautiful, Melanie. Does it really fly?"

"You bet it flies. You've never seen a plane before?"

"Sure I have. When I was real little there used to be tons of planes. We lived below one of the air paths so we'd see the big jets going overhead. I flew a few times to visit family and stuff, but it was a while ago. After the Holes started, a lot of machines quit working like they were supposed to. It got too dangerous to fly."

Walter frowned. Ezra could tell he shared her misgivings. He said, "That's what I want to know more about. Things not working. Things like airplanes. Because as you said, the Holes are just getting thicker."

David said, "Well, I don't know about a plane exactly, it was just machines in general. After the Holes started to get bad, things didn't always do what they were supposed to. It was the electronic stuff first, computers and radios. Then motors quit turning. Cars and lawnmowers, even garbage disposals just quit. But that was all at home. Once me and my brothers started getting further along, closer to the center, *nothing* worked. The compass pointed straight only half the time, even zippers would jam, or coat buttons would just quit holding on. None of it ever made sense to me. Things just quit being all there."

Melanie added, "You mean they quit being real. It's kind of like back in town. The whole town isn't real anymore. But sure, there are a few things around here that maybe don't work exactly right. And it's not that they shouldn't, it's that they just don't. It's all the same thing."

"What kind of things?" Walter pressed. "Things like planes? Things that if they quit working would drop out of the sky and kill us all? Things like that?"

"No. Not like that." She winked. "Light bulbs, mostly. Anything electric. I used to think it was 'cause the power plant wasn't real, but flashlights and batteries all went a little flakey too. But don't worry. This here plane is more mechanical than electric. The beacon is the real worry."

David asked, "What's a beacon?"

"That, is this." Melanie held up a metal object covered in knobs with a large antenna stretching from one end. "There are two kinds, one that sends a signal, and one that receives them. We've been using beacons around here for years. During the war, it was too dangerous to cross the river without some way of being found. Not many people go that way even now, but I sent a distress beacon with the sage just in case. He said he'd turn it on if he got in trouble, or once he got where he was headed. We're too far away to pick up a signal from here, but our range will be better from the air."

David scratched his head. "Wouldn't he run out of batteries after a while?"

"They last a really, really long time."

"Then it's settled." He clapped his hands. "We'll leave tomorrow."

Ezra furrowed her brow. "Wait. We haven't decided about this for sure. If that plane quits working, it's over for everyone. Do you think it's worth the risk?"

"If we don't try, the whole world may run out of time. Who else is going to risk it if we don't? The sage is already out there. And if Melanie's right, we could meet him tomorrow! And then it'll all make sense, and we'll know what to do and—"

Walter placed a hand on David's shoulder. "We don't know if the sage knows any more than we do."

Melanie sighed in exasperation. "If you'd quit flapping your jaw and listen for a sec, maybe you'd think differently. Like I said, he told us all about what he was doing. He was heading off to talk to some folks who might know some real answers. But even if they did or didn't, he was still pretty set on meeting up with you too. Think of it like this whole thing's a puzzle. He's got a lot of pieces, but so do you. So even if you ninnies don't want to go, I'm not missing out. I'm leaving with or without you."

Walter's jaw dropped. "*You're* coming with *us?*"

"Well, which one of you knows how to fly? And which of you has ever been west of the Mississippi?"

"I've been west," Ezra stated.

"Well, congratulations to you, Ms. Hunter," Melanie replied. "There's still the plane. Oh, and the beacon."

David folded his arms. "And you'll need me to find the Holes."

Melanie smiled. "Well, of course you're coming, David. But what about you two?"

Walter exhaled. "I'm coming. I made a promise. I've seen what these Holes can do. We're in this together."

All heads turned to Ezra. She had known this moment would come. She had enough teeth to wind out her remaining days, and without fear of withdrawal—if she paced herself. But there was something else as well. Like it or not, the chimera were linked to these Holes. If the war was to start again, the hunters would need to know why. This was an opportunity to gain the upper hand. Perhaps this was a chance to win the war for real.

"I'll go." Ezra paused. "But what *does* happen if the engine stops? Is that the end?"

Melanie squinted one eye and propped her hands on her hips. "No. Not the end. Bad. Really, really bad. But not the end. I've never had to do a dead landing, but they can be done."

"But what then?" David asked. "We'd be in the middle of nowhere."

"Hey, we're not flying back no matter what we do."

"What do you mean?"

Melanie walked to the side of the aircraft and gave a few hard thumps on the wing. "This little guy's not built for long-range. We'll be stretching it as it is. And that's assuming your maps are right and the headwind doesn't beat us down too much. Where we're going, we're probably not gonna find much of anything, much less a place to refuel."

Walter said, "We can get fuel off that tractor we saw back near the Hole. It should have plenty."

She shook her head. "We've already got a full tank. This isn't about gas, it's about weight. The plane can only carry so much, and there are four of us. Getting off the ground'll be a bit of work in its own right. We're going to need help."

"What kind of help?"

"Now you're thinking. But it'll just have to be a surprise."

●

Night fell across Memphis. And as each star flickered into view, Melanie's compatriots filtered into the tree house. The steady clink-

clink of boots on metal gave them all plenty of warning. Her friends weren't all her age, though many proclaimed to be her schoolmates. There were twenty-five in all, and by the time the last person arrived, the tree house roared with life. Despite her claims to the contrary, and despite her age, Melanie ran the place. When she strolled through the room, people turned to look, to listen to what she had to say. She had a pilot's confidence, a trait no one could match. She could leave at any moment, to be free from the bleakness of a town that no longer *quite* existed. The others recognized it.

"Hey there, David. Having a good time?"

Melanie sauntered through the crowd. With a wave of her hand, a young boy leaped out of the bean bag next to David to make room for her. She plopped down beside him and shot him a smile.

"You bet, Melanie. This place is great. And everyone is so friendly. I can't believe you'd want to leave. How long have you lived here?"

"Pretty much ever since the town quit being real. A month? A few months? Afterward, everyone who was left just kind of banded together. Most of the farmers stayed at their homes. The people here are just city folk lucky enough to be out of town when it happened, and who didn't have anywhere else to go."

"I don't get it. How come nobody else heard about all this?"

Melanie's brow wrinkled. "That's our fault, I guess. The survivors got together after it happened. People were shaken up, you know. They all decided that if you stayed, you stayed. But if you left, you didn't talk about what happened. You never know how people will react to this kind of thing, and we were all a little done with trouble for a while. And sometimes, if you make yourself try to forget, you actually do forget, start to believe it was a bad dream."

David looked at her with skepticism.

"Look, I *know* we should have told everyone… but how can you? It's crazy. It's all crazy." She remained silent for a few seconds.

"Anyway, those of us who stayed behind, well, we keep close. We get together like this every night. We try to make everyone feel a part of the family. I think it would be too hard otherwise." She turned to face him. "Where's your family, David?"

"Home, I hope. I haven't been there for a long time. No telling what's left anymore. It could be like Memphis, for all I know."

"I guess you can't go check on them, can you? That's why you're here."

David didn't answer right away. His eyes scanned the laughing and smiling faces of Melanie's friends. These people had gone on living, even though nothing was left behind. "Honestly, it's hard to be optimistic. I try, but I've never seen a Hole go away. Not one. It gets to you after a while. I put on my best face, but when I see them…" He shuddered. "I guess that's why I'm out here."

Melanie's face turned dark. "Come with me, David. I want to show you something."

The wild-haired girl rose and helped him from the floor. He followed her to the great stairs and down to the base of the fire tower. They walked back to the north, back to the Hole. The night was calm, no hint of bustle, not even the stray call of a coyote or chirping of birds. Animals, David supposed, knew better than to linger here. As they walked, Melanie thrust her hands into her pockets. She dropped her voice low.

"David, what do you see out there?"

"I see the Hole. I see… well, nothing. It's just black. Black and dark and nothing. At night, it's like looking across the water. A big, black lake."

"Well, that's not what I see." She pointed out at the darkness. "I see the spire of the old church. I see the roof of the building where I went to school, where my dad went to work, the museum where I would visit with my brother. I used to come here every night just to watch, just to throw one more rock to see if instead of disappearing it would hit, and crack and bang. And then you came and ruined it."

David looked at Melanie. The curls hanging in front of her eyes hid her expression. "What do you mean?"

"You say you don't see anything. You say there's nothing there. I may know there's nothing there, but it's worse that you actually see the nothing. It's like it's fading away. I could at least hope I'd wake up tomorrow and it would all be normal. But you say that isn't true." She flipped her hair from her face. Tears ran down her cheek. "I'm not going with you just because I want to help you. I'm going because I want to show the sage he's wrong. He wants to know why the world is dying. I want to prove it's alive."

"Melanie, I…" a strange lump caught in his throat. He wanted to comfort her, but he'd seen the end. He, too, was traveling because he had hope. But how much was left? "Melanie, where I came from there were a lot of Holes. The whole world was Holes. Things never went back the way they were. I want to believe I'm wrong too. But I don't know how. That's why I need to find the sage. Maybe he knows something. Or at the very least, maybe I can help him figure something out."

A long moment stretched between them. David looked into the black and wondered what she saw. Was it still and dark, or did she see the lights of buildings that didn't *quite* exist?

"Come on, let's go inside," Melanie said. "I need to say goodbye to my friends. We may not be coming back at all. I know that. So I'm going to make sure I say goodbye this time. That's something I didn't get to do with my family. My real family."

"Go on without me. I'm going to wait here for a little while. I need to think. Would you let Ezra and Walter know where I am? Don't want them worrying."

David sat on the still-warm dust and looked out at the Hole. He could hear Melanie's footsteps as they grew softer and softer, until the only sound was the buzz of conversation from the party. That, and the stir of wind rolling down from the hills to meet the Mississippi.

He knew he didn't belong here. Melanie made that clear. In a way, he never belonged back at home either. He'd always played with the notion that by seeing the Holes he was special. But maybe he just couldn't see the hope left behind. Maybe that was why other people couldn't see the Holes. Not because they lacked second sight, but because they believed more than he did. So did he not have faith? Was he gifted, or tragic?

Twenty minutes passed as he sat and pondered. His thoughts were disturbed by the crunch of footsteps on gravel. He turned to see Walter standing behind him.

"That girl said you'd be down here." A pause. "Mind if I join you? I'm not much for these kinds of parties."

"And Ezra?"

Walter chuckled. "Ezra is the center of attention. Someone found her a bow and some arrows. She's been shooting cans off the tower while they place bets. Great fun for everyone." He shook his head. "It's a sucker's bet though. She doesn't miss."

"Good for her, I guess. Have a seat."

Walter settled cross-legged beside David. He kept his eyes straight ahead. "You looking at the Hole?"

"Yeah."

"What do you see?"

"Same as always," David muttered. "What do you see?"

"Out here? Not much. There's a warehouse over there, an open yard, maybe used to have stock or something. Over to the right side are some houses. They are all pretty small. A few look like they might not have had anyone living in them at all. Up there in the center looks like the main road into town. I can see a church or something a little farther in, but after that, it just looks like buildings. Just kind of empty. Why do you bring it up, David? What did that girl say to you?"

He looked over to meet Walter's kind, brown eyes. "She said I took away people's hope. She said that when I said there was nothing there, it was a slap in the face. It was saying nothing could ever get better. Who needs someone who's hopeless?"

"Now David, there's hopeful and there's ignorant. When you know what's happened and look for the best, that's being hopeful. When you know what's there and choose not to believe it, that's ignorant. No matter how you spin it, it's always important to know what you're dealing with."

"You mean you have to know the truth?"

"If you want to call it that, yeah."

David frowned. "So does that make Melanie ignorant?"

"Not at all. She can't see what you can. So when you say it's nothing, it's like you're only seeing the worst. It's just a matter of perspective. It's like back in town when the storm came. If you, as someone who didn't know better, looked up at the sky and saw clouds, and then out of the blue said you thought it would be a hurricane, well, that's just being a pessimist. There's no reason you should think that, so why even say it? But if I look at that same sky that same day—and I've sat through some twenty-odd storms in my life and know how to read the winds—and *I* say it's a hurricane, that's just the way it is. I guess that's what your sage would call truth."

"So you think truth can vary from person to person?"

Walter shook his head. "No. I think it stays constant. What you know, and how you use that knowledge is what changes."

David smiled. "So you don't think I'm a bad person?"

"No. I happen to think you're a pretty good person—you just have a few more pieces of the puzzle than the rest of us do. That's why we need to get you to your sage." Walter stood up. He offered David a hand and pulled him to his feet. "Now let's head back—and put some bets on Ezra."

16

WEST

As soon as morning came, David began his patrol. He started at the fire tower, then moved in concentric circles until his path took him to the edge of the great Hole. Throughout his patrol, he only found one other Hole. It was small, barely eighteen inches across, and sidled up to a corrugated metal shed. David knew even an "ankle grabber" was deadly if unmarked. He built his barricade, circled it with the orange tape Melanie loaned him, and then returned to the runway to meet the others.

The dual-prop plane glistened in the morning sun. Rays shone off the polished fuselage. The plane was at the far eastern end of the runway, wheels only inches from where the pavement turned to grass. Fifty feet in front of the prop plane—also glistening in the sun, but with an ebony sheen—was the muscle car.

As David approached, he could hear Melanie barking orders at her minions.

"Not that way, you idiot! You need to thread the straps through the loops on the plane, not the car. If the wrong end releases, and we get webbing in the propellers, then… well then what do you *think* is going to happen?"

Melanie was dressed from head to toe in a leather flight suit. She shouted commands at her friends, Ezra, and Walter in turn as they rigged bright blue straps from the car's bumper to the front of the plane.

"What's going on here?" David asked.

"Aha!" Melanie shot David a grin. "Top of the morning to you, inspector Hole-detector. Any luck out there?"

"I found a little one over that way. I marked it off." He looked around him. "What's all this?"

"It's my idea. Though the big fella deserves credit for bringing up the problem. He was whining—as he seems to love to do—that my little plane couldn't carry us all. That started me to thinking. What if it *can't* carry us all? I mean, it's got the engine to pull it off, but we're going a long, long way so maybe we should conserve fuel the best we can. And *that* is where your car comes in."

David looked from the plane, along the length of the blue straps, to the muscle car, and back to the plane again. "You're going to tow the plane? Like a kite? What good is that going to do? We have to cross the river, right? If we could have driven, we would have."

"No, no, no, no, no. You're missing the point. The plane has to work the hardest to get up to speed and into the air. So, if we can give it a little boost, then that saves us precious fuel." She folded her arms. "Maybe it'll matter, maybe it won't. We've got a long way to go, right? All the way to Kansas, which if I've got my bearings locked in, ain't none to close."

Melanie gave David a long, silent stare. After a while, the gaze made him uneasy.

"What? What are you looking at me for?" he spouted.

"Well, are you ready to go, or not?"

"Yes, I'm ready. Are you ready?"

Melanie grinned. "Sure am! Let's roll."

David walked to the dual-prop plane where one of Melanie's friends stalked around, clipboard in hand. As they approached, the boy unfolded a door that opened into a set of three steps. David climbed up and took a seat behind the pilot's seat. He could see that Melanie's friends had packed food and water on the floor in back, as well as several duffle bags. Moments later, Walter climbed up and into the passenger's side seat. Ezra came next, her face more uneasy than her normal stoic expression.

The hunter nodded in greeting. "You all ready for this?"

"Ready enough," Walter replied.

For a minute, the three sat in uneasy silence until Melanie appeared at the open door. She had subdued her mane of hair under a tight aviator's cap and donned a pair of reflective dark glasses. "No, no, no. This won't work at all. We have to balance it out. You, hunter-lady, you're behind me in the pilot's seat. Big fella, you're next to the hunter. David, you're up front with me. We hafta make this thing balance or…" Melanie launched into a dramatic pantomime, miming a crash complete with sound effects. "Now come on, let's go. Move!"

Once Walter, Ezra, and David had taken their appropriate positions, Melanie settled at the helm. The door was pulled shut, sealing them inside. Using hand signals, Melanie motioned for the starboard engine to be pull-started, then the port one. Once both engines whirred, the wild-haired girl began flipping switches, checking dials, and murmuring to herself. After her checks were complete, she looked up, smiled, and waved once more to her friends.

David heard the now-familiar rumble of the muscle car, though the sound was just an undertone next to the twin engines.

"And here…we… *go.*"

As the muscle car rolled forward, the blue straps pulled tight. The plane lurched ahead. The car strained at the unusual weight, then moved forward, taking the plane with it. The progress, at first slow, grew to a rapid pace, faster and faster until they were halfway down the runway.

Melanie grinned. "Now it's our turn."

She dropped the throttle down and the plane's turbines changed from a low rumble to a high-pitched whine. The plane roared ahead. The pull of both car and turbines, however, was unstable. Melanie signaled to her friends, and the straps were released. The car veered out of the way, and the plane was freed of the tethers. David gripped his seat as the end of the runway came closer, and closer—and then they were up. The wheels cleared the ground, and the little plane was airborne.

"Lady and gentlemen, we have liftoff." Melanie kept her eyes dead ahead. She pulled on the plane's controls, sending them into a low arc as they swung around to head west.

David looked down, amazed not only at the speed but the incredible contrast of the blackness of the great Hole next to the muddy waters of the Mississippi. And on the other side, green as far as he could see. Higher and higher they rose, climbing until the trees wavered to a blur.

"And that, my friends, is how it's done."

David looked behind to see both Walter and Ezra, the color drained from their faces. While Walter's hands gripped his seat, Ezra's eyes darted left and right, looking from one window to the other.

"Oh come on," Melanie chided. "The hard part's behind us. It's all smooth sailing from here on out."

"This isn't sailing," Ezra grumbled.

Walter had a different take. "I would think," he swallowed hard, "that landing would be the hard part."

Melanie shrugged. "You're both right. And don't worry about landing, that part doesn't happen until the end. And we don't even know when that is. Which reminds me, Mr. Walter, would you grab the beacon?"

Walter reached into his coat pocket and handed Melanie a radio-like device. This was how they would find the sage. Melanie passed it to David.

"Ok, you're on signal duty. Here's how it works. Turn that big knob up top."

David twisted the black knob and a panel on the front of the beacon flickered to life. There was a three-digit display and an arrow which fluctuated from side to side. "Ok, what's this mean?"

"The numbers are the signal strength. Anything under ten doesn't mean diddly. But you get above a hundred and you've got the real deal. What's it say now?"

"It's jumping around. Three, eleven, seven, zero, one…"

"Then that's just static."

"So what do I do?"

"Just keep your eyes on it and let me know if anything changes. If there's a signal, we'll find it."

David nodded. "And if the sage never turned his beacon on?"

"Then we'll just see him in Kansas."

●

At first, Ezra was mesmerized by the bird's eye view. But she soon found herself staring down in search of the chimera. Like many hunters, she had gone into these lands after the war. She had found nothing. And yet, she wondered.

Ezra fingered the pouch of chimera teeth. She'd tried to prepare the mixture earlier, to use her second sight. Melanie had put her foot down. No open flames inside the plane. Period. She'd gone on for twenty minutes about fumes and oxygen and altitude and combustion, but Ezra paid little attention. If Melanie wanted to be lord of the air, so be it. They wouldn't be up here forever. Ezra knew her time would come.

There was a click and a series of beeps coming from the front seat as David adjusted the knobs on the beacon. He had barely looked up from the device since they had taken off.

Walter leaned forward between the pilot and co-pilot seats. "Does that help at all? Playing with it like that?"

Melanie shrugged but didn't turn to look. "Doesn't hurt. The beacon broadcasts on several frequencies, so we should pick it up regardless."

The thrum of the engines rang loud in Ezra's ears, but it bled into the background. The engines could well have been the breeze or the crash of an ocean wave. The sound was peaceful, in a way, provided she could forget they weren't on solid ground. She shuddered. Probably best not to think at all.

"What was that?" David looked up. He darted his head around. "There it was again. Did you hear that?"

Ezra strained her ears. A sound reached over the engine's whine. It was dull, like bursts of gunfire. *Thud, thud, thud-thud.* Each boom was varied—some louder, some so soft they may even have been imagined.

"I hear it."

"Sounds like thunder," Walter said. "Looks clear enough out here though."

Ezra shook her head. "It's not thunder. We've heard this before, back in Cinderwood. We can hear it, David. But can you see it?"

David turned to face the hunter, his eyes wide. "They're everywhere."

"What's everywhere?" Walter caught himself. "Holes? Are we hearing Holes? What do you see?"

"Really big ones. Like, field-sized. Some are smaller, but I can't hear those. They're opening everywhere. I… I've never seen it like this."

Ka-THUD.

A thunderclap sounded. The plane dropped, falling fifty feet before catching the wind once more. The aircraft convulsed and shook, with Melanie cursing in time. "This doesn't make any got-darn…"

David shook his head. "That one was right below us. Really big."

"Wait, David," Walter said, gripping the seat in front of him. "I thought there weren't Holes in the sky. What was that?"

"It wasn't in the sky. It was underneath."

Melanie's knuckles whitened as she gripped the control stick. "Wherever it is, it's screwing with the air. If this keeps up we're in for a real bumpy—"

Ka-THUD, Ka-THUD.

Two more cavernous booms and the little plane was sent into a freefall. Adrenaline surged in Ezra's veins. Her breakfast swung in her stomach. She managed to keep herself from vomiting, but only barely.

David tugged on Melanie's sleeve. "Can we get any higher? Would that help?"

"We're flying about as high as we can. The air gets thinner further up, less to hold on to."

Thudthudthudthud, thud…

The thunder of opening Holes ricocheted around them, but this time the little plane did not get bucked by the wind. Ezra watched as David's head jerked in all directions. She didn't need to stand helpless, unaware. If she could prepare a tooth, then she could see what was happening as well.

KA-THUD!

Another boom and the plane dropped once more. Ezra yelped in surprise, a sound barely audible over Walter's frantic screams. Only Melanie remained calm.

The plane jerked violently, the shock throwing Ezra forward. Her head came down hard, banging on the seat in front of her. Pain shot across her brow. The cabin erupted in electronic bleating as alarms blared and lights flashed.

"Melanie!" David shouted. "What's going on? What's happening?"

"We've lost the number two. Something ruptured. I may have to put her down."

Walter's eyes went wide. "The number two? The number two *engine*? We lost an engine? How can we fly without an engine? And what do you mean, put her down? Put the plane down? Where? Where could we possibly...?"

"Shut up, everyone," Melanie barked. "Don't distract me." The rest of her words were drowned in the rattling of fuselage and blaring of alarms. "There! I can put it... *there*."

Melanie banked hard, the throttle convulsing in her hands. Ezra saw where she was headed, a small lake—pond, rather—nestled in a grove of trees. Did the plane even float? Was that possible? Could it land on water?

"Melanie? What are you doing?" David's voice was frantic.

"The lake. I'm headed for the lake."

"No! Not there. It's not a lake, that's a Hole. You have to go farther. We have to keep going."

Melanie wrestled with the controls. Ezra could see her arms flexing from the effort. "How... about... that... one..." Melanie nodded with her head. Ezra saw another lake, this one far smaller.

"No Holes there," David shouted. "You can do it, Melanie. Go for it!"

The plane screamed as convulsions shook the cabin. There was an enormous bang, and then silence as the second engine died, leaving only the howl of the wind and the thud of opening Holes. Ezra gritted her teeth. They were dropping fast now, somehow still moving forward, but the flying was done. The lake drew closer, closer. They just might make it.

Another crash as the plane clipped the top of a pine tree. Ezra was hurled forward, the seatbelt punching her in her midsection. But before she could cry out, they had crashed into the water. The plane skipped, then splashed, waves streaming on all sides of them. And though the plane slowed, the lake's shore was fast approaching. Ezra huddled low and braced for impact.

And then the blare of alarms, rattling wings, and howling wind was gone, replaced by the steady rush of water, as the plane began to sink.

●

David lay on a bed of moss and watched dragonflies flit across the edge of the water. The pond had finally become still. The only testament to the crash was the mess of wreckage and the bits of floating debris. He hurt. His body, his mind, his stomach, every one of his muscles throbbed in pain. But he was alive. And except for the cuts and scrapes covering them all, his friends were alive as well—even if not alive *and* well. Ezra had fared the worst. She'd lost a lot of blood from a deep cut across her forehead. Walter patched her up using strips of clothing as gauze. The hunter was battered, but she should pull through.

David watched the others from the corner of his eye. While Walter sat hunched in concentration, Ezra sorted her belongings, strung and restrung her bow. Melanie, on the other hand, was furious.

"This is crap, I'll tell you. This does not count as a crash, and this does not ruin my record. Supernatural, reality-punching Holes and generalized Armageddon do *not* count as ordinary flying conditions. Or even extraordinary ones. This doesn't count!"

David regarded Melanie with a querulous eye. She'd shed her aviator cap, and now her wild blond hair sprang out in all directions.

Walter folded his arms across his chest and stared at Melanie. "So you're mad you crashed? Not because the plane is gone, or we're stranded—but because it messed up your record?"

"Yes!" Melanie cried. "You just proved my point. It's not you who crashed the plane, or the gloomy-Gus hunter, or the Hole-seeing-boy. It was me. The pilot. It doesn't matter the world is dissolving away and screwing with the wind. No, that doesn't matter at all, because it was *Melanie* who crashed the plane. It's always the pilot's fault. Isn't it?"

David thought it better not to respond. He leaned back on the mossy ground and closed his eyes. He could feel the Holes out there. He'd seen a storm of them from above, so there was no denying it. The dull thuds still reverberated in the distance. He shuddered. The rumble had become commonplace.

"Melanie?" Walter asked.

"What now?"

Walter paused, sighed, then continued. "How far did we make it? Is this Kansas?"

Melanie shrugged. "We made it a long way. But I don't really know where David's Kansas starts. I'd say we're maybe two hundred miles to where I'd plotted on the map." She blew a raspberry with her lips. "So now what? What's the next step? We're on the ground. So it's time for this here pilot to take a back seat."

Ezra, mostly silent since the crash, drew herself up to her full height. She did that a lot, David mused. No matter how much she hurt.

"We make camp. Take stock of what we have. Salvage what we need. Then we keep going. I don't think we have any more—"

"Shhh." David strained his ears to listen. "Do you hear that?"

"Holes?" Melanie asked.

"No, it's not that. It's like a little beeping something. I can't quite make it out, but it seems to be coming from…"

Melanie's eyes lit up. "The beacon! It's the beacon." The girl lunged for the collection of baggage and debris from the plane. She tossed aside bags and sacks of food, all sodden from the crash. She emerged triumphant with the device in her hands. "Read it and weep, boys and girls. We've got us a sage to find."

David stared in disbelief at the pulsing red numbers. The reading, though it fluctuated up and down, was well above two hundred. The sage was close.

17

THE BURROW

Despite David's pleadings, Walter's grumblings, and Melanie's inborn impatience, Ezra convinced them to wait until morning to follow the signal. They were still miles away, according to Melanie, and they all needed to rest and recover. Ezra didn't mention that she felt too weak to go farther, even if she'd wanted to. Her head throbbed, and focusing remained a challenge. What's more, she had seen something in those first minutes after the crash. When the rest of them thought the hunter was too battered to unload their cargo, she had done the only thing she knew to do. She'd used another tooth. Not much, but enough to broaden her sense of the world. And in doing so, she had found the chimera. Not close, not many, but they were out there.

Ezra walked to where Walter had gathered a collection of sticks. "No fire, Walter. It's too dangerous."

"I'll clear a fire ring. This wood shouldn't be much for sparking anyway."

"I'm not worried about burning the forest down. There are chimera nearby."

Walter paused. "You're sure about that?"

"I am."

"Then we need to get out of here. They would have seen the plane go down. Damn. They'll be on us in minutes."

Ezra shrugged. "I thought about that. I expected them here by now. I don't think they're ignorant to our presence. I think they're scared."

David ambled over to join the conversation, leaving Melanie alone with the beacon. "If they're scared of us, then what's it matter if we've got a fire?"

"Maybe they were scared when we landed. Maybe now they're getting brave. They missed their chance to hit us right at first, so maybe they'll wait until night. I don't want to tempt them. And I don't want to make finding us any easier. No fire. Understand?"

"No. I don't understand," David said.

Ezra regarded him coolly. "The fire will let them know we're here. They'll see the smoke and track us."

"I understand that. What I don't understand is how those things—those giant crazed mega-bug things that can change shape, look like people, and seem to take out anything that isn't *you,* Ezra—can possibly be scared."

The hunter shook her head. "The chimera aren't bugs. Not even mega-bugs. And they have fears, just like us."

Walter chimed in, "Well, that's a new one. I've heard people say they are mean, tricky, deceitful, and dangerous—killers every one—but everyone agrees they're bugs. And never scared."

"Well that," Ezra replied, "may be the popular version. But it's not the whole truth. I can explain if you'll listen. Without a fire, of course."

They all muttered assent, except for Melanie. She simply glared.

"Very well. Then let me tell you what we learned of the chimera after the war ended."

●

"After the first Chimeran War, when humankind fled to the new continent, the people knew they wouldn't be safe forever. The hunters could give warning, but it wouldn't be enough. So the people improved their defenses. They increased their arsenal from steam engines, to combustion engines, air flight, radio, and better weapons of course. But as for their knowledge of the creatures, they learned nothing more.

"What they did know, and had always known, was the enemy was intelligent. You didn't reason with them—not because they *can't* reason—but because they won't reason with you."

Melanie squinted. "What? Reason with one? Why would you even try to do that?"

"Because," Ezra said, "if we'd known what they wanted, then perhaps a truce could be reached—if it ever came to that."

"Or," Walter added, "if you knew what they wanted, they'd be easier to fight."

Ezra nodded. "Correct. Which is why when the second war began, we hunters tried our best to capture them. But, despite our efforts, not one chimera was ever interrogated." She looked around at the others. "But *sometimes* they would capture us."

The hunter closed her eyes. "One of my mentors was one such captive. He'd been held for almost three years during the war. In that time, they questioned him. He realized by cooperating—by speaking with them as much as possible—he could learn about them as well. And so he told them everything. By the questions they asked, he learned what they cared about, what they wanted." Ezra paused. "What's the matter, Walter?"

"What's the matter? You're kidding, right? First, you pretend we didn't know anything about them, and now you're saying the hunters did all along? Why didn't you tell us?"

"I'm telling you now."

Walter's face reddened. "But why wait until now?"

"It was a secret, Walter. A secret of the hunters, and the last great one. It was also—more importantly—a secret kept from the chimera. Knowledge is a powerful weapon."

"I guess so." Walter scuffed the dirt with his boot.

"May I continue?"

"Please."

Ezra looked around at her listeners. "The first thing he learned was the chimera consider people to be wasteful, hurtful, and useless. They believed the wars necessary as humans needed to be eliminated. They thought we couldn't be trusted to live on our own without growing and spreading until nothing was left. They had every intention of exterminating us.

"But during the second war, things changed. The chimera had learned something. Something terrible they didn't fully understand. What's more, the chimera became convinced that if the war went on— and if they won—the whole world would be destroyed. Even if they *lost* the war, the world would still be destroyed. A victor, any victor, would bring ruin.

"And so the chimera decided they would no longer fight. They would retreat, sink deep into their burrows, into the woods, and across the seas. They would not be defeated, as their numbers would remain strong. Nor would they try to defeat us. They would still attack, occasionally. And in doing so the war has never completely ended."

David looked up in surprise. "That's kind of like what the chimera in Cinderwood told me. Not about the war, but about the sage. It said I needed to keep looking for the sage, but I shouldn't ever find him. It didn't want my search to end. Kind of like not wanting the war to end."

Melanie put her fists on her hips. "Ok, so we're getting somewhere now. Why don't they want things to end? There has to be a reason."

For a while, no one spoke. Then Walter exhaled deeply. His brow furrowed. He opened his mouth several times, and then shut it once more. "Ok, I've got an idea. A completely unfounded idea with no real evidence, but bear with me on this one."

Melanie, David, and Ezra nodded.

"Ok, so we know the chimera know about and can see the Holes. They can fly in and out of them so that's a given. We also know they are concerned about the world ending. Like Ezra says. So it's not that big of a leap to think they were worried about the Holes."

"I'm following you so far," Ezra murmured.

"Thanks. That means a lot to me." Walter gave a hint of a smile. "Essentially, things ending—wars or searches or whatever—leads to Holes."

Melanie raised an eyebrow. "And why's that?"

"That's as far as I got."

David looked up. "Then maybe we should ask them."

"Who?"

"The chimera."

Walter's eyes went wide. "No… I think we keep with the plan. Try to find the sage and go from there. We don't want to push them."

David shrugged. "Maybe you're right. All I'm saying is if we do see them again, I want to talk to them. They must know *something* we don't. And maybe this time I can get them to tell us."

Melanie blew a raspberry with her lips. "Good grief. You're all crazy people, you know that? Normal people don't talk like this."

Walter smiled. "Not your cup of tea?"

"Not exactly. I'm a here-and-now kind of girl. But if I could back way up, I've got a question for Ms. Hunter over there. If you knew the chimera stopped fighting on purpose—and that just maybe the fate of the world was at risk and all that—why keep looking for them?"

Walter snorted. "The tooth."

Ezra gave the farmer a long, hard glare. "That was part of it. The other part was having purpose. A hunter with no chimera has no reason to live. I kept looking to recapture that purpose. I knew nothing else. I needed that reason to exist. Nothing else mattered."

David caught the steely eye of the hunter, but he did not reply. Perhaps Ezra had stumbled onto the missing piece of the puzzle.

●

They had just finished a cold breakfast of dried granola and fruit. As Ezra still forbade a fire, both cooking and cleaning had taken no time at all. David thought this for the best. They needed no more delays.

Melanie sprang to her feet, which in a way was the only way she did anything. While she leaped, darted, charged, and bolted, she just never walked, ambled, meandered, or took her time. The wild-haired girl dusted the leaves from her aviator suit and placed her fists firmly on her hips.

"All right. Someone has to take charge here or we'll be sitting around all morning. Now is everybody ready to sign off?"

David shrugged in acceptance, though he wasn't quite sure what she meant.

"All right, I've got the beacon and have a lock on Mr. Sage's signal. We're only about six miles away, tops. Ms. Ezra, how are things on the chimera side?"

The hunter responded without hesitation. "There are a few in the vicinity, but they are farther south. I can sense others, but nothing too close."

Melanie nodded curtly. "Well, we're heading north, so just let us know if they start getting closer. Mr. David, how's the Hole situation?"

"There's one on the west side of camp, I showed you that one already. I didn't see any of the big ones before we crashed—I mean landed. Sorry, Melanie. Either way, I'll keep in the lead while we're walking."

"Sounds good. And Mr. Walter… any special talents you'd like to bring to the table?"

He scowled. "For one, I'm carrying all our supplies. And more importantly, it's my job to keep the rest of you from doing anything ridiculous. That good enough for you?"

Melanie stuck out her lower lip. "Fine. If you want to be that way about it. We appreciate you too."

"Likewise."

Melanie pulled the beacon from her pocket, spun around once, then pointed into the trees to the north. "Thataway, folks. Let's find ourselves a sage."

After pulling on their packs, David took the lead. Melanie followed with the beacon in her hand, and Walter came third with the gear. Ezra trailed a few feet behind the others, bow in hand and an arrow knocked and ready. The travel, however, was slow. Without any discernible path, David had to pick through the forest. Even then, though he and Melanie had an easy enough time fitting through some of the narrow openings (and Ezra slid through everything), Walter struggled more. By the time noon came, they were all drenched in sweat.

"There's another one." David pointed straight ahead, then turned sharply to the right. "About fifty feet across."

"Roger that," Melanie said. "Once we get it well behind us, what do you think about lunch?"

Walter sat down on a nearby log. "How about right now? Lighten this pack a bit. One of you want to give me a hand?"

David shuffled to help Walter with his pack. As the straps were released he was sent tumbling under the weight.

"Walter! Good lord… what are you carrying?"

Walter ran a sleeve across his glistening brow. "Water, mostly. You said this Kansas of yours is a pretty dry place. We may see another creek soon, we may not. Better to be prepared."

David looked over his shoulder. "Ezra?"

"He's right. We don't know what's out there. And we don't know what we'll find when we get to the signal. Water is a good idea. Lunch too."

Walter smiled at Ezra. "And what makes you so agreeable all of a sudden?"

The hunter smiled back. "I don't know what you mean. I'm always in a good mood."

David didn't like it. Ezra was *never* in a good mood. He didn't want to say anything, but he suspected the hunter's steady diet of tooth had something to do with it. Not that the drug wasn't in their best interest, it had helped them steer clear of the chimera. Nevertheless, David noticed the pouch around her neck, which held so many teeth after Cinderwood, was less than half its former bulk. What's more, her eyes were becoming increasingly bloodshot. They needed to get to the sage quickly. Who knew how much longer Ezra would last.

When they started up once more, David noticed something peculiar. Melanie's hand, which had held the beacon thrust straight out when they'd started hiking, had begun to drop, lower, lower, and lower.

"Hey Melanie, I thought that thing was supposed to be level or it wouldn't work? That's what you told me."

The wild-haired girl scrunched her face in concentration. "It's not that. It's the signal. It's starting to drop."

"Drop? Like off a cliff or something?" He looked back at Walter. "Did you bring any rope?"

Walter nodded. "I did. But I don't think that's what's happening."

Ezra came to a stop. "It's not a cliff. It's a burrow. There's one ahead, and not far away either. It's old. Almost abandoned, but I can sense chimera within it."

"How many?"

"Six. Maybe more." Ezra dropped to a crouch to tighten the laces on her boots. "They're not moving around much. And I don't think they know we're here. The beacon must be down there."

"And the sage too. Right?" David asked.

Ezra shrugged then turned to Melanie. "How close do you think we are?"

"Maybe a mile. Why?"

Ezra gritted her teeth. "Going into a burrow isn't suicide, but it's close enough. We shouldn't head down unless we absolutely, positively have to."

Walter shrugged. "You're the expert. So how do we know if he's down there, or if the chimera just took a souvenir off him?"

"There's a way I can check." Ezra closed her eyelids. David could see the hunter's eyes twitching fiercely behind them. "But it might be dangerous. There's a chance, since the sage isn't from our world, I might be able to see him like I once saw you, David. But…"

David interrupted, "But you've used the tooth a lot lately. You could get hurt."

"Yes. To do this the dosage will need to be high. Very, very high."

Walter folded his arms across his chest. "I'll do it. I did it once, I can try again."

"No, Walter. I don't doubt you would see something. You may have another vision perhaps, but this requires precision. It's a risk, but still better than going into a burrow blind. But first, we get as close as possible."

●

Ezra prepared the tooth as Walter, David, and Melanie watched. David looked on with concern, Melanie with interest, and Walter with perplexity. She ignored them, focused on her work.

"That's an awfully strong batch," Walter said. "Is that... *four* teeth at once?"

"Yes." She resumed grinding with mortar and pestle.

Walter continued, "How much did you give me that one time?"

Ezra held up a single sliver of tooth to demonstrate. For someone like him, a sliver was all it took, and all he could handle. But she wanted to be sure. Because even if she didn't see the sage, she planned to look much, much further west. To the end.

"Ok. I'm nearly there." Ezra set the mortar and pestle down. She used a needle to prick the forefinger on her left hand and then squeezed three drops of blood into the powder. After returning the needle to her collection of instruments, she held the bowl over her candle. Within a minute, the powder had cooked into a bubbling mixture. She was ready.

Walter said, "How will we know what you see?"

"I will have a vision, but I'll be here physically. Even if I can't hear you, I'll be able to speak to you." She pursed her lips. "Now please, I need to concentrate."

Ezra looked down at her leg. She pulled her trousers up above her right knee. With three strokes of the razor, she sliced her exposed skin. She waited until the cuts seeped blood before applying the mixture. The olive-tinged fluid took on a life of its own, running the length of all three cuts, and then disappearing below the skin. As the tooth was absorbed, the cut healed.

The hunter took a quick breath. At first there was nothing, the last pause before the tide began—then a searing flash as the drug took effect. As always, an enormous weariness seized her. She struggled to maintain her consciousness, to fight against the potency of the teeth. Panic ran through her veins alongside chemical fire. But there was no turning back.

"Here it goes," Ezra said—or at least thought she said. She could neither feel the movement of her lips nor the vibrations in her throat. Perhaps she only imagined the words. "First comes the mundane. The natural world."

Her mind rocketed upward and she looked down on the earth below. Rocks, dirt, boulders, and streams were shown stripped of life. She *saw*, she *knew*. Ezra experienced the full understanding and awareness of every rock below her. She could see the snake and arc of the chimera burrow beneath the forest. The tunnels had no rhyme or reason, at least none she could deduce.

"I can see the burrow. It's deep, but the tunnels are intact. I don't see any collapse, only…"

She trailed away as the second layer of reality replaced the first. She saw trees, plants, moss, and lichen. Organic life covered the surface of the ground, even as it inundated the soil below. But pieces were missing. Ezra could now see the Holes—or at least the absence caused by them. Thankfully, the Holes did not pierce the chimera's burrow. That would be one less worry.

Some part of her knew she should comment, to tell the onlookers what she saw, but she didn't know how to describe it. As the second layer of reality was replaced by the third (fish), fourth (fowl), and fifth (beast), she no longer thought of her immediate surroundings. The teeth burned white-hot, intensifying her senses. She lingered for a moment to watch the heartbeat of a doe several miles from where she sat. She observed the ballet of trout as they wove through the rivers. Ezra felt herself slipping, her identity merging with those of the creatures around her. Then the next layer was revealed.

The sixth layer, the layer of man, returned Ezra to the task at hand. She could see her own body, lying on the forest floor. Walter and Melanie hovered over her, skittering back and forth with worry. She saw the somewhat-unreal form of David, his aura a tinge apart from the others. She cast her mind further.

"I see him!" Ezra cried. "It's him, it's the sage. He's in the burrow. Deep. He's standing. No, he's pacing. He looks trapped." She paused. "He's sick. I can hear his breathing. He's been underground too long. He needs to…" But she couldn't finish. Whether or not she spoke the other words, she didn't know. Her mind was splitting. The penultimate layer, the layer of the chimera, snapped into view. She could now see why the sage paced. He was trapped and guarded. Three of the creatures stood vigil. But that wasn't all. Miles away, she could also see other burrows, and still others beyond them. The land teemed with the life of her ancient enemy. The chimera were here. They hadn't died or disappeared at all. They were alive and well, thriving. And now she'd found them.

Ezra's vision flashed once more as the layer of chimera was stripped away, revealing the final level of reality: that of mathematics, gravity, and the laws of nature. This layer, mundane so many years ago, now shone terrible. Once more, she saw the ethereal signature of the sage, and the flare intensity of David. But she also saw their destination.

In a place surrounded by Holes so thick that darkness swallowed the land, Ezra saw a pinpoint of energy. This was David's epicenter. This was their goal. If only she could look closer.

The hunter strained her vision, trying to catch a glimpse of the source, but the pain was too much. Agony spread over her body, consuming her in both fire and ice, cold and electricity, as well as enlightenment, fury, joy, madness, despair, envy, and lust. She pressed on, she forced her vision to focus on the center. And there, in the white-hot blaze of nirvana—

She became lost.

●

David stared at the hunter. Ezra's eyelids were half-open, the pupils twitching back and forth. The last thing she said—before she collapsed—was that the sage was in danger. After that, she was silent. Her mouth had opened and closed; her face had twisted into every expression. But she did not speak. They tried to rouse her, but she didn't respond to their shakes or calls.

David looked at Melanie and Walter, then back to where Ezra lay. "What do we do now? How long will she be like this?"

Walter shook his head, his face grave. "I don't know. She was pretty weak from the crash to begin with. This may have taken her over the edge."

"I've seen this before," Melanie said. "Hunters would sometimes come to Memphis before crossing the Mississippi. Sometimes they'd do just what Ezra did and use a whole lot of the tooth at once. Some woke up right away, some took days." She sighed. "Sometimes, they never woke up at all. They might drink water, or eat a little food. But it was automatic. They didn't know what they were doing."

David asked, "So what then? Do we just wait and see? Do we have time for that? Should we be worried?"

Walter, who had been pacing back and forth, took a seat. "Look, David, if you're not worried, you need to look around. There's a good chance none of us are going home. You knew that going in."

"What are you saying?"

"We're here to find your sage. Thanks to Ezra, we know he's in that burrow. I say we go get him."

"But what about her?"

"We'll be back soon enough."

"No!" David barked. "She may wake up any minute, just like Melanie said. Then what? We're all gone? One of us should stay behind."

"That rules you out, David," Walter replied. "Just in case there are Holes. I'll go with you. I may not be a hunter, but if there's a fight, I can hold my own."

"Uh-uh. That's all changed now," Melanie said. "We can't fight them, not down there. Not like Ezra could. If we're going underground, we need to be quiet. And sorry to break it to you, Mr. Walter, but I'm sneakier than you. Besides, I'm better at using the beacon. It's tricky to maneuver once you get close. Flux lines and such."

David scratched his head. "I can't believe we're arguing about this. But I'm with Melanie, quiet is better." He looked at Ezra. Her muscles jerked; her jaw clenched. "And if a chimera *does* show up, someone needs to protect her. You're bigger than us."

"I guess you're right," Walter grumbled. He pulled his pack in front of him and fished through the main compartment. He came up with four flashlights and a long stretch of rope. "Here, you'll want these."

"We only need two lights," David said. "You keep one."

"Backups. Better safe than sorry. Take this too." Walter pulled out the gun he'd been carrying since Cinderwood. "Just in case."

Melanie draped the rope over her shoulder and took two of the flashlights, handing the others to David. "You ready?"

David bent down next to the hunter. He rested his hand on her shoulder. "Ezra? Come on Ezra, wake up. We need you for this."

"David, are you coming?"

"I'm coming."

As soon as they left the small copse of trees, David and Melanie lowered their voices. Without Ezra, they couldn't be sure how close the chimera were. And while they might have to face one eventually, they didn't know what to expect. So they crept through the last grove, emerging where grass, bushes, trees, and leaves stopped entirely. The once-vibrant forest ended in a barren stretch of rock. And in the middle, an opening, little more than an arm span wide. The entrance to the burrow was perfectly circular, much like the Holes. Only this hole wasn't empty.

Melanie turned on her flashlight, and David followed suit. The tunnel dropped straight down for six feet or so before twisting out of view. David looked for something to tie the rope to, but there was neither vegetation nor nearby rocks on which to secure it. He said, "I wish we had something to use as a stake."

"Why? We can't leave the rope up here. If the chi'merrys see it they'll know we're inside."

David squirmed. "Then how will we get back out?"

"I don't know. You can stand on my shoulders or something. We'll figure it out later. Now are we going to do this or not?"

"Fine." He sucked in his breath and tucked the flashlight in his pocket. He lowered himself into the tunnel until his arms were fully outstretched and he hung only by his fingertips. Then he let go.

David landed on a sandy floor. As soon as he moved aside, Melanie dropped in beside him. The two pulled out their flashlights and peered around the antechamber. The walls were stone, smooth except for spiraled grooves that twisted this way and that. Some grooves cut through rock, others were carved through dirt. Above them, the ceiling was low to the point they couldn't stand upright. And underneath, the floor was covered with fine powder. In addition to the opening above their heads, there were six other tunnels, all a little more than four feet in diameter.

Melanie shone the beam of her flashlight from one opening to the other. "Man, we're gonna get so lost in here, aren't we?"

"Kind of looks that way," he agreed. "I guess we can always follow our footprints back out. If we don't cross paths, that is. Or maybe mark along the wall." He crouched to take a handful of the fine white powder. The grains sparkled as they dropped through his fingers and back to the cave floor. "What do you think this is? Quartz?"

Melanie shook her head. "Probably a byproduct of their digestive process."

"Huh?"

"I think it's poop."

"Gross."

Melanie pulled the beacon from her flight suit and twisted it around. "Oh yeah, the signal's definitely strong in here. With any luck, the rock won't mess it up at all."

"So which way do we go?"

"Down."

David and Melanie started their descent. The burrow was a honeycomb of tunnels, as though colossal worms had chewed through the rock leaving the borings behind. At first, he tried to keep track of the twists and turns, but as they reached junction after junction, fork after fork, it became impossible. He had some hope they could retrace their footprints, but worried the chimera would use those same tracks to find them.

"Are we getting any closer?" David whispered as they reached yet another dead end. He turned around, the lead reversed as they backtracked. When they reached where they'd made their last wrong turn, he drew a line on the ground, marking off the dead end.

"Closer. Yeah, we're getting closer. But not fast. And these tunnels aren't branching out as much. So that's good. Take a right up here."

David ducked to his right. He shuffled in the half-crouch, half-crawl that he was getting better at. He used one hand to steady himself and the other to grip the flashlight. But when he reached the junction, he froze.

"Why did you stop?"

"Shhh," he whispered. "Look at that."

On the floor of the crossing tunnel was a series of long thin lines, like something had been dragged along the surface. They weren't footprints, clawprints, or hoofprints—but they were something. Were these the tracks of a chimera?

Melanie slid past him to look at the trail, careful not to disturb the markings. She glanced down at the beacon and then turned the display for him to see. "Go left here. I'll bet if we follow these tracks or whatever down that way, it'll take us right to him."

"Or right to *them*." David felt a lump growing in his throat. "Wait… they make tracks!"

"I can see that."

"No, I mean they make tracks and these are the first ones we've seen."

"So what? Finish your thoughts."

He spoke hurriedly. "If we haven't crossed their tracks before, then they didn't come in the same way we did. Which means they *don't* come in the same way we did. Which means they won't see our footprints and follow us here. What I'm saying is all we have to do is be able to get back here and we'll know the way out. And get away clean!"

"Won't they see our tracks if we go farther?"

To answer, David pushed past Melanie and stepped into the crossing tunnel. He stretched his feet wide so that each foot pushed into the wall above the crystalline trail below him. He flashed a grin and started down the tunnel. And while his movement was much slower, he no longer left footprints. Melanie, however, didn't follow.

"David... David, what's that noise?"

He strained his ears. Something was echoing down the hall, a strange skitch and ruffle sound punctuated by clicks and chirps. "Something's coming," he said. "Head back. We need to get off the path."

Panic rising in his gut, he twisted around and scurried into a side tunnel. He shut off his light and tried to be quiet. Darkness swallowed them, a blackness as deep as any Hole. The skitch and chirps came closer. The sound grew louder and louder until the rustle filled his ears. Whatever was coming—chimera or some other nasty thing—it was big. And it wasn't slowing down.

David held his breath as the scuttle reached a crescendo, one sustained for thirty seconds before slowly ebbing, becoming softer, and softer still. Soon, he couldn't hear it at all. After a minute, he turned the flashlight back on. He shone the beam at Melanie. Terror showed in her eyes.

"Should we keep going?"

Melanie didn't respond, only nodded and glanced at the beacon. She mouthed the words, *We're close.*

●

As night fell, the forest filled with sound. Walter didn't know what to call these lands. Anything west of the Mississippi had always been "the Wilds." The only other name he'd heard for it was from David. But whether they had reached Kansas, or whether their destination was far off, he couldn't know. Strange, he thought, to be in a place without a name.

To his right, Ezra lay curled on the ground. Walter had laid a blanket down and then rolled her onto it. He'd covered her with the only other blanket they had. She looked so small like this. And for the first time, Walter saw the years weighing on her. When awake, Ezra was white-hot steel wrapped in barbed wire. Now, she was just another old woman. In a way, she reminded him of his father. Both were wiry, had their own inner strength. And while Ezra was flat-out dangerous, his father had his own resolve. After all, raking oysters in your eighties wasn't a path everyone chose.

Walter swallowed hard. He'd left before they'd even had the funeral. He knew his family would understand. He had told them what his father had asked of him. But paying off that debt now seemed impossible.

"He used to hit me, you know," Walter muttered to the unconscious Ezra. "When we were kids, he'd go out drinking and come back angry. He'd beat my mother and us kids. For two years, it was like living with the Devil. Then one day—for no particular reason—he woke up, realized what he'd done, and vowed never to drink again." Walter laughed mirthlessly. "That lasted about a week before he was back out again. But he did change, you know? He'd still get drunk— powerful drunk—but he never beat us."

He folded his hands across his lap. "When I got older, I had my own problems with the bottle. They say that's common enough, runs in the family. But I've always thought that just an excuse. I almost lost my family 'cause of it. My wife, my kids. It actually took my father to set me straight. And he did too. You think that would be enough for me to forgive him, but I didn't. Maybe it was because when I looked in the mirror, I'd see him looking back. I always felt like I couldn't shake that. I always felt like I needed to prove myself. Maybe that's why I came all this way."

Walter shook his head. No. That didn't explain it. The answer had to be simpler. This wasn't about retribution. He must be crazy. That's it, he was crazy. Crazier than his father when he got drunk. Crazier than his mother when her mind began to slip. Crazier than that old radioman, and just slightly less crazy than David.

"I wish there was some way I could help you," he said. "I'm sure you'd know just what to do if it was me with too much tooth in my brain. Of course, you never saw fit to mention it. Would have been helpful."

Walter rolled the thought around in his head. He tried to think of anything that might help. If it was poison, he could make her vomit. But the tooth was in her blood. There was no getting that out. Unless, he thought, Ezra had come prepared for something like this. Of course she would have. The hunter was ready for everything else, why not this?

He opened her pack and set the contents on the ground. Despite his complaining about carrying the bulk of the weight, most of what she had was group gear: food, water, a cookpot. She had a poncho, two changes of socks, and a long length of bundled cord. There were no trinkets, no keepsakes, no mementos. Perhaps she wasn't sentimental. Hunters weren't supposed to be.

And that was all. Nothing remained in the pack, and even a patting down of the leather revealed no hidden compartments. Then his eye fell on Ezra's instruments for preparing the tooth. Walter shuffled over to the black silk square and spread it flat.

He'd never taken a full look at the kit; he'd been too distracted by the process. There was the small scalpel, the needle, and the mortar and pestle. But there were other implements as well: a piece of flint and some matches, some kind of screen, a strainer, and an array of hooks, picks, and files. Lastly, unnoticed at first, was a small leather box with the word "anti" branded on one side.

Walter removed the case and popped it open. There was a syringe inside filled with purple liquid. But there was no writing, no label, no hint as to the use. Perhaps this was an antidote for chimera poison, or a simple snakebite. Maybe it was a way to commit an honorable suicide, an antidote to life itself. Or perhaps this was what he hoped for, a countermeasure against the tooth. If so, it could bring Ezra back from her trance and—God willing—make her useful again.

There was one other option to consider. Seven teeth remained from the massacre of Cinderwood, a mere fraction of what Ezra started with. Perhaps the overuse had made her sick instead of the single large dose. Maybe her system just needed to turn out the tooth in good time. Or, maybe she needed a jolt. Maybe giving her one last hit of tooth would put the fire back in her veins.

A screech echoed behind Walter. Acting on reflex, he hunched down and remained as quiet as possible. He knew that sound from Cinderwood. The chimera had taken to the skies. Maybe they were looking for him, maybe not. Maybe they already knew where he was and were simply getting others. Either way, waiting for Ezra to wake up wasn't an option. He needed to act.

As the sound of the creatures faded, Walter looked back at Ezra. He hefted the pouch of teeth in one hand, and the syringe of antidote in the other. "Which'll it be, old girl? There's not much time, and those kids need our help. I can't have you lying around all night. So which is it?" He studied her face, looking for some hint of direction. All or nothing. One or the other. Something had to be tried.

"Here we go. Let's hope this does the trick."

Walter looped the bag of teeth around his neck then scooted over to the hunter. He removed the purple syringe, pulled off the top protecting it, and looked for a suitable place to inject. Though he hadn't a clear understanding of what to do, he decided to start with the source. He'd deliver the shot in the same place she'd administered the tooth. He swallowed hard, and pushed down on the plunger.

Time passed. The stars above changed from grayish blips to intense jewels in the ebon canopy. Ezra, however, did not stir. Walter checked her pulse. Her heartbeat was weak, her breathing shallow. Whatever had been in the syringe didn't appear to have done anything at all.

"Ok. Time for plan B." Walter went back to the instruments. He pulled one of the remaining teeth from the pouch, then picked up the razor. He ran the blade along the length of the tooth to make the long clean sliver that Ezra had done with such grace. But the process was far more difficult than he expected. Chips and splinters filled the bowl, but there was no beauty to it.

Next, Walter moved to prepare the tooth with the mortar and pestle. When the powder had been ground, he removed the needle Ezra used to prick her finger and mix in the blood. Walter at first went to prick himself, then realized that maybe the mixture wouldn't work without a person's own blood. He pulled Ezra's hand from underneath the blanket and pricked her finger.

And at that moment, the hunter stirred.

Walter flinched. Ezra's eyes slowly opened, and she pulled herself to a seated position. The hunter regarded him as grogginess gave way to lucidity.

"The tooth," she rasped, "is its own kind of poison. Poison can't cure poison. It doesn't work that way. If that was indeed your plan."

"Ezra!" He yelped, then forced himself to a whisper. "You're back."

The hunter cast her eyes at the night sky. "I've been out a while, I see." She glanced around. "David and Melanie?"

"They went in the burrow. They've been gone a few hours." Walter grimaced. "I was getting anxious."

"And so you thought to poke me to pass the time?"

"I was trying to wake you up."

"And so you…" Ezra froze; her face blanched. She pointed to the empty syringe. "Walter? The antidote. Did you… did you use that on me?"

"I think it woke you up."

She shut her eyes and leaned her head back. "Yes, yes it would. It counteracts the tooth. It is to help those who have gone too far. As perhaps I did."

Walter smiled. "Lucky guess, then. I was worried it was—"

Ezra winced. "And it's permanent." She leveled her gaze. "I'll never be able to use the tooth again." Her jaw tightened. "Don't tell the others."

"Well, that's up to you."

Walter waited, a lump thick in his throat, but the hunter spoke no more. Then slowly, soft at first and building strength, Ezra's bitter sobs filled the night.

●

David edged forward. He peered down the corridor. Whatever had passed by was now gone. The dual line markings had been swept away, replaced by a different signature, two thin streaks on the outer edge, and a single jagged imprint in the middle. Perhaps each chimera left its own particular footprint.

Melanie pointed down the tunnel, and David continued. He splayed his feet wide to avoid leaving tracks. He moved forward, and down. The tunnel spiraled as it descended, each corner just out of sight.

David turned to Melanie. *How close?* he mouthed.

She responded by holding up the face of the beacon. The number read "567" but that meant nothing to him. She gestured for him to keep going.

As they rounded the next bend they dropped straight down a steep slope. The tunnel leveled out before snaking again to the right, then left, then right again. As they twisted, the character of the tunnel changed. The grooves on the walls became more spaced. The passage widened. Tunnel broadened into chamber, and then chamber into cavern. What's more, there was light here. He flicked off his flashlight, and Melanie followed suit. A weak amber glow pulsed in and out of view. At first, he could barely see, but as his eyes adjusted, the cavern stretched ahead. No longer overpowered by the flashlight's beam, the cavern filled out. The cave bulged, the walls no longer regular. He felt he was inside a massive, half-deflated pool toy. But something was nestled in the corners and nooks. Something moving.

David dropped low. The chimera were huddled against the walls. As in Cinderwood, each held a different form, though all a variant of insect. The opaque wings, the sickly black carapaces, and the segmented legs twitched back and forth. Did the chimera not see them? Were they asleep? He looked down. His footprints were easily visible on the floor.

A high-pitched sound filled the air. After the squeal came a flutter, the maraca of the chimera changing shape. The shriek stopped, then started again, this time accompanied by other squeals of different pitches and intensity. When the sound had become so loud, so unbearable, that David thought he would scream, another noise rose behind it. The clicks and squeaks ceased, replaced by the buzzsaw of chimera wings. Though afraid to look at them directly, he saw the shadows of the creatures swarming the cave. The buzz of wings peaked and quickly diminished. He looked out from his hiding spot to watch the last of the chimera fly through a passage on the far side of the cavern.

"They left," David whispered.

Melanie's eyes were wide. "All of them?"

He shrugged. "I don't know. But this might be our chance."

Melanie sprang to her feet. With beacon outstretched in her right hand, she scurried along the cavern floor. Her direct-line path shifted as she moved in a parabolic arc, then closer, closer, until she stopped at the far wall. She placed her hand on the stone.

"This is it. The beacon's just past here."

David shuffled next to her. He knocked tentatively against the rock. "Hello? Hello, is anyone there?"

No response.

Melanie said, "It's on the other side. We have to get in somehow. Do you see any way through?" David and Melanie split. He moved down the left side of the wall, and she moved down the right. "I think I found something," she whispered.

He skipped over to her side. There was a tunnel bored into the rock. But unlike elsewhere in the cavern, this one was blocked by a loose pile of stones. Though the rocks were large, there were small openings around the edges. He flipped on his light and peered around the corners. "I think I can squeeze through. Pull me out if I get stuck." He dropped to his belly and slid forward. He found that if he put one arm out in front of him with the other behind, and if he angled his shoulders just so, then he could… maybe… just… fit.

David squeaked in surprise as a dry, calloused hand grasped his forearm. The grip tightened as it pulled him forward and through the pile of rubble. He peered up in disbelief to see the shaved-smooth head, the drooping mustache, and the grinning face of Dr. Remus Alabaster. The sage.

18

REMUS

David looked up at the sage. Much of the man was the same as when last they met. His head was shaved clean, his skin smooth, his complexion immaculate. The man's bright blue eyes twinkled with inquisitiveness, a sentiment that reached to either end of his long mustache. As for the rest of him, the sage appeared somewhat the worse for wear. While his muscles rippled with the physique of a yogi-master, his jeans were now cut-off and frayed. The sage's *Rolling Stones* T-shirt bore holes and stains. He didn't appear to be a beaten man, only one bereft of civilization.

"Well, well, I believe this is a twist of the plot of our own good story." The sage's grin spread wider. "Here I was, desperate to escape so I could find you, and you're on my doorstep. In my doorstep, rather. But my word, David. How are you? Wonderful to see you again." The sage thrust his hand forward in greeting.

David was dumbstruck. He'd been so focused on finding this man, he hadn't thought about what he would do next. "Um, Mr. Sage…?"

"Call me Remus. The hour of our formality has passed."

"Ok, Mr. Remus, we need to get out of here."

A muffled voice sounded from behind them. "Hey! Hey David. Is he in there? Is he ok?"

David twisted around and peered through the rubble. "Yeah, he's all right. How do things look on that side?"

"No sign of the chi'merrys," Melanie called. "But no telling when they'll be back. We need to move."

"A capital idea," the sage said. "But I must ask, are they all gone, or just the guards?"

"I'm pretty sure they all are," David said. "They flew out in a hurry for some reason." The thought flitted across his mind that he and his friends might just be that reason.

"Well, then subtlety aside, and with a lookout in place, I think the time has come to take this carnival elsewhere." The sage called into the tunnel. "Hello, how many on the other side?"

"Just me. It's Melanie from…"

"Oh yes, Melanie from Memphis. I remember you. Five-three, blond hair, penchant for idioms, and fetish for conditioner. And such a delightful story you tell. Melanie, I need you to help get David back through."

"I can do that."

"Excellent." The sage bounded to the back of the cave and reemerged with a thick rope, a green canvas bag, and a knotted collection of cords that trailed from the opening. The sage opened the sack and pulled out a long, cylindrical shape. "David, this is an explosive. A bomb. I've made several for the occasion. I want you to crawl back out the way you came, then pull the bag behind you. Once you're out, place these charges around the door on all sides, like so." The sage pointed at the edges of the door. "The one thing you're not to do is break these wires. I'll use those to detonate the charges. Once everything is set, you and Melanie get as far away from the door as possible. Hide behind a rock or something."

David scratched his head. "Where did you get bombs?"

The sage winked. "I made them. It's not important right now. Anyway, I thought you said we were in a hurry? Understand what to do?"

"Yeah, I think so."

"Splendid. Now off to it. We haven't much time."

David hopped to action. He tied the rope around his right ankle and then shimmied back through the gap in the rocks. The squeeze was much tighter this way, but with the sage pushing from one end, and Melanie tugging from the other, he was soon through. He pulled on the rope to retrieve the canvas bag, and then set the charges as directed.

"Ok, sir. They're ready."

"Great. In twenty seconds. Ready? One, two, three…"

David took off at a run, pulling Melanie behind him. Without much time to pick a spot, they crouched behind a pile of large rocks near the exit. He ticked off the seconds in his head, keeping the mental count alongside the sage. After reaching "seventeen" a great hissing began. Daring a peek, he saw a trail of sparks burn from the entry of the cave and move along the fuses. He snaked back into his hiding spot. He shut his eyes and covered his ears.

The charges erupted. A muffled thud sounded, followed by a wave of flame. Fire licked around the edges of David and Melanie's shelter, then flickered to nothingness. Waiting several seconds before daring to look out, he edged around the boulder.

The cavern had been transformed. Explosive residue dripped from the walls, coating the floor in fiery patches. As for the rocks blocking the tunnel, more than half had been scattered. David watched as the remaining stones shifted, then tumbled outward. The sage stood triumphant in the opening, his grin shining through a layer of soot. He disappeared for a moment and then emerged with a heavy leather bag in one hand. He swung the pack onto his back and winked.

"And now, my friends, I trust you know the way out?"

Melanie skipped over to his side. "You bet we do, Mr. Sage."

"Please, call me Remus."

"Whatever floats your boat, grandpa. Now come on."

Melanie took the lead as they crossed the cavern and climbed back to where their tunnel had opened up. If hesitation remained in her mind, David couldn't detect it. When the passage narrowed, Melanie straddled the crystalline powder lining the bottom of the tunnel. "You've got to stand like this. That way they can't see our tracks."

Remus nodded. "I think speed is more important than tracks. In case they heard me open the door, so to speak. I am curious, though, how did you find me?"

David pointed to Melanie. "It was her idea. She has a beacon."

The sage nodded thoughtfully, then grinned once more. "Very nice. That's what I assumed. Though in a world such as this, with hunters, second sight, chimera, and teeth, I did not jump to conclusions. But as you mentioned, we should probably get moving."

David took the lead to watch for Holes with the sage following. Melanie lagged behind to listen for chimera. They shuffled along the corridor until they were back to the junction where they'd first seen the chimera tracks. David shone his flashlight down the side passage. At the end of the beam's range, he could see his and Melanie's footprints.

"This way," he whispered. He set off down the passage, and soon he was back where their tracks had led. This was the part that made him nervous. They'd taken more than one wrong turn on their way here. And except for the marks he'd made in the powder, they had no other signs to guide them. He took a deep breath and moved forward.

David crept in silence, the sage and Melanie on his tail. And though his mind brimmed with questions, secrecy was more important. All the answers in the world meant nothing unless they escaped. With his flashlight down, he moved as fast as he could, retracing his footprints. But whether by luck or fate, the path remained clear. And so they ascended, up and up and up, until finally he was forced to stop.

In front of them lay a seven-way junction, one of several at the upper reaches of the burrow. David knew they must be near the topmost passages. But here the footprints stopped. The marks had been wiped clean, replaced by the etched trail of a chimera's passing.

"This is bad," he mumbled.

When Melanie caught up, she poked her head around the sage. She continued in the stage whisper only one hair quieter than her regular voice. "You're right this is bad. This means we've got a chi'merry sliding around up here."

"I believe," the sage interrupted, " the issue is not just the chimera, but our path. What do you propose?"

"You're asking me?" David looked at the sage in horror. "What can we do? There are six wrong ways, and only one right one."

"No, David, not so many. Think. Six ways to go, seven if you count the way we came, but are there truly six paths?"

David wrinkled his brow, why was the sage doing this? It was like he knew the answer, but didn't want to tell. And though confused, he stumbled on the solution. "No, you're right. There are only two ways to go. The others don't have our tracks, or chimera tracks, so we couldn't have gone through there."

Melanie sighed. "So what, flip a coin? Give one a shot? Break up? We could still get pretty lost, but I'm game."

The sage tapped his chin in thought. "Now, my friends, while I believe this affords an excellent teaching opportunity, I'm afraid we must pass it by in the interest of haste."

David and Melanie exchanged confused looks with one another. In response, the sage removed a metal box from his pocket and flicked it open. With a spark, a flame appeared at the lighter's head.

"Don't breathe."

The sage concentrated on the flame, and then David saw it too. The flame flickered as it moved, leaning first one way then the other as it tilted in the direction of the tunnel. "The flame," the sage explained, "moves as the air moves. If we are near the exit, then no matter how slight, there would be an exchange of air above with below. And while I give no guarantees, I believe this is the right way to go." The sage snapped the lighter shut and pointed to the leftmost tunnel lined with chimera's tracks. "After you, my young friend. And do be careful. We're not alone down here."

David took the lead once more. But with every twist and turn, as their own tracks did not reappear, he wondered if they were simply following a chimera. Nevertheless, they continued to climb until he saw something ahead that made him want to weep with joy.

Melanie spoke first. "Look, guys. It's light! We made it."

David nodded, but the fear in his belly wouldn't subside. He moved forward until he stood just beneath the entrance. Cool moonlight streamed in through the opening above them. The smell of fresh air filled his nostrils.

David turned to the sage. "Remus sir, would you give me a boost?"

"Gladly."

Melanie and the sage each held one of David's feet and hoisted him upward. David stretched his arms, and then his fingers found purchase on the rim. Kicking and scrambling, he emerged into the topside world. Before making another move, he scanned the area. But while tracks circled the entrance, he saw no chimera.

"Are we clear?" Melanie shouted from below.

"Looks that way. Come on up."

With a boost and a scramble, Melanie soon knelt beside him. David prepared to lower a rope for the sage, and was surprised when the man leaped upward, his fingers pressing hard against the walls. The sage scurried up the passageway with the ease of climbing a ladder. Once topside, he collapsed beside them and laughed.

"Ah, freedom," the sage sighed. "Glorious, glorious freedom. Wonderful it is, if only for a moment."

David looked at him. "What do you mean?"

"I mean him."

The sage pointed into the darkness at the edge of the clearing. A man walked toward them. He wore a neatly-tailored black suit with pointed black shoes and a pressed black shirt. The man smiled at them, perfect teeth glinting in the moonlight. His face was chiseled, strong. But the smile was more unsettling than friendly. And then David realized just how familiar the face was. The clothes and hair were different, and the mustache was missing, but it was the face of the sage.

●

The man in the black suit walked steadily toward them, his hands folded behind his back. In that time, the grin never wavered, though his eyes flicked from the sage, to David, to Melanie, and back to the sage once more. When he had come within ten feet, he stopped. And waited.

Finally, the man in black spoke. "My dear Remus, where are your manners? First, you leave without saying goodbye, and now you fail to introduce your friends. Perhaps you do need to get out more."

The sage scowled. "Don't be fooled, kids. This is a chimera. And as they don't give themselves names, I've been calling him Johnny Cash on account of his wardrobe. And we're not twins."

The man in black bowed low.

"And," the sage continued, "before he charms you. Know that he's also the duplicitous ass who sealed me up down there. Don't trust him."

Mr. Cash's smile widened. "You were ever quick to judge, Remus. And you forget I acted in the interest of my world. You had to be waylaid. As you must be again. As all of you must. I'm afraid that hasn't changed."

David said, "You don't sound like other chimera."

Mr. Cash nodded. "I've had considerably more practice with speaking aloud. It is, shall we say, my specialty."

The sage turned to David and Melanie. "They aren't as faceless as you'd think. They're organized. There's no queen bee or anything. But they have a society."

Mr. Cash responded, "Telling stories once more, Remus? How easily you fall into your old ways. But I think such things are of little interest now. There are, if you will, more pressing matters."

"How did you find us?" Melanie asked.

The chimera chuckled. "You exploded a bomb in a burrow. We could have stopped you there, but I thought it more interesting if you made it to the surface. We must stay interesting, after all. And I would hate to miss this opportunity to chat. With all of you. Now your other friends, they are different. They are too dangerous to be left alive. My brethren will find them soon enough, and so our conversation can be undisturbed. Once they are back, no doubt they will resume with their silly plan."

Melanie stepped forward. She glanced up and down at the chimera shaped like a man. "What plan? You just said there was a plan. So what plan are you talking about? Why is it silly?"

The sage grumbled. "I'll tell them. You speak prettily enough, but you haven't the art of explanation. Do you mind if I provide the context?"

"Not at all." Mr. Cash folded his arms across his chest. "I suppose they deserve to know. Call it a last kindness."

The sage nodded in acceptance. "In that case—and since we are all being civil here—what do you say we step a bit away from the burrow? If one of your family does come out, then I think our 'nice little chat' will be over."

Mr. Cash bowed deeply. "Very well, I'll take your lead. But not too far."

David took a step forward, moving the same way they had come in. His mind flashed to Walter's pistol sitting heavy in his front pocket. Perhaps all he needed was an opportunity.

♦

"I first met Mr. Cash," the sage began, "after learning I was stuck in this world. Once I accepted that unfortunate fact, I no longer made a secret of what I was doing. So I sought out others who might aid the evaluation of my data. There was a scholar in New Amsterdam, a teacher in Columbia, and a philosopher in Cinderwood. All of these thinkers helped me develop my ideas. But they were provincials, so to speak. But once I announced my presence, the chimera came looking for me, with Mr. Cash as their envoy. He told me he had visited other worlds, that he was as familiar with the Holes. I didn't care he wasn't human. I needed allies." The sage gestured to the chimera. "Would you like to take it from here?"

Mr. Cash nodded. "Certainly. Your friend Remus was closer to his answers than he knew. But his premise was incorrect. He sought an abstract. He hoped by gleaning truth, bit by bit, he would understand the Holes. Our approach was more direct. We looked for trends. And just as Remus had traveled down from world to world, so did we ascend. We passed *up* to the other planes of existence. We looked both at dying worlds and ones already dead. We found no single cause, but we did find a pattern."

David looked up expectantly. "What was it?"

"The Holes," Mr. Cash answered, "always follow a fight, a great event, an amazing feat, or a monumental struggle. And once that struggle—whatever it may be—is concluded, then the Holes appear. The events themselves could be quite dissimilar. In some places, it was a war between people, in others the achievement of travel through the stars, and in others the conquering of disease. But no matter what the struggle, once over, the Holes would come."

For the first time, Mr. Cash's grin disappeared. "We developed a theory: Every world has a destiny. And each destiny is punctuated by a final battle. That battle is the reason worlds exist. But once the battle is won, the vitality of a world fades. It no longer has a purpose; it no longer has a reason. The Holes are the rusting of a world without use. Think, my friends, a story with no conflict has no reason to be told. We did not wish that to happen to *our* story."

David squinted in concentration. "So you did quit the war to stop the Holes." He paused. "But it didn't work."

Mr. Cash shrugged. "Yes. Perhaps we were mistaken that there needed to be a victor. Perhaps when we quit fighting, the resolution was reached all the same. Not all endings are requisite of bloodshed."

"But what about the sage?" David asked. "What about Remus? What does any of this have to do with him? Or me? Why didn't you want me to find him, or him to find the source of the Holes? If the Holes are here, this world is already dying. So why do you want to stop us?"

The grin dropped once more from Mr. Cash's lips. "Your task, David, is as great as any of the final struggles in any world we've seen. Greater. We believe it may be the struggle of *all* worlds. This struggle could be the linchpin—the element holding it all together. *Everything.* If you or Remus were to succeed, there may be no reason for *any* world to exist. After all, the Holes are the only problem tying all worlds together. Why wouldn't discovering their underlying cause be the greatest achievement of all? And if so, it could mean the end of everything. You are a linchpin of linchpin."

"Wait." David squinted one eye. "How can stopping the Holes bring more Holes. Wouldn't they be stopped at that point?"

"I didn't say stop them. I said understand them. They can never be stopped. But they can be delayed. And they must."

The sage ground his teeth. "And that, David, is why the chimera don't just kill us. If they did so, then the battle would be lost. And if they turn us loose, and we succeed, then the battle would be won— which is just as bad in their eyes. Either way, the chimera think they'll lose. So they lock us away and hope they're right about it all. The linchpin won't move, and the conflict will never find a resolution. The story will go on."

Mr. Cash shrugged. "Not exactly. But close enough."

●

Clouds passed in front of the moon, rolling in from the west and plunging the night into darkest black. The dimming bulbs from their flashlights provided the only light. David, Melanie, and the sage were all seated now. Mr. Cash knelt in front of them, his grin re-affixed.

The chimera said, "That's why I can't let you continue. Surely you understand what's at risk. Everything."

"You're wrong." David balled his fists. "The Holes are already here. We can't ignore them and hope they go away. We have to stop them. You're just ignoring what's already happened. You're just…"

The sage broke in, "Shutting the door after the cat's already out. I've been saying that all along."

Mr. Cash's smile took on an air of condescension. "You think too small, David. Perhaps this world will be lost. But others still live. We can't risk those as well." The chimera's eyes gained a faraway look. "But I don't particularly care. After all, I don't believe you and your friends are the *only* ones on this quest. In my opinion, destiny is inevitable."

A chill crept over David's skin. "What do you mean?"

"Destiny can be delayed, but never stopped. And whether we put you in a prison, or whether you are stopped more forcefully, one day someone will fulfill that destiny. *Someone* will unlock the secret of the Holes. It doesn't have to be you. You aren't special. And you aren't unique."

The sage stood from the ground and dusted the dirt from his jeans. "And that, my friends, is his way of saying he intends to kill us after all."

David scrambled to stand beside the sage. "Then why even bother explaining? Why not just do it?"

"Shhh," Melanie whispered, "don't provoke him."

Mr. Cash shrugged. "Think of it as a parting gift. But now David Winters, Remus Alabaster, Melanie Wrightshift, I'm afraid *your* destiny has arrived. *Your* story has come to an end."

Though David stood frozen, Melanie acted. She did not squeal or scream. She simply ran, sprinting into the trees. Mr. Cash followed her with his eyes, grinned once more, then he transformed. The chimera rippled as the color drained from his body and clothes. Mr. Cash's formal attire morphed into an oily black slick. The creature's chest split open, as though turning inside out. Spines bristled from the open shell, which changed to an arachnid's legs tipped with spikes. The body of Mr. Cash folded backward, and then back on itself as oily skin hardened into armor. Rows of segments knitted together as the creature reared up.

"*Run!*" the sage shouted, as he dashed in the other direction.

David dove to the side. He wrestled to pull free Walter's gun. But the chimera (that was once Mr. Cash) still had its sights on Melanie. David drew the pistol and fired. He shot three times. And from the chimera's screech of pain, each shot had connected. The beast wheeled to charge him. But even as it leaped forward, a flash of light greeted him, followed by an explosion.

"Forget someone, Johnny?" The sage came up grinning. He clutched a familiar cylinder that showered sparks as the fuse burned down. "This is for locking me away!" The sage hurled the device at the chimera. The tube detonated as it hit, sending Mr. Cash flying back. David took the chance to shoot again. He emptied the remainder of the bullets into the shrieking monster.

But whether its ancient age, hardened cunning, or simply that not all chimera were created equal, the beast did not fall. Mr. Cash reared up. Several tentacles hung lifeless from its back; much of its body now burned with residue from the sage's bombs. And yet it was not defeated. It loosed a roar and lashed out again. The first strike missed. The attack steered off-target due to another explosion. But the second attack landed, tearing into David's arm, and flooding his body with agony.

David dropped, the pain too intense even to move. Now the chimera shifted his focus to Remus. Just as the creature turned, the sage threw another explosive. But this time the chimera was ready. It plucked the bomb from the air with its tentacle and tossed it aside. The chimera paused. He watched.

"Last one, Remus," it hissed.

"It's all I need," the sage sneered. And then David realized why. The bomb Remus held was several times the size of the others, and the wick was nearing its end. The sage was waiting until the last moment so that the bomb couldn't be deflected again. "Time to meet *your* destiny."

The sage hurled the device at the chimera, and Mr. Cash reacted. The right side of the creature lurched forward, separating from the main body and flying to meet the bomb. The fragment of the chimera transformed as it flew, shifting into a mass of black substance, which spread out like a net and then wrapped around the charge. Milliseconds later, the bomb exploded. Fire and residue of chimera flew everywhere. But while much of the chimera had been destroyed, some remained. The surviving part morphed once more, shifting into a humanoid shape, though with insect legs, reptilian arms, and the slender wings of a dragonfly. The creature may not have retained its former bulk, but it looked just as deadly.

The chimera spoke. "It's more satisfying this way. Better this than slipping and falling, catching a corner of a Hole, and being dragged down. This is a real end." It reared back, the reptilian arms transformed into serrated blades. There was a hiss in the air, followed by a hollow "thwock." Mr. Cash screamed in pain.

The shaft of an arrow protruded from the creature's right eye. On the opposite side of the clearing, Ezra stood tall, Walter and Melanie flanking her. The old hunter held her bow at the ready. She drew another arrow, pulled back, but did not yet release. She didn't need to. The chimera gave one last cry and then took to the air. But as it rose, it exploded. Fragments of the creature splattered and dissolved in all directions. Nothing else remained.

"And now," Ezra said. "We run."

19

SIDEWAYS

When David awoke, the sun was at mid-morning high. Light streaked through the trees onto emerging grass mottled with leaves. He tried to push himself up and was rewarded with searing pain along his left arm. The night had been a blur of pain and panic. They had run. Through the woods with no light, no direction, no path, and the distant buzzsaw of chimera wings at times far, and at times far too close. They'd gone in periods of reckless sprints and quiet huddles, as they tried in turn to get as far from the burrow as possible, and also to remain unseen. At last, when far past the point of exhaustion, they had taken refuge under the wide, sweeping branches of an oak. Even then the had scattered, staying a dozen yards from each other in the event that the chimera did come, that not all of them would be lost. Over time, the sound of the chimera became less, and David succumbed to exhaustion.

Walter walked over to where David lay. He nodded and handed him a canteen. "Morning. How do you feel?"

"Awful. Why didn't you wake me up?"

"You needed the sleep. We all did. I think Ezra is the only one who stayed up all night. She thinks we're safe for now."

David scanned the campsite. The morning's activities held no trace of last night's terror. Ezra was busy doing something with her bow. Melanie was leaning against a tree paging through a book. And as for the sage, he had no less than nine books fanned around him on the ground, which he flipped through while scribbling notes. Remus caught David's eye and flashed him a smile.

"Well, well," he clucked, "I guess that's everybody. So do we get to it now, or do you need to catch your breath?"

David yawned. "I wouldn't mind something to eat. I'm pretty hungry."

"Of course you are." The sage smiled. "Walter, grab the boy some food. Melanie, Ezra, you two gather round. We need to discuss our plans."

Walter fished some dried fruit and nuts from his backpack and handed them to David. "Our plan was to find you. That's about all the plan we had."

Ezra shook her head. "No, Walter, you've got that wrong. The plan has always been to find the source of the Holes. We must keep heading west."

The hunter pulled a sheet of paper from her pack. On one side was the map they had taken from Joby at the radio tower. But on the back, there was an intricate drawing, complete with topographical lines, rivers, mountains, and other landmarks.

David gasped. "How did you do this?"

Ezra tapped her forehead. "My vision. I wanted to get the detail down before the memory faded." She pointed to the center of the map. "That's the middle. That's where we're going. From what Melanie and I estimate, we've got a hundred and fifty miles to go. If our pace is good, we can be there in two weeks."

"That's assuming," Walter remarked, "we have no more run-ins with chimera, bandits, fanatics, or hurricanes. But you're kind of a magnet for that, huh David?"

David ignored him. "I doubt the chimera will quit looking for us. Even if Mr. Cash is gone, there are still the others." He looked around the circle. "Did Remus explain what the chimera said?"

Walter answered. "About the end of the world? If I've got this right, either we learn what causes the Holes, which will make the world end, or we don't figure it out, and the world ends anyway."

The sage chuckled. "My friend Walter, I am impressed with your ability to summarize a situation of inter-dimensional 'damned if you do, damned if you don't' regarding the very fabric of reality, into one sentence. Bravo."

Walter chuckled. "Hey, someone has to get to the point. Either way, it's trouble."

"Indeed." The sage laughed again. "So it's just a matter of point A to point B. But I don't recommend walking."

Melanie frowned in disgust. "Well, Mr. Remus, the plane is busted, we left the car back in Memphis, and I don't see what else we can do." She squinted one eye. "Unless *you've* got an idea."

The sage flicked the end of his mustache and released a snicker. "Hah! I've collected a million tales of triumph in over a hundred worlds. It's not a matter of whether I have ideas, but which one we should use."

"Ok, so what are your ideas?" Walter asked.

"Well, we could walk, as Madam Hunter suggested. On the other hand, we could try to capture and domesticate a horse, or repair the plane, or trick a chimera into carrying us... Aha! We could fashion a hot air balloon and sail to Kansas! It would be very L. Frank Baum of us, which has both a poetic element about it and is a decent idea to boot. Now there is the matter of prevailing winds usually blowing from west to east, but I could puzzle that out if given enough—"

Ezra set her jaw. "Sage Remus. The chimera are looking for us. And as you know, they can fly. A balloon would be taken in minutes. As for your other ideas," she ticked them off on her fingers, "you can't trick a chimera; it would take longer to repair the plane than it would take to walk; and the same goes with finding and domesticating animals."

The sage narrowed his eyes. "So what do you propose? I'm all ears."

"I propose," Ezra growled, "that you just tell us your *real* idea and quit wasting time." When the sage opened his mouth to protest, Ezra cut him off. "Don't even start. I've seen your calculations, I've seen your measurements, and I've seen your lists."

"So, you were spying on me."

"I don't know you, sir. I was being cautious. Do you have a plan or not?"

The sage stuck out his lower lip. "I've never found a group of individuals so opposed to suspense and intrigue in all my life. But very well. If you insist, I do have a plan. And it's one I arrived at only after exploring all other options, which you seem so incapable of doing, trusting instead I will make the correct decision in a vacuum—which is a very unscholarly way to go about it."

Ezra delivered another glare at the sage, this time joined by Walter and, to no small part, Melanie. David, however, simply waited.

The sage continued, "I've spent years of my life sliding down from one world to the next. Which was fine until I came here and could drop no lower. So I thought, what if I moved in a different direction? If the chimera can ascend to worlds above, why can't I?"

David frowned. "We don't need to get to another world. We need to get to Kansas. We're so close."

"And I'm not finished. If you weren't so impatient, I'd have continued to say that what I was more intrigued about was whether I could not only move from world to world, but if I could do so precisely. Perhaps I could choose not just my direction, but my location. And if I can move from world to world, precisely, then why not move from point to point, precisely? I'm speaking, my friends, about a sideways Hole."

Walter raised an eyebrow. "So no hot air balloon?"

"Certainly not. Don't be ridiculous." The sage grinned. "No balloons, no horses, no saddled chimeras, and certainly not plain old walking. We simply start here, and end there." He pointed to Ezra's map. "Well, maybe not the whole way there, that might be dangerous. But near enough we can walk without too much trouble."

"And you know how to do that?" Walter asked.

"I think I know enough to try." The sage reached into his pocket and pulled out a folded list of ingredients. He handed the paper to Ezra. "Here are the things I'll need. What do you think?"

"What about the chimera?" David asked. "Won't they be looking for us?"

Ezra shrugged. "Perhaps. And if so, I'll be ready. Nevertheless, we shouldn't linger." She turned back to the sage and tucked the list in her pocket. "I think I can find most of this. But if I decide I can't, we start walking."

Walter frowned deeply. "Wait. I don't get it. If you could make a sideways Hole, then why didn't you just make one to escape?"

The sage snorted in disgust. "If I thought they'd have brought me all those things, I might have. But it was hard enough just to get what I needed to make those bombs. The chimera can be gullible at times, but they're not stupid. At least not conventionally so. And even if I had all I needed, there was also the matter of being underground. I wouldn't want to wind up a hundred miles away, just to be buried in dirt." He tapped his chin. "Now can we get to work? You four start collecting. I have to refine my calculations."

●

They started out together. Ezra took the lead with David right behind looking for Holes, Melanie and Walter trailing. Whenever the hunter pointed out one of the ingredients on the sage's list (whether mineral, herb, or otherwise), they'd collect it and retrace their steps to the campsite. They spent three hours like that, gathering the various items until they were down to just a few specimens. At that point, Ezra sent Walter and Melanie to help the sage with his preparations, while she and David went for the last ingredients.

Ezra and David traveled through the forest, following a game trail near the hillside.

"Wait," David said. "Not that way. There's a Hole, three feet across. It runs right up to the cliff. Want me to take you around it?"

Ezra squinted at the hillside. "Can you see that plant with the little yellow flowers? Below the slope, next to the pointed brown rock."

"Nope. Just the Hole."

The hunter shook her head in disgust. She sat cross-legged and motioned for him to join her.

"David, there's something you need to know. I can't see the Holes anymore. Not even in the partial way I could."

"Because you're not using the tooth?"

Ezra hesitated. "That's right, but not just that. You see, I was too far gone. Walter used an antidote on me. I can't ever use the tooth again. I can't help in the way I used to."

David gave her an accepting smile. "It's ok. Don't forget you've still got me." His smile broadened. "I don't need you stealing my thunder."

Ezra frowned, her face worried. "But what if *you* couldn't see the Holes anymore? Would you feel like you still belonged with us?"

"That's a weird question. Yeah, I mean I guess I belong with you as much as anywhere. To be fair, I don't really belong here at all. I kind of think that's why I want to keep going. As long as I'm moving, it's almost like I'm still with my brothers."

"On your way to save the world?"

"Yep."

For a few moments, David remained silent. It had been over a year since he was back home. Was his home even still there? He looked back at Ezra. The pained look was still on her face. "Are you ok?"

"I'm adjusting. You see, the tooth is… it's part of being a hunter. For a long time, that's all I've had."

"You're still a hunter, Ezra. Tooth or not, that's who you are." He smiled. "But come on, we've got work to do. Do you remember seeing any more of those flowers? I think the Hole ruins this one."

Ezra's eyes snapped back to alert. "Yes. Yes, of course. Follow me. It's just over that ridge." A pause. "No Holes that way?"

"Nope."

"Thank you."

David and Ezra trekked over the hill where they found a small patch of the flowers. Though the sage's list called for only two, they took four. They'd grabbed a double dose of everything. That had been Walter's idea, in case the sage made a mistake or wasn't able to make enough of whatever he was mixing. If anything else, it would save them from making a second trip. And if it actually worked, maybe this same trick could eventually take them home.

Once the flower had been obtained, David and Ezra returned to the campsite. The area had been transformed. Pots and pans, boots, gloves, cord, knives, and tools had been repurposed into a chemistry set. Canteens bubbled with purple gas. The coals from the fire heated six dishes of percolating mixture. And—to Ezra's visible dismay—the hunter's mortar and pestle were in heavy use grinding up ingredients.

The sage grinned as they approached. "Ezra, David, I hope you found my yellow-spotted marigold."

David handed the flowers to the sage, who promptly chopped off the roots, then tossed the rest of the plant aside.

"We're lucky for this forest," Remus said. "Such abundance and diversity of life. This makes gathering materials rather easy, if I do say so myself."

Walter, who was working to chop oak leaves into fine bits, looked up at the sage. "Mr. Remus, I know you say this is a science of sorts, but it sure looks like witchcraft to me. I don't know how I feel about that."

"Humph, you speak as if there's a difference. In some worlds this *is* witchcraft, in others just a matter of chemistry. And I'll tell you, Walter, it doesn't matter if the active ingredient is mumbled worlds, newts' legs, or dianhydrides. The result is what's important. If you sweat the details of the how then you'll never get anywhere."

David squinted one eye. "Isn't the whole point of this trip to get the details of 'the how'? I think it's probably really important."

"Nonsense," the sage replied. "I think we'll find that whatever our underlying truth is, the 'how' won't matter. But that's just an opinion. Anyway, who's ready for a test run?"

Unsure of what the sage intended, David was reluctant to answer. Melanie, however, never let silence stretch for too long. "Sure thing, Mr. R. Show us how it's done."

"Thank you, my dear." The sage shot a smile around as Walter, Melanie, David, and Ezra gathered close. "In this container, I have the product of all the wonderful ingredients you were so kind as to bring me. And when put together, we get this." The sage held up one of their canteens. A purple fog drifted out of the open spout. "All we have to do is set a Portal on one end, and a matching Portal will appear at our destination."

"I thought you were making sideways Holes," Melanie said.

"Oh, I am. But I've decided to call them Portals so we don't get them confused with Holes of the nasty death-dealing variety. Other questions?"

"Where will it go?" Walter asked. "How are you going to test it?"

The sage winked. "Patience, and all will be made clear." Remus walked to the side of the camp, where one of their sleeping mats was hanging up to dry. He tilted the canteen upside down, pouring a fluorescent violet mixture on the mat. At first, the liquid simply ran down in a straight line. But instead of dripping to the ground, it simply stopped moving in the middle of the mat. The liquid gathered together, then spread out into a perfect circle across the surface. The fluid brightened, becoming intensely colored, and then...

<Pock-ffffttt>

The liquid disappeared, and in its place, a Hole. Though instead of being pitch black, this one pulsed with violet light. A Portal.

<Pock...>

David leaped in alarm as the telltale sound started behind him. Without pausing to think, he dove forward, grabbing hold of Ezra and Melanie's shirts as he went. "Look out!"

<...ffffttt!>

He jerked his head to look at the newly formed Hole. But this wasn't a black Hole, it was another violet-hued Portal. It, too, hung vertically. But instead of being on a mat, it was suspended in the air.

The sage clapped his hands in delight. "It worked! I think. Or at least it's worked so far. Now to test it."

"Wait just a minute." David hopped back to his feet. "You can see it?"

The sage frowned. "Of course I can see it. It's right there."

"But you can't see other Holes."

"This isn't like other Holes. It's a Portal. Just like the Holes that pass to other worlds are also Portals. I could see those too." The sage frowned. "But you're missing the point, David. The point is to test it to make sure it does what we both hope and want it to do. All we need is a traveler. But I'm not quite ready for human testing." The sage glanced around him, then pulled out one of the shoes he'd used as a beaker. "This'll do. And now," he paused dramatically, "to boldly go where no footwear has gone before!" With a flourish, the sage threw the shoe into the violet Portal. He then spun around to look at the opposing opening.

Nothing happened.

"That was mine," Walter muttered.

The sage scratched his head. "Hmm, this is peculiar. I kind of expected it to come out the other side. Perhaps it's because the shoe, although leather, is still largely inert despite being organic. If we're going to do this, maybe we need something alive. I don't know, like a frog or something. Do any of you have a frog? How about you, Walter?"

The large man folded his arms across his chest. "Do I look like I'm carrying a frog? Just in case I thought you might need one later?"

"No. I was simply asking—"

Ezra interrupted, "If you need a frog. I can get you one. David, looks like we have…" She didn't finish her sentence. Because at that moment, Walter's shoe flew out of the opposing Portal and hit Melanie square in the back.

"Ow, ow, ow. Why did you do that? How do you think that feels?" She picked the shoe up from the ground and wound up at the sage.

Remus clapped his hands with joy. "See? See? It works, it works, again it works! Melanie dear, would you hand the shoe here… not so much hurl it. I do believe you are missing the point of the exercise. We have a confirmed working Portal." Melanie switched her style, under-handing the shoe back to him. Remus turned it over and over in examination. "No excessive temperature shifts, no discoloration, not on fire or anything. I suppose that's good."

Walter gaped in disbelief. "Mr. Remus, just exactly how scientific do you claim to be? I'm just saying because I think there's a difference between something not being on fire and actually being safe. Don't forget we need to go through it too."

The sage looked aghast. "When did I ever say I was a scientist? I'm a storyteller. A story collector if anything. Maybe a bit of a philosopher when the mood strikes me. But certainly not a scientist."

"But… the…" Walter's face reddened. "Then what are all the mixing and bubbling and talk about precision and coordinates and all that? If you're not being scientific, then how are we supposed to trust we won't end up in the middle of nowhere, or in the sky, or just disappear entirely? Why should we believe you about anything?"

The sage frowned. "Because you just saw it work."

Walter's voice nearly squeaked under the strain. "But do you *know* how it works?"

"Well, how do your legs work?"

"I don't know. But what's that got to do with…?"

The sage grinned. "You still walk, don't you? Still manage to move around? I'm a man of stories, tales, and history, Walter. Not a scientist. So as a storyteller, all I'm asking for is a little suspension of disbelief. Everything will work out fine."

"Even though there's no reason for it to?"

"Because there's no reason for it *not* to." The sage's grin took a mischievous slant.

Walter glanced at the other bystanders. "Do any of you have a problem with this?"

David patted Walter on the shoulder. "To be fair, I gave up on understanding things a long time ago. But the shoe did make it, and I did get here through one of his Portals. So I guess I'm ok with it."

Before anyone else could respond, the sage piped up. "Listen. I'll put your fears at rest. Observe." Without ceremony, the sage took a hop and a skip, then dove headfirst into the violet Portal. As soon as he had disappeared, Melanie, Ezra, and Walter wheeled around to look at the other opening. David counted the seconds in his head, *One-one thousand, two-one thousand, three-one thousand…* And then the sage emerged headfirst, his dive shifting to a somersault as he rolled and then sprang to his feet once more. And though his body was covered with sweat, and his eyes looked a little redder than average, he appeared otherwise fine.

"Ta-da!" The sage threw his hands in the air like a dismounting gymnast. "Is that proof enough? Now I won't pretend it's not weird in there. But I do consider our Portal tested. So enough delay. Time to pack our things and hit the road, so to speak." The sage winked. "After lunch of course."

●

Walter could feel the apprehension in the air. He was about to jump into a glowing purple Hole and emerge God-knows-where. To be honest, the Portal didn't bother him. The thought should have been the source of more dismay, but what concerned him was the destination.

The world was ending. In the time he'd spent with David, Walter had come to accept that as a matter of faith. True, he hadn't seen David's Holes. But he'd felt them. He'd seen things disappear into nothing. He'd heard them open, from pock-fffftttts to thunderclaps. And he'd seen the chimera. That the creatures feared the end was the most convincing argument of all. But he'd be lying if he said he knew what they'd find at the center. Was something making the Holes? What can make nothing?

Walter was concerned that looking for the center of the Holes was like looking for the center of a forest fire. For a fire, it doesn't matter if it started by lightning, a poorly doused campfire, or from being set deliberately. Once going, the burning trees were the issue, not the first spark. Assuming they did make it to the center, Walter expected nothing more than a great big Hole.

"You not hungry?" Melanie tugged at Walter's sleeve. He looked down at his untouched jerky and cheese.

"Preoccupied."

"Still," Melanie said, "you should eat something. Who knows what's on the other side."

Walter looked over at the boy. "David, you've been to the center once. What was it like in your world?"

David looked up, his eyes cold. "Holes. Holes everywhere. They covered at least half of the ground. More in places."

Ezra asked, "And the terrain?"

"Rocky. Sandy. Like a desert. Which, I understand, wasn't always how it was. We should be ready for anything."

Walter coughed. "Could you be a little more specific?"

"Right, right." David wiped the sweat from his forehead. "The farther we went, the weirder things got. Like, sometimes the days would be really long, or the clouds would be funny colors, or you'd hear this strange buzzing in the air. But there were weird creatures as well. Giant spiders with bodies like centipedes, or huge snakes that swam through the air. Oh, and these little tornadoes that would chase you and throw you if they caught you. Every day was something different." He swallowed hard. "I don't think that when we come out of the other side, we should expect things to be the same as back in my world."

Ezra nodded. "There is a chance it won't be that bad."

Walter gasped in astonishment. "Ezra the optimist? Reality *is* breaking down."

"I simply meant," the hunter growled, "that David's world could have been further along. There is a chance we're ahead of it."

Walter opened his mouth to reply but was interrupted as the sage came crashing back into the circle. The man's eyes were afire with a mischievous light. He tugged at the straps of his backpack. "All right travelers, the potion is calibrated and we're ready to go." The sage waggled a canteen in front of him. Purple mist poured from the mouth. "Let's hup-to."

Melanie, David, and Ezra lumbered to their feet. Walter waited a few seconds, took a deep breath, then followed them. He took a last bite of his lunch, crammed the rest in his pocket, and pulled his pack on as well. "All right, Remus. Any pointers for this?"

The sage smirked. "Just hop right through. Easy as pie. Are you volunteering to be first?"

"If that's what you need."

"No," Ezra gruffed. "I'm first. Give me five minutes to clear the area, then follow."

Walter looked at the hunter to see that as well as wearing her pack, she clenched her oversized knife in one hand and had her battle chain gathered in the other. He agreed with her. If something nasty was on the other side, she had the best chance of all of them.

"Hey, David," Walter said. "You still have that gun?"

"No. I must have dropped it when we ran."

The sage scowled at them. "People, people. We are not crossing to fight a war. We are simply journeymen. It's entirely the wrong mindset to expect to kill something every time you go through a door. Where is your sense of optimism and adventure?"

Walter raised an eyebrow. "So *you* want to go first."

"Ahem, no. Ezra already called it. But we can still be optimists. Anybody not ready?"

No response.

"Then here we go."

The sage walked up to the hanging mat. The previous Portal had dissipated, though Walter was unsure how long it had lasted. The sage poured the mixture on the mat, and once again the glowing substance pooled together, spread outward, and then…

<Pock-fffftt>

A Portal opened on the surface. Vivid purple light poured through, first pulsing and then growing steady. The Portal had scarcely stabilized when Ezra, weapons in hand, disappeared inside.

Walter swallowed hard. He knew the anticipation might kill him even if the dangers on the other side didn't. "I'll go next. In case she needs help."

David said, "No. There might be Holes around. I'll go next."

Walter nodded in agreement. After Ezra's requested five minutes had passed, David leaped through the Hole, followed a minute later by the sage.

"Just you and me left, Melanie. Do you mind?"

The pilot gestured with her hand, then started tucking her hair up beneath her aviator's cap. "After you, Mr. W."

Walter adjusted the straps on his pack one last time. Positioning himself perfectly in line with the opening, he took a deep breath and jumped through.

But instead of being filled with light, motion, or all the magic and wonder he had anticipated, he simply landed in the dirt on the other side, his boots plopping in the same place he'd stood minutes earlier.

"It didn't work," he muttered to himself. "Hey, Melanie, I don't think that it…" He turned around, but the pilot was nowhere to be seen. The rock on which she had been standing not ten seconds earlier was bare. "Melanie? Melanie, where did you go? Did you see anything happen when I…?"

Walter let the words trail off. An uneasy feeling gathered in his stomach. The woods were quiet. Completely quiet. There was no singing of birds or chirping of insects, not even the smallest wisp of a breeze. Then, faint at first but growing stronger, a delicate rush filled his ears. The sound was like a faraway ocean, moving in and out with the rhythm of the waves. The rush became louder and more pronounced, until it completely encompassed him. And then so loud he likened it to standing beneath a waterfall.

Off in the distance, the land rocketed upward. The dirt erupted like a volcano, as trees, hills, mountains, and rocks exploded skyward. He saw the land swell like the surface of the ocean. And with that thought, he realized he was in an ocean—of sorts. He had dropped into the ground, floating among a now-fluid collection of dirt and rocks. Walter struggled to stay afloat, but his pack was filling with liquid. He fumbled with his straps, but his fingers had gone numb. And in that moment, that last flail of panic, the wave hit.

20

TERMINUS

Walter came to his senses on all fours, fingers gripping trampled prairie grass. The rush of sound was gone, as was the viscous world. He could feel the sun beating against his neck, and the familiar sensation of sweat running along the backs of his arms and down to his fingers.

David's voice broke him from his trance. "You need to move, or Melanie's gonna land on you. Just crawl out of the way."

Walter did as he was told. He clambered about six feet and then flipped over to his back. He popped out of his pack and stood— promptly stumbling and sinking to his knees.

He gasped. "I can *see* them."

"We all can," Ezra replied.

Walter marveled at his surroundings. And despite David's descriptions, he still wasn't prepared. They were in a plain, a great wide prairie covered with amber grass, but that was hardly all. Holes were everywhere. A fragmented night sky lay at his feet.

He struggled to stand. "I can see them," he repeated. "I can see the Holes. What does it mean?"

The sage hopped forward. "I have a theory."

"Right. Of course you do," Walter muttered.

"The Holes aren't *really* real. They are gaps in reality, and thus they are nonexistence. You weren't able to see them before, because there was nothing to see. Instead, you saw the trace of reality the world thought should be there."

"So why can we see it now?" Walter asked.

"Because, quite simply, these Holes have so thoroughly consumed this part of reality, even the vestiges of the real are gone."

David turned to the sage. "So how come my brothers couldn't see them?"

"I don't know. Maybe we're closer than you were. Maybe their minds weren't ready. Or maybe going through the Portal triggered something."

David replied, "Either way, stay close. In case there's a Hole I can see but you can't. Just until we're sure."

A crash sounded from behind him as Melanie passed through the Portal and hit the ground.

"Ouch! Well, that was weird." Melanie hopped to her feet and dusted herself off. "I don't know what happened to you guys. But it was kind of like…" Her eyes went wide. "HOLY CRAP! Ho-ly Cr-ap! So *those* are Holes? I can see the Holes! Can everybody see them?"

Walter walked over to Melanie. He brushed some of the debris from her pack. "Sure can."

Melanie grunted. "Well, now I know what you were talking about. It would have made a lot more sense if I'd been able to see them all along. But I guess it's good for now."

Walter noticed David had his eyes firmly set on a point in the distance. "What's up, David?"

"Guys… is it just me, or can any of you see *that?*"

"See what?"

David pointed to the north where there was a bolt of lightning, but not one that struck and faded, one that was continually striking, the terminus never moving. The energy danced all around.

"What is it?" Walter asked.

David turned to face the others. "That's the center. It has to be. That's where we're going."

Ezra nodded. "I've seen it before, in my visions. That's the end."

"Woooo!" Melanie giggled. "I just got the chills. Did anyone else get the chills? Come on now."

Walter allowed a grin to break through. "Yeah… I did too. You got me, Melanie."

"Well then, what are we waiting for? David?"

"Yeah?"

"Lead on! Destiny awaits."

With David in the lead, the travelers set off. Sometimes their path was straight, other times an intricate weave as they circled, sidestepped, and threaded between the Holes. The tall grass slowed them somewhat, and made seeing the smallest Holes difficult. Every time they passed a Hole, David would point to check if the others could see it as well. After two hours of walking, he no longer asked. They forged on, the never-ending strike of lightning growing steadily closer.

After the sun dropped low on the horizon, Ezra signaled their halt. They were all tired and sunbaked. And since they wouldn't reach the spark before nightfall, they would rest until the sun rose again. For whatever the strange energy was that came from the center, it cast no light on the land.

After camp was set and dinner was eaten, Walter decided to wander off by himself. He hadn't done so since they started this mad adventure for fear of falling into a Hole. He'd missed the solitude at first, but now he only missed his family, his sons, his wife. He wanted to believe they were proud of him. But he still wasn't sure what he was here to do. Would tomorrow justify all of this? Would it make it worth him abandoning his family with their home destroyed by hurricane and Holes? Is that what his father had wanted?

He dropped to his knees and allowed himself to shed a few tears. He'd done as his father asked, and now he was here. Now he should do as his mother would want, and pray.

And so he did.

●

David couldn't sleep. He wasn't anxious. He simply wasn't tired. At all. He hadn't been tired all day. When the others had stopped for water, or had wiped the sweat from their brows, or heaved from heat and exhaustion, he had not. Restless energy flowed through him. He felt he could drop his pack and run to the center right now. Nothing could stop him.

On the northern horizon, the light flickered and danced. The spark extended not just into the clouds, but beyond, as if striking from the furthest reaches of space. What was it? Was it anything at all? Or was it the signpost leading them to the center? To lead *him* to the center?

Linchpin. That had been Ezra's word for it. The element holding the world together. Or, if Mr. Cash had been right, all worlds. So was he the linchpin? Were they all linchpins? Was the question even important? If he and his friends were going to the center, did such a thing even matter? Or was this an afterthought, just another coincidence?

David crawled from beneath his blanket and got to his feet. He wasn't going to sleep, that was certain. With the campsite at his back, he walked toward the spark until reaching the edge of a lake-sized Hole.

He sat on the shore between existence and nonexistence and watched the light dance.

A half-minute later, he heard footsteps behind him. A voice called, "Want some company?"

David turned around to see the sage, hands thrust in his pockets and his T-shirt ruffling in the light breeze. He smiled weakly. "Sure."

The sage took a seat beside him and looked north. "You want to talk about it?"

"Talk about what?"

"It."

The sage left the word hanging in the air. The flood of emotions that David had kept so long at bay came surging up.

"I don't know what you mean."

"Yes, you do. I know what you're thinking about. What the chimera told you. Let's talk about that."

David winced. "It's ridiculous, you know. This whole 'linchpin' thing. How could I be holding the world together? The chimera can't be right. Can they?"

The sage nodded thoughtfully. "Well, David. I think they are."

"You do?"

"Yes. At least partially. But I don't think they're entirely right, and I don't think they are right for the right reasons."

"I don't understand."

The sage looked back across the Hole. "The chimera say worlds die after some great event, and I've seen that to be true myself. But I think they are missing the bigger question."

"And what's that?"

"The question is 'But why?'."

"But why?"

"Precisely." The sage began to speak rapidly. "'But why?' is the difference between a scientist, which I am not, and a historian and storyteller, which I most certainly am. You see, a scientist determines mechanics: gears, the combustion of stars, physics, chemistry, et cetera, et cetera. But a historian asks 'but why?'. And what the chimera are missing is not that worlds end, *but why* they end. They're missing the *truth* behind the truth."

David replied, "You don't think the answer is scientific?"

"Certainly not. The rules of nature, physics, chemistry, and such aren't consistent from world to world. So how could science be the answer? But events and ideas and conflict and passion *do* stay the same. That's why I collected stories, to see if I could find trends. I now see where I was wrong. I was looking for a trend in the stories, but I missed the important thing. Stories *were* the trend. Every world had stories. And in a way, every world *was* a story."

"So the chimera were right. We shouldn't go farther."

The sage shook his head vigorously. "Of course we should, because we need to discover the '*but why?*'. We need to know why conflict keeps worlds alive."

"And what do you think?" David dropped his eyes to his feet. He carried his gaze from the ground to the edge of the Hole.

"I don't know." The sage sighed. "I thought I'd have figured it out by now, but I haven't."

David didn't respond right away. "You know, according to your friend Levi in Cinderwood, it's impossible to figure it out. Did I tell you that?"

"What did he say?"

"He said when it comes to the truth, revelation was the only way to ever know anything. He said it was the only solution to the Carta… the Carts…the…"

"The Cartesian Crux." The sage stroked his mustache. "The limits of logic, never knowing anything beyond your own existence. Levi was right in part. You can never empirically know anything else, and that's something I've accepted. I never solved that problem either. But I did find a way around it."

"Really?" David looked at the sage in disbelief. "How?"

"By realizing it didn't matter. Dropping from world to world taught me maybe ultimate truth isn't cut and dry. Maybe truth can't be ultimate at all, only relative. I call it 'relative reality'."

"I don't understand."

"Ok, I'll back up a bit. When Rene Descartes, of the 'I think therefore I am' fame, was developing his theory, he tried to rule out the things you could and couldn't trust. He decided you couldn't trust anything. He postulated that everything you saw, heard, smelled, or felt might not really be real. It could all be a vivid dream, and you'd never know for sure. Nevertheless, as long as you can think, then you must exist. 'I think, I am.'

"So what's relative reality?"

"That's simply embracing that whether the things you see are real or not doesn't matter. Because they are still real relative to your perceived reality. Your relative reality."

David furrowed his brow. "But how does that help? It's like the all-important 'but why?' doesn't matter after all. If it all just matters relatively, then there is no 'but why?'."

The sage ticked the points off on his fingers. "I disagree. I think relative reality allows us to get closer to the 'but why?' than otherwise possible. After all, it allows us to take our facts at face value. Relatively speaking, they do have value. One, Holes exist and keep popping up. Or down. Two, they exist in other worlds and show up after an event. Three, the Holes are here."

David grumbled, "Four, they never go away. I don't see how this is helping."

"Well, maybe it doesn't. All relative reality says is to get up off your backside and don't feel so hopeless just because you may—*or may not*—

know what really is—*or is not*—real. It's real to you, so deal with it. And the Holes are real to you, David. They are more real to you than anyone else. Just think. Until this morning, I'd never seen one myself."

"So *I'm* the one who has to deal with it?"

"Yes." The sage rose to his feet and looked down at him. "But you don't have to do it alone. That's what we're here for. Not to just give you the answers, but to help you along. Maybe you are a linchpin of sorts. And maybe you aren't. Or we all are. Or maybe there aren't linchpins and it doesn't even matter. So let me ask you this: Are we going to the center tomorrow?"

"Yes."

"Then get some sleep." He offered his hand to David. "Because whatever happens, I think it'll be interesting."

"Relatively speaking."

"That's the spirit."

David couldn't help cracking a smile. "*But why* is it interesting?"

"And now you're being a smartass. Let's go, my boy. Don't want the others getting worried."

●

David wasn't certain if he had slept that night. His restlessness never stopped, and yet with eyes closed, he couldn't tell where his thoughts had drifted to dreams or when back to thoughts again. All he could do was try to relax, though the thunderclap of Holes forming all around them, and the smaller pock-ffffttts close by were not helping. So when light crept over the horizon, he had to shake himself to meet the day. Like it or not, his fate stood before him.

By the time he got up from his blanket, Walter, Melanie, Ezra, and the sage were already moving about the camp, scraping together a breakfast and packing up their things. He noticed they spent a lot of time gazing out over the plains. No doubt they were trying to grasp what it meant to see the Holes. He had once done the same thing.

"Don't worry guys," he said in a cheerful tone. "You get used to it after a while. Next thing you know, it'll seem normal."

Walter shook his head. "It's not that, David. *Look*."

He looked north toward the spark. His jaw dropped. The world between their camp and the spark had simply ceased to be. Holes covering Holes, next to Holes and overlapping Holes had transformed the land into a single and all-encompassing sea of darkness. And while patches of ground remained, the remaining strands appeared to be nothing more than a spider web across the chasm.

"Oh my god." David squinted at blackness. "Do you think we can find a way through?"

Walter shrugged. "We were discussing our options."

"Well, we're not going back." David set his jaw. "But I don't know how to get through."

The sage, indefatigable as always, hopped up with a smile. "Just a minor setback, folks. Now, I don't think it's our destiny—since you people seem awfully fond of throwing that word around—to get lost in a maze of Holes."

Walter perked up. "What about that hot air balloon you were talking about. Would that do the trick? I mean, sure, we may need to have Ezra scan for chimera first, but floating over that mess seems preferable to walking."

The hunter shook her head. "I can no longer sense the chimera, remember."

Walter bit his lip, "Right. I guess I didn't think about that."

Melanie said, "What's she talking about?"

Ezra kept her face stern. "When Walter woke me up from my trance—for which I am grateful—he used the antidote I carried. It's not a solution without consequence. I can't use the tooth anymore."

The sage said, "Well that's inconvenient. Not bad, just inconvenient."

"Shut up," Melanie cut in. "I see a way through. Look." She traced a path with her finger. "Left then right, then around the side. Happy?"

Walter looked straight at David. "What do you think?"

He squinted as he studied the sea of Holes between them and the torrent of light. There were indeed splintered paths leading to the center, a place that looked free from Holes. *Of course it is,* David thought. *We didn't come all this way for one more Hole.*

"She's right," he said. "There's a way through. We need to keep going."

The others did not argue with him. Even though they could all see the Holes, something had shifted among them. There was a deference to him that he couldn't place his finger on. Or perhaps it was just concern. David gestured for Melanie to take the lead.

The party broke camp and followed the wild-haired girl toward the spark. Whether her experience as a pilot or just her relentless confidence, she ordered every step they took. When they started, the path had been wide. But the farther they walked, the narrower the trail became.

At regular intervals, Melanie climbed up on Walter's shoulders for a few extra feet of vantage before setting off again. And though they twisted and turned, hooked and dog-legged, they steadily progressed to the lightning. The energy was incredible. The spark twisted, fluctuated, danced, and spun—and yet the strike never faded.

When the sun had risen directly overhead, the sage signaled a stop to collect their thoughts. The best they could manage was a twenty-foot span of land. The grass of the field was brown and long dead. The blades of grass crumbled in desiccated piles as the party shuffled around and cast their bags aside.

"How close do you think we are?" Walter asked.

"I'd put us at a mile away," Ezra replied. "Melanie, do you see a way?"

"You betcha. I think it gets a lot cleaner up ahead. Which makes no sense at all. I mean, if we're going to Ground Zero, or whatever we want to call it, then shouldn't we be in one big Hole from start to finish? And that lightning … that doesn't make sense either. So Holes are nothing, I get that… so why should there be a something in the middle of them? Again, no sense. None of it makes sense!"

Walter chuckled. "And the rest of it does?"

She scowled at him, then her face split into a grin. "Good point. So to answer your question, Mr. Sage, yes. I can get us there."

A voice boomed from behind them, refined, and yet forceful. "And why, exactly, should I permit that to happen?"

David turned. There, in clean black clothing, unblemished except for a scar across his eye, was Mr. Cash. Or at least someone who looked exactly like Mr. Cash. In other words, like the sage.

Ezra leapt to her feet, her knife sliding from its sheath and the battle chain dropping to the ground. Melanie and David jumped back in panic, while the sage backed away slowly. Walter, however, didn't flinch. He folded his arms across his chest.

"Mr. Cash," Walter said, his voice dripping sarcasm, "aren't you aware it's impolite to not stay dead?"

The chimera grinned, an emotionless but mocking grin. "I can take a thousand shapes in a thousand worlds—you think I can't pretend death?"

"Why?" David asked.

"To escape. I was outnumbered, and you had a hunter." Mr. Cash nodded at Ezra. "But now I'm here of my own accord. You made it this far, you must have some reason to keep going. Or is making it to the center what it's all about? Why continue, when you have nothing to gain but the death of us all?"

David felt his pulse quicken. He studied the eyes of Walter, Melanie, Ezra, and even the sage. None of them gave any indication of reply. And so if this was it, if he was a linchpin of whatever sort, then David knew he had to respond.

"But why?"

Mr. Cash frowned. "That's a question, David. You can't answer my question with one of your own."

"I am answering it. You say if we go to the center, we'll die. *But why* is that the case?"

"I've told you once," Mr. Cash growled. "Each world has a destiny. If you fulfill that destiny, the story will be complete, the destiny reached, and the reason for worlds to exist will die. The story will have come to its end."

David persisted. "*But why?* Why would reaching the end make it die?"

The chimera furrowed its brow. "It doesn't need a reason, it just does. It's been proven one hundred times and over again. So why do you keep going when you know what will happen? Tell me, or I call my hive and we end it now."

Walter, still exuding calm, answered. "Mr. Cash, sir, if you think this is a story, then why do you think we know the ending? What's more, why do you think we *should* know the ending? We're looking for answers ourselves. David wants to know why the Holes began, Melanie wants to know why her hometown disappeared, and I suppose Ezra wants to know if she's been on the right side of the fight."

"And you?" Mr. Cash asked, his tone mocking. "What do you want?"

"I made a promise to my father. I want to keep that promise." Walter squinted one eye. "What do you want, Mr. Cash? Do you want to see this finished? Or do you want to keep wondering about it until the Holes really do eat through everything? Come on," he matched the chimera's grin, "you said it yourself. You're curious."

"Yes. But not foolish."

Walter folded his hands across his chest. "So what do *you* want?"

The chimera answered, "Perhaps… in some small part, I also want to see this finished. I want to see what happens when he reaches the end."

"Who? David?"

"The linchpin, yes."

Walter stepped forward, bridging the gap between man and chimera. "Then come with us. Tell us what you know and let's face it together. This wouldn't be a destiny if there wasn't a chance we'd win."

The chimera shook its head. "You say you'd trust me. But can I trust you?"

Walter set his jaw. "I think this is bigger than what's past. But I can't convince you to come. It'd be a matter of faith."

Mr. Cash reared up, the jet-black suit exploding into a mass of points, until a dragonfly's wings formed on its otherwise formal attire. "I cannot do that. But perhaps, I won't stop you either. And I'll keep my family from doing the same. For now." Mr. Cash looked directly at David, the whites of its eyes now consumed in the black ichor of the chimera. "Good luck, linchpin. Hold us together."

●

Once the chimera left, David, Walter, Ezra, Melanie, and the sage gathered their things once more. The feeling of hope that sparked for a brief instant had died just as quickly. As they resumed their walk, the silence and weight closed around them. The grass was now gone, replaced by rock, sand, and dust. What little path remained had become quite narrow, and at times they had to jump where a small Hole broke the ground between them. Other changes happened as well. The temperature dropped. The once oppressive heat of the direct Kansas sun faded, as did the sun itself. At first, David thought this only an illusion brought on by the creeping haze. But it was as though the sun wasn't covered by haze, but had instead become haze. The sky had shifted to a slate gray, as though a storm raged overhead. But no rain fell, and no lightning struck, save for the constant spark at the end of their path.

Due to the brightness, they grew dependent on Melanie and her darkened aviator glasses to move forward. The rest of them kept their eyes down, and their hands on the packs of the person in front of them. To look directly at the spark was to be blinded.

But the closer they drew, the paler the light became. After a while, it no longer hurt their eyes. Its movement also stabilized. While it still danced in the upper reaches of the atmosphere, the base looked constant, defined. When at long last they reached the spark, it was not just stable, it was as motionless as a marble column. The glowing mist resembled smoke trapped within a glass cylinder, one hundred feet around.

The sage was the first to approach. He took step after tentative step. With each foot he progressed, he would pause, look, listen, and then inch forward again. When he was within reach of the spark, he slowly extended his hand to touch the column. His fingers came to rest on the surface. Solid. He pushed, and then rapped on the outside.

"It's hard as a rock," Remus exclaimed. "I'll be damned if I know what it is, but it's solid. At least down here. Not up high of course. We can all see that. So perhaps it only appears solid and is instead exerting a type of repellant force. Magnetism, or antigravity, or repulserflex, or just a force field of the old-fashioned variety. Or perhaps…"

Though the sage kept speaking, the words dropped to a mumble in David's ears. He moved forward until he could see nothing but the light. Slowly, he reached out to touch the glowing mist. Unlike the sage, he met with no resistance. He turned to see the others staring at him.

"David…" Melanie whispered, "how are you doing that?"

"I don't know. It's… I don't know."

Melanie, Walter, and Ezra tried to replicate his feat, but the column was just as solid for them as it was for Remus.

The sage turned to face David. "I imagined this might happen."

David shook his head. The feeling of dread consumed him. "You did?"

Remus grimaced. "I am an observer, David. I have been lucky in the things I've seen and the places I've gone. I have crossed worlds and seen stories. But they were never my stories. It is not for me to take this final step. I hope you have learned from me. I am grateful to have played some small part. But it is you who must continue. My story ends here as well."

"What are you saying?"

Walter patted him on the shoulder. "I think he's saying good luck—in his own way. You need to go in alone. We'll wait for you to come back, of course. But for us, this is the end of the line. We're not meant to follow you."

David looked from face to face. He could feel tears beginning to well in his eyes. "Should I say goodbye? I don't understand what to do here."

Ezra smiled gently. "You say good luck."

"But what do you think is in there?"

The sage tapped his chin. "If we knew that, then we wouldn't have come all this way. You go find out and tell us."

David unclasped the waist belt of his backpack and laid his things on the ground. He took one last swig from his canteen. "All right, then. No goodbyes. Just good luck."

Well-wishes echoed around him. David took a step forward into the luminescent fog. After another step, he was completely immersed. He could make no distinction between air, sky, or ground. Even his boots faded to gray at the ends of his legs. He turned back once more, but his friends were obscured by the mist. He walked ten steps, twenty, fifty. Had he reached the center? Had he gone past it? Was this the middle of it all? Not black nothingness, but a white nothingness instead?

"Ok," he stated, "I'm here."

No response came from the fog, though he heard a soft sound below him, starting in a single hollow pop, like a cork snapping from a wine bottle, and ending in an outrush of air.

<Pock-fffftttt>

21

THE LINCHPIN

David felt the ground drop. The cracked earth didn't tumble away in a cascade of rock. Instead, it simply sank, becoming loose and elastic until the membrane of existence released entirely. And then he was falling. Air rushed past in a roar, but he saw nothing. The luminous fog annihilated all vision. Not that he couldn't see, for he could see the white. But without color or texture, he was blind.

As time passed, the rush of air diminished, as did the whistle of wind in his ears. He wondered if he was falling, or floating, or if he'd ever stop. What's more, he wondered if the things he felt were real at all. Was this what it was like to be in a world that didn't exist? What clues did he have that anything existed? With senses gone or rendered uniform, he was without bearings. But was he gone? David struggled with the thought until the words of the sage came back to him. Even if nothing else could be known, there was one fact that couldn't be shaken. As long as he could think, that meant he was still there. He existed. He would continue to exist.

His senses returned.

David's vision was back, as was his sense of touch, taste, smell, and hearing. Stretching his sensory muscles gave him little satisfaction. While he could see once more, he had little understanding of how he came to be where he was. He sat cross-legged on a polished floor of dark marble tiles which fit together in a hexagon mosaic. A pool of light gathered around him, though he couldn't locate the origin, as there was nothing but black above him, and no light nearby. Somewhere in the distance emanated the click and whirr of machinery. The industrial sound was overlaid by a thick aroma of grease, oiled metal, and the hint of a long-ago chemical fire. Temperature was evident as well. But instead of a factory's heat, a chill pervaded, frosting his breath and prickling his skin with goosebumps.

David heard a shuffle behind him and spun to look. There, hands in his pockets and a perplexed look on his face, was David. Correction, it wasn't exactly him, though they looked much alike. This boy's face was somewhat rounder, his eyes more heavily set. His longer hair hung near his shoulders in matted ringlets. The clothing, however, was the same. Soiled shirt, pants tattered from overuse, and shoes so worn the laces were nothing but frayed knots.

"What are you doing here?" the boy asked. "Most don't make it the whole way down. Usually they just… sort of disappear." He pointed above their heads. David looked up to see the empty space occupied by falling objects. Men, women, children, pets, livestock, wild animals—all drifted and dove, before becoming clouds of dust.

David stood to face his doppelgänger; the boy looked back expectantly. Perhaps he wanted his question answered. But David simply didn't know how to respond. So he uttered the only words that came to his lips, the thought that had pulled him from the void.

"I think, therefore I am."

The boy rolled his eyes. "Oh brother. You're one of them, aren't you?"

"One of who?"

"It doesn't count, you know." The boy wrinkled his nose in disgust. "It has nothing to do with you thinking at all. I don't know what you're thinking, and I don't know that you are even thinking. And if I don't know it, then it might as well not be true. And if it's not, maybe you're just another figment of *my* imagination."

David shook his head. He looked up at the objects falling and dissolving, at the light which surrounded him, and then back at the boy who could be his twin. "Is that what this is? Your imagination? Is that what keeps things going?" He paused. "Are you… God?"

The boy snorted. "Everyone asks that too. No, I'm not God. But I don't have to be for you to not be real. None of them are real either."

"If I'm not real, then what am I?"

"I don't know. Why do you think I should know? I guess I know more than you, but it doesn't always make sense."

"Well, what's your guess?"

The strange boy screwed up his face. "If you're like all the rest, you're probably just an old memory. I don't remember you, though."

David replied, "You don't remember me? You look just like me!"

"Oh, that." The boy looked ashamed. "Sometimes when I read things, if I don't have enough to go on, I kind of imagine myself in the story. You must be from some old book." The boy's face lit up. "Of course! That must be it. So which one is it? What's it called?"

David stuttered. "I, I don't…"

"Right, right. Of course, you wouldn't know the name. But you know where you came from. How did you get here?"

"I was near the center. There were Holes everywhere, and this glowing light in the middle. But no one else came to the end. They said they wanted to, but they couldn't."

"*Who* didn't come with you?"

David ticked off the names on his fingers. "Well, there was Walter, I met him in Greenwater's End where I fell. Then Ezra the hunter. There's Melanie—she was a pilot. And of course the sage, Remus. I guess there was also a chimera named Mr. Cash, but I'm not sure if he was following us, or if he ended up leaving."

"The Hunter and the Chimera?"

"Ezra was the hunter, Mr. Cash was the chimera."

"No. I mean that's the book. I remember it now, *The Hunter and the Chimera.*" The boy wrinkled his nose in disgust. "Man, I haven't thought about *that* one in a long time. Terrible book, if you ask me. I mean, it was off to a good start and all, but it just fizzled out at the end. Tell me how a book with no ending even gets published?"

"It was a book?" David paused in disbelief before a feeling of defensiveness crept over him. "You know, it wasn't that it didn't have an ending, it just didn't have one yet. It was unresolved."

"Yeah. And boring." The boy thrust his hands in his pockets. "Nothing happened. Why it's hardly worth remembering at all. Book without an ending… I mean, it's unique to say the least, but that's all."

David's mind raced. A thought formed at the tip of his awareness, and then bubbled away. "So did you write that book?"

"Naw. I found it on the exchange shelf at the library. Which makes sense, of course. Who would pay for something like that? No offense, you being a character and all. I don't remember you, though. Sorry."

"I'm David." He paused. "So this isn't your imagination. And you didn't write the book. And you're not God. But you've got to be the linchpin… nothing else would make sense. So what are you?" David paused, but didn't wait for the strange boy to answer. "I… I think I understand."

"You do?" The boy smiled. "Great, because I sure don't. And the other people who fell the whole way down without disappearing didn't understand it either. Though they all seemed concerned about it. Just to warn you, they all disappeared eventually, even if not at first. I don't want to lead you on or anything."

David closed his eyes, squinting them hard against all light. "It was never me. I'm not the linchpin. And it was never about my struggle, or my adventure. Or any of our adventures. The chimera were wrong. It's you. You're holding it together."

"I told you, I didn't write the book."

"No, but you didn't need to. It's not the writer who gives a story life. They know it's just a story. It's the *reader*, the person who receives it. That's where it becomes real." David gritted his teeth, but the words kept coming. "Those other worlds ended when the conflict ended, but not because any destiny had been fulfilled. They came to an end because their stories were put down and forgotten. The world I just came from, the one with chimera and hunters, you forgot it because it didn't have an ending. Maybe that's why it slipped away so fast."

The strange boy stuck his hands on his hips. "Look, kid. I'd take you more seriously if I thought you were real. But I don't understand a word of what you're going on about."

David shook his head. "You don't have to understand it; you just have to remember it. That's all it takes."

Frustration covered the boy's face. "Well, to be honest, it's been a few years since I read *The Hunter and the Chimera*. I mean, I remember bits and pieces, but that's all. And you know what, you being a figment of my imagination hardly gives you the right to get all up in arms anyway. Like I said, I definitely don't remember you."

The words caught in David's throat. He looked around at the strange dark world with nothing but tile beneath and falling things overhead. And at the boy, who looked so like him, standing with judgment in his eyes.

A chill crept across David's skin. "Would you mind if I told you a different story?"

The boy cocked his head. His eyes twinkled with interest. "Would you? That'd be great. But I don't want to just hear *The Hunter and the Chimera.* Do you know any other stories? Maybe one I haven't heard."

David looked back at the boy. "I sure do." He took a deep breath. "I call this story *The Linchpin.*"

"You said that word before. What's a linchpin?"

David ignored him. "I was nine when I first saw the Holes…"

22

CODA

Ezra, Melanie, Walter, and the sage waited for David to return from the fog. When he had been gone twenty minutes, the first of the changes happened. The sun, no more than a blur overhead, parted the strange mist and shone down once more. The next change was less conspicuous. In fact, Ezra was unsure how much time had passed before they noticed it. But as they awoke on the second day, the hollow booms of the enormous Holes had stopped. They heard no more opening of Holes at all, only the sound of the wind. And still, they waited.

On the third day, the first of the Holes began to disappear. They did not snap shut as abruptly as they opened. Instead, they wavered, becoming less and less defined until the land was exactly the same as if there had never been a Hole at all. Melanie was the first one to walk where a Hole had been—after testing with rocks, sticks, and her own shoe. Whatever David had done, the world was beginning to heal. No one spoke of moving on, and so they waited.

To pass the time, the sage told stories about the worlds he had visited. Ezra listened as intently as the rest, but her thoughts were of

David. And those thoughts had turned grim. After three days, Ezra shared that sentiment with the others. She hadn't been alone.

When finally, their provisions had run dangerously low, they spoke of their options.

Walter tried using the tooth, but he could make no sense of his visions. The sage tried as well, but with no effect at all. Finally, Melanie gave the drug an attempt. The visions as she described them were more defined than Walter's, but no more helpful. She saw many things, but she didn't see David. And received no clue of what to do next.

And on the tenth day, they had to decide.

Their best option, the sage said, was to open a Portal back to Memphis. He'd spent his time making the calculations and was certain he had them correct. If the Portal was successful, they could pass through. If not, they would navigate back out of the maze of Holes on foot.

"All right." Remus uncorked his potion. He looked into the canteen as the purple mist spewed forth. "This worked once, so we can only hope it works again. But no promises."

Walter raised an eyebrow, though the normal sarcasm that tinged his voice was gone. "No promises? Like you said, it worked before."

Remus replied, "Yes, but things are odd here. It might not be exactly the same, and the world is changing. But we'll have to try." The sage lifted the vial but Ezra stopped him.

"So we're just quitting? We came to the center of it all, and now we're just quitting? Isn't there something else we can do while we're here? Isn't there something you should study, or test, or something like that? Maybe a way to break through that mist?"

The sage lowered his hand. "I don't think we're just quitting. Something changed when David went in there. The Holes are disappearing, maybe not all at once, but it is happening. And I can't put my finger on it—but a weight is gone. There's life in the air. Don't you feel it?"

Melanie nodded. "I can. Something's different."

"Or maybe," Ezra snapped, "you just want to think something's different."

The sage placed one hand on his hip and gestured with the vial. "And maybe it doesn't matter. We've nothing left to eat or drink. If we don't go back, where do you suppose we go?"

"Down." Ezra gritted her teeth. "That Portal can probably take us back, I don't doubt that. But when's the last time you tried your *other* potion, the one to cross worlds. When's the last time you tried that one? Maybe we're unstuck."

The sage dropped his hand to feel the yellow vial on his belt, the same potion that had transported both him and David into this world. "All right," Remus said. "I'll do both. I'll open a Portal to Memphis, and another to the next world down. I'll leave you to choose."

The sage held up the small, tinted hourglass, and with one hand snapped the vial in two. The yellow potion spilled onto the ground and then disappeared into the dust. Nothing happened.

Walter put a hand on the hunter's shoulder. "It was a good idea."

Ezra shrugged him off. "Well, Remus, what are you waiting for? Time to run away."

The sage uncorked the container. Purple smoke oozed from the opening. Then he held the bottle high and upended it. A purple liquid fell, then widened, flattened, and became round. The liquid expanded into a perfect, glowing vertical disc. "This should take us outside of Memphis," he said. "And if for some reason something goes wrong… it has been a pleasure." The sage shouldered his pack, took two quick steps, and jumped through the Portal.

Ezra looked over at Walter and Melanie. "You two can go ahead. I need a few minutes. I want to say goodbye."

"I'll stay with you," Walter said.

The hunter shook her head. "I prefer to be alone."

"Well, I've got no problem going ahead," Melanie chirped. "So long, David." She blew a kiss at the glowing fog. "See you two on the other side." Melanie jumped through the Portal and vanished.

Walter turned to the hunter. "Why does this feel like goodbye, Ezra?"

"Because it is, Walter." A strange emotion built inside her. Her eyes watered, and then a tear dropped down her cheek.

Walter set his jaw. "You're not coming with us, are you?"

"I don't have a place in this world anymore." Ezra cleared her throat. "I never planned on going back."

"I'll come with you."

"No. You kept your promise to your father. Now keep the promise to your family."

"And you?"

"I need to keep a promise to David."

Walter rested a hand on her shoulder. "You're all right, Ezra. We could never have made it without you. I hope you find what you're looking for."

Ezra nodded.

Walter turned back to the Portal. Ezra watched as the farmer disappeared in a purple flash, leaving her alone at the end of the world. She walked to the edge of the fog and extended her hand. And though she had tried the same thing every day for the last nine days, this time the mist parted.

Just as she knew it would.

The hunter took one last look around her, at the Holes, the fragments of grassland, the clear blue sky, the midday sun, and the Portal whose light was beginning to wane.

She stepped into the light.

●

Walter landed face down in a brackish mixture of salt, detritus, and the unmistakably thick mud of the marsh. He cursed and pulled himself upright. Wherever he was, it certainly wasn't Memphis. Wheeling around, he was greeted by the gentle lap of the ocean's waves against the south jetty.

The south jetty!

The realization ripped through his mind. He knew this place. He wasn't more than ten minutes from his father's oyster grounds. In fact… this was where they'd found David. He was practically home.

Walter paused. Where was Melanie? Where was the sage? Shouldn't they be here as well? Or did the Portal drop each of them where they belonged? Maybe Melanie was in Memphis, just as he was here. And what about the sage? What would he call home? Or was he even in this world anymore? Either way, Walter decided not to wait any longer. He had to make sure his family was all right. And so he waded through the marshes to make his way to Greenwater's End.

Three hours later, Walter stood in the ruins that was once his home. The buildings looked the same, but the damage from the hurricane, and the Holes which peppered the ground, were reason enough the town had been abandoned. He walked into town anyway. He wove around the Holes, thankful he could still see them, and wondered if they would close up here as well. He hadn't gone fifty feet toward the church when he heard a familiar voice behind him.

"Walter? Walter Lofton? Well I'll be, boy. We ain't never thought we'd see you around here again. You must-a found what you were looking for."

He turned to see the smiling face of his father's friend and fishing buddy, Douglas. "What do you mean?"

"You went looking for the problem right? But you don't have to look anymore. We can see the problem now, plain as day." Douglas squinted at him. "You *can* see these here Holes, can't you?"

"Yes. I can see them." He paused. "Can everyone?"

"Sure they can." Douglas grinned. "And if what they say on the radio is any proof, it's getting better."

"I don't understand."

"They're disappearing. Bit by bit, but they are. So maybe it's over."

Walter bit his lip and nodded. "Not completely, though."

"Maybe not yet. But where we've started building, there ain't but a handful of Holes at all. And if they all fade away, we can come on back." Douglas's grin spread even wider. "But are you going to stand here and gab with a sorry old man all day? Let's get you home."

"I'd like that."

●

Melanie emerged from the Portal headfirst, facedown, and six feet high. Reacting with some as-of-yet untapped reflex, she twisted to land deftly on her feet. And though she was unbalanced, she did not fall.

Laughing at her dexterity, Melanie stood upright—and then gasped. Not two inches from the tips of her toes was a Hole, one large enough to rival those at the end of the world, a sea of ink. She shuffled backward, her movements slow, and then turned, nearly tripping over a pile of debris.

Realization and familiarity set in. The combine, the mill, the cracked pavement, and immobile cars. She had returned to Memphis— just outside it rather—and was seeing it for the first time with the illusion of reality stripped away.

Remembering her last time through a Portal, she stepped aside in case Walter came barreling after her. Despite her own elegant entry, she suspected he would drop like a stone. But after a minute had passed, the Portal first diminished, and then disappeared entirely.

"Huh." Melanie squinted in confusion. Had the others been waiting for something? Did David reappear and delay their departure? Or had they decided not to follow her at all? They could have at least let her know.

BRAAAWWWWGGGGGGHHHHH

The blare of the foghorn snapped her back to the present. She squinted south to look at the fire tower she once called home. The structure stood only a quarter-mile away and was clearly visible in the morning sun. A grin spread across her face. Down the steps and ladders of the fire tower, swarms of people descended and raced toward her.

In less than a minute, she collided with her friends. The refugees greeted her in a storm of grins, backslapping, and hugs. She bathed in the warmth of being reunited with her adopted family.

"Melanie! I can't believe you're back!" Yancey, one of the younger boys, exclaimed. "Did you see what happened after you left? It all changed. Can you see the Hole? We all can."

Melanie turned on her heels, took in the colossal Hole with a casual glance then turned back. "Of course I can. Been seeing them for days. And if you can too, then I'd say our work here is done."

"What do you mean?"

She snorted in mock-disgust. "Well, you think anyone's going to fall into that thing by themselves? No way. Let's get out of this dump and find somewhere a little less Holey. Now bring my car around. It's the black one with the flames and such."

"What happened to your plane?"

"Oh, that? Had to bring her down in a hurry. Couldn't be helped. I'll tell you all about it. But for now, let's start packing. Time to fly this coop."

Yancey looked up expectantly. "But where will we go?"

Melanie shot back a grin. "I was thinking the beach. I may even know someone who'll put us up until we get settled." She set her eyes to the rising sun. "Here we come, Walter. Ready or not."

●

The sage looked down at the last few strokes of his pen. He felt deeply unsatisfied.

"I don't like this at all. I was supposed to get some sort of conclusion. I was supposed to end up with ultimate truth and ultimate understanding."

Across from the sage, in a heavily oiled red leather chair, sat Mr. Cash. As usual, the chimera had shifted its form to look impeccably dressed in a three-piece black suit. Mr. Cash held a glass of brandy in one hand—also a mere representation—and shrugged. "Something happened out there, Remus. You have to accept that maybe your ultimate truth was found. Perhaps by David, or perhaps it was merely a coincidence."

"I don't believe in coincidence."

"And neither do we." Mr. Cash waited patiently. "So that's it? All of it?"

"Well, it's as much of it as I know. Not a particularly satisfying ending, but that's the account as I saw it." The sage slapped his hand down hard on the manuscript. "So there's your book, Cash. Can we talk about your side of the bargain?"

"Ah yes, the top." The chimera smiled a long, thin smile.

"You've got it. The topmost world there is. Truth is still out there, and I intend to find it. And now that I can see the Holes, I think that gives me a bit of an edge."

"And what if you don't find your truth this time either? What if you make it the whole way back to this bottom world with no answers?"

The sage winked. "Then you give me another ride to the top. I won't live forever, but I'd like to find an answer or two before this thing is up. So will you take me?"

"Of course." Mr. Cash stood and gave a polite bow. "But I have business here first. We'll go tomorrow."

"Wait."

"Yes?"

The sage thumped the book. "You never told me why. Why do you suddenly care so much about stories? I thought you'd dropped your idea of the linchpin."

"Oh no, we haven't dropped that idea at all. I just don't believe we've found him, or her… or it."

"And my story?"

"Perhaps it can help. We aren't done looking for truth ourselves."

The sage grinned. "Tomorrow then. To the top!"

"To the very top."

●

The linchpin clapped his hands. He rocked back and forth in delight. "Splendid, splendid! That's a great story, David. I must say, this is the first time an imaginary person has ever told me a story."

David replied, his voice hoarse from speaking for so long uninterrupted. "So… you don't think you're going to forget this one?"

"Of course not. *I* was in it. How could I forget that? I've never been in a story before."

David smiled wanly. "I thought the same thing." He heard a sound from behind him and turned to look. There, leaned against a pillar, her arms folded and face taut, was Ezra. The hunter looked even more worn down and tired than before, though had an easy smile on her face. He scrambled to his feet and ran to embrace her.

"You were listening?" he asked.

She nodded. "Yes. And now I understand." She straightened and turned to face the strange boy sitting across from David.

Ezra asked, "So you're the linchpin."

"That's what he says."

She nodded. "Good. Then it's time you showed it. It's time for you to send David home."

The linchpin frowned. "But I don't know how to do that."

"Of course, you do. It's part of the story. It's a part of every story." Ezra turned to David. "Well, finish it up."

A smile crept across his face. "Finish it? Do you mean, something like, 'happily ever after'?"

"Yes." Ezra nodded. "Something exactly like that."

Acknowledgments

The past year has been an adventure into the world of books. I'd like to thank Sarah for her encouragement from the beginning—and grounding when I needed it. Thanks to Maggie and Ellen for their boundless enthusiasm for this endeavor. I would like to recognize Scott for his wisdom and insight into early drafts of the story, and the members of the "Third Thursdays" writers' group for their camaraderie. I also must give my appreciation to Maria and the Old Rock Library, as well as Jen, Arvin, Danica, and the other good people at Townie Books for the support of community. I also want to thank Liz and Cherie who gave the work its finishing touches. Lastly, a heartfelt thanks to all those I may have missed, and those I have yet to meet on this journey.

About the Author

After college, Phil left North Carolina for the west and then never managed to go home again. When not living and breathing books, he likes to hike, mountain bike, ski, and appreciate being where the air is thin, and the cows outnumber the people.

His books and stories are all about taking an idea and then pushing it far beyond the bounds of our own reality. After all, we have more than enough real life in our real life.

Phil currently lives in the mountains of Colorado with his wife and two daughters.

Web: https://www.philcolemanbooks.com
Facebook: https://www.facebook.com/philcolemanbooks/
Instagram: https://www.instagram.com/philgoodbooks/
TikTok: https://www.tiktok.com/@philgoodbooks